THE SECRET LIFE OF US

Evan Wylde was born in Mt Waverley, Victoria in 1976, and has lived in Kew, Yarraville, and Wonthaggi. He was educated at Mt Waverley Primary School, where as the winner of the book prize in Mrs Nance's Grade 3 English class, he was awarded 'Dot And The Kangaroo'. In Year 11 at Yarraville Secondary College, Evan lost his virginity behind the dunnies during the athletics carnival. Evan studied and was kicked out of creative writing at the Royal Melbourne Institute of Technology, and has had short work and articles published in local magazines and street press. He now lives in the Melbourne bayside suburb of St Kilda where the events of *The Secret Life Of Us*, his first novel, take place. He is currently working on his second novel *Fitzroy Street Kisses* and is also a grandmaster in the art of hackeysack.

Evan Wylde is, of course, a fictional character in the hit Australian TV drama *The Secret Life of Us*.

THE SECRET LIFE OF US
A Novel

Evan Wylde

First published 2002 by Channel 4 Books
an imprint of Pan Macmillan Ltd
Pan Macmillan, 20 New Wharf Road
London N1 9RR
Basingstoke and Oxford
Associated companies throughout the world

www.panmacmillan.com

0 7522 6504 0

9 8 7 6 5 4 3 2 1

A CIP catalogue record for this book
is available from the British Library.

Typeset by seagulls
Printed by Mackays of Chatham

ACKNOWLEDGEMENTS

I am indebted to the following people for their help along the way: R.M.Fehim; Samuel Johnson; Amanda Higgs, John Edwards, Hamish Wright and Cathy Payne at Southern Star; and Annie Schafheitle, Charlie Carman and Sean Garrehy at Channel 4 Books. I also thank my two muses Christopher Lee and Judi McCrossin. But my main thank you goes out to my friends – without their positivity and encouragement, but most importantly their weird and wonderful lives, there simply wouldn't be a secret life of us.

1

There's living it, and then there's Living It. We all know that, right? There's getting out of bed, sitting at a desk in some shitty job, waiting on some shitty pay cheque that just about gets you through Friday night. There's that constant low-level yearning for sex, that nameless desperation to fuck anyone who'll let you. The waiting, always waiting, for the someone who won't; for that inevitable unrequited thing. Spending half your life wishing you'd fall in love and the other half wishing you hadn't, always looking for that forbidden line just so you can cross it. There's beer, good times with your mates, some warm memories that kid you that your friends are your real family and with them at your side nothing can touch you and all of you will live forever.

There's the odd joint, a couple of pills maybe, living out your youth to the last letter of the dictionary definition and then there's the next day and the next. That's the way I live life and that's the way I love living life: in your face, right now. Instant karma come and get me. But as much as I love loving it all right now, I've found out there's more. Something more than the chicks and the highs and the women and the highs and the girls and the highs. There's me and my laptop.

I've got it planned. An extra-curricular addition to the high-octane partying, to the finding true love, as many times as I can, with whoever I can, forever. A plan that means that I can live each moment for all it's worth – free and easy for sure, but with an ultimate purpose. That when I do croak, it won't matter; in fact it'll be cool, because by then I'll be immortal.

Isn't that what we all want? Everyone you know and you. Everyone I know and me. Like Miranda wants first-night applause on a stage that counts; like Richie wants to hear his name at an awards ceremony in the States. Like Alex wants love and a good night's sleep. Like I want this, my book, my words, to mean something to me and to you and everyone I know and everyone you know, today tomorrow and always.

Maybe immortality's not for everyone. Maybe just those fifteen minutes in life's spotlight, even in love's spotlight, is all they need.

But I need more. I need forever.

So I've got it planned.

And plan A is to stop planning and start doing. Plan A is to take us – Alex, Richie, Miranda, Will, Kelly, Jason and Gab – all of us and me and to recreate us. To turn our head life, our heart life, the secret life of us, into screaming, kicking, going-for-glory Living.

And it's all right here.

~

The world has changed. For the first time maybe ever the world has changed and changed us all, everyone in it, all at once. For the first time there's no pretending it's someone else's problem.

There's been a seismic shift in world order that sends aftershocks that ripple and ripple through every day altering everything for ever and ever and yet ...

Even when I'm not there I know exactly where they are right now. The Fu Bar, night; Kelly pours the beers. The TV is on, the news. Alex is there, she's looking beautiful, tucking her dark hair behind her ear the way she does when she's tired, when she's angry, when she's flirting. Alex is talking to Simon:

'I think we went wrong right back in September. Bush responded with revenge and that's morally reprehensible. And to respond with ...' Alex pauses, looking around, searching the air for the right word.

Simon watches Alex struggle with his characteristically raised eyebrow.

'Such ffff ...' It's an F-word she's looking for.

'Fever?' Simon suggests.

'No,' Alex sighs.

'Favour?' Simon questions. Alex rolls her eyes and tucks her hair behind her ear again.

'Simon! You're putting me off ... Fervour! That's it. Fervour.' She beams at Simon for a moment like a pleased little girl before collecting her thoughts.

'Now, what was my point?' she asks Simon, a serious frown setting between her brows.

Simon backs his eyebrow-raising antics up with a shrug.

'No idea.' Alex laughs and punches him lightly on the arm, relieved she's off the stage of world politics and back on a stool at the Fu Bar, the hub of our own little universe.

Here's Richie now, shoulder back, chin up and verging on celebrity. The episode where I almost accidentally outed him almost gone and forgotten, but he's still a beginner at being gay. He thinks he might only want half of the gay lifestyle, and he's not really sure which half. Simon is acutely aware of Richie's entrance, and suddenly everything about him changes slightly, his poise his tone, his smile. It's obvious to nobody but me, and I'm not even there, that Simon can barely contain his crush on Richie.

We can trace Simon's bedroom eyes back to the night he kissed Richie right there in the bar, mid-karaoke duet emboldened by beer and Richie's consciously unconscious flirting, smoking a joint and talking French. Simon sang 'You're Gorgeous' to Richie and meant every word of it. Richie sang 'You're Gorgeous' to himself and meant every word of it. There they were, laughing and stumbling through all the double meaning and sexual tension of it all, and then Simon just kissed Richie.

And Richie kissed him back.

Our world changed in that moment, our world order shifted and crumbled and began to slowly rebuild itself. Miranda found out that the man she loved, loved men. The precious relationship that she had spent so long building and nurturing, bearing the brunt of, crumbled in the few moments it took Richie to say, 'I slept with another man'. She'd always suspected that it would end one day despite all due her care and attention, but she'd never expected it to end the way that it did and somehow she felt cheated. There were tears and recriminations and everyone changed places again, altering the world of us forever. And our world order is not something that can be phased into background noise on the television news. Whatever happens to one of us happens to all of us. It buzzes in our blood.

Anyway, it's clear as day that Simon thinks he is in love with Richie. You'd think, wouldn't you, that flatmates would be able to realise when there's a secret love thing going on …?

Changing the subject now.

There's Miranda sitting with Will, raising her chin as if she's waiting to be kissed. She has almost finished putting herself back together now – almost. It helps that she's getting good reviews for the work she's doing. It helps that she is the new Pores Afresh model, that her bank balance and profile are both happily secured for the foreseeable future. She's finding she can make her own way without Richie. She's gradually discovering that Richie isn't essential.

Will's there – I mean he's physically there, he's smiling, joking with Miranda, even talking about picking up a cute chick at an opening night party they are going to. But we wonder, you and I, and we can't quite see from here – is his heart there? Is his soul? Will guards himself well, the foot soldier of fate.

Alex is back on her high horse now, this time pontificating to Jason.

Jason's looking good, happy with his lot like he's accepted that his and Gabrielle's relationship is finally over. Like he never fucked Alex on her best friend's – his girlfriend's – sofa ten minutes before she came in through the front door to make them both dinner.

Happy like a cash-rich corporate lawyer's job, girlfriend Caitlin and fatherhood, his instant family is all he'll ever need.

Once again the fault line opened up, swallowed familiarity whole and then closed again, until we'd all got used to the new view.

Now Nathan. The new me. He's been staying in my room while I'm away and falling in love with Kelly. Look at Kelly, she's radiant; I've never seen a woman more altered by love than Kelly. She's so happy her thoughts are written all over her face. She's thinking, 'It's funny how a relationship can sneak up on you. You're single one day, then you have a date, then a few more. Then you start reserving your Saturday nights and then you have a boyfriend – a steady proper boyfriend – who you love.'

She shuts her eyes as Nathan kisses her.

'And who loves you,' Kelly savours the thought and looks forward to going home with Nathan.

And so it is. There's a new world order in our lives. The old partnerships have all dissolved or been ripped away and new alliances formed. The elements are the same but the configuration has changed forever.

Now we all have to work out where we stand in it.

And I'm not even there.

2

Alex dribbles a little olive oil over the pasta and stands back as Kelly stirs in the pesto sauce. Kelly looks sideways at Alex and looks resolved.

'A postcard came today. He's in Cuba.' Alex studies the salsa she is dressing, feigning disinterest – badly. Kelly looks at the tension that runs along her shoulders and – determined to follow her resolution through – takes the postcard out of a kitchen drawer and reads it out.

'All I've got to say to you, babes, is Guantanamera.' She reads it in a carefully constructed neutral monotone, without the humour and zest with which it was written. Alex lifts her head and shakes it in disbelief.

'That's not it?'

'That's it,' Kelly confirms bluntly.

'He's unbelievable.' Kelly tries desperately to read Alex's thoughts.

'It's a lovely picture – look,' she says brightly, holding out a hip black-and-white photo of Che Guevara. Alex turns her head away.

'Don't even show it to me,' she says. But she looks anyway.

'Life would be easier for everyone,' Kelly thinks, 'if men just did what women wanted. Why hasn't Evan written to Alex? Why isn't he trying to get her to wait for him to resolve his place in her life? Why isn't he acting like I would if I loved someone who was far away? Why isn't he acting like a woman?'

Alex has never told Kelly everything that went on in that taxi the night that Evan left for the States. She didn't have to tell her that anything had happened, it was all there in her face, which was bruised with kisses and tears. One look at Alex's face and Kelly could see everything that happened, or the way she imagines it ought to have happened.

Kelly, Gab, Miranda, all the girls. They'd all sensed it, the build-up to that moment, even if they hadn't seen it all happen. They all sensed it and despite their twenty-first-century selves they'd all believed in it, believed that it would mean true love forever. All of that unresolved sexual tension couldn't fizzle out to nothing just because it was stretched over a few hundred miles, could it? Alex and Evan; in the top ten of TV couples they were meant to be TV couple number one. Except this wasn't TV, of course, Kelly reminded herself.

All those weeks that Alex and Evan gradually spent getting closer, cautiously taking down one barrier after the other, crossing each line as if they were walking in the other direction when in fact they had been running, racing to each other's side. Alex pretending she was only joking. Evan pretending that he hadn't loved Alex since the first moment he saw her almost three years ago. Neither of them wanting to say the word love in case they had gotten the definition wrong, neither one of the wanting to admit to love in case reality didn't live up to the dream.

But it's easy to live up to the dream in the back of a taxi on the way to an airport.

'We'll kiss again,' Evan told Alex as he left. 'I promise you.' And in that moment they believed they loved each other.

And from that moment so did Kelly.

'Do you want the male point of view?' Nathan cuts though the stressed-out silence. Alex meets his gaze with determined resolution.

'Yep,' she says shortly.

'Don't wait for him – just go and have fun. Just go and live your life.' Nathan smiles mildly and Alex, weary of all those weeks of wondering and dreaming and building and imagining, sees that the whole charade might just amount to nothing, not even a hill of beans.

'Alex isn't waiting,' Kelly tells him staunchly. She doesn't want Alex to be embarrassed into letting go of her dream, which is half of Kelly's dream too.

'You're right, I am waiting. And Evan's not. Three postcards in three months. That's not waiting.' She pushes her hair out of her face and lifts her chin. 'I'm gonna get out there and meet people and take up every single opportunity that I can.'

'Onya,' Kelly says, but she's sorry – sorry to see the romance of the year begin to fade away to nothing.

'Onya,' Nathan says, and he's glad that Alex is being practical because although Nathan believes in love he believes in being practical, and being in love and being able to live the way you must doesn't always mix.

That night Kelly and Nathan take Alex out.

Kelly knows Alex is in mourning for her dream and Nathan knows

Alex is struggling to alter her mindset, but neither of them have seen her as crazy mad as this in a long time. Drunk crazy. Flirting crazy. Crazy mad crazy. The kind of out there 'Look at me I'm mad!' craziness that Alex and Kelly know, that anyone who'd stop to look at her closely would know, translates as, 'Don't look at me, I'm hurting.' Kelly and Nathan follow her from bar to bar trying to keep her out of trouble.

'My God,' Kelly whispers to Nathan, 'I think I preferred her when she was depressed and whinging. She was so much more attractive!' They exchange a little smile, but Kelly keeps her eyes on Alex. To Kelly believing love will find a way is essential, because it's like, well, it's like if you don't keep clapping Tinkerbell will die.

~

Down the road in the foyer of a theatre Miranda looks at Will and then Julie and back at Will. Julie looks at Will. Will looks at Julie. No one looks at Miranda. Suddenly Miranda finds that she is regretting pushing Will into picking the kind of girl he'd go for out of a crowd, because now the self-same is standing right in front of him, smiling at him despite her supercool self. She's a hip, remote maybe-but-maybe-not kind of girl.

Miranda looks her up and down, long blonde curls, hippie chick chic, too much eyeliner. Miranda wouldn't admit it to herself but she likes her style. Suddenly a deliberately suppressed memory pops up.

'Oh I know you! You're Julie,' she says, all but positioning herself between the two of them to break eye contact. Julie turns to her, a look of disinterested 'I can't fuck you, now can I?' resignation written all over her pretty face. Miranda bites back her instinctive dislike. 'You were at the audition the other day, the one for the part of Eliza – do you know who got it?' She finishes with a wide-eyed Miranda smile.

A catlike look of triumph spreads over Julie's face, and Miranda's faux-friendly smile freezes on her face. She knows what Julie is going to say and she can't do anything to stop her.

'Yeah, I got it.' Julie instantly drops Miranda back out of the conversation. 'So Will, what were you saying …?' Miranda bites her lip again, it hurts. 'Damn it, damn it,' she thinks. 'Never bring up a bad audition in conversation …'

'Would you like to sit with us?' Will asks Julie. Miranda's trying to read his face but she can't tell what he's thinking or what he wants. Julie studies her drink for a beat longer than is strictly polite and with

the smallest look at Miranda she half smiles at Will and says, 'Okay.'
Miranda wonders 'What has she just said okay to?'

~

'Your burger looks yummy, is it yummy? Why don't you try it?' Kelly
is trying to get Alex to eat something, but instead Alex leans back in
her seat, pushing her hair of her face and holding it off her neck. A
sheen of alcohol-induced perspiration gleams faintly under the fluo-
rescent strips of the burger bar they have finally managed to bring
her to. Suddenly Alex's eyes widen and she points excitedly.

'Oooh – look, cute attack at 2 a.m.!' she says, in a not very quiet
stage whisper.

Kelly looks around to 2 a.m.

'No, Kel. That's 10 a.m. Over there …' Alex giggles, clapping her
hands over her mouth before whispering. 'I mean 4 a.m., duh!' She is
pointing anyway, so the subterfuge is somewhat wasted. Before Kelly
can find him, he finds them. And he's coming right over to their table.

'Alex. How've you been?' he says pleasantly. He's what Kelly
would call classically good-looking; tall and well built. 'Dark and
sweet,' Kelly thinks absently, 'with hands you could imagine gripping
your forearms moments before he kisses you with that strong, firm
mouth.' Kelly blinks herself back to reality and squeezes Nathan's
knee under the table, feeling a little guilty. Alex laughs. She doesn't
know who the hell he is but she isn't about to admit it.

'Excellent,' she says with amused conviction. 'And you?'

'Really good.' He smiles and looks at her closely. Kelly and
Nathan exchange cringes. Alex giggles.

'Cor, look at you, hey?' She laughs at Rex like a mischievous five-
year-old.'

'What?' Rex half smiles, the way people do when they're not sure
if they're in on the joke or the butt of it. Alex leans forward and
pings the Lycra of his cycling shorts.

'Can't hide anything in there, can you!' She is hysterical, finding
herself very funny. Dark and Sweet shifts from one foot to another.
Kelly wants to hug him.

'Er, right, well I'll see you another time then,' he says, a little
embarrassed and a lot confused (but still very cute, Kelly thinks).
And then he is gone.

A chance meeting like that can change the world again. The
butterfly effect.

3

Trust me, nothing ever turns out the way you imagine it. Nothing. Richie Blake, standing on the verge of world domination, finds it is nothing like he imagined, for example. In fact, since he landed the part of hot hunk on hit soap *The River* it's more like being a naughty schoolboy in front of the headmistress – at least when he's in publicist Pia's office. She looks him up and down with those bullshit-blasting eyes of hers and he can feel his artistic integrity wither like … well, like his dick frankly.

'So you're cool with that, yes?' She asks him. He knows Pia wants his assent and wants him out, but he pauses, feeling like Dorothy in front of the Wicked Witch desperately clinging onto his red shoes. Pia continues, 'Because we're putting a great deal of effort into promoting you as a heartthrob – so we'd like you to follow through with that.' She couldn't load her voice with any more double meaning if she tried. Richie must act straight for his supper.

'Sure …' Richie references his self-image and double checks Pia's version of it against his own Personal and Artistic Integrity. Her expectant silence almost crowds him out of the office door, but he stands his ground.

'The thing is Pia, on reflection …' Pia sighs and taps her pen impatiently against her desk. 'I don't mind doing the interview but I'd rather not do interviews that involve my preference in partners …' Richie looks at his feet and then up at her, half-wincing already in readiness for her inevitable rebuff. Instead she regards him calmly, appearing unconcerned, still and silent.

'It's just that I'd rather focus on my work.' Richie's preference is sucked silently into the vacuum. Pia puts her pen down and pauses, picking up a magazine.

'Richie, this is your work. You're a soap actor; people want to know about you, about your perfect woman. Make something up. Is that really too much to ask?' Richie falters for a moment but then remembers his Integrity.

'I'd rather not answer questions like that,' he says with more conviction than he feels, waiting for the fall-out. He is more afraid when there is none.

Instead Pia turns her back on him and over her shoulder says mildly, 'Then there's really no point in doing the spread, is there?' Richie blinks at her back. It tells him, 'Discussion over.'

~

Jason never imagined that in a few short weeks he'd feel so strongly for the unborn baby that Caitlin carries. He loves that baby more than anything he has ever loved before. Even himself.

It would all be sweetness and light. Except Jason never imagined that in a few short weeks he'd feel so strongly the way he does about Caitlin. He cares about her, he likes her, he wants her – but he knows with total conviction that he doesn't love her. All the expectations and hopes of their first few days together up until and after the conception have come to almost nothing.

If it had happened to a mate, to someone else, Jason would have been horrified. If someone else he knew had rushed into a relationship and a kid just weeks after the catastrophic end of a one-day marriage to the woman formerly know as the love of his life he'd have laughed his head off. He'd have laughed his head off and told them they were mad and bound for failure.

Only it's not so funny when you find out you've done it to yourself. Jason doesn't love Caitlin and he suspects he never will and he doesn't know what to do about it, except to try; because like his mum would have said, 'You've made your own bed, Jason ...'

So when he sees her in the Fu Bar that night he kisses her and calls her sexy and to everyone else, including Caitlin, they look happy and Jason thinks that trying might be enough.

~

After the half-remembered misadventures of her night out with Kelly and Nathan, Alex never imagined to run into her so-called 'cute attack' guy again.

There she is at the pool treading water, missing her daily gossips with Gab, when she sees him surging through the water towards her. She notices his powerful shoulders, distorted though they are beneath the water.

'Hey!' she's calling out even before she knows she is going to, touching his foot as he turns into another lap. He stops and rises out of the water like an aftershave ad. (Alex's cultural references tend to be the more populist ones.)

'Hi,' they greet each other and make small talk in the water.

'Never seen you here before,' Alex says, wondering about her swimming costume and how it looks.

'I've just started coming here,' he tells her, stretching his arms out along the pool. Alex laughs. Why does Alex laugh? What's funny?

'I run into you everywhere,' Alex says. That's not funny. Not unless you're flirting, Alex. Alex, are you flirting? Cute Guy laughs too.

'I know, can you stop stalking me?' he says with a one-sided, much mirror-rehearsed smile. Alex returns it with one of her sideways looks and pulls herself out of the water, sensing him watching the water sparkle on her skin.

'Have you got time for a coffee?' he asks quickly.

Alex pauses and looks at the water dripping from her skin as it splashes against the poolside tiles. She thinks about me and I'm not there.

'OK then,' she says. 'How about my place – it's just around the corner.'

Now I have imagined a lot of things about Alex since I've been gone. But I never imagined that.

~

When Alex and her guest walk through the door Gabrielle is waiting for her, luminous with weeks spent drinking in the sun.

'You look amazing,' Alex tells her as she rushes over to her. They hug for a moment, relieved to have each other back.

'So do you!' Gab returns the compliment. 'God I've missed you!'

Gab raises her eyebrows at the guy and Kelly thinks, 'Mmm, Dark and Sweet again, what does this mean?' Alex almost jumps as if she has half-forgotten he is there, politely waiting to be introduced.

'Oh yeah, right.' She turns to him awkwardly. 'This is Gabrielle, my best friend – she's been overseas for two months – and this is Kelly, my flatmate.' She flounders, wondering how to escape her social faux pas hell, she still hasn't found out his name and she's still pretending she knows who he is.

Kelly to the rescue.

'Yeah, we've met actually, sort of. What's your name again?' She smiles sweetly at Alex as she says it and Alex breathes an inaudible sigh of relief.

'Rex,' Dark and Sweet tells her.

'Rex,' the girls repeat in unison. They all smile a lot trying not to look at his Lycra.

'Um, is there somewhere I can put some clothes on?' Rex asks, feeling three pairs of eyes drawn to his Lycra.

'Yeah, use my room, it's just down there.' Alex tries to look nonchalant as she makes the coffee but the girls are on her immediately, Gab with her big blues bigger than ever.

'So?' she asks, all anticipation.

'Nothing.' Alex shrugs.

'Nothing.' Gabrielle repeats flatly, staring at her, seeing through her.

'I'm telling the truth! Nothing!' Alex is flustered.

'So who is he, then? How do you know him? What does he do?' Gabrielle is determined to get some information. Alex looks embarrassed.

'I don't know,' she says sheepishly.

'Don't know what?' Gab asks.

'Anything actually. I just can't seem to place him ...' Gab looks at her for a long moment before resting back on her heels, deciding to keep what she wants to say to herself, at least for the moment.

'OK, well I only dropped in to say I'm back and that I have this ...' She delves into her bag and brings out a video tape. 'It's from Evan, he made it for you.'

She holds it out to Alex, who stares at it for a while as if uncertain about taking it. Finally she does.

'Really?' she says. 'When's he coming home?' Her voice is so absent of intonation or intent that to Gabrielle and Kelly it simply speaks volumes.

4

Alex is focused, in her place, in her world, where she is queen and in control, far away from thoughts of coffee with half-remembered Rex and an unwatched video tape gathering dust on her bed. Alex is at work.

'I think you've dislocated your shoulder,' she tells some teenage kid, all dreads and dread. 'What were you doing?' She smiles reassuringly at him and quickly puts a drip into his arm, expertly, efficiently.

'Crowd surfing,' He winces and wonders if his moshing days are over.

'OK, I'll put it back in but I'll give you pain relief first.' She looks at the nurse, 'Give me seventy-five milligrams of pethidine and five milligrams of medazolam.' The nurse nods and steps back as Alex slowly injects the drugs into the boy's drip, watching closely as he fades out of consciousness.

'Right,' she says, calm when any other mere mortal would have faltered and failed, 'he's stopped breathing – probably due to us stopping the pain stimulation. We'll have to put in an endotracheal tube and help him breathe for a while. Can you get the anaesthetics registrar – just in case?' The nurse nods again and is gone. Alex works on. She is calm, she is in control. This is her place in the world, a place where she can finally bring order.

'You okay?' Alex nods looking up for a moment from her work and sees Rex. Now she remembers, she smiles at him but quickly returns her attention to the boy.

'He needs to be intubated, can you give me hand?' she asks him. Rex take control and Alex watches him as he works, talking to the unconscious boy as he inserts the tube into his throat. Calm, in control.

Alex looks at him. 'This is his space too,' she thinks, watching as Rex takes the time to make sure the boy is comfortable, padding his shoulder with a folded tube so that the ventilator tube doesn't rub his skin. When he's finished Rex smiles at her for the first time since he arrived on the scene.

'You really didn't know who I was, did you?' he asks her.

'I do now.' Alex smiles back.

'Do you want to go out for dinner tomorrow night?' He cuts to the chase with heroic speed.

'Yes,' she doesn't hesitate. They smile at each other, a reflection of each other.

'I'll pick you up about eight, then.' He holds her gaze for a beat.

'Yes,' she says again and he is gone. Alex turns back to her kingdom, crowned in glory.

~

Will can count the number of days he felt like a king, just for a few short weeks. It began in that first moment after he'd finally crow-barred his nightmare ex-girlfriend Leah out of his life for good and just before he flew his homemade kite for his new girlfriend, Sam, on the beach.

'Will loves Sam,' it proclaimed as it danced in the sky and it hadn't been until Will had seen those words carried on the wind for all the world to see that he realized he had meant it. He really meant it. Will loved Sam and he was king. For three months twenty-six days and eleven hours, Will was king of the world.

And then Sam died. Maybe because of Will. Maybe, he didn't know for certain, but he did know that the girl he loved crossed the road when she was cross with him and she didn't make it to the other side.

'Look left, then right, then left again,' Will repeats to himself under his breath. 'Look, damn you.' He looks at the wind in the branches of the tree he is sitting under and feels the world spinning on its axis and he waits for – wishes for – gravity to let him loose of its bonds.

'How are you, mate?' Kelly's voice brings Will back down to earth with an invisible thud. He looks at her as though she had always been there.

'Do you think she looked to the right instead of the left? Why didn't she cross at the lights? Do you think she tripped?' he asks her, demands of her, anger and resentment burning just beneath the timbre of his voice. Kelly sits beside him and wraps her arms around his shoulders, wanting to bury her face in his neck and put out his pain with a smother of love, but knowing that she can't. Knowing that for all his bravado, for all his strength and outward show of getting on with it, Will's grief is like a mad dog: it sits at his feet quietly for hours and then without warning it leaps up and sinks its teeth into his throat.

'Maybe … maybe you could go to where it happened and see it for yourself?' she suggests, almost able to watch her words fall away from the wall of Will's resistance.

'Do you think she said anything as she was dying or was she just dead?' he turns to look into her eyes, the whites of his almost entirely red. 'Can it happen so fast? Can it?'

Kelly sits back helpless and hopeless, for once at a loss.

'I don't know,' she says simply.

~

Tonight, for the first time in a while, Alex feels like herself – or like she imagines she should feel – as Rex escorts her into the restaurant. She knows she is looking good. She knows he's looking good. The prospects for the evening are looking good until …

'Hi, how are you!' A blousy blonde is suddenly in her face. Well Rex's face to be exact, and he looks slightly uncomfortable with it.

'Hello,' he says simply. 'Alex – this is Jennifer.' Jennifer gives her a cursory glance.

'Hi. And you know Hamish McManus, don't you Rex?' Rex nods and they all greet each other.

'Join us!' Jennifer demands, sweetly enthusiastic. Rex and Alex attempt excuses but the force of Jennifer's will seems unstoppable and all at once Alex's starring role in her own date has turned into the supporting act – no, make that an extra extra – in Jennifer's world.

'Ooooh, Rex, let's share oysters,' Jennifer says with a sex-filled giggle and Alex thinks, 'I knew this couldn't happen to me.'

~

Kelly almost feels guilty for being so happy and she almost feels doomed, certain that a love as perfect as hers surely can't last. Curled up on her bed right now as Nathan smiles indulgently at her, listening to the latest of her theories on how to achieve the perfect balance in life.

Kelly, as always, had a theory on how to achieve the perfect trifecta (Love, Work and Domestic Bliss) since the day she breezed into our flat and our lives. She left halfway through a sentence, abandoning her mobile and half of her personal life. Alex and I both knew that she'd be back for both and we knew she'd fit perfectly into the world of us.

Nathan does love her, more than she even knows. To think she almost didn't date him because he was too perfect, and yet now his perfection is everything that makes her heart sing and tremble. Kelly's seen a lot films and read a lot of books. She's afraid that nothing that is perfect ever lasts, that her happiness will be martyred to the laws of the universe. She's afraid but so in love she can almost forget the fear.

~

Jason's life is waiting for him when he gets in from work. A beautiful woman carrying his child – it's all he's ever wanted but now he can't make himself want it enough.

'How's my beautiful baby?' he asks. He's later than he said he'd be; he watches Caitlin's face, trying to judge her mood.

'How was soccer?' Caitlin doesn't take her eyes off the TV. It's bad.

'I scored the winning goal!' He plays the cute and contrite card.

'I was thinking about when I go back to work after the baby is born.' Jason folds his hands and sits next to her, suddenly deflated.

'Oh really?' Since they had gotten together Jason had a hard time picturing the future; even tomorrow seemed like a long way off.

'I think I'll go back quite quickly.' She still has not looked at him.

'How quickly?'

'Eight weeks.'

Jason studies his hand for a moment, trying to keep the anger out of his voice.

'I think that's a bit soon,' he says. 'Your maternity leave is six months.'

'That's too long, I don't want to completely blow my career,' she says bitterly, feeling the full weight of pregnancy weighing heavily on her spirit. Jason tries to reassure her.

'It wouldn't be the end of the world. I earn good money!' As usual his trying doesn't seem to help.

'Yes, but how long are you going to be around? I don't know that.' She watches his face, closely searching for a hint of the answer she's looking for.

'I'll always be around to look after my baby,' Jason says deliberately. Caitlin swallows hard and looks back at the TV.

'I meant how long will you be around to look after me?' Her voice is full of tears.

~

Richie? Well, right now his world domination seems in peril. His Integrity seems to have let him down; he's not one of 'The River Boys' featured on the cover of this week's TV listings magazine Simon's left out for him. Pia has been as good as her word. Richie feels the horror of exclusion as keenly as Pia planned. He takes a moment to rationalize.

Richie makes a call.

'Pia, it's Richie here. Listen I've thought about few things and I think I will do those interviews. Yep. Yep. I'm happy to talk about that sort of stuff. Yep, okay. Okay. Bye.'

Richie has decided that he and his Integrity should take a bit of a break from each other.

~

What the writer guy knows is that romance isn't hearts and flowers clichés. You can't predict it, it's out-of-the-blue spontaneity.

That's why when Alex gets home tired and dejected after bailing from the date that the lovely Jennifer hijacked, she isn't ready for it when it truly arrives.

The doorbell goes and it's Rex, complete with Chinese.

'Have you eaten?' he says, but he means 'Do you still want me?'

'No,' she says. But she means 'Yes.'

5

The last thing you ever want to see first thing in the morning, when your hair's mussed up and your face is still creased with sleep, is the more perfect version of you sitting in your kitchen. But this is exactly what's happening to Miranda.

Julie is breakfasting in her kitchen.

'Hi, how are you?' Julie says brightly.

'Hi.' Miranda's reply is just about polite. She smoothes down her hair and butters her croissant studiously. When Will walks into the room her eyes bore into the back of his head. She's not exactly sure why she's so angry. She knows Julie makes her angry, with her curly hair and her make-up already on and her fresh, clean skin. (Shouldn't the Pores Afresh girl be the one with the luminous skin?) She knows Will's still broken and she's pretty sure it's not Julie who can fix it. And she knows that Julie got the part and she didn't.

'Ready to go?' Will asks Julie amiably. Miranda scans his tone for intentions but like so many things about Will recently it's devoid of any, or anything else.

'See you tonight M,' he says to her in exactly the same tone. She watches them goes and eats her breakfast alone.

~

Working on no breakfast to speak of, Alex walks quickly through her kingdom ready for whatever other people's fate has to throw at her. She's ready and poised for action but all the same she's thinking about saying goodbye to Rex last night and their goodnight first kiss. About how she sat on her bed hugging her knees up to her chest thinking about how nice it was to say goodbye to him, knowing she'll see him again, yet half-afraid that she won't, feeling all sweet-sixteenish anxious with anticipation.

'Will I see you tonight at the residents' drinks?' Rex appears by her side, a daydream made flesh.

'Yeah, I was planning to go.' She half-masks her pleasure at seeing him appear so suddenly – not because she wants to, but just because she feels she ought.

'I'll see you there then,' he says, his dark eyes crinkling in a smile and then he's gone again like a vanishing wish.

Alex and Rex. Some people, Kelly for example, would say that they look exactly right together – Christ, they even sound right together. Kelly would rest her chin on her arms and look at the stars and say that sometimes two people look exactly right together – like two halves finally fitting.

Kelly would say that. Your narrator would beg to differ.

6

Maybe it's the promise of a daydream half come true, but when Alex gets home that afternoon she finally feels ready to watch the video tape, just in case there's an outside chance that last week's daydream might come true too.

When the static clears abruptly to reveal Video Evan's face she's shocked to find her heart racing. She turns, looking around to make sure she's alone.

'Well, here I am at the writer retreat and so far it's fantastic …' She listens to Video Evan whisper. She watches him talk – and slowly, very slowly, her Evan smile finds its home amongst her features. She remembers how much she missed him and she's waiting, waiting for any sign at all that's he's missed her. For a few moments, Rex is nowhere.

'I've been here for two weeks now,' Video Evan whispers. He's in bed, his face close to the camera just moments away from the closeness of a kiss. 'I've been a bit lonely.' He pauses again. 'Alex I've … goodnight.'

Alex swallows hard, waiting for the message for her to wait.

She watches Video Evan in Cuba, dancing, talking. She watches as Gabrielle joins him, laughing, flirting with the camera. She experiences all their fun second-hand and ever more remotely. Father and farther away from the taxi cab kisses.

Gradually her Evan smile fades out.

'There's nothing on the tape,' she tells Kelly later. She shrugs. 'Nothing.'

'Yeah, but he's interested in you, obviously. Or he wouldn't have made you the tape.' Kelly's not sure how much of the bright side she is supposed to see. Maybe Alex wants there to be nothing on the tape. A clear way for Rex. Kelly concludes that maybe Alex isn't sure either.

'Aren't you going out with Rex tonight? Some residents' thing?' Kelly asks, testing the water.

'I don't think so, I'm not up to it.' Alex looks tired, lonely and defeated and Kelly can't bear it.

'You should go to the residents' drinks,' Kelly says firmly, doing her best imitation of her Nanna, who always knows best.

'Why?' Alex responds like a little girl.

'Because Rex is a babe and because he wants you to go and because there is nothing on the tape. Go.' Alex looks at Kelly, gathers her resolve and stands up.

'OK, you're right. I'll go. I'll go.' And in that moment she packs away all of her Evan dreams. It seems that Video Evan didn't quite cut the mustard. Sometimes you can hold back too long.

'Wear something cute!' Kelly shouts after her as she goes to her bedroom to get ready. 'And leave your hair down!'

~

Alex shuts the apartment door behind her and wonders how on earth two dates in a row could be ruined so entirely by the same person, by this Jennifer woman. The Jennifer woman and taramasalata, that is.

'Hi,' she says dejectedly to Kelly and Nathan, trying not to notice how perfect they look with each other, entwined in easy relaxation.

'What happened?' Ever-sensitive Kelly pulls herself out of Nathan's arms and leans over the back of the sofa.

'Oh my God.' Even deep in depression, Alex knows a good story. 'I did think it was going well, we were really clicking there for a bit, and then out of nowhere it all went downhill fast. First off I spilt taramasalata on my boob! And then Rex was, like, trying to wipe it off while not looking like he's trying to cop a feel! He just made it worse and I'm going all red and he's going all red. And then that bloody Jennifer from the restaurant? Oyster woman? She comes over all glamorous and, "Oh, Rex darling come back to mine for a private party!" or something like that and sees the bloody dip on my tits and shout it out to the whole bloody bar! "WE NEED A CLOTH OVER HERE, SHE HAS SPILT TARAMASALATA ALL DOWN HERSELF." Like I'm a retard. And then she goes to me, "Oh my God your dress is ruined! You should go home." I left. I got the hell out of there.' Alex flops down on to the sofa. 'It'd be funny if wasn't typical of my whole bloody life! My whole life is a taramasalata stain on my boob.' She half-laughs for Nathan and Kelly but she doesn't feel any better. Their affection for each other is like a palpable presence in the air and Alex just can't bear to breathe it in at the moment.

'I'm off to sponge this,' she says with an heroic smile, and Kelly watches her go.

'She's faking that laughing-it-off thing,' she says to Nathan. 'If Evan had just said what he felt none of this would have happened. That's men for you, that is,' she tells him gravely.

'You don't know how Evan feels. The way he feels might be better left unsaid, at least until they are face to face again.' He strokes the length of her forearm with the tip of his finger. 'Isn't it time for bed yet?' he runs his gaze over her body.

'No, Nathan, it is not. You know I have to attend to all seven areas of my life to create perfect harmonic balance. We did love life this morning – I still have intellectual and social life to attend to.' She looks at him mock seriously. 'I'm going to be up till midnight.' Nathan snakes an arm round her neck and pulls her in close for a kiss.

'Come on, let's do love life again.' Just as she's about to crumble the phone rings. Kelly leaps up, enthused. 'I'll get it! If it's for me I can pass it off as social life!' Nathan smiles to himself as he watches her go to the phone and wonders, 'Is it possible for any one person to be so charming?'

As she pick up the handset her face falls.

'Hi, how are you,' Kelly asks deadpan. She turns to Nathan and mouths 'It's Rex.' 'Oh yeah, sure. Hang on.' Kelly puts her hand over the mouthpiece. 'Cheeky bastard,' she mumbles to Nathan. 'Alex! Phone!'

Alex takes it, weary and worn.

'Yep?' she says shortly.

'I just wanted to make sure you got home safely.' She listens to Rex's voice for traces of embarrassment and pity.

'I'm fine,' she says, uncertain that she has heard either. 'Are you at Jennifer's?'

'No, I'm in my car … I'm not far from yours, actually.' In the space of a heartbeat the whole of Alex's evening changes.

'Do you want to …'

'Can I come over?' They speak together.

'Yes,' Alex says and she means it.

Twenty minutes later and Kelly stands for a second outside of Alex's bedroom just before she makes her way to her own. She listens to the low murmur of conversation; Alex's giggle deep and flirtatious. Rex says something and then she hears nothing. She pads into to her room and curls up beside Nathan,

'Nathan, there's a new world order again. I haven't seen Alex like that with a guy since Evan left, which of course, begs the glaring question … What's going to happen when Evan gets back?' Nathan laughs and buries his face in her neck.

'Come on Kel, remember the balance. It must be time for love life by now.'

7

Traffic rushes by. The sound of horns booms and shrieks in his head. Cars are hurtling towards him at speed; crashing into his dreams. Horns scream, and brakes screech so loud he can hardly bear it and then the dark, dead sound of a body hitting the road punching him in the heart.

Will wakes up sweating and remembers. Sam is dead.

He walks slowly to the shower and waits for the water to heat enough to boil away the pain.

Will feels as if he might as well be dead too.

~

Alex is glad to be alive. Her fingers run over Rex's warm brown skin and she feel her pulse throbbing in her fingertips.

'I've prepared your breakfast, doctor,' she flirts, fluttering her lashes at him. 'It's waiting for you in theatre.' Rex's eyes travel the length of her legs and then, in a second, his face – which had been full of delightfully nefarious intent – changes.

'Hey, I know! I can show you golden ratios!' He sounds like a little boy at show and tell.

'Oh can you?' Alex says in an ill-fated attempt to re-fuel the flirtation.

'Yeah, the perfect breakfast cereal.' He smiles at her proudly. 'The Fibonacci numbers.'

'I'm sorry?' Alex is lost. 'Fibonacci?'

'0, 1, 2, 3, 5, 8, 13, 21, 34 and so on. That's the sequence.' He acts like he's reciting his ABCs.

'Right …' Alex says, taken aback. 'Why?'

'It's the answer to a problem,' Rex tells her, mildly distracted by the proximity of her body. 'Have you ever counted spirals on a sunflower? Twenty-one going one direction, thirty-four the other. Consecutive Fibonacci numbers. Pretty amazing huh?' Alex wants to be part of the enthusiasm.

'I guess …' she says uncertainly.

'If I drew a logarithmic spiral where all the angles were equal, based on the sequences, you know what I'd get?' He runs his finger down her shoulder and just inside the rim of her robe. 'The curve of your breast.'

Alex smiles at him, but somehow the symmetry of the moment is bent out of sequence.

~

Miranda is glad to be alive and enjoying the simple pleasure of squeezing a blackhead.

'What's up?' Will appears behind in the mirror in true horror flick style. She jumps and smiles at him, before returning her concentration to the mirror.

'Oh, I've got a blackhead.' Will looks at her reflection.

'A blackhead?' He laughs, but he laughs like it isn't funny.

'Yeah it's a bitch,' Miranda says to her own reflection. Will shakes his head and now he can't stop laughing, can't stop laughing like it isn't funny. He picks up a Pores Afresh packet from the sink. Miranda instinctively takes a step back from him.

'You get paid shitloads of money … your picture is all over the city and you even use the things …' Miranda continues to back away from him, half smiling, confused by his sudden hysterical aggression.

'I do use them,' she defends herself, almost drowned out by his laughter. 'Will, stop it!' Her raised voices catches his attention and the laughter stops. He looks at her dumbly, like he's just been woken from sleepwalking.

'What were you laughing at?' she asks him. For a second, Will looks at her like she is a stranger.

'I wouldn't have clue,' he says. And he doesn't.

~

Will still can't solve the mystery as he passes the last scaffolding pole up to Davo. He can still hear the faint rush of traffic in his ears like he's listening to a seashell gone wrong, but he tries to block it out. He tries to find rhythm in the routine of his work.

'Is that it Will?' Davo shouts down from the very top of the scaffold.

'Yeah,' Will shouts back – loud enough to make himself heard in his own head.

'All right – smoko!' Davo yells and just as he pulls off his glove, he stumbles forward and grabs onto the nearest piece of support. 'That was a close thing,' he thinks and as he breathes a sigh of relief he sees that he's kicked a pile of rivets over the edge of the platform; rivets and a scaffolding pole plummet down to earth.

Every motion slows right down.

'Get out of the way,' Davo shouts out, but Will can hardly hear him over the traffic. He looks up and sees the scaffolding pole heading right for him. He takes off his hard hat. He waits.

It crashes to the ground at his feet, the rivets arriving right after like a shower of hard rain.

The crew is all around Will then, his mates shouting, running, worrying, shocked and elated.

'Are you all right?' someone asks him.

'I'm okay,' Will whispers. The foreman arrives, the clamour rises, different version, and eye-witness accounts all told in harmonic discord.

'I'm okay,' Will says, a little louder.

'Jesus …' The foreman looks at him in disbelief. 'Are you …?'

'I'M OKAY!' Will shouts. 'I'M OKAAAAY!' He wrenches the pole out of the ground and looks the foreman in the eye.

'Look to the right. Look to the left. Then look right again.' The foreman shakes his head at him, and starts to tell someone to call an ambulance.

Will is running away.

He runs through the crowds on the sidewalk, he runs through the traffic, knowing the traffic can't hurt him. The street noises fade in and fade out. The world focuses in and focuses out, and then fades out to black.

Gravity releases him at last and Will faints.

When he opens his eyes he sees a clown. 'Yes, a clown,' he thinks. 'That'd be right.'

'You all right mate?' The clown asks him.

'Yes, you're right,' Will nods. The clown looks uncertain but presses a flyer into his hand. He gets paid by the leaflet market his kids' party business.

Will reads the message the clown has been sent to give him.

'YOU'RE FREE.' Will reads. 'That's right, you're a clown. I'm Free.' He struggles to his feet and laughs. 'Sam,' he says out loud. 'I'm coming to see you.'

Minutes later and Will stands on the brink of Sam's road feeling the pull of the racing traffic. He closes his eyes, trying to feel for Sam in the warm exhaust-filled air. For a moment his dreams fill his mind and he hears the thud of her body hitting a car. The world spins away and he opens his eyes, desperately searching for a point to focus on.

Across the street he sees Julie, sitting outside a café. Cool and untroubled in a world of confusion. Will nods to himself. It's a sign, after all. He's Free.

He steps off the curb and follows in Sam's footsteps. He doesn't hurry, he doesn't look, because he knows he doesn't have to. He's invincible; he's Free. The traffic can go around him but not though him, no way. Traffic can't touch death-defying Will. Julie has seen him from across the street, her face white and frozen.

'She's Free too,' he thinks and leaving a cacophony of chaos behind he calmly joins her at her table.

'Are you crazy?' she asks him, laughing with horror and delight.

'No, I'm not crazy.' He smiles. 'I'm Free.'

~

Later on Will tears through the weekly soccer game like a Brazilian whirlwind, fantastically fast and fabulous. Making all the moves, hitting all the strokes, scoring all the goals. The rest of them watch him in awe.

'Mate, where'd that come from?' Jason asks, a little envious.

'I've just had the best day,' Will tells them. The others gather round, smiling, glad to see he's feeling happy for once.

'Yeah, it started off a shocker ...' He shakes his head and smiles.

'Yeah? How come?' Miranda remembers how he was with her this morning. Is that what he means?

'Well, there was this accident at work and I nearly got killed ...' The group stops dead.

'You almost got killed?' They all know Will isn't one to exaggerate.

Will looks at them and realizes that they don't understand, they don't see the big picture, all they can think about is the details, the 'almost getting killed' bit.

'Incidental,' he wants to say, but somehow he's too tired.

He doesn't want a fuss, so he lets Miranda lead him to Alex. He lets Alex poke and prod him about. He sits under her quite intrusive gaze for as long as he can bear it.

'Will, have you been thinking a lot about Sam?' she ask him levelly, as if she were asking the time.

'I've been having dreams ... I thought maybe if I saw the place ... Anyway, I met Julie there and we went to Luna Park.' He smiles to himself. 'It was nice to be with a girl again.' Alex frowns.

'Tell me about your dreams,' she says. Will shrugs and makes a car out of one fist and Sam out of the other.

'Ka-boom!' He giggles.

'Will,' Alex says gently. 'I think you might be in a little bit of shock.' Will rolls his eyes and sighs. Why does nobody else see it the way he does?

'I'm Free, see?' he says and he shows her the flyer as proof. Alex frowns again.

It reads 'Children's Party Quotes Free!' but she says nothing, not really sure of what she can say.

8

'So I bought this pair of boxers,' Alex tells Gabrielle as they wiggle their toes in the water, their old lunchtime swim routine re-established at last.

'Oh yeah?' Gab laughs. 'Kinky.' Alex smiles sheepishly.

'Yeah well, not really – they were joke ones. I thought this guy's so obsessed by numbers, so orderly, that it's got to be something … wacky.' Alex rolls her eyes. She hates the word 'wacky'.

'Got it. Right … and?' Gab is eager for the story.

'And so he looks at me like I've handed him a stick of dynamite. Not even a smile, nothing. Not even an ironic smile.' Alex shakes her head, disbelieving as she remembers. '"What do I do with them," he goes and I go, "You wear them!" And he goes, "I can't wear these, I wear jocks …"' Gab laughs out loud and lifts herself out of the water in one easy movement.

'Jesus, that is a bit super straight …' she says. Alex follows her out of the pool.

'No, no just wait, wait till you hear his reason for only wearing jocks.'

'Go on then.' Gab is intrigued.

'OK, so he goes, "I can't wear boxer shorts – everyone can tell when you've got an erection!" The girls laugh together.

'You're joking?' Gab says, incredulous.

'I'm not,' Alex replies, deadpan. 'So I said to him, "No one's going to know you've got them on" – and then it dawned on me – "not unless you get erections at the hospital!" And you know what, he does!' She gazes at Gab, her face a picture at the unfathomable mystery of men. Gab shakes her head.

'Now you are joking,' she says.

'I'm not. He told me cool as a cucumber,' Alex continues. 'So then I ask him, "Which bit of the hospital do you get these erections in?" And he goes, cool as you like, "I get an erection at two forty-five every afternoon."'

Gab claps her hands over her mouth. 'Two forty-five?' Gab is almost speechless.

'On the knocker, he says.' Alex looks at the bright blue sky with a wry smile. 'Tell me, how did someone like me get to be with someone that anal?'

'Mmm, good question.' Gab considers it seriously.

'That time I was joking,' Alex sighs.

~

'Three!' Will shouts out to Julie just before taking a second to look out at the flickering lights of the city. It's a pretty good view up here – and to think that Miranda almost stopped him leaving the apartment. But she couldn't stop him; no one can stop the unstoppable Will tonight. No one and nothing.

That's why he's here on the very top board of the diving tower at the pool, even though the pool is closed. That's why he could bring Julie – powerless to resist him – here and tell her to close her eyes while he undressed her down to her stockings and to keep them closed until she heard him count to three.

'I feel like jumping off something very high,' he had told her. He can see her looking up at him now, very far away, her mouth open.

'Fuck me dead,' she says awestruck, but Will can't hear her.

'I could really handle "The Mark of Cain!"' Will calls out to the night and sure enough the night provides the music kicking out the jams.

Will balances on the very edge of the board and looks out into the sky.

'Yeaaaaaaaaaaaaaaaaaaaah,' he shouts as he dives into the pool. Julie flings herself into the water after him; catching up and pulling him to her, she clings to the heat of his body in the cold water.

'I didn't know you could dive,' she says breathless.

'I can't,' he says and he kisses her like he's never going to stop.

He's still kissing her as they tumble through the door half an hour later. Miranda sits waiting for him on the sofa, cradling a cup of tea in her hands, the way that worried women do.

'Hi, Mum,' he says wearily.

'Are you all right?' Miranda looks at Julie, unable to stop her disapproval spilling into her voice. Will hangs his arm around Julie's neck.

'Are we all right?' he asks her, his words are slurred, but not from alcohol.

'We're amazing.' Julie is super superior. ''Night Miranda.' She makes her way to his room like it's her that lives here and Miranda is the cuckoo in the nest.

'Look, Will …' Miranda begins earnestly, clumsily trying to take his hand. 'Julie isn't Sam …'

'No, Julie isn't Sam. Julie's Alive and I'm Alive and Sam's Dead! Gone. Finished. No more dreams.' He breaks away from Miranda.

'Don't let the bed bugs bite.' He bites her head off.

Miranda winces as he slams his bedroom door shut.

Thirty minutes later and Will sees Sam's body slamming into the oncoming car. He's dreaming again. Struggling like a man drowning in the water, fighting for air, fighting for consciousness. Finally he breaks the surface of his sleep.

Julie lies undisturbed at his side, silent and peaceful.

'You know what,' he whispers to her. 'I need to jump off something very high.'

~

'Three,' Will whispers to himself. He takes a moment to look out at the lights of the city and the traffic rushing by on the freeway. There was no one to stop him coming here either. No one to stop him standing on the very top of the scaffolding he helped to build this morning. It seems like a lifetime away.

He eases himself to the very edge of the scaffold.

'I could really handle "The Mark of Cain"?' he asks the night, uncertain now and alone. The night is unforthcoming.

'Doesn't matter,' Will lies to himself, 'I can do it, I'm Free.'

And he lets himself fall just like the scaffolding pipe did, just for a moment before the fear smashes him back from the edge and he grabs on to the frame like he's never going to let go.

Will curls up as tight as he can and he knows that he doesn't want to die and he knows he isn't Free.

~

Alex stretches out her arms into the morning and opens her eyes to see the boxers she bought Rex flung over the back of a chair, unworn. 'Evan would wear them,' she can't help thinking. 'At least Evan's got spontaneity.'

Rex's strong arm snakes around her waist and draws her into the curve of his chest. Alex pushes any more thoughts of Evan out of bed.

~

Miranda had been trying to work out what's been going on since

Julie slammed out of the apartment this morning. All she knows is that Will was gone and that Julie didn't seem to know – or care – where.

'Did Will even tell you he nearly got killed yesterday?' She'd shouted at Julie, unable to bare her smug facade any longer. Julie looked stung but she landed her own right hook before she left.

'He probably left because he couldn't face dealing with you!' she'd replied and slammed out of the flat. And Miranda has been waiting and worrying ever since.

When Will bursts in through the door, relief and anxiety race each other across Miranda's heart at equal speed.

'What's happening to me?' he asks her, lost and confused. 'I was Free … the flyer said so, but then it stopped working and there wasn't music any more and I wasn't Free. I was just me and I was scared again.' His eyes are filled with tears.

'What's happening?' he repeats.

'You've had a shock,' Miranda whispers as she leads him to his room. 'It's wearing off. You'll be all right.'

'But I have to go to work.' He makes a half-hearted attempt to walk in the other direction.

'Shhhh, shhhh now.' Miranda lies him down and brushes the hair from his forehead. 'Don't worry. I'll phone work. Go to sleep.' She watches and waits until he is sleeping and she watches and waits while he is sleeping.

She wishes she could make everything all right by just being there. What she doesn't know is that she can.

9

Simon strolls into the bar like a man at peace with the world, brimful of sun and relaxation. He watches Kelly on her hands and knees clearing up the latest customer catastrophe.

'How's it going here?' he asks her. She stands, feeling a slight kink in her back and the sheen of the heat on her forehead.

'Yeah, fine. There was a fight earlier – I sorted it. And the stock taking, and the cashing up and I had a quick look at the book and jotted down some ideas for a theme night.' She smiles at him, but the smile is absent of the usual Kelly sparkle. She doesn't mention the college course books she's been hiding under the cash register for the last week and she neglects to mention the speech she's been practising, about the reasons why she feels she has to quit this dead-end job. She neglects to mention it and decides that now is not a good time to say it. It never seems like a good time to say it.

'Kel, can we have a word, please?' Simon beckons her over. Kelly shrugs and pulls a stool up at the bar.

'God, do you know I think that's the first time I've sat down all day.' Kelly shakes off the comment with a smile. She doesn't want Simon to think she's complaining. Simon shakes his head gravely at her.

'Kelly, you're fired,' he says lightly and pours her a drink. Kelly looks around at all the work she's accomplished in only one day and feels her lip quivering. Over-stretched and over-tired, her resistance is low.

'What! Why?' she asks him furiously.

'Because it's the only way you'll ever get out of here and go to college, of course!' Simon grins at her. Her fury swiftly evaporates but her confusion lingers on.

'You know I want to go to college … How do you know?' she asks slowly.

'Keep up, darling … I'm gay, everyone knows homosexuals are more intuitive,' Simon says deadpan, just the edges of a smile teasing at his mouth. 'Kel, it was bloody obvious and anyway you've a face made of glass and you didn't hide your prospectus very well. I found it two days ago.' Kelly laughs. Relief flooding her face, she stand down her speech.

'Listen,' Simon continues. 'I know that I've been working you like a slave the last couple of months – and I know you're the kind of person who can't say no, just wants to help and all that. And that is the kind of attitude that's going to get you nowhere fast and me the best tan of my life and middle-aged spread. But I'm not that kind of guy. So you're fired.' Kelly laughs feeling unburdened and light, looks inward, assesses her dreams and aspiration and then sighs hard and feel her spirits sink. And all in a fleeting Kelly moment.

'Simon, do you think I sell myself short?' Simon huffs out his exasperation.

'God yes,' he says seriously. Kelly considers this for a beat.

'So do I. I want a qualification. I want to be a professional woman with my own business. I don't want to end up being a ... being a ...' She falters.

'Bartender?' Simon finishes for her without reprieve.

'Well, yeah.'

'So you're fired. Now look, I have this position to fill on a part-time basis. It would be ideal for ... say ... a student such as yourself. Do you want the job?' Kelly laughs.

'Yes, please.' Simon really is a top-shelf guy.

'Good. Now go get your qualifications. I've always thought you have a natural aptitude for marketing.'

~

Will opens his eyes and waits for the ceiling to come crashing down on him. He holds his breath for as long as he can and then he realizes that for the first time since Sam died catastrophe hasn't struck him hard in the chest the moment he opens his eyes. Will feels something almost like peace. He looks from the ceiling to the chair in the corner and finds Miranda.

'How long have you been there?' he asks her. Miranda shakes her head mildly and half shrugs.

'Not long, I don't know.' They watch each other closely for a moment, each of them searching for traces of the morning's turmoil in each other's faces.

'Thanks,' Will says finally, slowly, like he's learning to speak again. Miranda says nothing, but accepts his gratitude with a quiet smile.

They spend the rest of the afternoon careful around each other but happy and close; like good friends are when they've come through stormy water. When one good friend has guided the other safe to shore. Maybe that sense of comfortable ease is what makes it so hard for Will when he sits opposite Julie later that night.

Everything that makes him feel so at ease with Miranda makes him uneasy and uncomfortable with Julie. He considers conjuring up the heated moment of the swimming pool kiss again, but he finds without surprise that the memory frightens him.

'… It's a great idea, and I'm trying to write it with this guy but he's just not getting into it, you know?' Julie tells him excitedly. Will feels guilty. He led her on and now she's feeling secure in his company when security is the last thing he can offer her.

'So what do you think?' Julie asks him brightly. Will notices that she's left lipstick on her glass, a perfect negative impression of her swimming pool lips.

'Are you listening to me?' She repeats, her voice just as bright but now brittle.

'Julie, I need to tell you something …' One look at her face and Will knows he wouldn't have to say another word if he didn't want to; she knows. 'That dive last night – in fact, the whole of last night. That wasn't me.' Julie grips the stem of her glass hard.

'I know,' she says, without meeting his eyes.

'I had this accident, but it's not just that – there's all this other stuff going on and …'

'I know,' Julie repeats, lifting her chin this time and bravely holding his gaze. 'Miranda told me.' She pauses and smiles at him, a cautious half-flirtatious smile. 'It's OK …' she begins to say.

'No!' Will snaps at her vehemently, pulls himself back into control and then finishes deliberately quiet and soft. 'No. No it's not OK. Something happened to me yesterday. Something that meant I could dive off towers and walk through traffic and meet a girl and not be afraid. I thought I was Free. I thought I would always be Free. But I'm not. I'm not like that guy. I'm just a scaffolder.' Julie presses her best smile home.

'But …' she begins. Will shakes his head.

'I'm not the bloke for you,' he says with finality.

'And am I the girl for you?' Julie asks despite herself.

'I don't know,' Will says out loud at last. But he's given her his answer and they both know it's no.

~

Will walks out of the evening and into the night and through the early hours, trying to get lost. He's happy to be alone and not knowing where he's going until he gets there. When he gets there he finds Miranda.

'What are you doing here?' he asks her. Not until he speaks to her does he realize that he's come back to his work place, the scene of the accident that seems a lifetime away.

'You weren't at home,' she says simply. 'I figured you'd be at Sam's road or here.' Will looks up at the platform; a wave of fear surges in his gut as he remembers the last time he went up there. He swallows and steels himself to put it all behind him. He's glad Miranda is here.

'Come on,' he says, holding out a hand to her. 'Let's go up.'

Just as they reach the top of the scaffold the sun begins to seep over the city's skyline. Will looks at the same old streets, familiar buildings touching the sky and the crease of the roads busy with traffic and he sees everything with perfect clarity.

'Everything's changed,' he says to the dawn and then to Miranda. 'Everything's new, like I have to learn it all again.' Miranda hears the little boy in his voice and her hand slips along the cold metal of the scaffolding railing until her fingers find the warmth as his. As they wait for the day to arrive in the city, an early international flight sinks into Tullamarine airport.

10

Alarm bells are ringing in Alex's ears, but they're not the ones that should be. She fights sleep off and stretches taut against the strength of Rex's body.

'We have to get up,' she smiles a whisper to him.

'Oh yeah?' Rex presses his hand into the small of her back. Alex musters willpower she does not feel.

'We really do have to get up,' she repeats with paper-thin resolve. She is letting herself melt into his embrace when she hears the knocking on the apartment door.

'Christ, who's that?' Rex growls. 'Ignore it,' he instructs her but Alex pushes him away and pulls herself forcibly out of his embrace.

'I can't ignore it. It might be important, an emergency.' She shivers as she pulls her robe around her. 'I'll be back before you know it.'

Rex grumbles, pulling the covers over his head. 'Why do women always think everything is an emergency ...' he complains to the pillows.

Alex is already smiling at the thought of going back to bed when she pulls open the door. Her face falls fifty feet.

'Hi.' Alex looks at me as if I've flown in from another planet, not Cuba. I let my smile settle into my face and decide to let jetlag to take the blame for any emotional impropriety the sight of her may have sparked in my eyes. I let the moment fall flat.

'I lost my keys ...' I tell her, hoping she'll stand aside and let me in, or throw her arms around me and hug me or something, anything – please.

'Er ... right.' She stands aside, waving me into the apartment with a stiff and formal gesture. It's maybe not the option I would have preferred. Rex walks out of her bedroom, still warm with sleep and wearing a hastily grabbed pair of comedy shorts.

'Hi,' I say to him, briefly raising my eyebrows questioningly at Alex. It seems a bit early for sincerities anyhow. Alex rakes her fingers though her hair and visibly pulls herself together.

'Oh God, right. Rex,' She smiles at him theatrically. 'This is Evan,

Evan my flatmate.' She takes a deep breath. Evan this is Rex, Rex my … Rex.' Her Rex.

I've been three months and ten chapters away from her and now she's standing here in front of me I can't think of one right thing to say or one right thing to do.

'I like your boxers,' I say to her Rex and I go in search of coffee or whisky or both.

No, just whisky.

11

The bad thing about jetlag is that you go to sleep with your nose in your beer. The good thing is you get to do stuff you'd normally put off, things like sticking up the souvenirs, sorting out your travelling life into your roots down, turned around up-rooted life.

You get to use the kitchen when everyone else is asleep, or otherwise engaged anyhow, which is handy because you're hungry and restless and so wide awake you get the feeling you'll never sleep again. And I need to sleep again, because if I know one true thing it's that I won't be able to stay up all night listening to Alex and her Rex … talking, or whatever they doing, for even one more night. Ultimately jetlag is like a bad night on speed, and it's very easy for things to get you pissed right off.

Little noises, sex-type sounds. That kind of thing means I'll be right here in the kitchen making a castle out of Weetabix waiting for silence and morning and noise.

'I hope you're going to eat all those?' Kelly makes me jump. We regard each other with bleary-eyed smiles for a moment. 'Thought you were an hallucination,' she mumbles. 'What's with Fort Knox?'

'I got bored, my body clock's still in the US somewhere.' I sit uneasy in my chair, too hyped for coffee, too edgy to relax, wanting to talk but not to Kelly. Half-wanting the reunion with Alex that taxi cab kisses deserve, half-glad that it's all being taken out of my hands. And the third half crazy as hell that it has. Kelly shakes herself awake and looks quizzically at me as I leap into sudden, decisive action.

'Are you making brekky? I don't think I have ever seen you make breakfast.' She ponders the thought.

'Ah, it's not for me, it's for her majesty and what's-his-name, who seems to have moved in.' I feign nonchalance, badly. 'How often does this guy stay over anyhow?' Kelly shifts from one bare foot to another.

'Just every now and then?' she says hopefully.

'On a scale from one to ten?' I have to get a frame of reference here. Kelly buries her face in the coffee jar.

'Five,' she mumbles into pure ground Colombian. I cast about for something to say that isn't too much or too little.

'Christ, I go away and you two turn the place into Bonk Central. I'm making him eggs,' I declare, thinking I've pulled off 'offhand' with manly and practised aplomb.

'Oooh, that's a sweet gesture. Very nice. Good boy,' Kelly says. I fear she's not reading me quite the way I've written myself.

'So how come I don't get the royal treatment?' she asks me sweetly. Time to set her straight.

'Because I like your guy,' I say firmly.

'Oh,' Kelly looks slightly anxious. I lift the tray on the flat of one palm.

'Stand back – I'm going in.' I swerve up the hallway and into Alex's room like a hybrid waiter-come-knight of old, ready for duelling with a smile.

I don't bother knocking – surprise is the best form of attack. The bed is empty of everything but Alex and I'm pretty sure she's naked under there.

'Are you naked under there?' I ask her. (A writer always confirms his details.)

'Brekky … how cute!' She ignores my question. Definitely naked.

'Where's "whatise"?" I ask, dismayed to find my quarry gone. She frowns a smile.

'He's gone; he's on an early shift.' She laughs with delight. 'Have you really made me breakfast?' she asks, eyes glowing. I nod sweetly and work out my next move.

At moments of change you have to step back into your world from a new direction. Life doesn't come in a straight line – it's more of a dance and you've got to know your moves.

12

Mid-morning lights slide off the polished wood of the desk and Gabrielle ponders her next move beyond smoothing her skirt over her knees again, crossing her legs at the ankle and maintaining eye contact. She's been in this interview for fifteen minutes and already she thinks she's stuffed it up for sure.

The stuck-up woman, Siobhan, defiantly hates her. Hates her for being younger, blonder, more beautiful and braver than she is. That Craig looks like a walking idiot anyhow, a glove puppet for Siobhan's stiff little fingers. As for the other one, the generic European guy, Dominic, just looking at him makes her feel stupid.

'So, why did you leave your last position?' he asks her. She tries to remember her rehearsed answer but find herself fumbling instead.

'Just felt … like I'd done it, I suppose?' she all but asks him. His smile makes her feel worse, like she let him down. Siobhan sniffs loudly, dismissively.

'Would you describe yourself as a team player?' she asks huffily. Gab struggles to remember her rehearsed answer again and thinks if she tries very hard, and avoids looking Dominic in the eye again, she might just be able to pull off a performance.

~

'He made you breakfast,' Kelly tells Alex, in case she might not believe her eyes.

'Mmm, almost edible too, apart from no milk and sugar in my tea.' Alex smiles, feeling really happy for no real reason, and even if she knew it she wouldn't want to put her finger on it anyhow.

'I heard that!' I say, wandering into view. The girls prepare to be right again.

'Evan, by now you should know how Alex takes her tea,' Kelly tells me gravely. I take my cue from Alex's smile.

'Why on earth would I know something like that!' I clown for her. Her smile vanishes.

'Three years, Evan,' she says. 'Because in three years I've always had my tea the same way.'

Life is a dance and I just trod on her toes.

I'd have expected her to still be smarting by the time we make it to soccer, but it's like nothing ever happened and she's happy again, full of light and movement. Anticipatory and girlish. I'm not getting her down and it's driving me crazy.

Will kicks off and the dance commences.

The dance. Sometimes it can be like one of the old barn dances, where you prance around doing the do-si-do stuff, and then you turn around to find someone new is standing right there in front of you. Like Will bumping into Miranda, sending her flying, picking her up, dusting her down. Smiling at each other a little coyly. Touching each other with just a little more ease and intimacy than they used to. And as the look on Richie's face perfectly displays, sometimes you can find your partner standing in front of somebody else.

I decide to take a leaf out of Will's book. I get the ball at my feet, control with the left edge of my right foot, dribble it past Kelly and run with it, free, up the field to where I can see Alex, I'm about to take her on one to one when ... the music stops and Alex leaves the floor.

Rex has arrived. As she runs into his arms the dance begins again.

Pain shears up my shin and I see the back of Gab as she dispossesses me of the ball, going for goal. I lay sprawled in the grass like a clumsy kid, and not the Fred Astaire of football I had meant to be. Alex and Rex move in for a smooch.

The thing about the dance is that sometimes you choose, and other times you get chosen. But there's a third position. Wallflower. These are the people who watch.

I lag behind on the way to the bar, limping in unseen intent of practising hating Rex.

' ... Evan says a tard, a deadshit and a fuckwit are all the exactly the same thing ...' Alex is telling everyone when I arrive. Still talking about me. Good.

'No they're not,' Rex says with conviction. Bastard. Seems I don't have to practise too hard. Good.

'Yeah! Evan said.' Kelly gently takes the piss. Time to take control of this melee of literates.

'No I did not. You lot've got NO colloquial lexicon ...' They shout me down with a torrential display of typical layperson's ignorance. I wave them down.

'It's all right, it's all right,' I tell them. 'You know the trouble with you lot is that you've got no art in your heart.' I head for the bar; one-nil to me. Simon, Richie and Jason lean against the bar, waiting for me to help prop it up.

'Welcome back shithead,' Simon says to me kindly. He lines the stubbie up on the bar. 'Everything different?' he asks. I shake my head.

'So the same, I cannot tell you.' The cold beer takes the sting out of my battered shins. I let myself linger on the Alex/Rex combo for just a moment too long.

'Not everything is quite the same ...?' Jase says, waggling his eyebrows at the other guys. I try to shake it off but I can't quite let it go.

'What is it with these guys? Alex and Rex, Nathan and Kelly ...?' I am appalled to hear a playground whinge in my voice. Jason ruffles my hair.

'What's a matter, your two women don't need you any more?' he teases.

'Ah shut up and get me a beer. Who needs the hassle of chicks anyhow,' I say, with all the cavalier bravado I can muster. As if specifically to prove me wrong, the beautiful Gabrielle arrives just at that moment, draping her tanned arms around my neck. I notice Jason's shoulders tense imperceptibly.

'Enough of the beers, Simon, rack us up some Mojitos, hey Evan?' she says. I laugh and nod, remembering the cool, sharp edge of the mint and the slow-burning warmth of the rum in our favourite Cuban cocktail. I circle my arm around Gab's waist and from across the room Alex watches us for a moment, noticing how our adventures have made Gab and I dance partners of another kind. I don't know if I should go to her or not.

Do I sit this dance out and watch? Or do I get in there and tap someone else on the shoulder? Jason is just wondering the same thing when he sees Caitlin across the bar with a friend. She sees him and smiles and then she sees the lithe, golden Gab and her face falls. You can tell that she has never felt so ungainly or so pregnant before this moment. Jason bites his lip and heads over to her. We all try not to eavesdrop and fail.

'How was soccer?' Caitlin asks him, too eager to smile. Jason looks distracted already.

'Great. Why are you here?' he asks, with more brute force than he means. She looks hurt.

'I just bumped into Emma,' Caitlin looks pointedly at Gabrielle. 'You said you were going out with the guys ...' She watches him closely for a lie.

'These are the guys,' he rolls his eyes and makes her feel stupid and foolish.

'I just don't get it,' Caitlin says, unable to pull herself back together. 'I love it when you meet my friends ...' Jason lets her plea for an invitation slip over his head and into the rafters with the smoke and the gossip.

And so the old dance continues. The problem is knowing who's dancing, and who's not.

This all depends on your point of view.

~

Later on, back at the apartment, neither Rex nor Nathan are anywhere to be seen. I'm hiding the fact that I'm happy to be back with just the old team again.

'Do you want tea? Alex asks Kelly and I, no doubt looking forward to being able to demonstrate just how well she knows our tea-drinking habits.

I say yes to please her, and to please her I go to the bedroom to retrieve the teapot, standing cold and alone where she left it this morning. I'm not a nosy man, but I am a curious one. Writers needs to be curious, it's our stock in trade. In the interests of my art I happen to slide the top drawer of her bedside cabinet and accidentally pull out a string of condoms, each neat little square still chastely attached to the next. Almost a whole packet. Perhaps you're not so red hot after all, hey Rex?

~

As we're sipping tea and I'm secretly smiling at my own private joke, Will's considering the rights and wrongs of his next moves. He lies on his bed feeling the warmth of the night against his bare skin and listens to the faint noises Miranda is making somewhere else in the flat.

He can't help but see her differently now and the thing is, he's not so sure that he should. I mean, even with Richie so firmly out of the closet, to do something about it would be letting down a mate. But the last few days have changed everything again for Will.

Miranda is no longer just Richie's girlfriend. She's Will's friend first now. Maybe his best friend. He watches the shadows on the ceiling and takes an experimental walk to his bedroom door. It seems like a good idea to turn to the safety of the bed.

After a few moments he tests out the door theory and then, in an impulsive moment of madness, opens it with an excuse to himself that he needs a glass of water.

Miranda is standing on the other side of the door.

The glass of water excuse seems redundant.

He pull her into his kiss and lets his reservations melts into the shadows.

When the morning light chases away all the shadows, Will's reservations stand starkly at the bottom of the bed.

Miranda looks him in the eye.

'Oh shit,' she says with a giggle.

'Yeah, I know!' Will smiles and they laugh all their worries under the bed.

13

Sirocco, Santa Ana, Diabolo. Hot, crazy winds that blow all day long and into the night. In Melbourne we just have the Northerly, straight off the Simpson Desert. Not quite as poetic but with all the same mind-altering properties of those other, more illustrious winds. When the Northerly's in everything goes haywire.

Murder rates rocket, allegiances shift, and all of the old secrets come out the closet, even when you think you've packed them safely away.

~

Warm air lifts the sweetly stale smell of the Fu Bar floor directly and fills Richie's head with fumes; he's feeling slightly dizzy, almost like a man suddenly cured of vertigo teetering on the edge of a cliff. It's either the wind or the tequila. He's enjoying this moment. Being one of the lads with his best mate and his dad, he feels like one of the family for once. Will stands at the head of the soccer table, preening like Pelé.

'OK, who's next?' he asks them, ready for more action. Both father and son wave him away, slurring their protests and leaning into each other's shoulders to steady themselves.

'Oh right, scared I'll win again are ya Gordon!' Will swaggers from the table to join them, falling into his seat and downing his shot in one easy, fluid movement. Gordon, the perfect picture of Richie in thirty years' time, after a lifetime of sun and hard work has thickened his neck and shoulders.

'Soccer is a girl's game anyway, any decent bloke knows that,' he nods, feeling vindicated, and downs the next shot.

Will laughs and, letting his tongue get a little loose, he says, 'That should make you blokes experts.' Will tries to catch Richie's eye but Richie wades in with a diversion.

'It's true. All that kissing and bum patting ...' He laughs along with his dad, but in the back of mind – in the small, lucid part of his mind – he's started a countdown. Ten, nine, eight ...

'I'm surprised you're no good at it then,' Will says, having so much fun with his own private joke: seeing just how much he can make Richie Blake squirm. Richie's face warns him off but Richie's brain is still counting seven, six, five …

Gordon claps a heavy hand on his son's shoulder and grips his wrist. 'Is he questioning the superiority of the Blake family talent?' he asks Richie.

'I believe he might be,' Richie looks at his father in the eye, blearily searching out his father's approval.

'Ah, you're nothing but talk, son,' Richie's dad tells Will. He hands him another tequila. 'Get this down your neck, it'll put hairs on your chest.' Both Richie and Will laugh hard together, tears streaming down their cheeks. Richie hasn't told his dad that he had his chest hair waxed clean away for his part in *The River*. Hurt like a bastard, it did. Will gestures broadly at Richie.

'Go on then, give it to him,' Will says. Richie shakes his head.

'What do you mean?' Gordon asks.

'Come on smoothie, flash it for your old man!' Will is almost helpless with laughter. Richie reveals his baby-soft skin with a thespian's flourish. His dad's eyes nearly pop out of his head. Four, three, two …

'Christ son, you look like a poofter!' Gordon bellows.

One.

'That's lucky, 'cos I am a bloody poofter!' Richie says lightly. Will blinks two red-rimmed eyes. Richie's dad freezes for a second and then claps his son hard on the shoulder.

'You almost had me there for a moment, son,' he says, wiping a damp palm over his hot red face.

'No joke, Dad. I am a poofter. I'm gay.' Richie tells him.

And we have lift-off.

~

The wind makes brave men out of fools and jerks out of the rest of us.

Just as that gust of hot air knocks Richie's dad's world for six, Alex is drowning under the touch of Rex's lips. Right on the other side of that door he's telling her how beautiful she is and kissing every inch of her throat, moving slowing downwards.

There are only two ways to deal with the madness the wind brings. You either shut all the doors and windows and wait for it to blow over or you try your level best to block it out. Loud, loud music, that's what I need. Loud music in my head, twenty-four seven, even if it drives me mad – anything, anything not to have to listen to them making love. Fucking.

~

Back in the bar Richie's waiting for his dad to go out of orbit; so far he's just floundered in his seat, looking old at last and confused.

'But Will?' he says. His son's best mate, more like him than Richie'll ever be. Even dependable Will seems to having nothing to say this time. Richie tries to make eye contact with Gordon.

'Leave him out of it, Dad. Talk to me for once.' Richie feel instantly sober, more lucid and in control than he's ever felt. His dad shakes his head.

'I don't get it ...' He looks at Richie likes he's a stranger.

'I'm a gay man. I don't know how else to put it. I'm gay, Dad,' Richie reiterates.

Gordon reaches for a beer and takes a long draught. He stares at his hands, at the table, anywhere but at Richie. Will tries as best as he can to sink back into the cushions of his seat until he is no longer there. Richie leans closer to his father.

'Dad, say something, anything.' he pleads, but before Gordon can react Miranda bounces into the bar, bright as a button, a living, breathing example of the life Gordon had always expected for his son.

'Hi! Sorry I'm late. Drinks anyone?' No one answers her. Richie just watches his dad, waiting.

'Dad?' he says again. Will struggles to his feet and taking Miranda by the hand leads her away from the table.

'Dad?' Richie repeats, feeling that in this moment his entire existence is frozen in stasis, that he is waiting for his father to move the hands on the clock ... His father shakes his head as if to clear his mind and shrugs.

'Well what? You are what you are, I obviously don't have much say in that any more. What else is there to say?' He meets Richie's eyes, not angry or hurt. Just blank. Richie feels his reaction almost as if it is an anticlimax. He can't believe what's he hearing, he can't believe that it might be this easy.

'You can say exactly what you think, Dad.' He steels himself.

'You're my son. That's all there is,' his dad says. But Richie doesn't quite hear the cold, empty bleakness that's just crept into his voice. Richie sinks back into his chair contemplating the enormity of what he's just done.

~

Kelly's nanna always says it's an ill wind that blows no good. Sometimes it takes an ill wind to make you tell your deepest secrets, the kind of wind that's rattling the shutters of Alex's bedroom windows and creeping under the door.

'You've got beautiful ears,' Rex tells her. She giggles, tracing a fingertip into his hair.

'And you've got wonderful hair,' she whispers, enjoying the game.

'And I love the way your chin sticks out, just a little bit,' Rex kisses her lightly on the chin, tightening his arms around her waist. Alex luxuriates in feeling wanted.

'And I love this little mole that you have, just here ...' She drops a light kiss on the end of his nose.

'I love you, Alex,' Rex says, lightly, like those three words are just part of the game. Alex waits for the moment to rewind.

'Sorry?' she says, when it doesn't, breaking the moment despite herself.

'I love you,' Rex repeats, with more gravity now

'This is it,' Alex thinks, 'this is the moment I've been waiting for, dreaming of for so long. But if this is it, why I can't I say it back?'

She opens her mouth but the words don't come out.

'Thank you,' she says tenderly and kisses him deeply, wanting to blot any more meaning out of the night.

~

Miranda shuts the door behind her and crosses her arms at Will.

'C'mere,' he says, his voice low with sex. She neatly side-steps his lunge and pours herself a glass of water.

'So Richie's out to his dad, just like that. Can you believe it? His dad seemed to take it pretty well. What do you think?' Will leans back against the counter, waiting for the small talk bit to be over.

'Yeah, I thought he was going to shit himself!' he giggles. 'Come here.'

'Richie must feel great, free,' Miranda says, more to herself than to Will. 'Relieved.' Will launches himself off the counter and comes back to earth with his arms around her waist.

'Come here.' Third time lucky?

'You're pissed,' Miranda tells him with a small smile. Will hiccups.

'Yes, but not blind.' His hands run up from her waist and over her breasts. She pulls them away and turns to look at him.

'I am really exhausted,' she says, pushing him away to arm's length.

'I can cure that,' Will tells her with a swagger. Miranda knows you never try to talk about 'US' with a man who is silent, leaving or pissed. But Miranda's never been one to go by the book.

'Are we a secret?' she asks. Will tries to work out if being a secret means she will sleep with him or she won't.

'No, yes ... no? Tell me what you want us to be?' He's still hopeful. Miranda rises to the challenge with more enthusiasm than Will expected.

'All right. I'd like to go on a date. A proper one. I want to feel special. I want you to appreciate that I'm not just here at your convenience. I ...' Will tries to demonstrate he's got the message by kissing her.

'Don't forget I'm a man, I can only do one thing at a time,' he tells her sweetly, making it really clear which one thing he'd like to start with.

'Then you can start by taking yourself off to bed. Goodnight Will,' Miranda kisses him on the cheek and shuts her bedroom door behind her, leaving Will staring blankly at the wood.

14

Even in the early morning the heat of the wind stings your skin like it's still full of sand. Richie flinches against the sun as he leaves Simon's flat and then flinches again when he sees his father waiting for him.

'Dad?' he says.

'Whose house is this?' Gordon looks up at the windows.

'It's Simon's, he owns the bar we were in last night,' Richie tells him. Gordon pauses.

'Right-o. Is he your ... boyfriend?' he asks. Richie hides a smile.

'He's just a friend, Dad.'

'But he's "gay" too, right?' In the cold light of sobriety, Gordon struggles over the word. Richie hears it but tries to ignore it. He nods.

'Yeah, but he had a spare room. You knew he was gay before.' Richie begins to wonder if he might have gotten away with it a bit too easily last night.

'I'm just trying to get my head round you, son.' Gordon takes two small steps backwards as Richie walks towards him.

'Don't worry, Dad. I'm not going to turn into some screaming queen and turn up at your site singing The Village People.' Richie laughs as he visualizes the image, but his dad doesn't.

'I bloody well hope not!' Gordon says with conviction.

'Dad,' Richie says quietly, 'I'm still just me.' His father thinks a few things over for a moment.

'How about a drink later?' Gordon asks. Richie's face is flooded with relief.

'Yeah, OK. I'll have to move a few things around,' Richie thinks aloud.

'Oh no, don't bother if it's too hard.' His dad is immediately on the defensive. Richie tries his best to look like it's the easiest thing in the world to do.

'It's no problem,' he says.

'I mean if you're too busy ...' Gordon says.

'Dad. I'll see you later, OK?' Richie feels in control.

'OK,' says his dad. He doesn't.

15

The thing about the wind in Melbourne is that just when you think you've had enough of watching the flatmate you are not in love with walk half-naked out of the shower after a sex-filled romp with her boyfriend, just when you wished you'd never left Cuba ... just at that moment, whatever you think it may promise, it always delivers something else entirely.

'Evan, phone for you. Some chick.' Kel hands me the phone, raising her eyebrows speculatively. I shrug. Since landing back on these shores I've been discovering the joys of celibacy with as much cynical irony as I can muster.

'Who is it please?' Kelly asks in her best receptionist's voice. Her face falls when all hope of romantic intrigue fizzles out to nothing.

'It's someone from Everson Clarkes – a publishers?' she says with an interested smile and she returns to her breakfast to eavesdrop some more. I take a deep breath and take the phone. Is this my destiny calling?

'Hi, Evan?' A young woman's voice. My mental imagining goes into overdrive: sexy, husky brunette, intelligent party girl. Promiscuous.

'Yes that's me,' I say to my vision.

'Hi Evan, I'm Lauren Sanderson, Commissioning Editor, Everson Clarkes. You've heard of us? I just wanted to give you a call and say how much I enjoyed your chapters ...' I think that I know enough not to believe the hype but somehow whatever she says it sounds so alluring that I'm finding my usual unassuming modesty hard to maintain and I happily acquiesce under her lavish praise.

'So anyway, Evan, how about lunch on Thursday? I'd really like to discuss your work with you,' She cuts to the chase. My chest puffs out, and I feel like the little boy who wrote the story about the stamp again.

'I'd be thrilled. Lunch it is. See you then.' So when the wind changes suddenly to bring you a bright young woman with compliments and an expense account and maybe even a small advance, well all I can say is thank God I'm home.

~

Two women take a break from their lives in an oasis of their own creation, a park bench hydrated by caffeine.

Alex lifts her chin to the sky like a sunflower searching for the warmth of the sun. How many spirals which way? She tries to remember.

'Rex told me he loved me last night,' Alex says to Gabrielle. Gab nearly drops her coffee.

'No! Did you say it back?' For a moment the pair of them look exactly the way they did discussing boys at the back of the class, ten years or more before. Alex feels time standing still as she gets older and tries to shake the sensation off.

'You know I really wanted to, but I just couldn't. As if the words wouldn't come out of my mouth.'

Gab tries to diffuse her melancholy with a dirty joke. 'Were you giving him a blow job at the time?' Alex laughs and punches her lightly on the shoulder. 'Seriously,' Gab continues. 'I thought you really liked him.'

'I do. He's fantastic.' And the big fat 'but' that neither of them can put their finger on floats into the sky like a helium-filled balloon.

'Well take my advice: don't let yourself get caught up in the past. Don't end up like me, a bitter and twisted old spinster who can't move on.' Alex takes her hand, glad not to be talking about herself any more.

'No one likes to see their exes with another person. That doesn't make you bitter and twisted.' Alex squeezes Gab's fingers.

'It's not even him, or them. I just wish I had something more. For me, you know?' Gab says as she watches an elderly couple stroll by still hand in hand. Alex nods.

'You're moving on, it never happens all at once,' Alex assures her. Gab half smiles.

'How … how comforting,' she sighs.

'No really,' Alex teases. 'I mean, look at you. Your hair's sparkling, it's obviously moved on. And your skin, your skin is glowing. Your skin is so over Jason it's not funny.' Gab knocks Alex gently in the ribs with her elbow and they laugh in the sun, able to comfort each other the way that only old friends can.

'So how's the new job going anyway?' Alex asks her, thinking she's on safe ground.

Gab studies her painted toenails.

'Um, I don't know,' she says cautiously.

Alex looks quizzically at her. 'What do you mean, you don't know?' Alex feels a rumble beneath her feet.

'Well, it's my boss, Dominic. You know, he's old and married with children and kind of balding, with like long hair at the back?' Alex wrinkles up her nose. 'Yeah I know!' Gab says. 'But ... I don't know. There's something about him. Maybe it's his accent. He's got that whole European thing going on.' Gab wrinkles her brow and wafts her hands about, a generic visual impression of being European.

'Do you have a crush on your boss?' Alex laughs. 'It's powerful men; never fails to attract gullible young things like us.'

'No! No. I don't have a crush on him, he's married with children. It's just ... it sort of seems like there's this sort of "thing" between us. For some reason it's awkward, I don't know why.' Alex raises her eyebrows with a 'you have a crush on your boss', look but she doesn't say a thing.

A sudden rush of wind lifts Gabrielle's hair back from her face and everything about her looks different.

~

Miranda hears the wind chimes sounded by a hot blast of air seconds before she hears the front door go. When she opens it, Gordon is standing there, looking lost and lonely, his hands empty of any explanation he can understand.

'Gordon,' Miranda says with resignation. 'Hi, come in ...'

'I just thought you might be able to shed a bit of light on few things for me,' Gordon says.

'Sure,' Miranda nods and sighs at the hallway as she closes the door. She thought everything had gone too smoothly. It's less than an hour later when she watches Gordon retreat down the same hallway. She hopes she's helped Richie a little bit.

'He just needs your acceptance. It's so important to him,' she told Gordon, trying to see in his eyes if he could give it.

'It's a big ask.' Gordon finds a smile for her. 'I'm still in bloody shock!'

'Just talk to him, 'Miranda says softly. And she hopes she's said enough.

Sitting in his car Gordon looks up at her apartment window and thinks about what a nice girl Miranda is, kind and caring. The sort of girl who'd make a great mum one day ... He reaches for his phone and calls his son.

'Son? Look Richie, I'm sorry mate. I'm not going to make it. I'm flat out.' He hears the disappointment in Richie's voice.

'Oh OK,' Richie says. Gordon remembers his meeting with Miranda.

'I ducked in to see Miranda before, but it's just gone nuts since.' A silence crackles in the empty air.

'I moved things around, that's all,' Richie says, wanting to show his dad how much he needs to talk to him, almost sounding like the little boy his dad had so many dreams for once. Dreams that are impossible now. Gordon pinches his forehead, hard.

'Look, I'd better go, they need me on site this arvo. I'll call you later.'

'Sure,' Richie says. For a moment after he's hung up, Gordon stares at the driving wheel, feeling the guilt churning in his stomach. 'I just don't know what to say,' he says out loud to his tricolour air freshener, and to himself he thinks, 'What do you say?'

~

Cool water, paddling pool. A joint, a beer, a beautiful woman to shoot the breeze with. There's very little in life that could be finer. Gabrielle and I on the roof pretending this blow-up pool is a Cuban cove and that real life isn't happening to us any more.

Gabrielle screws up her eyes and looks at the palace, taking a deep drag on the joint.

'You know, if you squint it could almost be the Plaza de la Catedral. I just need to have you pining for Alex and the picture would be complete. Go on, look all sad and incomplete,' she grins. I give her a hard stare.

'I never pine,' I tell her flatly.

'Oh you were a veritable forest.' Gab thinks she's funny.

'No, see, I'm your more tortured romantic soul.' I want to change the subject.

'Romance involves a certain amount of honesty which you, amigo, are incapable of.' Gab thinks she's clever. I press for that subject change.

'Romance is my stock in trade, writing is all about romance. For example, name your top ten TV couples.' For some reason I've been dwelling on this since I went to the States.

'What? It's not the same thing at all!' Gab is intrigued, the subject is changed. Almost.

'Oh yes it is. In at number ten Bruce Willis and Cybill Shepherd in *Moonlighting* ...' I take a deep toke, warming to my subject.

'Are boys born with these lists or do they actually spend time thinking them up?' Gabrielle asks the heavens. 'This doesn't prove a thing,' she says to me.

'Sure it does it's all about URST. I am an expert on URST. My book is all about URST.' I attempt a sage-like smile, but my lips seem to have gone numb.

'URST?' Gab looks confused. 'Is your book science fiction or something? URST? What the fuck does that mean?' I've noticed that Gab is always more foul-mouthed when she's stoned.

'Unresolved Sexual Tension. The punters can't get enough of it,' I tell her. Gab looks at me like I'm Yoda and I admit the power of all-seeing wisdom feels pretty cool. Pretty cool it feels.

'Shouldn't that be UST?' She asks, with less reverence than I'd hoped for from a disciple.

'No, URST sounds better. It's artistic licence.' Gab looks at me like I'm mad.

'So this URST business,' Gab says seriously. 'Does it happen in real life? Like with us, in our lives, does it happen?' Up wake and the coffee smell, young mistress, I want to say to her in a Yoda voice. But I hold back – girls so rarely get *Star Wars*.

'That's my point. Fiction and reality, it's basically the same thing.' It's never occurred to me until this moment that I really have a razor-sharp, almost touched-with-genius kind of perception of the world. No, wait a minute, yes it has. It must be the weed affecting my short-term memory. What was I walking about? Oh yes. 'Definitely. URST happens to you. To me. To all of us, baby.' No doubt about it, I'm a guru.

'Shit,' Gab looks distressed. 'In that case I definitely have URST with my new boss.' I see a new chapter coming and prick up my ears.

'What's happened?'

'Nothing, he's married with kids,' Gabrielle recites. 'It's just that whenever I go into his office it's awkward.' She sighs and sinks a beer.

'That's not URST, that's you having a crush on him,' I say, sinking deeper into the pool, as deep as I can go, which is about six inches.

'I do not have a crush on my boss!' Gab snaps. 'It's tension, it's definitely tension, like you said. It's URST.'

I shake my head knowingly. 'That's not tension Gab. That's frustration.' Gab almost drowns me with a look.

'Anyway, as I was saying,' I continue, keen to avoid her wrath. 'The number-one all-time URST in a TV show. Maxwell Smart and Agent 99 in *Get Smart*.' I wait for the applause, fairly sure she's too stoned to notice that couples nine to two have gone astray.

'Didn't they get married?' Gab asks, missing the moment.

'Exactly, then it was crap. Once the URST is gone no one wants to know any more.' Another one of life's bitter ironies.

~

Richie blows in through the door like a hurricane. Like a hurricane that thinks it stills lives here, Miranda thinks. Will watches them, trying not to get in the middle again.

'What did you say to Dad?' Richie demands, bypassing social niceties. Since he spoke to Gordon, he has been living and reliving the conversation and the one bit that keeps coming up is, 'I popped in to see Miranda …' It must be something Miranda said that rocked the boat.

'I didn't say anything,' Miranda says defensively.

'Why were you even talking to him?' Richie asks shortly. Miranda looks at him, at a loss.

'He turned up at the door. What was I supposed to do? Slam it in his face?' She wanted to add, '… like I was never a part of your life?' but she bites back the words. Miranda tries to calm Richie down. 'Listen, don't put this back on me. You dropped a bomb on your dad the other day. Don't expect it to be easy for him or you.' She holds his gaze. Richie returns her look with contempt.

'So you think I shouldn't have told him, thanks a lot for your support,' he tells her, his words clipped with fury. Miranda bites back a whole lot of other words.

'I didn't ask to be a part of this,' she says, her voice brittle. Richie looks disgusted.

'It's easy for you. As soon as I'm out of the door you start fucking my best friend.' Richie makes his exit as loud and dramatic as he can, slamming the door. Miranda slumps next to Will, letting her head fall onto his shoulder.

Will finds that he is stuck in the middle again.

'M, I'd better go after him,' he says cautiously. A moment passes. Miranda stands up abruptly and goes to her room.

'You do that,' she says before she slams her own door.

Miranda isn't sure how long she's been staring at her bedroom ceiling before she hears a knock on the door. 'Better not be any one's dad again,' she mumbles to herself as she drags her feet answering it.

It's Richie. He looks contrite. Maybe Will said something to him on her behalf after all.

'I think this belongs to you.' He holds out the front door key, his best Richie Blake rueful smile making a guest appearance.

'Thanks.' Miranda takes it, remaining reserved, waiting.

'I'm sorry Miranda. I shouldn't have taken it out on you. I've been a dickhead haven't I?' Miranda half smiles.

'Yeah, you have.' She steps back from the threshold. 'So are you coming in?'

Will did not come to Miranda's room that night, but the next morning, when Miranda got up and when she went to the fridge, she found he'd left her note, a great big note on orange spotted paper reading '8 p.m. tonight, be ready. I'll pick you up – it's a date!' Miranda smiles to herself. For a scaffolder, Will knows a thing or two about romance that even a writer could learn from.

And Will is the kind of guy that can always sense when the weather's about to change. For the rest of us it is never that predictable. Sometimes you talk yourself out of something you want more than anything without even knowing it. Not until it's too late, that is.

16

'How's the book going?' I jump, sharply wrenched out of my version-vision of our world. Alex stands there, a picture in the door frame.

'Not bad, doing another polish,' I grin at her. I grin at her a lot these days in lieu of something meaningful to say.

'Do you think it'll get published?' she asks, and I love her for asking.

'Funnily enough, I sent a few chapters off on spec to this one place and I've had call from the editor. She wants to meet me,' I tell her. I do a characteristic chair twirl for her benefit. 'Power lunch.' Alex bites her lips and clasps her hands together before looking like she might actually come into my room and then deciding to take a step just out of the threshold instead.

'Evan?' she says, a small prelude to her question in my name. Her tentative tone puts me on red alert.

'Mmm?' I say as non-committal as possible, carefully studying my pen.

'Are you happy to be back?' she says. She's skirting, but I'm not sure what around. I tread carefully, looking for clues.

'Mostly,' I say, master of ambiguity, which in this case forces Alex's hand just a little more.

'Is there anything you'd change?' Ah-ha so she's talking about her and Rex. She thinks that now she's happily ensconced in her grown-up relationship she can come in here and gloat at lovesick little old Evan. Well I won't let her think my whole world revolves around her, because it doesn't for one thing and for another thing … well, it doesn't.

'Let's see,' I say, deliberately offhand and casual. 'I walk in the door and it's all exactly the same as it was before I left, which is depressing the shit out of me.' Alex's face wonders if by that I mean her and me, so I press home with. 'On the other hand, it's hot, I'm being paid to write and later on today I've got a "date" with a very sexy publishing person who might change my whole life.' I leave out the bit about not ever having met Lauren and emphasize the word 'date' instead.

'Date, right.' For less than a second Alex looks indescribably sad. 'So you're happy with the way everything turned out then?' And there it was. Alex's cool breeze of reason coming up of the Bass Strait just when you least expected it. I hold my nerve.

'Sure I'm happy.'

She looks at me levelly.

'Good luck on your date then,' she tells me simply and she is gone.

I look at the space she has left in the doorframe and it dawns on me too late: that was my last chance. Alex has gone, feeling free to tell Rex that she loves him – even if she doesn't – and our moment is gone for ever.

~

I feel like the Titanic reaching New York unscathed as I swagger into the restaurant to met Lauren, happy to be the ship that passed Alex's iceberg in the night. Hyped-up and hyper from a battle fought and possibly lost but maybe won, eager to grasp hold of the Next Thing and move right on. My plan is that Lauren should be the Next Thing – she is, after all, the person who may hold the key to my immortality. It can surely only help to woo her and win her, regardless of how her looks fits her voice. Luckily she is slim and sexy, wearing typical publishing type bohemian retro chic, blonde and warm. The very negative of ice-cool Alex.

She stands to greet me.

'Evan? Hi, I'm Lauren Sanderson. I'm pretty excited about the potential of your book,' she says.

'I would really love to go to bed with you,' I hear. I'm in the zone, picking up all the vibes, the master at work.

'Great,' I say, with my best unassuming smile.

'I thought maybe we could discuss where you might see it going and then you might do a bit more work on it for me. I think it's fabulous, but it has to be word perfect to get it past the Editor-in-Chief's beady eyes,' she laughs, deep and throaty; set to defrost. 'If you and I work well together I don't see why we can't get you a two-book deal.' She fingers the beads that hover just above her cleavage, doing a very good job of looking as if it's unconscious.

'Great,' I say, struggling to keep eye contact. Chicks really appreciate eye contact, particularly when wearing a low-cut top. It demonstrates respect.

'You could be hot Evan, are you ready for that?' she purrs. Can you even get more of an overt subverted come-on than that?

'Ready as I'll ever be,' I tell her manfully and I sink back another glass of wine and feel any remnant reservations melt, and the warm air builds and builds in the room as Lauren talks about the chapter I've sent her so far.

'I love that part, I really relate to Sasha.'

'Oh yeah?' I'm suddenly glad I changed all the characters' names for the publisher's draft.

'It's autobiographical, right, the book?' she asks me. Writers hate it when they are asked that question. It makes them look like slackers without a fresh idea or free imagination. Like they should be off researching medical terms for some crime thriller about a lesbian pathologist who likes cats.

'Inspired, by life,' I nod sagely. Lauren brushes off the bullshit with a flutter of her lashes.

'It's actually kind of sad, isn't it?' she says mischievously.

'How so?' I say with a cautious smile. Sad isn't how I would have described it. More poignant.

'Well, you know that Harry is really in love with this Sasha character and you know that she feels the same way. And they miss out. All because he can't tell her how he's feeling.' She studies me for a reaction.

'And she can't tell him either,' I say quickly, not wanting Harry to take all the blame.

'Yeah, but Harry wouldn't meet Sasha halfway. It nearly killed her to get there and he backs away. So he's the coward.' She smiles reasonably.

'No see, you've read that wrong,' I tell her, more concerned than is cool. 'I see him more as a tragic romantic, more caught up in the idea of romance than in the everyday consequences of it.' She smirks.

'Classic writer's evasion,' she says.

'Besides, I'm not Harry,' I say, with finality.

'Good job too,' she splutters into her wine.

'But you do like him right?' I say tentatively. Lauren leans back in her chair until the material of her dress stretches taut across her breasts.

'Well I have always been a sucker for the hopeless case,' she says with a catlike smile. I'm in.

'So do you know how to cure one?' I drop my voice and lean across the table to her. She holds my smile.

'Are we talking about Harry or Evan?' she says slowly. I move in for the kill.

'Why don't you come home with me and find out?' I say quickly, wanting the words out there before they sound corny and sordid.

'Is that what you think I meant?' Too late, she's offended. Lauren pulls back from me and thunder claps above our heads.

'I just …' I stutter.

'I think it's time you learnt the difference between fiction and reality,' she tells me with a lightning strike of venom. My confidence is electrocuted and desiccated.

'I didn't mean to offend you,' I say quickly, embarrassed, mad and for the first time since I arrive shocked into full consciousness.

'And I certainly didn't mean to encourage you.' She stands up, waving her credit card at the waiter and then, just as she's leaving the table, turns to me and says, 'I'll be in touch about the book.'

I watch her back retreat and see visions of my book at the bottom of the slush pile, under outdated outback sagas and yesterday's Chick Lit.

The static in the air begins to clear.

~

By the time I've staggered back home and have sunk simultaneously deep into the sofa and depression, Will and Miranda are watching the sun set over St Kilda, sitting on the bonnet of his Ute. Miranda feels the evening breeze in her hair and as she watches the remains of the day spills out into the night the early effects of intoxication make her feel like a sea bird riding a thermal.

'So this is how you charm the girls is it?' she says charmingly.

'Oh no this is just for the special ones.' Will doesn't look at her but his pleasure in her pleasure is reflected in his face.

'So am I special?' Miranda treads through the romance of the moment carefully. Will reaches behind her and pulls out a non-specific meat pie.

'I bought you this, didn't I?' he says with a mock-sincere face full of real sincerity. Miranda suppresses a smile, takes her gift of a pie and returns her gaze to the view.

'So I am special?' she asks again, mildly.

'Definitely in the top five,' Will tells her and he gently takes her hand.

~

The sun has gone out and the sofa and I have become one by the time Alex and Rex tumble into the flat. Alex looks kind of relieved, carefree and laughing.

'Shoosh, I'm trying to learn about numbats,' I tell them stupidly. Luckily I think they are too drunk on beer and each other to really hear me.

'How'd your date go?' Alex feigns interest.

'Fabulous, since you asked.' I fail to sound like I mean it. Alex ignores me anyway and goes to bed.

Rex watches me for a moment longer and goes after her.

I know exactly what's going to happen next.

'You're a pretty great guy, do you know that?' Alex pulls Rex onto her bed and rolls onto his chest.

'Just trying to impress my girl,' Rex shrugs; his hands run the length of her back.

'Well, it worked,' she tells him. She pauses and take a deep breath. 'I could fall in love with a man like you,' she says, letting the words ride on a rush of outward air.

'I'd rather it was me,' Rex smiles a quiet, small smile.

'Then, it is you,' Alex tells him.

And it's over.

17

The next day Richie watches his dad from a distance, as he leans on his truck, his sleeves rolled up, discussing plumbing or something with one of his team. Richie briefly imagines marching over there in a pair of chaps and nothing else and launching into 'Y.M.C.A.', and a small smile curls up the edges of his mouth. But he loves his dad. Despite all the years of never quite feeling the way he suspects a son should feel, Richie loves him. He wants his understanding and approval more than anything right now.

'Dad!' he calls out, and on seeing him Gordon turns and strides quickly towards him. Richie pushes back the idea that it's got something to do with him not wanting his mates near him. Just in case he starts flopping his wrist or lisping or something.

'I thought you'd be knocking off about now,' he says levelly to his dad.

'I am,' Gordon examines him, looking for changes. 'I'm sorry I haven't rung ...' he begins.

'Yeah,' Richie interrupts, as if he doesn't believe him.

'But I haven't thought about anything else since you told me.' Gordon looks like he hopes that might be enough to appease his son.

'And?' Richie waits.

'Look, you're young. You actors, you mix with all sorts, it's natural you want to try different things. I'm not as old fashioned as you think I am.'

'Yes you are,' Richie thinks. 'It's not something I'm playing at,' he says out loud. Gordon looks at his boots, choosing his words.

'What I'm saying is, it's not too late to turn back, son.' Richie feels the ground fall from under his feet.

'Shit Dad. This isn't something that's going to go away. I'm Gay. End of story.'

Gordon looks uneasy. 'Keep your voice down,' he whispers.

'I don't care what they think,' Richie says, nodding at the workmen.

'Well I bloody well do.' Gordon reins in his temper. 'Look mate. When your mum died ... well, I never told you this before, but I saw someone then. A counsellor and it really helped me get back on track.' Richie swallows hard.

'Dad, you just don't get it, do you?' he says quietly.

'I want to help you, son. I'll even pay for you to see someone ...' Gordon implores him.

'What!' Richie's plummet from his father's grace ends with a devastating crash. Gordon thinks of Miranda, and her soft, kind voice.

'What about me? You don't know how much I was looking forward to having grandchildren.' Richie looks at his father for one moment longer and then turns his back on him and walks away, wondering if he'll ever look at him again.

Both men feel desolate.

~

Gabrielle and Alex gossip in the Fu Bar.

'And then there he is,' Gab tells Alex, her eyes wide with horror at the memory, 'wearing Speedos for God's sake, and it's all I can do not to look at his ... you know, and he goes, "Oh thanks for bringing these papers over to me Gabrielle, it's so good of you, blah, blah" and then, "because Speedos never look good on any man," and I go, shit, I go, "Not unless he's got a huge ... Oh shit!" I stopped myself with inches to spare.' Alex bursts into laughter.

'You've got to do something, Gab. All this knee brushing, hand touching, sexual tension's going to kill you.' She says it with a light tone, but she's serious.

'Nothing's going to happen, he's married with children. He's really old,' Gab says. She's been saying that a lot recently.

'But what if it did happen, what if he actually came on to you?' Alex tests her.

'Oh gee, I don't know, what would you do? What would you do?' Gab asks her defensively. Alex winces; her marriage-wrecking affair with Jason is not completely forgotten.

'Come on Gab, this isn't about me. It's about you.' Gab shrugs.

'I'd set him straight. I'd tell him where to go.' She sounds likes she's convinced herself. Simon comes over to join them.

'Do you want another glass of wine, Gab? On the house?' he says, pouring her one without waiting for a reply. Alex holds out her glass but it remains empty. She frowns at Simon and his raises his eyebrows at her, before topping her up.

~

I frown as I watch them and Kelly leans across the bar and whispers the news in my ear and it all becomes clear. Caitlin went into labour this morning.

I walk casually over to join them and drop into the seat next to Gabs, draping an arm around her shoulder.

'You OK there, Gab?' I ask her. She looks at me suspiciously. Smart girl our Gab, didn't get that high-powered union job for nothing. When Will squeezes into the space on the other side of her she says:

'What's going on?' Kelly brings over a tray of drinks and we all sit back, relieved.

'Caitlin's gone into labour,' Kelly says, gently placing another drink in front of Gab.

'Oh right.' She smiles brightly, looking round at us as if she hasn't a care in the world.

And then she bursts into tears.

'I can't believe it! I'm supposed to be over this!' she wails, leaning into the curve of Will's arm.

'Your body remembers Gab, you don't have any choice,' Kel says sagely. Will and I exchange a glance of 'what?' over the top of Gab's head, but we say nothing.

'Jason's having a baby ...' Gab sniffs. As fast as she wipes tears away more come in their place. 'And not with me!'

'It'll pass,' Alex says. 'You won't be like this about him forever.' She talks as if she has experience. I forgot for a moment that she does.

'I will! I'm going to be alone for ever!' Gab sobs, in the kind of moment that can tip the balance forever that she has been so studiously and precariously maintaining.

'You've still got us,' Will says and Gab believes him, but even all of us isn't enough.

'What are you to me?' she snuffles a smile.

Battered from his meeting with his Dad, Richie joins the group. Relying on Simon to fill him in, his own problem etched into the line of his face.

'How'd it go?' Simon takes a moment to ask him.

'Don't ask,' Richie says sadly.

'It's not over yet, mate,' Simon reassures him and Richie is glad of it.

The phone on the bar begins to ring and the group falls silent, watching it for a frozen moment.

'I'll get it,' Alex says like a doctor and we all wait agonising seconds.

'It's a boy!' she calls across the bar. '3.7 kilos – a whopper!' Alex can't help but smile. We look at Gab, ready to take our cue from her, waiting to see how happy we can be for Jason right now.

'Do they have a name?' she says quietly.

'Angus,' Alex tells her as she returns to the table.

'Angus Kennedy,' Gab says, mustering a genuine look of pleasure. 'That's a good name.'

One crazy wind is all it takes to topple empires, but after the storm has passed it's the people who are left standing that count. And sometimes you've just got to gather your family around you and weather the storm.

18

The last couple of weeks all I've been doing is watching Alex and Rex be romantic.

Sometimes you can just tell a couple won't last. That it's all just not right, it doesn't click. The vibe's all wrong. You might have to look really hard but the signs are there if you pay attention. All these moonlight picnics, days in bed. Flowers for no reason, all that 'I know what you're thinking' billing and cooing. It's just papering up the cracks, trust me.

The other day Rex even said to me, 'You wait around a long time to meet a woman like Alex and when you do, you don't stuff it up. You hang on to it and you make it work.' All smug and Mr Know-it-all. 'The trick, of course, is to know when you've found it,' he finished, all *Men are From Mars* ... style.

And then, the other night, I hear them laughing in the kitchen so I go to see what's up and this guy, this Rex, he's cooking an omelette with one hand and giving Alex a foot massage with the other! Is he even real? Alex doesn't want someone like that, trust me. All text-book perfect.

It won't last, you can just tell. I spent the rest of that night lying awake telling it to myself, so if anyone knows, it's me.

Anyway I was just thinking I might call Lauren, see how the land lies.

~

Gabrielle can't see the signs like I can and Alex's picture postcard love life has been bugging her, even though she won't admit it. What with Alex all rosy and flushed with love and Jason and Caitlin all proud parents, she feels the spaces in her life even more keenly. Even Miranda's and Will's badly-kept-secret affair gets her down. So she's gradually lets her Dominic daydream creep ever more into her real life, working late every night to be near him a little longer

'Still here?' Dominic sees her at her desk. 'The workers would be proud.'

'Oh, hi.' Gabs smiles like she hadn't been waiting for him.

'This paper you gave me ...' he holds out a folder to her. 'Really great. Incisive and brief. I can't tell you the amount of crap I usually have to wade through, so thank you.'

Gabrielle glows.

They look at each other for a moment.

'Don't stay too late, OK?' he tells her, all paternal.

The thing is, delusion is easy. Under any circumstance we tell ourselves what we want to hear, believe what we want to believe, so Gabrielle wonders, 'Did he come in here to compliment me on the report, or was there something else going on?' She smiles to herself and lets her daydreams slip into the evening.

~

Kelly smiles to herself as she watches Will walk into the bar. 'There's just something about him,' she thinks. 'Something so masculine without being overbearing. Something reassuring. He makes me feel all girlie.' she suppresses a giggle and catches his eye.

'Hey Will, you look happy?' She's pleased to see it.

'Me? Just the same as always, Kel,' he says, but there is a peace in his eyes that he can't hide from Kelly. 'How are you and Nathan going?'

For a split second Kelly lets herself believe that Will is a tiny bit jealous.

'Great! Well … actually I don't know. Since Evan came back and he had to move out again things don't seem the same …' She frowns at the bar. 'The other day I woke up and I just missed him being there, so I thought I'd be all spontaneous and I got up and put my coat on over my PJs and just went round there, first thing, to seduce him.'

Will shakes his head with a laugh.

'Only you, Kel. Did it work?' he asks.

'Well he wasn't even there. So I waited on his doorstep and it turns out he'd been jogging and came in the back way. I'm all "Come let's pash" and he's all "Oh hi Kel, I'll be late for work." You're a man. What does that mean?'

'That he was late for work? You don't want to be in someone's face all the time, right?' Will replies.

'But I do, I do want to be in his face. And he should want to be in mine.' Kelly feels the panic rising and the universe turning.

'Kelly, he's mad abut you. I'm a bloke and even I can see it,' Will tells her with just the right amount of assertion. Kelly smiles her thanks to him.

'How's Miranda?' she asks casually.

'Why?' Will snaps his head up and then gathers his wits. 'She's fine, I mean. Normal.' Kelly knows all she needs to know and sighs a wistful little smile.

~

Life in the Kennedy household has not been the same since little Angus arrived on the scene, one small person with the power and force of a horde of screaming banshees. Jason tries his best, but his best is not enough to stop Caitlin from dreading the slam of the front door when he leaves for work.

'He smells so beautiful,' he tells Caitlin, dropping a gentle kiss on the baby's head just before he leaves.

Caitlin waits for her own kiss, but it doesn't come.

'Have a good day,' she says to the door and she tells herself it's because he's tired.

19

Masterstroke of genius. I called Lauren's office anonymously and I found out she was going to be here in this bar, another potential author lunch. I see her double-cheek-kiss another woman goodbye and I bide my time, waiting for her to relax over her coffee.

'Lauren Sanderson,' I appear at her shoulder. 'The answer to all my questions.' She looks me coolly up and down.

'Evan Wylde, Australia's answer to Irvine Welsh.' I think she might be being sarcastic, but I gloss over it. I sit in the vacant writer's chair.

'Lauren can I take you out?' I say. She smiles at my nerve.

'Gee, I thought I kind of snubbed you?' Her voice is cool but her eyes look friendly.

'I know, the last time we met I was all overly artistic and rude.' I'm really good at modesty.

'Which is why I never date writers. You're all the same.' Ouch, the woman knows where to strike.

'I'm prepared to beg,' I say. She sits back in her chair. 'Really. Let me see ...' I sink out of my chair and onto my knees at her feet. People turn and stare. 'Please go out with me, please go out with me, please go out with me,' I repeat endlessly, taking her fingers in mine. She loves it.

'OK, but on one condition. This will in no way affect whether or not I recommend your book to my boss. If it's shit it won't go in, OK?' I look at her, taken aback.

'It isn't shit,' I say. 'But OK.'

'OK, how about Friday?' she says.

'How about tonight?' I shoot back. She's pleased that I'm demonstratively keen.

'Eager, aren't you?' Her aloof act is getting harder for her to keep up.

'I'm just keen to move on, to get this thing moving, I mean,' I say. 'When you know what you want, why stuff around?'

'I think I like that,' she says. I knew she would. 'You can come with me to this launch I've got on tonight.' I hesitate, disappointed. Work do. It'll be busy – less chance to flirt.

'I was hoping we could have a proper date?' I try my luck.

'There'll be free booze ...'

'I'd love to.' Well, there's always a bright side.

~

I had wanted to see Alex's reaction when she opened the door to Lauren, but I was still getting ready when she arrived. It takes a long time to look like you haven't taken a long time to get ready.

'Evan!' Alex called me out of my room. Her face was implacable.

'Oh, you're Sasha in the book!' Lauren told Alex. Alex looked at her like she was a retard.

'Not really, it's a book of fiction,' Alex said and she threw me a look over Lauren's shoulder like, 'Who have you dredged up this time, Evan?' It was pure jealousy. Lauren looked wonderful, all glitter and lace.

'Oh really?' Lauren looked delighted. 'Only Evan said that ...'

I hastily interrupted. 'Evan says it's time to go!' I took her arm, enjoying the fifties glamour of her Coco Chanel aroma and guided her out of the door.

'Have fun,' Alex said. She didn't mean it, so I determined that I would. And I have.

It's official. I am in love. Lauren Sanderson. It's like this.

'Hi, this is Evan Wylde, he's going to be hottest writer in Australia.'

'Meet Evan Wylde, sexiest writer in Australia.'

'Have I introduced you to Evan Wylde? Shake the hands of a future literary god.'

'Evan Wylde – writes like a dream.'

Stuff like that could go to a man's head. So I ask her: 'Do you believe that stuff you say about me?' She grins, sipping a martini.

'At least half of it,' she tells me. I lift my chin.

'Which half?' She looks me seriously in the eyes.

'Your name *is* Evan Wylde, right?' I laugh.

That's when I decided that I loved Lauren Sanderson. I kiss her like the lovelorn fool that I am all the way back in the taxi, I don't stop kissing her. I let the world spin on its axis with my kisses, until she's the only girl I've ever kissed in the back of a cab. Finally she pushes me back and touches the tip of her tongue to her tender lips.

'This is my stop,' she says.

'I'd love to see your place,' I say, ready for the next stage in our whirlwind relationship. She smiles but shakes her head.

'I don't fuck on the first date,' she tells me.

'Fair enough, what are you doing tomorrow?' She laughs and pushes me aside to climb out of the cab.

'It's been great,' I call to her.

'It has,' she says, and just before she goes into her house she turns and looks at me.

I have to accept Alex and I missed our moment together. Now she's got Rex and I've found Lauren. You've got to grow up and see life as it is, not in some lovesick teenage way. I sit back in the back seat and feel pleased with myself.

'Driver,' I say, 'I'm ready to move on.'

~

I'm so in love I almost can't wait for it to be morning so that I can tell Alex. As soon as I hear her in the kitchen I get up. She is surprised to see me so early.

'Great date. Great girl. Great night,' I say, apropos of nothing.

'Great,' she says, shortly. She must have got out of the wrong side of bed. Great.

'Yeah. We're a good match, you see. I think that's what's so great. Common interests. She's in publishing, she's a party girl. I'm a writer, I'm a ...'

'Party guy?' Alex interrupts with deadpan sarcasm.

'I like the nightlife, sure,' I say, determined to stay up with the beat. Alex looks at my door.

'I haven't seen the sleepy-eyed Lauren yet ...?' She is superior.

'No, well, when you find the right person you don't want to rush it,' I say, listening to my own voice say someone else's words. Alex turns her back on me as she pours tea.

'Not like you, you normally have a high rotation going on,' she says. I wait for her to turn back to me; I need to see her face. When she does, it is composed.

'Why don't we all have dinner together,' I say, pressing for a reaction. 'I want you to like her. I like her. We're friends, I want you to like her. You and Rex.' Alex scans the room, searching for something else to look at.

'We're busy,' she says. She's angry.

'I haven't said a date yet,' I say slowly, trying to interpret her anger.

'Look, if she sticks around the whole week we'll have dinner. OK?'
She leaves the room.

OK. I don't know why I'm doing this either.

~

Gabrielle has been waiting all day for Dominic to talk to her. When
he does her heart skips fifteen beats and her cheeks burn brightly. He
picks up a copy of her favourite book from her desk and smiles.

'Oh, I love this book, it's terrific.' Gab shines like teacher's pet.

'It's great isn't it, the movie's just out?' She has no idea why she
tells him that like a question.

'I can't remember the last time I went to the movies,' Dominic
says, with a wistful tone. 'I'm an old married man, old married men
don't go out.' Gab gives him a radiant smile.

'I don't think of you as old,' she says warmly. Dominic gives a
European gesture which loosely translates as 'Pah!'

'I'm twice your age,' he says with a laugh.

'You're exactly fourteen-and-a-half years older than me,' Gab
replies promptly, and the flush that warmed her cheeks creeps down
her neck and over her chest. Oh Christ, she can't believe she said
that. Dominic gives her a little frown-crowned smile.

'Is that right,' he says, obviously amused. He replaces the book
and goes back to his office.

Gab reaches for the phone on reflex, tapping her pen incessantly
on the desk, counting the number of rings until Alex picks up.

'He says,' she tells Alex with no preamble, 'that old married
people don't go out any more. So is he saying he's dissatisfied with
his life and attracted to me or ...' Alex interrupts her.

'Gab! I think you should ask yourself why you are so obsessed
with this man.' Gab listens to the words but doesn't hear them.

'I'm not,' she says on autopilot. 'He's married with kids.'

'You never talk about anything else!' Alex says, a little wary.

'I do!' Gab is indignant. 'It's you, you're reading all this URST
into because you're so obsessed with sex. It all this Rex and Evan
stuff ...' Alex loses patience.

'What the fuck is URST?' she says.

'Anyway.' Gab ignores her. 'I've decided that Dominic and I are
friends. I could really value that, friends.' She sounds like she might
believe it. 'So anyway, I'll see you.'

Alex listens to the dial tone and thinks, 'Oh, Gab.'

~

I've pulled a brilliant coup over on Alex, in a bid to help us move on. I waited until I was on my own with Rex and then I say to him, 'So you and Alex should have dinner with me and my new girlfriend Lauren.' Rex looks pleased. He wants me to like him, because he knows how much Alex likes me.

'Yeah, great – when?' he says.

'Alex is off tonight, I think?' I say. 'Are you?'

'Yeah, tonight it is then,' Rex says.

So now Alex is sulking. I try polite chit-chat.

'Where's Rex, he's still coming isn't he?' I say, trying to please her.

'Gone to get wine.' She's monosyllabic. Not a good sign. 'What is it with you?' she says, almost angry. I shrug.

'I just want us all to be friends. It seems like the mature thing to do.' Alex snorts.

'I've never known you to be so big on the mature thing,' she says, clearly impatient for wine. 'And since you just met this girl maybe you should just wait and see if you even like her before we all have to join the party.' She is clearly impatient for the wine.

'Are you jealous?' I ask her. It was begging to be said.

'Me?' She is incredulous.

'Good,' I say, not waiting for her to say no. 'You shouldn't be. You've got Rex, I've got Lauren. We're lucky people, we've moved on. There's no need for awkwardness between us.' I sound convincing.

'Whatever could've happened between us is past,' I say, testing my believability. We stare at each other for a moment like kids playing chicken.

'I know,' she says finally. Some part of me had been expecting her to deny it. The tension still hangs in the air when Rex arrives with Lauren in tow.

'I found her on the stairs,' he says, but he looks from Alex's face to mine, trying to discern our civilized smiles.

A lot of wine later and Lauren looks like she's in her favourite soap. I want to show Rex which one of us is king of the kitchen, so I have a little surprise.

'And now for the main course ...' I serve omelette.

'Omelette?' Alex looks at it as if with disdain. She didn't look at Rex's omelette that way. 'It's a dinner party and you're serving us omelette,' she says again.

Lauren laughs. 'That's so Sasha,' she says with a huge grin. Alex shoots her a dagger look.

'What?' she says, pronouncing he 'h' in 'what'. She only ever does that when she's really narked.

'Hey, when someone is good enough to prepare you a meal you should have the grace to appreciate it,' I say cheerily to her.

'My God, it's like being in the book!' Lauren says to Rex, who looks like the only adult in an unruly kindergarten. Alex seethes.

I see only one option to diffuse the situation.

'Eat it,' I say, picking up a forkful. 'Try it.' I flick it at her face, a small piece of cooked eggs clings to her cheek before plopping onto the table. She looks straight at me for a moment before throwing some back at me and before you know it it's the two of us again, Evan and Alex, fighting it out to the death with cooked egg, just like we always used to. Well, you know what I mean.

We're still laughing three courses later, showing a reluctant Rex and a polite Lauren our old photos.

'Oh remember this?' I say to Alex. She laughs at the memory.

'Have you still got that hat?' she says. I run off to my room to retrieve it, happy to be making her happy.

'I believe in style …' I say, striking a catalogue model pose for her when I return.

'It's getting late,' Rex says. He looks distinctly uncomfortable. Lauren tries to catch my eye, but I deliberately avoid looking at her. Alex reaches up and take the hat off my head.

'I didn't know you kept this,' she says smiling at me, the way she used to before the taxi cab kisses. Rex virtually growls his displeasure

'I'm working early, so I might hit the hay.' Rex's hint misses its mark by a mile. Alex is all shiny eyed with memories. 'Coming?' he says to her, but his word falls on deaf ears.

'I might just go and check out your room, Evan …' Lauren tells me with heavy suggestion. I wave my assent at her with a preoccupied hand.

'Oh Evan do you remember this?' Alex says, clearly not for bed. Over her shoulder I see Rex scowl and makes his way to the bedroom alone. I sit next to her on the couch, taking one corner of the photo between my thumb and finger, so that we are both holding just a few centimetres of glossy reminiscence between us.

'Oh yeah, that old guy kept saying we looked like the perfect couple,' I say. I remember the evening. Alex with a flower in her hair. Under the moon. When the old man had said it, I thought Alex would have been bound to see it too then, that then would have been the night for us. But she just laughed it off as a preposterous joke. Of course, I had a really bad crush on her back then. All that's gone now.

'That's right.' The curve of Alex's cheek rises in a smile. 'He said we'd always last.' And for a moment she's quiet as she remembers. I watch her as the lamplight picks out the perfection of her profile and before I know what I'm saying the words are out humming in the air with fatal resonance.

'You looked so sexy, that night,' I whisper to her softly. We watch each closely, feeling our lost chance like never before until the ache passes or at least dulls.

'I'd better go …' Alex says, confused and suddenly sad.

'Yeah, me too,' I say. 'Mustn't keep the lady waiting!' Alex manages a feeble smile and collects up her own pieces before she opens her bedroom door.

When Alex closes her bedroom door Rex is waiting for her, but not the way she expected, not warm and in love with her, no shelter from the storm of her feelings.

'You were together, you and Evan, weren't you?' he asks her, bluntly.

Alex frowns and shrugs the comment off.

'No,' she says, hoping that will be the end of it. Rex looks disgusted

'Alex, don't lie to me on top of everything else.' Alex sees that he's not going to let it go.

'We had a fling, it was nothing. It means nothing.' Rex watches her undress.

'So why didn't you mention it?' he asks her.

'Because it meant nothing,' she says again, weary with emotion and wine. 'There is nothing there. Now, can we get some sleep?' She climbs in to bed and pulls the cover over her head. It's a long time before Rex gets to sleep.

When I close my door I see Lauren, beautiful blonde career-making or-breaking Lauren, stretched out on my bed and ready for love. I can't believe that I'm going to say this.

'Lauren,' I say. 'I really can't do this right now, I'm sorry.' She raises a cool eyebrow.

'You mean fuck? Are you gay?' she asks lightly.

'No!' A man's got his pride. She shrugs and examines her nail polish.

'Impotent then?' she challenges me. I climb onto the bed and kiss her hard until I'm hard, waiting for the moment when nothing else but having her takes me over, drowning everything else out. But it doesn't.

I break the kiss and look at her, miserably.

'OK, so you're not impotent,' she says and she wriggles out from under me, smoothing the creases from her dress.

'No, no. Look I like you, a lot,' I say to her, realizing that I really do, 'and normally this'd be great, but ...' Lauren interrupts me.

'There's Sasha,' she says diplomatically. I see no point in denying it.

'Yeah and even though she's with someone else and you and I could still have sex, because there's nothing to stop me just using you sexually ...'

Lauren says what I can't say: ' ...You can't. You just want to be with her.' I nod, helpless.

'It's pathetic and tragic, isn't it?' I say, sadly. Lauren gets up and tidies her hair.

'Oh well, you'll live.' She kisses me goodnight on the cheek, not one of her feathers ruffled. I prepare to kiss my career goodbye.

'Hey, you should put this in your book. Yeah, in the next lot of pages you're going to send me. It would really work!'

She gives me an encouraging smile.

Lauren is exactly the kind of woman I would be in love with if I wasn't in love with Sasha. My moving-on epic has just ground to a halt.

The very next morning and Gabrielle decides to test her friendship theory out with immediate effect. She takes extra care over her hair and make-up in preparation. She waits for a good reason to go and see Dominic and then when one doesn't present itself quickly enough she takes a bad one.

'Hi!' she says brightly, handing him a fax she'd managed to find by the machine. It's an advert for office cleaners. He looks at it.

'Hi,' he says, puzzled.

'Hi, listen I thought we could go and see that film?' Realization dawns on his face and to Gab he looks terrified.

'Gabrielle, I'm a married man …' He trails off. Gab is defensive.

'I know that, but we're friends, aren't we?' She's aware of the high-pitched note of desperation that has crept into her voice.

'I'm your boss too,' he says. He pauses and looks as if a whole jumble of words are struggling to be made sense of in his mouth. 'Look it's just inappropriate. OK?' Gab can feel his discomfort, like he'd leave the room if only it wasn't his office Gab was standing in.

'Highly inappropriate,' he repeats to her, looking meaningfully at the door. Gab takes the hint.

'No, no. Right, I totally understand. OK, well, I've got to go anyway. I've got to do something now. Something that involves leaving the room.' She closes the door behind her.

'Shit, shit, shit!' she says and reaches for the phone to call Alex.

We delude ourselves about who we are, about what we want. It's insane, but sometimes it seems the only sane response to getting through life.

Kelly is sashaying down the street looking like a million dollars, because Kelly believes that if you are going to apply for the job of your dreams you should be fantastic and fabulous just to deliver the résumé. If you were watching Kelly from the other side of the street right now, or if you caught her eye as she was passing, hoping to catch some happiness from that infectious smile, you'd wonder, 'What's she got to be so happy about?' To you and I that might be a mystery, but to Kelly there is nothing more simple in all the world. She's in love with someone who loves her back – of course she's happy.

Kelly lifts her chin as she arrives at the office of her prospective employer, strides through the double-fronted glass doors and up to the reception desk, striking just the kind of balance that means other women admire her fineness, but instinctively like her too. Two suited professionals stop mid-conversation with the reception-ist, to bask a moment in the reflected glory of her shining light and the receptionist beams at her. Kelly hands over her résumé and bestows one last smile on her people before sailing serene and complete out of the building.

Kelly is in love, she's happy at home and her dream job is just around the corner. Her mythic trifecta is in sight – of course she's happy.

~

I look at Alex lying on my bed and close my eyes briefly, waiting for the flashing images of her in a less platonic setting to fade away.

'So you're having a problem with this Sasha character?' she asks me, casually, as if she didn't know that everyone so far who has read my work and knows Alex, knows that Sasha is Alex.

'Well, Lauren had a bit of problem with her character as it stands. She says she has a "suspect moral code"', I say, pretending to look at my computer screen.

'What's a suspect moral code?' Alex asks me, furrowing her brow, the way that she does. I shift uncomfortably in my chair.

'You know, she er ...' I read from the notes Lauren sent me as if we'd never had an intimate moment in our lives. 'Flits from one empty relationship to another, neither learning nor changing from the experience,' I say as if reading from the back of a cornflake packet. Alex guffaws.

'First of all, that isn't a suspect moral code. A suspect moral code is when you thinks it's all right to hang people, or shoot puppies. Second of all, I never thought of Sasha that way. She's just searching, that's all, she's on a journey.'

'That's what I think,' I say. 'Also she thinks that Harry and Sasha should, you know, get together.' Since the night of the omelette fight dinner party Alex and I have been so carefully nonchalant around each other, that I think we can safely detach how much we might have once felt for each other from the characters I am writing.

So in these few nerve-racking moments that I'm waiting for Alex's opinion on Sasha and Harry's relationship I can honestly say that there is no hidden subtext here about us. No siree.

'Well, yes. I think that is fair. The reader needs satisfaction,' she tells me in measured tones.

'As a woman, and as Sasha is loosely based on you, I thought maybe you could have a read before I submit it again? What do you think?' I ask her. She smiles, pleased.

'Of course I'll read it. I'll be brutally honest.' She takes my pages and I resist the urge to snatch them suddenly back. Just as I surrender my words to her, her mobile rings, as soon as she picks up the call her whole body language changes. It's Rex.

When you've known someone for a while, been through some life together, everything operates on a different level. It's like every word is loaded with some other meaning. Every gesture I understand and interpret.

'What am I doing?' she says to him. 'Oh God, nothing, boring, boring, boring ...' She walks out of my room still talking, my pages in her hand and I turn and look at my keyboard for a long, long moment. Before I can shake Alex's words out of my head a bird starts singing right outside my window and suddenly that is all I can hear.

22

Kelly arrives on Nathan's doorstep dressed to kill with all the fatal beauty that a woman in possession of two-thirds and a bit of the mythic trifecta can muster. When Nathan opens the door to her he is momentarily dazzled by her light but his smile freezes on his face when he sees her disappointment. This is not going to be as easy as he'd hoped.

'Nathan! You're not dressed!' she tells him, mortified at his track-suit bottoms and gone-grey T-shirt.

'Ah yeah, the party. Kel I forgot.' Nathan says and Kelly knows – they both know – that in six months of being together Nathan has never forgotten prearranged dates; he is the original Mr Reliable. Kelly walks in, takes in the cold beers on the table, the bowls of nuts, the sports channel.

'You'd better get dressed then,' she says, giving him a chance to back out of his corner without confrontation.

'Oh well, look Kel. I was thinking maybe you could go without me?' He gives her his hopeful half-smile, which usually melts her resolve in five seconds flat. This time Kelly's face freezes for a moment before she turns the tactic back on him, setting her ray-gun smile to stun.

'I really think we'd have a great time together,' she says sweetly. 'Come on, let's go out and have some fun!' She waits for Nathan to catch her enthusiasm but instead he shuffles on the spot and looks at his bare toes.

'Kel, it's just … it's all your old schoolmates. I won't know anyone there and there is this really big game on tonight and …'

Kelly interrupts him. 'Nathan, look this is important to me, OK. It's important to me that you go. I need you to go with me. When I was at school I was this far from being a dag; just on the very edge of the cool team and they only let me hang around them because I could make Shona Mathews laugh until she pissed her pants. I never had a boyfriend, I had really bad skin and I never had the right clothes.' She walks over to Nathan, taking his hand in hers, saying softly, 'Now I am going to Shona Mathews' party and I am wearing great clothes, I have great make-up on, no spots and I am taking with me a gorgeous, smart, funny, drop-dead sexy boyfriend ...' She moves in closer until her lips are millimetres away from his.

'You're coming,' she tells him.

Nathan takes one last longing look at the telly and goes to get changed.

~

I thought birds were supposed to have an allocated time slot dependent on species, hemisphere and evolutional circumstances – that kind of thing. Like early in the morning dawn chorus, or maybe as the sun goes down, evensong, or sometimes at night, a nocturnal kind of groove. The bird that now lives outside my window is an aberration of fucking nature. Since the moment Alex left my room this morning it has never shut up.

It's the fucking antichrist of birds. I can't write. I can't think. I can't sleep. All I can hear is the sodding bloody bird, singing its little heart out.

I'm going to kill it.

'Do Harry and Sasha get together in this version?' Alex's voice makes me jump. For a moment the bird is blocked out, the relief makes me forget our new-found friendly distance.

'Lauren wants that to happen. Do you want that to happen?' I ask her tentatively. Alex stares at me for a long moment, made heavy by the sudden bird-free silence.

'I think that is what the reader would want, yeah, for sure,' she says.

'You know,' I throw caution out of the window, hoping it will flatten the bird, 'Harry really does like Sasha, he just can't tell her.' Alex edges closer to the door.

'Maybe he should show her,' she says quietly, her eyes scanning the posters on walls like she hasn't seen them a thousand times before.

'Show her?' I ask. 'Like have sex? Really hot passionate sex?' I swallow as those images flash hot behind my eyes again. Alex retreats further.

'Sasha wouldn't just have sex with him, just like that,' she says defensively.

'No, I know, but maybe that's where it could be going? What do you think?' I am lost now in a maze of my own construction, unable to separate fiction from reality. Alex decides to save us both.

'Whatever happens, your writing – it's just improved so much. You're amazing.' She smiles at me before she leaves and I settle back into my chair, drunk on her approval. It's almost a whole minute before the bird starts in again.

~

In the space of twenty-four hours Kelly has gone from the brightest sun in the universe to an all-consuming emotional-energy-draining black hole. She has imploded into antimatter and it has something to do with a party. Alex puts an arm around her shoulder.

'Kel, what happened?' she asks gently. Kelly sniffs.

'He doesn't felt the same about me any more, I just know it. It's only been six months and he doesn't feel the same!' she sobs into Alex's shoulder.

'Come on, tell me all about it,' Alex says.

'Well, so we finally go to Shona Mathews' party and you know how important it was to me to go, with Nathan and everything?' Alex nods. 'OK, so we get there and instead of making an effort to meet people and to mingle, he just sort of sulks. He just goes into the kitchen and sulks and, you know, maybe I wasn't at his side the whole time but only because I was catching up with my old mates, and maybe he was a bit bored, but he wasn't even making the effort, Alex!' She pauses for breath. 'And then, and then he just left! He left without even saying goodbye. Can you imagine what the others thought of me then? It was just like back at school. It was worse. I could see they were all thinking: "Same old Kelly, still a loser at heart. He doesn't like her, not really. He just felt sorry for her." It was awful ...' As if by magic Alex produces chocolate from her bag and hands a piece to Kelly, who ingests it like it's a drug.

'So ... so I go round to Nathan's and I say to him, "Why did you leave me?" and instead of being all kind and sweet Nathan, instead of apologizing, he says, "Kel, you were just using me, trying to be someone you're not." Like, I'm not good enough to be Shona Mathews' friend!'

'You're way better than her,' Alex murmurs sympathetically.

'Anyway, so we both just keep saying the wrong thing, neither one of us being sorry and something's wrong and I don't know what it is but something is and then I can see it's just going to go on like it, so I just ... leave ...' She stares at Alex in disbelief. 'I left him! And now I don't know what's going to happen, I just don't want it to be over. How did this happen to me? Yesterday I felt like the queen of the world and now I feel like the person who cleans toilets for the servants and lives in the barn with the pigs and has bad hair and spots.' Alex suppresses a smile and feeds Kelly more chocolate.

'Well, I'm not calling him. No way. I always do the calling,' Kelly declares. Alex gives her a small, affirming hug.

'Good onya,' she says.

'Yeah right,' Kelly says and she takes the rest of the chocolate out of Alex's hand.

23

Since the omelette-throwing dinner party, since that last moment between Alex and I where anything could have happened has past, I really think there should have been some kind of mourning from both parties. I've done my bit; I've passed up casual sex with a beautiful, potentially career-enhancing woman. I have become a martyr to the bird, who woke me up so early this morning making so much racket I could hardly think. Her singing reverberated through my bedroom walls, like she had moved in. But Alex doesn't seem to feel the need to feel that way. In fact, not long after the birdsong drove me out of my room she emerges from hers, her face a perfect picture of bliss, and Rex smug with the satisfaction of satisfying her not far behind. Kelly watches me as I slurp my cereal, feeling miserable.

'That bird's really got to you, Evan,' she tells me, as if I didn't know. It's time to revert to plan A. Kill the bird.

~

Kelly went round to see Nathan to tell him that she wasn't going to call him; it's Kelly logic. When he saw her on his doorstep his face filled with joy, but Kelly was stalwart.

'I'm not coming in. I just want you to know that if you have been trying to call me this morning or if you intend to call me today I shall not be receiving your calls.' She gives him her best effort at an icy stare.

'Oh right.' Nathan melts.

'Oh and why is that funny?' Kelly asks archly.

'I'm sorry, I'm not laughing at you. I'm just so relieved,' Nathan tells her.

'What, relieved that I'm not going to accept your calls?' Kelly says, her composure crumbling beneath his smile.

'No Kel, that you're not really angry with me!' Nathan laughs. Kelly is mortified.

'Yes I bloody am!' she says, but she is lacking conviction, the remnants of which are shaken to dust when Nathan reaches out for her hand.

'Are you?' he says, softly as he draws her close to him.

'Yes, I …' Nathan presses Kelly into the wall and kisses her.

'Oh, you smell so nice …' Kelly says before she kisses him right back.

~

Later they lie in each other's arms, dreaming about Kelly's trifecta again.

'If you get that job, we'll have so much more time together,' Nathan tells her. 'No more shift work. You'll be a proper jellybean.' Kelly cuddles into him.

'Yeah, a nine-to-five jellybean.' She smiles.

'Nathan, I'm sorry about last night,' she says, wanting to clear the last bits of negative karma from their argument away. Nathan kisses her.

'That's OK,' he says, getting out of bed. Kelly waits for Nathan to say sorry too. He doesn't.

'Nathan, don't clam up on me now …' she prompts him.

'I'm not.' He rolls his eyes at the ceiling and Kelly feels her inner peace slipping through her fingers.

'But last night was awful, really awful for me and you seem to think it was nothing!' Nathan turns on Kelly, suddenly full of anger. Kelly flinches.

'I see, so I'm supposed to apologize, am I? For being treated like your fucking handbag?' He turns his back on her. 'Get a grip, Kelly.'

Kelly watches open-mouthed as he strides from the room.

'But you just have to admit you were wrong too …' She says to an empty room. 'Nathan, don't walk away from this!' she calls after him. But Nathan has gone.

Kelly dresses quickly, thinking hard. She wants to run after him, she wants to make it all OK, but she feels like she should make a stand. She feels like if she doesn't make a stand now their relationship will be doomed. She steels herself and walks out on him, for the second time in less than twenty-four hours.

And for the second time in less than twenty-four hours, Alex feeds Kelly chocolate.

'He'll call you,' she tells Kelly. 'I bet you money he'll call before tomorrow night.'

'Really? How much?' Kelly asks, as if the value will be in direct proportion to the likelihood that Nathan will call her.

'Fifty dollars,' Alex says reassuringly. Kelly half smiles.

'OK, but I hope I owe you fifty dollars by tomorrow night.'

~

The sodding bird has gone. I didn't kill it; I didn't get to kill it. Before I could find an effective way of shutting it up (couldn't hit it with a sling and the petshop didn't sell bird poison) it just upped and left. And now I miss it. I can't work without the sodding bird. That bird is fucking with my head.

'Hi. How's it going?' Alex asks me.

'The bird is gone,' I tell her sadly.

'Isn't that good?' she asks, giving me that 'why are you so strange?' look that she does from time to time.

'No. I miss the bird,' I say on a sigh. You think you want something and then when you have it you find that you don't. You pretend you don't want something and then when it's gone you find that you do, you really, really do.

'The bird has worked her way into my soul, my heart. I need the bird,' I lament. Alex looks at me that way again.

'I have to go, I'm late for work,' she says. 'You have to cheer up Kelly while I'm out, OK? Cook dinner or something.' I stare at her bleakly. She all but loses her patience with me.

'Evan! Come on, you never know, the bird might come back!' I brighten a little.

'Really? You think?' I ask her.

'Yeah, she's probably just out doing something birdie,' she tells me encouragingly. I clap my hand to my forehead.

'I threw things at her. I ignored her when she was singing for me. I've driven her away.' Sometimes it is a writer's prerogative to be over-dramatic. Over-dramatic doesn't light Alex's fire.

'Evan, get a grip. I'll see you later.' When she is gone I shuffle into the kitchen to cheer up Kelly. Maybe the theory of 'there's always someone worse off than you' might work.

'So you got that interview you wanted then?' I ask her as she puts the phone down on someone called Peace Piccardo.

'Yeah.' She doesn't sound too thrilled.

'Isn't that good, then?' I say. She looks at me like I'm insane.

'Don't you see, if I get this job I'm bound to split up with Nathan – no one ever achieves the trifecta and lives to tell of it. I should have known ...' I smile, despite my own despair.

'Come on Kel, let's go to the shops, we need fresh air. Alex tells me I'm cooking you two dinner.' Kelly looks at me.

'Aren't you working? The bird has gone,' she says, almost smiling.
'How do you know the bird has gone?' I ask her.
'She went to work,' she grins.
Goddamn bird.

24

I'm making risotto. Kelly is in her room meditating on her inner radiance and willing the phone to ring. Alex is grating parmesan cheese for me, my sous chef; we are both drinking wine as we work, a little faster than would be considered sensible on an empty stomach.

'How's the writing gone today?' she asks me.

'Slow, bird slow.' My voice brightens. 'But I've been doing a lot of head writing,' I say.

'Head writing,' Alex repeats, the beginning of a smile on her lips.

'Yeah, I do a lot of head work. I'm doing it right now, in fact. Observing, collating, and assessing the world ... humanity's infinite riches.' I notice there is a slight slur on the edge of my voice. Alex breaks into a smile.

'Oh yeah, what infinite riches there are to be had here in our kitchen,' she laughs.

I watch her, the evening light gliding over the planes of her face. I want her to want me instead of Rex. I don't know what I want after that but I can only think of one thing at a time.

'Well ...' I say, dropping my voice. 'The way you're grating that cheese ... I watch you grate away kind of inefficiently, missing big bits ... like there ... and I know at some point very soon you're going to want to lift that piece of hair from your eyes.' Alex stops grating the cheese, and almost stops breathing. I step a little closer to her so that she can feel the breath of my words against the back of her neck. 'But your hands are all cheesy now. A different person might use their cheesy hands to lift that hair away, but you never would.' Alex does not look at me.

'What will I do?' she says. Time runs downs to a standstill as I reach out and brush her soft dark hair off her forehead.

'Thank you,' she whispers and I want her to want me instead of Rex.

'There wasn't a day when I didn't think about you,' I say suddenly, desperately. Alex shakes her head in disbelief.

'I was in hell,' she tells me. I want to touch her, but how can I?

'Alex, I'm ... sorry. What happened between us in the cab that night ... I lived off that for four months, it was amazing; it was the best thing that's ever happened to me.' The ever-decreasing space between us crackles and sparks.

'Evan, three postcards. No phone calls, no letters, nothing. What did you want me to think?' Alex asks me. How can I tell her that I don't know?

'I'm sorry, so sorry. But I had you in my head, I took you with me everywhere I went. We had a great trip, you and I ...' Her eyes lock on to mine and I close the last of the space between us, pushing my fingers into her hair and pulling her towards me. I kiss her then, a slow and gentle kiss but full of more passion than I have ever dreamt of. I want her to want me and not Rex.

Finally she pulls back from me.

'Evan,' she almost says. But before she can say more there is a knock at the door. We exchange one more look before she goes to answer it.

It's Rex. He takes her in his arms and kisses her, but in that moment he knows everything that has just happened between us. In that moment everything between Alex and Rex changes. For the rest of the night he talks to everyone except Alex and before she can finally get him alone he leaves.

'I'm going home, I'm tired,' he tells her.

'Stay, stay and I'll make you feel better?' she asks in a hopeful, bright voice.

'No. I'm going,' he says and he is gone and Alex sits at the table after he is gone and she feels hurt and angry.

And she doesn't want Rex and she doesn't want me any more.

25

Kelly got her job. Peace Piccardo mistook her Nathanless misery as a cool and calm personality and offered it to her on the spot. Kelly felt the cool, calm misery all the way home. She knows that she is going to love her job, therefore she will never see Nathan again.

Alex doesn't look at me.

I've been waiting for her to talk about the kiss but she just won't look at me. Instead she watches the door and the phone, waiting for Rex so that she can make things better.

'Has he called?' Kelly's voice shakes her out of her vigil.

'No.' Alex means Rex.

'Oh.' Kelly means Nathan. Both women let the phone take them hostage in its mute grip.

'Oh Christ, just go over there!' I yell – anything to get rid of the tension.

'Really?'

'Really?' They both say together.

'Just go,' I say to Alex, but Kelly leaps to her feet, happy to be released from her pledge.

'You're right. I'm going.' Before she can make it to the door someone knocks.

Alex holds her breath.

Nathan is standing at the door.

'Hello, fifty bucks!' Alex laughs, happy for Kelly, her confidence in love renewed.

'Have you had enough space yet?' Nathan asks her, sweetly.

'Oh yes, more than enough,' Kelly tells him and they kiss right there in public, making everyone happy for them.

~

Alex gets tired of waiting and goes to find Rex. He's drinking coffee in the hospital cafeteria.

'Hi,' she says, with a carefully arranged smile.

'Hi,' he says. 'Never get used to working on Sundays.' Alex takes heart from his effort at small talk.

'Is everything OK?' she asks him, keen for the awkwardness to be over.

'Shouldn't I be asking you that?' he says levelly. Alex looks at him blankly.

'Alex, you've got me in a strange place. I don't know what to do,' Rex tells her. Alex feels the panic rise in her chest.

'What do you mean?' she asks, afraid of the answer.

'You and Evan. What's the story?' He has a fatal precision.

'Nothing!' she says too quickly. 'I don't know …'

'If I wasn't around, would you be with him?' He is unremitting.

'Look, I thought we'd talked about Evan …' Alex wants to run from Rex and to him all at once.

'But would you?' he repeats.

'No. I don't know. You are here, though, and I do know I want to be with you, Rex. I just want to be with you.' She hopes she has said enough.

Rex swallows the last of his coffee as if it is very bitter.

'I have to go,' he says, pushing back his chair.

'Can I take you out to dinner tonight?' Alex asks hurriedly, afraid.

'I'm not sure when I'll be finished,' Rex says over his shoulder and he is gone.

Alex feels the dread dead in her heart.

'I can never get this right,' she thinks and she thinks of me and just in that moment she hates me.

26

 have you ever noticed how your world has a habit of falling apart and reconstructing itself unrecognizably while you're not looking; how, while you were watching TV or having a beer, everything you know disintegrates into nothing and then reforms into something else entirely?

While I've been busy waiting for my bird to come back, waiting for Alex to say something, anything and everything has changed again. Richie and Will, best friends since seven, now ignore each other in the street – mainly, it seems, because Will is fucking Miranda. Will, in the meantime, has finally decided to use his savings and take off on a trip around Australia; he's trying to persuade Miranda to go with him. He knows that she isn't really his girlfriend, he knows that he isn't really in love with her – not the way he loved Sam – but she makes him smile and she makes his heart beat like a drum in his chest and when he's with her he remembers he's alive. She has become his lucky talisman.

And Caitlin left Jason for an 'extended break' with her mother in Sydney. Whatever Jason tried to do to make her happy it wasn't enough, and however much he managed to love her, that wasn't enough either.

Now Jason watches the empty corners of the flat where his son isn't, wondering how his perfect life moved out without him knowing and waiting for the next time he'll get to see his baby.

Since the night I kissed Alex she knows with absolute certainty that her world is about to crumble to dust; she senses that it's ready to disintegrate. All she can do is wait for the first breath of wind that will blow it away.

She watches Rex across the dinner table; she spent all afternoon making him a feast of curry with all the trimmings. She watches him closely, hoping that his pleasure might remind him about how to be happy.

'Can you stay the night?' she asks him? Only last week she wouldn't have asked him, he would have just stayed, but the tiny fissure crack that opened up between them that night that I kissed Alex has grown ever wider. Rex meets her eye for a moment before returning his gaze to his plate.

'No, I'm on call. I didn't bring anything.' Alex nods, mute with misery.

'That was lovely, thank you,' Rex's formality is crushing her.

'That's OK,' she manages to say, clearing away the plates in silence. She doesn't want to ask him the inevitable question, but she knows that she must. That he can't tell what her what he wants to on his own.

'Is there something on your mind?' she says, finally.

'I've been thinking a lot and I might consider doing an overseas term soon.' Alex feels the sudden urge to sleep, anything to escape the inevitable.

'Oh … where?' she asks.

'I'm not sure.' Rex shifts in his chair.

'Of course you're not sure,' Alex thinks, and she waits.

'I think it might be better with my exam coming up if we don't see quite as much of each other.' Alex sighs at his typical male evasion, but she holds firm. She wants him to say it.

'Oh sorry, I didn't mean to take you away from your studies. OK – that's fine.' Rex swallows and laces his fingers.

The silence between them crowds out the shadows thrown by the flickering candles until Alex feels as though she can no longer breathe in the near dark. The weight of Rex's unspoken words are crushing her chest. Finally she opens the door for him.

'Do you want to break up with me?' she says, monotone.

'No – it's just that we should see less of each other …' Rex fails again to find his mettle. Alex resists the urge to let her hope ride on this limbo for a single day longer.

'Are you seeing someone else?' she asks wearily. Rex snaps his head up and looks her in the eyes; she can see the anger burning there that he has been hiding from her for so long.

'I'm not seeing anyone else, no.' His words are clipped with restraint. Alex can't stand it any longer.

'This isn't a "let's see less of each other" conversation, Rex, and you know it. It's a "you're dumped" conversation, why don't you be a man and admit it.' Alex finds her own anger now struggling to rise from the surface of her sorrow. Anger stoked by Rex's blank wall of silence. 'Right, well thanks for the detailed explanation,' Alex adds bitterly, finishing her wine.

'It's mainly about studying,' Rex says again.

'Don't treat me like an idiot!' Alex shouts. 'Just tell the truth!'
Finally Rex pushes his chair out from under him and stands.

'Tell me, Alex, just what do you think the "truth" is?' Alex
searches for the strength of her anger but finds only a deep well of
sorrow again.

'That you don't want to be with me,' she says quietly. Rex
doesn't deny it.

'It just doesn't feel right, and I think it's better that I told you
now than let it go on,' he says.

'Oh, how noble,' Alex says, feeling numb, the edge of tears creeping into her voice. 'Would it make any difference if I said I don't
want to break up – will you stay then?' She knew she would plead
with him eventually.

'I don't think so,' Rex says, because he doesn't have the courage
to say no.

'Then stop trying to humiliate me,' Alex says. 'Just go. Just go. I
can't look at you now. I can't – just go.' Rex hesitates for a moment
and then reaches for his coat; he looks at Alex for a second longer
and walks out of the door.

Alex waits to hear it pull shut before she lets the tears fall.

Love is a balancing act. You love them more than they love you
then they love you more than you love them. Most of the time
you're walking along the wire, trying to get it right.

~

While Alex is walking slowly to her room, the rest of us are next door
playing Scruples, each looking for the card that will answer our problems. I'm looking for the one that reads, 'You kissed your best friend
in the back of a cab on the way to the airport and now you're not
sure if you want her or not but you know you don't want her to want
anyone else. Do you break up her relationship or not?'

Miranda is wondering if there is a card that says, 'You are having
the best sex of your life with a man you don't love. He wants you to
go away with him. Do you go for the sex and sod your career?'

Jason's would read, 'It's plain your new assistant really likes you
and would let you have sex with her. You have no romantic feelings
for her whatsoever, but you wouldn't mind a shag. What do you do?'

Kelly finds the card she wants, or rather she seems to. She looks
at Nathan levelly and reads it out.

'You are a very religious Muslim man. You fall in love with a non-Muslim woman. You know your family will reject you if she does not convert. She has made it clear she will never convert. Do you continue to see her?' Nathan pauses, plainly failing to see, or choosing to fail to see, Kelly's brick-heavy reference to the fact that he is Jewish and that she isn't.

'No,' he says with a happy smile. 'Not if my faith means a lot to me. If I was that religious then I couldn't continue to see her.' Kelly sighs and makes a mental note never to use board games again to get her Jewish boyfriend to admit that his religious differences mean nothing to him. Miranda chooses a card and giggles.

'Kelly, you're in a sauna and the only other occupants are this attractive young couple giving each other a massage. They offer to include you. Do you accept?'

'Yes,' Kelly nods affirmatively. The boys all cheer.

'I don't believe you, Kel,' Miranda laughs.

'I believe you,' I tell her happily.

'I want to believe you,' Will says and Kelly flushes with embarrassment.

'Not only do I believe you Kel, but I think we should go home right now and talk about it some more.' Everyone laughs and the game gradually breaks apart.

The corridor twists a little out of kilter as we swim back home and once inside I drift towards my bedroom like a little ship caught in a current. Kelly stops outside Alex's room.

'What's happened?' she says to Alex.

'I fucking fucked everything up again,' Alex says, distraught. 'I'm such a fucking idiot!'

'Don't say that!' Kelly says. 'Tell me, what's happened?'

'Rex. Doesn't want me. Any more,' Alex manages to say at last. Kelly feels the ground fall from under her.

'Oh no,' she whispers. She wraps her arms around Alex and lets her cry into her shoulder. It's a very long time before the wine and exhaustion send Alex to sleep.

27

I'm not sure if it is a perfect visual metaphor, but this morning I saw Alex leave almost before dawn dressed for a run and I ran after her like a fool, like a clown dressed in the only kind of running gear that I possess, which is none. She waits until I catch her up.

'Did you know Rex broke up with me?' she asks with a borderline accusatory tone. I nod.

'Kelly told me,' I say, and I run alongside her, wondering what role I have played in all of this, wondering what has been real and what has been a game. Alex stops, abruptly forcing me to run a few steps past and trip over my own feet in order to return to her side. She sits heavily on the grass.

'You think you want one thing and you then you think you want another,' she says, not looking at me. 'And now I just don't know.' I sit in silence beside her, feeling the spaces between us grow wide and harden.

~

Gabrielle has been working hard on just working with Dominic, pushing her crush on him so far to the back of her mind that she can almost believe it's not there. Instead she's all about being the best at her job, which is fine because that is what she had always been about. Except now she needs more than her own satisfaction. She needs Dominic's approval too.

'So, you've been to investigate that anonymous letter about bullying?' he asks her with a smile.

'Yeah, the garage owner, Vedda. Seems like an ignorant bastard. But anyway I did what I had to, gave him the leaflets, kept him informed. I doubt that he'll read them, though.' Gabs looks like she's spoiling for a fight. Dominic leans back in his chair and smiles at her.

'Ah well, you can lead a horse to water, but you can't make him read ...' he says, with a half smile.

'Oh, that should be "drink",' Gab corrects him helpfully.

'I know, I was joking.' Dominic looks at her in a way she has been trying to interpret for weeks, but now suspects means 'idiot'.

'Well, that does sound a bit patronising,' Alex tells her later as they lie, with Kelly, sprawled on Alex's bed eating chocolate. Gab is hoping an example of her own messed-up life will help Alex feel a little bit better in the world.

'I know, that's the trouble whatever I say, whichever way I mean it, it comes out the exact opposite.' Gab grins. 'Sincere turns into sarcastic, helpful to patronizing, distant and professional to lust-crazed schoolgirl passion ...' She examines Alex for any sign of amusement but there is none.

'There is no chance.' Alex drops the leaden words into the conversation, crushing any hope of levity. Gab thinks hard for a solution.

'Just tell him, tell him you want him back, that you love him,' she says. Kelly sees the bigger picture.

'What about Evan? Maybe you should sort that out first?' She is tactfully vague on what 'that' is.

'There's nothing to sort out. I let Evan go because he let go of me.' Alex is beyond tears for the moment. Gab tries to focus her mind.

'If you could choose one, if they were both here right now and you could choose one, which one would it be?' Alex looks at the wall.

'Rex,' she says without hesitation. 'You know what, he just didn't like me very much. He got to know me and he didn't like me. Simple as that.'

'No! Anyway, I like you,' Gab tells her helpfully.

'And me! I like you too!' Kelly hugs her.

'And me.' The girls look up to see Nathan's head appear around the bedroom door. 'I like you too.' Finally Alex smiles and Nathan feels safe to breach the sanctity of the female therapy session.

'Look what I got, invitations to Evan's reading!' He drops them on the bed. Alex picks up hers. It reads: To Alex and Rex.

She is crying again.

~

I'm nervous. The Fu Bar is full of people and they are all here to see me, hear me read from my stuff. I'm trembling with nerves, I'm a wreck – this is what I have always wanted. I want Alex to be here by my side, to be gently sarcastic and to tell me pull myself together, but although I know she is here I can't see her. She's hiding from me.

'This is great – free grog, free food. Will your book be free?' Will interrupts my fear.

'Ha ha,' I say to him scanning the crowds for the familiar tilt of Alex's head.

'Don't worry,' Miranda squeezes my arm. 'I'll buy your book.'

Lauren appears out of the crowd and places an arm around my neck.

'Where's your friend Richie Blake …' she asks. But before I can answer she spots him and calls him over.

'Hi Richie. Lauren. I love your work in *The River*, it's great.' Richie has yet to tire from this kind of admiration. Will mimes sticking his fingers down his throat and is gone; Miranda purses her lips and follows him.

'Why thanks,' Richie says.

Will talks to Jason.

'I've decided we need more sport in our lives so we're having a bowls day on Sunday.' Jason looks at him.

'Bowls? Like granny sport?' Will nods.

'Yeah, but you can drink while you play,' he says reasonably.

'Oh right then, I'm in,' Jason tells him with a grin. Both of them stop speaking when Gab appears by their sides.

'Wow, you look hot,' Will tells her.

'How are you,' Jason says, feeling the familiar ache of not being part of her life any longer even keener now that Angus isn't nearby.

'I'm okay. I'm good, great actually,' Gab smiles, choosing not to fill him in on her impotent affections for Dominic.

Finally I find Alex standing alone in a corner, holding on to her glass of wine as if it is a life belt.

'Hi,' I say to her.

'Come on, Evan pull yourself together, you'll be fine,' she says with brave predictability. 'You'll be great, don't worry.' Alex never lets me down, even in her hour of need.

The crowds mingles and changes forms and reforms, conversations are broken and renewed and before I know it it's time for me to read and I haven't had nearly enough to drink. I go to the podium like a condemned man and look stupidly at the mike for a moment. A sea of faces watches me for what must be hours and then at last I find Alex's upturned face in the crowd and I begin to read for her, knowing that while she's watching me I am Evan the writer, talented, confident and commanding.

'Looking back, I don't know when I crossed the line …' I begin to read and the crowd's quiet murmur fades to silence.

I'm flowing now, happy to be me in amidst my own words when I see my lighthouse, my Alex, leave the bar. I watch the back of her head disappear and suddenly I stumble over my words, taking a few sentences to regain my composure.

Even as I read I can see Alex outside, talking into her phone.

'Rex? I just got your message?' She's happy and excited. 'Oh right, you called about work. Oh right. OK what's the problem?' When Rex has hung up she looks back at the entrance to the Fu Bar and then turns her back on it and begins to walk home.

~

You'd look at us in our bowling whites, drinking shandies or beer from a glass and you'd think, 'Look at those people. Look at those friends. Everything there is all right with the world.' But you couldn't be more wrong.

Alex went to Rex's on the way here. She told him again how she missed him, and once again he closed the door in her face and left her standing alone in the sun.

I want to feel sorry for Alex but I can't. I needed her the night of my reading. I needed her to be there for me, the one person I could be sure would listen and understand. But she left. She left and now I am angry with her in ways I don't want to think about. Angry that she left. Angry that she is so hurt over Rex, angry that nothing ever turns out the way you imagine it will.

Jason misses Angus. Misses him so much it surprises him. He never thought he'd have to miss the one person he expected to never leave him, not his own son.

Gab flirts happily with all the boys until Dominic arrives with his son. She'd forgotten to mention to anyone that she invited him, and now that he is here she lights up like a flame in a sudden gust of air.

Kelly watches Nathan and wonders if he does love her and if they do love each other, which she's pretty sure they do, what does it mean? Now that it's been over sixth months, what will happen? Will they be together a year, two years? Will Nathan be the father of her children? Would Nathan even want a non-Jewish woman to be the mother of his children? If the mother isn't Jewish then neither are the children; Kelly found that out. Would she have to convert? She watches him play, smiling at her over the top of the ball before he bowls it and she know she shouldn't worry, she should just be happy in the here and now with this perfect moment. But Kelly is the kind of person who likes to know what the universe has planned for her, she doesn't like to leave her fate entirely up to fate. So she wonders and she plans.

Miranda watches Will bowl from behind, admiring his behind a little more than his bowling technique.

'Watch the master at work,' Will tells her before taking his stance.

'Maybe you need this,' Miranda interrupts him holding out a camping head lamp. She can't wait any longer to tell him what she's decided.

'Wow, that's so cool.' Will is a man who appreciates gadgets. 'Perfect for my trip, perfect for cooking ...' He puts the lamp on, tipping his own head back in an effort to get a look at it. Miranda laughs, she takes another lamp out of her bag and copies Will.

He laughs at her before he realizes what she means.

'You're coming too ...?' he half asks and when she nods he sweeps her up in his arms and twirls across the grass. Will is happy his lucky talisman is coming too. Richie watches them angrily, and chooses to ignore them even more.

Alex, always the alcohol lightweight, has had a little too much beer and rather too much shandy. She shades her eyes with her hands and, seeing that I'm about to take a shot, she lies down on the green with her arms outstretched in supplication. I make a poor attempt to suppress my irritation.

'Alex, get up!' I say, almost angry. She doesn't move. 'Can you just get UP!' I yell at her, running to her side. She stretches her arms out to me, lying in the sun half-drunk and half-happy; for a moment I forget everything except that I want her.

'Carry me,' she whines breaking the spell. I shake my head.

'Just get up!' And I hear her mumble as she climbs unsteadily to her feet and follows me across the green. I know that I look and sound like a five-year-old who's lost the game and tipped the whole board over, sending all the pieces flying. I know that, but all the same I can't quite turn the way that I feel around. I retreat to a bench to sulk.

Alex sits next to me and then, after a moment, leans into my shoulder, sinking down further until her head is in my lap. I sigh angrily but she misses the hint.

'Give me a head massage!' she commands me, lazily drunk. I ignore her.

'Pleeeeease,' she whines. I push her off me and stand up.

'Stop using me, Alex,' I say to her seriously. 'You are only acting this way because Rex dumped you. Stop it.' Alex frowns at me and shakes her head.

'I am not. You are not really my friend,' she says. I find I can't hold back any more

'No, you are not my friend. It wouldn't have killed you to stay for the book reading,' I tell her, my voice quiet with fury. 'You know how much it meant to me.'

Alex looks at me as if I am a stranger.

'Can't you see what I'm going through?' she asks me. 'Not everything is about you!' I know I should do something – hug her, talk to her, say, 'Yes I understand, I'm sorry, I want to help you.' But I can't. Instead I shrug and walk away from her.

'No, apparently everything is about you!' I call back to her, feeling cruel and somehow glad of it.

28

Alex lies curled up on her bed, in her pyjamas. Her hands are curled around her knees and she watches the hands of her alarm clock go by. She hears the apartment door go and some quiet voices outside; when Rex gently pushes her bedroom door open, she doesn't know whether to laugh or cry.

'Hi.' His eyes don't meet hers.

'Hi,' she says. She sits up, running her fingers though her hair, trying to remember if she took off her make-up or not.

'Are you all right? I just wanted to see that you were all right,' Rex says. Alex isn't sure but she's fairly certain she can hear real affection in his voice.

'I'm fine,' she says. 'I'm OK. I feel shit really …' She laughs gently, making Rex smile. He reaches out to her and folds her into his arms and for a moment the world seems right to Alex just as long as she can breathe in his scent.

'Will you stay the night?' she asks him in a small voice. Rex sighs.

'No, no Alex I can't.' He feels the tremble of her tears threaten across her shoulders.

'Please,' she whispers. Rex says nothing but slowly he lowers himself onto the bed and curls himself around her. For a long time they lie like this, looking at the wall. Some time, neither one knows when exactly, they both fall asleep.

When Alex wakes up the next morning she feels likes she always does. Then the sledgehammer of pain she has experienced ever since Rex left her smashes into her heart.

'Are we back together?' It's the first thing she says. Rex opens his eyes.

'Alex, please stop,' he says. He is weary too. Tired of being apart from Alex and tired of trying to stay apart.

'Did you fall out of love with me?' she asks him.

Rex pauses for a moment, debating whether or not to tell the truth.

'No,' he says at last, and it is the truth.

'What happened, then?' Alex can't bear it that he loves her and still he's leaving her.

'You don't love me the way that I love you. When I'm with you I don't see anyone else. When I'm not with you I long for you. You don't feel that way about me. You were the one for me Alex, but it's got to work both ways.' His shoulders fall. 'Oh look, I don't know, OK, I just don't.'

Alex watches him dress in silence and before he goes he bends and gently kisses her cheek.

When he closes the door behind him she lets her first tear escape.

29

Decisions in life are easy when the arguments are all one-sided. You just go with them. But if it's fifty-fifty, if it's six of one and half a dozen of the other, if it's the high road or the low road – that's when it gets hard to decide.

Take a look at Miranda and Will, crouching on their apartment floor, a huge map spread out before them.

'But I want to go to Alice Springs!' Miranda protests, bumping Will with her shoulder.

'We'll still end up there, we'll just come at it from another way,' Will tells her with a smile, enjoying the gentle rasp of her bare skin along his. Miranda falls back on the floor.

'Oh who cares,' she says, feeling the warmth of the sun on the rug.

'Not me, let's go your way,' Will joins her, stretched out on the floor and they smile at each other, each one enjoying this moment, the planning and the possibility, without even thinking about what it might be like to actually be out there, on the road alone – together.

~

Alex wanders home from a night shift and into the bathroom looking like a member of the undead who hasn't had a good night's sleep in two millennia.

'How are you?' I ask the back of her head.

'Fine,' she growls and slams the bathroom door behind her. Kelly leans on the breakfast table next to me and looks at that slammed door.

'How is she?' I ask her.

'Ratshit,' she tells me and we both exchange a look of 'Uh-oh'.

I have had a little bit of time to think about all of this now, everything that has happened since I got back, and I believe I have taken the mature approach. I am prepared to accept responsibility for at least some of Alex's misery. Alex means more to me than most, and after all is said and done, even after the kiss in the kitchen, even though she kissed me back, if it came to the crunch – her and me actually getting it together … Well, I'm not sure how I would handle it. I might run a mile.

Because of that I am determined more than ever to be the best friend she has ever had, to help her get over Rex.

Alex returns from the bathroom with a night of sleepless tears scrubbed from her face.

'Know what I'm doing?' she says to Kelly and I, pouring herself a hot cup of fresh coffee. 'I'm going shopping.' She nods in self-affirmation.

'Shopping? Since when have you been a shopper? You're not the shopping type?' I gently tease her. She slams out of her chair and pours her coffee down the sink.

'I am a fucking shopper,' she tells me, almost shouting, and bangs the empty cup onto the kitchen counter, making Kelly and I wince.

'OK, OK,' I exchange a look with Kelly, who shrugs and begins to surreptitiously open kitchen drawers in search of some chocolate-based sedative.

Alex sinks into her seat.

'How do I do it? One minute I'm in a relationship and the next ... How do I fuck it up every time?' She looks from Kelly to me and back to Kelly with wide-eyed misapprehension.

'You didn't fuck it up,' I say, almost adding, 'I did. I did because I wanted you to want me more than you wanted him. Trouble is, I didn't realize exactly how much you wanted him.'

'I can't stop thinking about him, every moment of every minute of every day. What am I going to do?' She looks imploringly at Kelly, who's found a packet of chocolate chip cookies and covertly places them on the table.

'I told you ...' I begin, but Alex snaps my head off.

'And don't say "I told you so!" That's a fucked thing to say. Besides, he had NOTHING to do with you.' The look of angry contempt shuts me up and I retreat to the other side of the room, grabbing a cookie on the way.

'Come on, I'll come shopping with you,' Kelly says gently. 'You should go to bed now though and get some rest. I'll bring you a cuppa and we'll go out this afternoon. OK?' Alex's look almost turns her to stone.

'I don't need sleep! I'm wide awake!' she shouts and then, more quietly: 'I'm sorry guys, I'm just ... I don't know.' Kelly takes her hand and leads her to her bedroom.

~

While Alex sleeps, Kelly tells Simon about her leaving party plans for Will. Oh, and Miranda too of course.

'So you get all the customers out by nine …' Simon blinks.

'I beg your pardon?' he says.

'You get all the customers out by nine, and that'll give me and Evan time to hang the banner and …' Simon interrupts her.

'Hang on, why am I kicking out my paying customers again?' Simon asks her. Kelly looks at him, hard.

'Because, I'm telling you …' she says flatly. 'OK. Next …' Simon puts his hand over her mouth.

'Kelly, shush! Now listen. What in God's name are we talking about?' Kelly realizes she might have left a vital piece of information out.

'I'm having a big party for Will. Oh, and Miranda. Because he – they – are going away.' Simon regards her for a moment.

'Here?' he asks.

'Duh, of course here, so I'll need a going-away cocktail, something special and …' Simon holds on to his patience with all his laid-back might

'Kelly I'm not kicking out paying customers,' he tries to tell her.

'Yes you are.' Kelly gives him that hard look of hers again. The one that means 'I shall not be moved.' 'So anyway the banner is going to read "Farewell Miranda and Will". Or do you think it should be "Will and Miranda"?' Kelly ponders on the thought.

'Well let's see, you think Will is Mr Gorgeous, so how about Mr and Mrs Gorgeous?' Kelly shakes her head, irritably.

'They're not a full-on couple – they are two separate people,' Kelly insists. Simon shakes his head.

'Kel, when two people living together root like rabbits, it means they are a full-on couple. Trust me on this one.' Simon watches Kelly's face fall a million miles.

'Kel? Did I say something wrong?' Kelly stare at him, her mouth working but no word coming out. 'Oh, Kelly, I'm sorry mate, I didn't know you liked him like that …'

'Oh I don't, not really,' Kelly says and as Simon runs away to serve a customer they both know she is lying.

Kelly sighs, and thinks, 'A full-on couple. Yeah I suppose it's true. It's not like there's anyone else around who Will likes, is it?' And she secretly, almost even keeping it from herself, wishes it might have been her.

30

I want to make everything the way it was before, before the taxi cab kisses, and Rex. I want to get back to those halcyon days when I knew that I wanted what I couldn't have, which made me want everything else even more. Or something like that ...

Some nameless need to help Alex feel better makes me follow her into her room when she'd probably rather be alone. I'm not sure if the need is for her benefit or for mine.

'There's nothing I can say, is there?' I ask her, for the sake of something to say. She shakes her head sadly. 'I wish there was, I wish there was something ... I've never seen you like this.' I sit on the edge of her bed and watch her face made up of shadows in the half light, a pillow clutched to her chest.

'I can't stop thinking about him. Why? I've broken up with guys before. If anyone is an expert on breaking up with guys it's me.' She manages a bitter smile.

'Maybe you didn't love them,' I say, not sure how much I want her to admit to loving Rex. Alex says nothing, only looking into the darkness for answers.

'Have you seen him? Maybe you can talk?' I suggest tentatively, but Alex ignores me.

'Why do I feel like this – what happened? This was working, wasn't it?' She turns to look at me, her eyes black and bright in the half light.

'Let's just go then,' I say to her then, almost overcome with the impulse to take her hand and just run anywhere, somewhere, right now. 'Let's go with Will and Miranda. Be the cuckoos in their little love nest?'

Alex's smile turns into a sigh.

'I'd love to,' she says, in voice that knows it would be impossible.

She turns her back on me then, folding her arms around her shoulders like school kids do when they are pretending someone is kissing them and I wait a while, but she has nothing else to say.

Back in my room I pace the floor back and forth, back and forth.

I have to do something to help her, even if it's to help them to get back together. Seeing Alex so heartbroken breaks my heart.

~

'You've got to do something, you're killing her,' I say to Rex the next day. I've been stalking him around the hospital for the last twenty minutes waiting for my moment, ready to pounce. He watches my face closely for a second and then begins to stride down the corridor.

'She's sent to you say this?' he asks as he walks. I struggle to keep up.

'Look just talk to her, explain things a bit more,' I say, finally matching his frenetic pace. He stops mid-stride and fronts up to me.

'What kind of man do you think I am? I did explain,' he whispers soft with anger. 'And this is none of your business.'

'Well, if you did talk you didn't do a good enough job of it, not nearly a good enough job. If you cared for her you wouldn't leave in this kind of state.' I hold his challenge. I'm not good at fighting but I'm prepared to give it a go.

'I was in love with her! It didn't work out. What else is there to explain, Evan?' he watches me for a reaction. After a moment he continues to walk.

'Please!' I try standing in front of him. 'Talk to her again,' I plead. He scowls at me.

'Get out of my way,' he says, his face is brimming with anger and remorse, as open as a picture.

'You still love her don't you?' I say. I know exactly what being in love with Alex looks like. We look at each other like reflections in a mirror.

'Don't you?' he asks. I ignore the question.

'So is the part where we do pistols at dawn?' I say, with a smile.

'No, this is the part where I tell you to fuck off.' Rex shoulders past me and marches down the never-ending corridor.

'Just do something!' I call after him. 'Anything to make her happy again.'

'OK, I will,' he shouts back and I can't make out if it's a promise or a threat.

When they asked the guy why he jumped out of the burning plane without a parachute, he said: 'It seemed like a good idea at the time.' Why do I have the feeling the earth's coming up at me at a million miles an hour?

~

Gab leads Alex to the end of the pier on the grounds that Alex said she was going anyway and Gab was half worried that unaccompanied she might just jump off the end.

'You know what I'd do,' she says sweetly.

'What,' Alex asks, brooding on the sea.

'I'd punch him. You ought to punch him.' Gab smiles brightly.

'What!' Alex is stunned; Gab gladly grabs her attention.

'You know, a double-whammy between his smug, martyrish eyes!' Gab tests the water to take the piss out of Rex. Alex lets one corner of her mouth curl up.

'I don't think I'm the type,' she says, wondering.

'Oh you are the type, I've never seen a woman more in need of punching a man. That makes you the type.' Gab nods sagely. 'And then your fists will be so over Rex it just won't be funny!' They both laugh at an old remembered joke and Alex is glad to have Gab there with her, anchoring her to the end of the pier.

'What about you?' Alex says, looking for the emergency exit from her life. 'What about Dominic?' Gab rolls her eyes in delight like the schoolgirl who felt exactly the same way for Tim Matherson aged fourteen.

'Oh my God, he's fabulous, I cannot tell you.' She give Alex a coy sideways look. 'Guess what?'

'What?' Alex looks at her.

'We're flirting. Big time.' Gab's eyes widen at the thought of it. Alex rolls her eyes in despair, exactly the way she used to at Gab mooning over Tim Matherson aged fourteen.

'Be careful, OK. You don't want to end up all puffy eyes and blotchy, like me?' She smiles weakly.

'I'm not going to do anything. He's the most married, married man in the universe. If God was married he'd be less committed than Dominic. He's married to his kids, he's married to his dog … he's married to his car ….' Gab tucks her arm into Alex's and leads her though the crowds concentrating hard on making her laugh and even harder on not thinking about how much she wants Dominic.

~

Before her next shift Alex decides she has got to move her life on and that to do it she has to confront Rex and bring things to a suitable conclusion. For her own peace of mind and his.

Once you make up your mind to face things, that's when you can start making changes. And not before. Nothing changes by itself, no matter how much you'd like it to. Alex's chosen profession was fixing lives, but the hardest life to fix was her own. When Rex left her without giving her any choices he robbed her of her independence, the very thing she had wanted to surrender to him all along. It was only now, now that he was gone, that she knew how much she wanted him. Determined to face him one last time, to reach her own conclusion and move on, she walked though the hospital looking for him.

'Dr McManus? I was wondering if you could tell me the whereabouts of Dr Mariani,' she asks her boss, with as much professional indifference as she can manage. He looks at some papers on his desk, gesturing to her without looking her in the eye.

'Sit down Alex.' Alex sits, intent on her own mission.

'I know he's rostered on today, I checked but no one seems to have seen him ...'

'He's gone,' Dr McManus cuts across her. Alex's mouth is left open mid-speech, and all at one she can feel a scream boil in the pit of her stomach and begin to well its way out, like lava forcing its way out of a volcano.

'Why?' she barely asks.

'I've sent him on a secondment. He seemed adamant that he should go, and told me that if I didn't agree he'd leave anyway.' Alex stares at him, stupidly. Whatever she expected, it wasn't this.

'Look Alex, he didn't give me reason, and looking at you now I'm guessing it's none of my business.' Alex manages a half smile and walks outside, out of the hospital, out as far as she can until she comes to the edge of the sea.

Whatever Rex was doing, maybe trying to save her from any more of the pain of being around him, he didn't realize that leaving her this way was only preventing her from moving on at all. Leaving her with no choices, with all the choices blank. Leaving her to begin again – from nowhere.

31

Kelly bustles around Gab and Alex and is far more tense about Will's party than she should be.

'I didn't think he'd do something like that,' I tell Alex, wondering if it had been me that had landed the final death blow to a relationship of two people who were essentially in love. She shrugs and I am relieved to see she doesn't suspect me. I consider telling her about my last talk to Rex, but I don't really think it will help.

'Evan, have you called all the people on your list for tomorrow night yet?' she asks me.

'Yeah, almost,' I tell her, fearing recriminations.

'Well get on and do it then!' she tells me, like my mum would about cleaning my room. Alex looks at Gab.

'Have you asked Mister Wonderful Married Man?' She raises an eyebrow.

'No, I would've last week, but … Oh he's so happily married it's just becoming sickening. And worse, he just suddenly snaps at me for no reason. Like last week, I thought I'd done a really good job protecting this kid, who was being bullied at work. And I don't mean they shoved his head down the toilet, they burnt him with cigarettes, all down his back. He was admitted to hospital,' Gab shudders at the memory she hasn't been able to talk about. 'At first Dominic was so kind and understanding about how awful it was. So I went down to see the boy's boss, a real bastard, read him the riot act. When I got back Dominic hauled me over the coals like you can't imagine, said I'd blown any element of surprise, played all our cards. Ruined a test case. I mean, maybe he was right that time, but since then he can't even look me in the eye.

'I think he hates me,' Gab finishes miserably. Kelly and Alex exchange a glance.

'No I think he loves you!' Alex teases.

'Maybe he's got trouble at home,' Kelly suggests.

'No way. It's all "sweetie" and "darling" and "I love you too schoompie" when they are on the phone.' Gab sticks her finger down her throat.

'Oh my God, his marriage is on the rocks!' Kel says, meaning it. 'You know those lovely-dovey relationships always mean that they are hiding from the terrible truth that their marriage bed is a desert empty of passion and tenderness.'

'Kel!' Gab laughs. 'They've been married for twelve years!'

'Exactly,' Kelly says simply, and wonders whether she should iron the party banner or hope that the creases fall out.

~

Miranda watches Will as he flops to the grass; the sunlight tangles in his hair and gives him a halo. She wonders how to tell him.

'OK, so we just get Kel's party over with and get on our way, what do you reckon?'

Miranda smiles and sits next to him. 'Will …' she begins.

'Australia won't know what's hit it,' Will says happily.

'I'm not coming.' Miranda can't think of any better way to say it. Will looks appalled.

'You've got to! It's for us! Kelly went to all this trouble, you can't just not show up!' Miranda shuts her eyes as she realizes he doesn't understand what she means.

'No, Will. I mean, I'm not coming, not coming.' Will is dumbstruck.

'Why?' he asks.

'I'm just … I'm not the sort of girl who can live in a van. I'm all high maintenance, you know that.' She attempts a smile.

'Why, really why?' Will repeats and then adds. 'I don't know if I even want to go without you.'

'You have to go, it's your dream,' Miranda says, although part of her wants him to stay, wants their happy limbo to remain in place. 'The thing is, you know the other day I went for that part in the Panther girl film. As third Panther girl?'

Will nods silently. 'Yeah, I thought at the time it was a bit suss, going for auditions the week before we're due to leave.' He looks at his boots.

'Well, see, I didn't get that part …' Will looks at her quizzically.

'… I got the second Panther girl role. They liked me so much they gave me the bigger part!' She can't hide her pleasure anymore. Will raises his head and begins to smile.

'Why didn't you tell me?' he asks her.

'Because I … I don't know. But I can't turn it down Will, I just can't.'

Will reaches over and hugs her hard. 'Of course you can't,' he says. They hold each other for a moment, fitting into each other's arms in easy comfort.

'So are we breaking up now?' Will asks her, a resigned smile on his face.

'Yeah baby, I reckon we are,' Miranda says, touching the tips of her fingers to his face.

'And we're not even yelling. How cool is that?' Will says, pulling her to her feet. 'So let me get this right, you only wanted me for my body, right?' Miranda laughs.

'Who wouldn't?' she says with a giggle.

'You slut,' Will says and they stroll along arm in arm.

'Second Panther girl, hey? Not bad,' Will tells her. It's easy for them to say goodbye like this because they know this way they will always be there for each other. Will doesn't need his lucky talisman any more Miranda has taught him how to breathe on his own again. And Miranda? Miranda feels that Will has given her back herself. She no longer feels like a leftover part of Richie's life.

~

Tonight, as I walk Alex to the party, something happens to us, something that puts us back where we used to be before the taxi cab kisses.

'You know what I've found these last few days?' Alex asks me and I brace myself for some kind of punishment. 'You're important in my life. I've never thought that before.' I watch the breeze in her hair for a moment and wonder what I can say.

'That's good,' I say finally, inadequately.

'I fall over and you're there,' Alex continues. 'You've never been there before.' I try not to sound hurt.

'Yes I have, you just haven't noticed.' Alex looks me in the eye.

'Have you really?' she asks.

'Always,' I say simply and we walk on through the dusk in silence.

~

The first thing that Will notices is that everyone is at the party except Kelly.

'Where's Kel?' he leans over the bar to ask Simon.

'Um, at work?' Simon suggests lamely, exactly the way Kelly told him to.

Will looks at his face, confused – why would he lie? Will thinks for a moment and then threads his way through the crowd. He finds Alex, whispers something to her and, taking her flat keys, leaves the party.

Twenty minutes later he lets himself in to our flat.

'Kelly?' he calls out; the apartment is quiet. Kelly emerges from the kitchen and stares at him in shock.

'Kelly – why aren't you at the party? It's not the same without you?' Kelly stands holding her mug of tea, unable to speak or explain until her heart slows to a manageable beat.

'I … I just didn't want to say goodbye,' she says finally. 'I didn't know how to.' Will take a step closer to her, a small frown between his brows.

'It's easy,' he says, with a shrug.

'No it's not … it's not easy for me to say goodbye to you.' Kelly can't look Will in the eye.

'Tell me, what's up?' Will says gently. Kelly struggles to explain.

'It's just that everyone always goes. Nothing stays the same. It's going to be different again now and you're the one who helps keeps us all together …' Will takes her hand.

'No I'm not, Kel. You are,' he says.

'You help keep me together,' Kelly says in a whisper and finally Will understands. They stand in the silent apartment and listen as everything they thought they knew about each other shifts just ever so slightly

'I'm not going for ever,' he says.

Kelly nods but she thinks, 'Yes he is, and after he leaves nothing can ever be the same. It'll be all of us and it'll be different. Without Will, there'll have to be a whole new us.'

Before Kelly realizes what is happening, Will places his fingers under her chin and tilts her face until her lips meet his. He kisses her softly, lightly on the mouth, but with all the tenderness and care that Kelly's heart deserves.

'Goodbye, Kel,' he tells her, gently.

'Goodbye, Will,' Kelly says and she watches him leave.

~

Watching Alex dance, I can see she is happy. Tonight in this moment, twirling and laughing as we dance together, she is truly happy. That strained smile and brittle bravado of recent weeks is almost gone as if she is finally getting over Rex once and for all. She pirouettes for me and throws back her head in a laugh. Then, suddenly, her whole frame is frozen for a second. I follow the line of her gaze and I see Rex standing in the doorway, watching her like he can hardly bear to see her. In an instance all traces of happiness drain out of her demeanour and she wilts. Without looking at me she walks over to him.

'I thought you were gone,' she says, her voice a flat monotone. She looks briefly over her shoulder at me, as if she misses me or at least the moments we spent together before Rex arrived.

'Not yet,' Rex studies her face. 'I went to your place but you weren't there …'

'Well, I'm here.' Alex says and then, with half-hidden hope, 'Do you want to have a drink?'

'No, I just came to say goodbye. I'm leaving on Monday …' They look at each other and wonder how anything as perfect as them could come to this.

'Yeah, I heard, six months.' Alex swallows.

'I gotta go,' Rex says at a loss. Alex waits for the magic words that will make this whole mess bearable.

'See you then,' Rex says.

'Bye.' Alex hides her eyes with her hair. He kisses her then, just gently before he goes. Even from here I can see how deeply his kiss moves her, more than our kitchen kiss ever did, maybe even more than our taxi cab kisses too.

The next morning Miranda wakes up at dawn and reaches for Will. Then she finds he is not there and she remembers they've split up. Smiling to herself she drags herself out of bed and as she goes to his room she calls out, 'What time did you get in? I waited for you but …' She sees a sheet of note paper tucked under a mug on the coffee table.

Miranda picks it up and rubs her eyes.

'Dear Guys …' It reads and that's all.

'Will?' Miranda goes to his room. It's empty, everything is gone. 'Oh, Will,' she says, sitting down on his bed. 'Bye then.'

32

'Hi Dom!' Gab tries to be nice as her boss strides past her desk.

'Morning.' He barely manages to be polite. Gab taps her pen against her desk for a few moments and then stands decisively, following Dominic to his office.

'I'm sorry to interrupt you, but listen I just don't know what I've done?' She holds the door handle hard.

'Nothing, what do you mean what have you done?' Dominic asks, flustered by her unexpected anger.

'I'm civil to you, always. But this,' Gab makes a general gesture. 'This isn't fair. I don't understand why you behave as if you hate me. Do you want me to resign? Do you?' Gabrielle is shocked to find herself close to tears.

'Gabrielle stop!' Dominic stares at her. 'You don't understand, do you? This has never happened to me in my entire life. Never. I'm going crazy. I can't eat. I can't sleep. I can't work. I think about you, I dream about you. All the time,' he finishes looking at her, waiting. Gab feels the terrifying weight of a wish come true on her shoulders and now she can't speak.

'I know this sound ridiculous Gab, but it's true. It's killing me.' Dominic sinks into his chair.

'Ahhhh OK. Right. OK, well, I ahhh um. OK.' She smiles brightly and shuts his office door behind her and steadies herself against the corridor wall until she can breathe again.

Her mum always used to say be careful what you wish for …

~

Miranda looks at Alex, who looks at me and I look at Richie, just to keep it going. Richie looks at the floor.

'He's just gone?' Alex says.

'He's gone and we weren't even talking,' Richie tells her. 'It wasn't meant to be like that.' He returns his gaze to the floor.

He just went and he never said goodbye?' Jason asks and the rest of us sit in silence, wondering.

'Kelly smiles a little secret smile to herself and remembers the taste of his kiss. 'He said goodbye to me,' she thinks happily. 'And in all my life I'll never forget it.'

33

There are those times when things are spinning off course. The ground is breaking apart under your feet and chaos is about to engulf you. Everyone's got their own way of getting back a bit of control over the universe. Marathon running, strict diets, making lists, filing ... For Alex it's work, it's being so good at her job she can hardly believe it herself. Super Doctor Alex saves lives, including her own. That sort of thing. And the good thing about Alex's job is that she can put other people's lives back in order while she's working on her own.

Miranda's way of getting back in the saddle after Will's abrupt departure is to fully enjoy the experience of living alone for the first time in her life. She moves all of her furniture to where she thought it always should be and organizes all of her belongings on a strictly colour-coded system. This morning she wakes up and stares around her flat in silent contemplation. She goes to her kitchen cupboard and takes out her cereal. She picks up her bowl, fills it with her cereal and her milk and finds herself one of her spoons. She sits down at her table and thinks.

Then she picks up her breakfast and goes next door.

Kelly opens the door to her and frowns.

'Hi,' she says looking at Miranda's breakfast.

'Can I eat my breakfast with you?' Miranda holds up a spoon like a question mark.

'Sure,' Kelly nods and stands aside to let her in. Miranda talks through a spoonful of Cheerios.

'I think I'm going mental on my own, I miss the sound of the loo flushing ...' Kelly nods in perfect understanding.

'Well you're welcome to come round here and listen to our toilet flush any time you like,' she says.

~

Since Dominic's revelation Gab has been happy to let her self-control slip ever so slowly though her fingers on a sure and certain downward spiral. Now whenever she sees Dominic she flashes her white teeth just a little more, throws her long hair back over her shoulders with a little more abandon and swing her hips just a little more than is strictly essential to make the short trip past Dominic's office to the photocopier. But she figures as long as nothing actually happens then it's OK to flirt a little.

Dominic finds it almost impossible to suppress his longing when he calls Gab into his office.

'Gabrielle, I had my secretary sort out the overnight accommodation for the conference, is that OK with you?' Gab looks at him, her brazen demeanour wilting a little.

'Are we staying overnight?' she asks in a small voice.

'Well the conference runs over two days so …' The possibility of that one night hangs silently like an inflated elephant in the room. They both ignore it.

'So that's fine,' Gab smiles and swing out of the office.

'Great,' Dominic says, narrowly avoiding to the impulse to rip out what is left of his hair.

~

Jason leans his ear into the phone and listens to the sound of Angus breathing.

'He's zonked out,' Caitlin whispers and he can hear the distance on the line between him and his son.

'God I miss him, I miss him so much,' he says with longing.

'We miss you too …' Caitlin says slowly. Jason knows what she wants him to say but he finds that he can't.

'It would be good to be all together again,' he says instead.

'We could be if you came up here?' Caitlin says quickly.

'What?' Jason asks her.

'You know, you me and Angus. Together. Mum could help out with Angus, it'd be the perfect set-up?' Jason says nothing.

'Will you think about it? Think about coming up here?' Jason listens and he hears the ultimatum.

'Yeah, I'll call you tomorrow,' he says slowly.

'OK, Jason I …' Caitlin listens to the dialling tone. 'Love you,' she says aloud. She looks at the perfect composure of her sleeping son's face and her heart breaks because she loves him so much.

~

'I don't even know where I'm going!' Jason tells Simon the next day.

'The bowling club?' Simon jokes mildly.

'No, no I mean in my life,' Jason tells him, earnestly missing the joke. Simon thinks, 'Here we go. Gay guy gives straight guy life advice. That old cliché.'

'Oh, you want life analysis,' he says out loud. 'You should be careful, the last time I did this it was for Richie and look what happened to him ...' Simon raises an eyebrow and Jason laughs awkwardly.

'The accidental father thing ... Wife, baby, corporate job. Everything out of nowhere. How'd it happen?' Jason looks at Simon for all the answers.

'Is it that terrible?' Simon asks him.

'It's not terrible. It's just that I didn't choose it ...' Jason tries to explain.

'Didn't choose Caitlin, you mean.' Simon cuts the crap.

'Yeah, I suppose so.' Jason sighs. 'She wants me to go to Sydney. She sounds so happy there. It would be great for her. I miss Gus so much; I miss the smell of him, you know?' Jason looks at Simon; Simon patently does not know. 'Well, anyway, I have completely lost the ability to make decisions.'

Simon smiles.

'Have you ever noticed how much harder it is to make a decision when it's about something that you don't want to do?' he asks. Jason frowns at him.

'Look,' Simon continues, 'don't worry about it for now. At least when you're bowling you can practise your parenting skills.'

'I can?' Jason asks.

'Oh yeah. Evan has a mental age of about eight.'

~

I see Jason and Simon and run over to them, out of breath, and skid along the grass to a stop. Some old people glare at me.

'Richie's not here, we're a player down, we need a player,' I pant, scanning the green and dismissing stray grannies until I see a sort of mate I had a few frames of pool and some beers with one night waiting for a chick who didn't turn up. He's just finished a game and is leaving. 'But oh look, see that bloke? I know him. Shall I ask him? I'll ask, him shall I? Shall I?' I run over to the bloke, whose name I can't quite place.

'G'day, I'm Evan, nice to see you again, mate.' I give him my best making-new-friends smile.

'Oh yeah, hi Evan. Christian.' He smiles. He's sweet. Sweet face, the kind of face girls really rate as genuine and sincere. I've always envied men who get to play the sweet card all the time. It's a killer with the ladies.

'Feel like another game, mate?' When men meet men for the first time they have to say 'mate' enough times to justify the platonic macho properties of establishing a new relationship. 'Our useless mate hasn't showed.'

'Oh yeah, mate. Always go another game,' Christian says.

My new mate. Good one.

~

Alex sinks her shoulders beneath the water. Twenty laps of the pool has almost numbed down the pain of missing Rex.

'So how can you bear it? All this sexual tension?' she asks Gab.

'I don't know, I swear sometime we are just millimetres away from ripping each other's clothes off!' Alex shakes her head.

'My God Gab!' she says with an anxious laugh.

'It's amazing, we kind of go about our daily business, all "Send this fax" and "Arrange this meeting", when really we're just saying "I want to fuck you brainless." Gab giggles.

'You can't go on an overnight trip with this man ...!'Alex shakes her head. 'You don't stand a chance.'

'No, it'll be fine. Although if I did want something to happen it could,' Gab says, with a half-smile of satisfaction.

'Gabrielle ...' Alex warns her in a low voice.

'Don't worry, I refuse to be at the mercy of lust,' Gab says, with some resolution.

'Right well. OK then. You'd better have a cold shower, my girl.' Gab laughs and leaps out of the pool with the energy and grace of someone who's got a secret romance on the back burner.

Alex struggles out, feeling ungainly and heavy.

'God, my boobs are sore,' she tells Gab, giving them a furtive squeeze.

'More than usual?' Gab asks.

'Yeah, a bit.' Alex frowns as she wraps a towel protectively over her chest.

'Sure you're not pregnant?' Gab asks her, with a mischievous smile.

'No!' Alex says, feeling a sickening sense of denial in the pit of her stomach. 'No it's just PMT. Me? The contraceptive queen, pregnant? Very likely.' Alex hurries into the changing room, pushing any worries to the back of her mind.

34

Kelly opens the flat door to the deafening din of an all-male kindergarten day trip.

'You got all your amenities close by, plus you're in the throbbing heart of bohemian St Kilda and did I mention the roof top area?' I tell Christian excitedly. I have had the brilliant idea that my new friend Christian can move in with Gab or Miranda. One or the other. The main thing is that he is my new friend and as such he's got to move in pronto. I never seem to manage to hang on to friends who don't live next door.

Kelly looks at me as if I've gone a bit crazy, which I have because Christian's my new friend and he laughs at my jokes.

'Kel, Christian. Christian, Kel.' Kel frowns at him. 'Christian is checking out the flats, seeing which one he is going to move into. Gab's or Miranda's.' I nod at her happily. 'Great, isn't it?' I refrain from adding that he laughs at my jokes.

Kelly looks at me stupidly as I lead the crocodile next door. I knock loudly on Miranda's door.

She opens it with a smile which quickly freezes as I lead my entourage of Jason, Richie and of course Christian into her home.

'Miranda, hi Evan Wylde, agent of fate, at your service.' Miranda scowls at me.

'Evan, what is it now?' she says.

'This is Christian, he has nowhere to live and I thought, well, we've got two apartments in our block with space for someone to live in, and Christian's a mate. So you know, problem solved.' I look at her happily; she does not return the sentiment.

'What?'

'Er, good day,' Christian says, feigning embarrassment.

'Hi,' Miranda gives him a quick once over, and decides he is not her type. 'Evan ...'

'So this is the lounge room, good view and through here is the ...'

'Evan!' Kelly's sharp tone stops me in my tracks.

'Kelly'd be your neighbour,' I say, trying a reproachful look, which is about as near to sweet as I get.

'Maybe Miranda doesn't want to live with a man she's never met. No offence mate,' she says to Christian with a polite smile.

'None taken,' he gives her his sweet smile back.

'Christian is a landscaper,' I tell Kelly. 'He can grow stuff on the roof. Plants!' A thought occurs to me. 'Hey Christian, can you grow weed?'

Kelly shakes her head in annoyance. 'Can I say something, please?' No point in trying to stop her when she's got a tone on. 'You can't boss people into letting other people move in,' Kelly hisses at me.

'I'm not bossing. I'm brokering a deal!' I say.

'He's the flatmate fairy,' Jason adds.

'A pretty bossy boots fairy,' Kelly reprimands me and I try to overcome an eight-year-old's impulse to tuck my hands behind my back and turn my toes in.

'I could go?' Christian asks with a unassuming smile. Genius move, mate.

'Evan you don't even know this guy,' Kelly lectures me. 'He could be an axe murderer! No offence, mate,' she says again.

'None taken.' Christian repeats, cleverly displaying his ability to remain laid-back in a tense situation. Ideal flatmate material. Kelly continues, 'It's like you picked up a stray dog …' Christian interrupts with a spontaneous memory.

'Once, I found a stray. A kelpie, down on the beach …' He smiles a puppy-love smile.

'Oh really? Dogs? I love kelpies.' Kelly instantly melts. I have never seen a man as smooth as Christian – barring maybe me.

'Yeah, Flash I called him. He was a champion dog. Got run over …' Christian gives a sad little sigh, followed by a brave smile. Kelly is now on his side.

'Oh, I'm sorry. You must miss him.' She gently pats his shoulder.

'Dog's dead, you can move in.' I state the obvious, happily.

'HANG ON!' We all look at Miranda.

'Right, thank you. Now Christian. Are you an axe murderer?'

'Nope.'

'Do you have a regular income?' Miranda says.

'Yep.' Christian is brief and to the point.

'Then you can move in if you want.'

The perfect end to a perfect afternoon.

'If you look any more smug Evan, I'll change my mind,' Miranda tells me and I keep a poker face.

35

Gabrielle watches Dominic at the bar, taking in the slope of his shoulders, smiling at that way he has of talking with his hands. As he turns back to her with the drinks she quickly looks away, but not before they have caught each other's looks.

'Staying in our separate rooms tonight is going to be harder than I thought,' Gab says to herself, as Dominic approaches her table.

They make a little small talk, Gab conscious of Dominic's eyes on her all the time and finding it hard to breathe air so polluted with longing. When you're besotted with someone, every little thing they do, even the way Dominic shreds up his beer mat, is evidence to Gabrielle that he is absolutely perfect and in the end you love who you love and you can't change it. Gab pulls herself out of the fog.

'Look, we've got that early meeting tomorrow. We'd better go to bed.' The word hangs in the air like a fiery brand.

'I mean me, I should go to sleep,' she says again, carefully.

'Yeah, I'll come with you,' Dominic says without thinking, because he can't think around Gab.

'No, no. You stay here and relax.' She gulps down the last of her drink and leaves with a hasty 'Goodnight.'

Gab is still trying to get in her room ten minutes later, when Dominic arrives. His room is right next to hers.

'Key trouble?' he asks. 'Let me try.' He stands close behind her and struggles with the key; she can feel the hard length of his body pressed firmly against her back.

'Enough!' Gab almost shouts. She breaks away from the door and leans against the wall.

'I can't stand this; we have to talk about this,' she says, almost breathless from the exertion of keeping apart from him.

'OK,' Dominic agrees. He opens the room door.

'No, not in there,' Gab says quickly. She sits down in the corridor, oblivious to what people might think.

'We can be logical about this,' Gab says.

'We can try,' Dominic agrees.

'OK. I would love to go though that door right now and fuck all night long ...'

'Right,' Dominic swallows, and places the folders he was carrying surreptitiously on his lap.

'But you are married, and I don't think you are the sort of man to cheat on his wife.'

Dominic nods. 'I'm not, I never have,' he says quickly.

'Good, because I respect that and I don't want to turn you into that kind of man. So we just go into our separate rooms and deal with it and get on with it, OK?' Gab says.

'OK,' Dominic says. 'But I want you to know, this is the hardest thing I have ever had to do.' They hold each other's gaze for one second of delicious wavering.

'You're a lovely man,' Gab tells him and she climbs to her feet and quickly shuts her room door before she can say anything else. When her mobile rings she snatches it up, hoping for some change of heart.

'Hi, are you alone?' Alex says, straight away.

'Yeah,' Gab sounds disappointed. 'You'd be proud of me.'

'Good on you.' Gab catches Alex's tone.

'Where are you? You sound a bit odd?' she says intuitively.

'I'm in the loos at work.' There is a short silence. 'I've done a pregnancy test – you know, to be on the safe side. I'm waiting to see what it says.'

'Oh my God.' Gab holds her breath.

'One line I'm OK, two lines I'm pregnant.' Alex says steadily.

'But do you think you are?

'No, I just wanted to make sure ... oh shit.' The line goes silent.

'Tells me!' Gab almost screams.

'One line,' Alex says, her voice brimming with relief.

'Thank Christ for that, it would have been a nightmare.'

'Yeah I know, I don't know what I would have done ... oh shit.' Gab listens but she can only hear distant echoes and Alex breathing.

'Alex? Alex? What's happened?'

'It's two lines, two lines.' Alex's voice seems very small. 'The other line just came up.'

'You said it was one!' Gab cries.

'Well, now it's two. Fuck.' Alex seems very far away.

'Oh God I wish I wasn't stuck up here. Shall I come back? I can, you know?' Gab tells her.

'No, no. I'll be OK. Look I've gotta go.' Alex ends the call.

36

When Alex walks in the door, Kelly knows something is up immediately.

'Alex, what's wrong? Is it Rex? Has he called?' Alex collapses onto a chair, trying to compose herself.

'No, no. I need to talk to you, Kelly.' She clasps her hands tighter and Kelly waits.

'I'm pregnant.' The silence in the room is palpable. Kelly takes control.

'Right, well let's be logical. Are you absolutely sure?' she asks calmly.

'Yes.' Alex avoids looking her in the eye. 'I never thought this would happen to me. Not me.' Kelly places a cup of tea in front of Alex. She doesn't touch it.

'Are you going to call Rex?' Kelly says. 'Do you want me to?'

'Should I?' Alex looks lost, lonely and so afraid, like she wants her mum.

'Do you want to?' Kelly asks her.

'I don't know,' Alex whispers. 'I don't know.'

You can think you've got the whole universe under control but then – whack – it pulls the carpet out from under you. And when you can't fix things for the people you love, that's when you feel the most helpless and out of control. That's the killer.

~

Kelly sits on the loo and watches Alex brush her hair.

'How are you feeling,' she asks Alex, almost afraid to ask. How does someone who is pregnant feel? Kelly wonders, let alone someone who is pregnant and alone.

'Okay, a bit sick. And I feel like I've turned into Pamela Anderson.' She manages a half-smile. 'Suddenly none of my tops fit and none of the men at work can look me in the eye.'

'You mean they could before?' Kelly's loud laugh echoes off the bathroom tiles.

'Do you want breakfast? I'll make you Vegemite on toast,' Kelly offers.

'Okay, thanks.' Alex smiles and follows Kelly into the kitchen.

'Have you written a list of pro and cons?' Kelly asks her as she slices some bread.

'Yeah, pros – I have a baby. Cons – I have a baby.' Alex looks blankly at the table; any sense of calm she had conjured up quickly evaporates. 'I should start getting ready for work, it's going to take me at least twenty minutes to find something that fits.' She leaves the table quickly.

'What about your ...' Kelly holds out the toast after Alex. Sighing, she sits down and takes a bite.

Caitlin and Angus are back. Jason had finally returned his family to the fold. He had managed to side-step the issue of him moving up to Sydney and he finally had his son back in his arms. Jason felt like, for once, everything was just how he wanted it. He was living with Angus again.

Caitlin looks around the apartment, looking as if she's looking for something.

'Flowers, lovely.' She smiles at Jason.

'Just a welcome home to my family.' Jason is so happy to see Angus that he has become generous with his affection. He lifts baby Gus from Caitlin's arms.

'You've got so big, you little fatso, it's all those mushed-up pears isn't it? Isn't it, hey?' Jason lifts Gus to face him until they are nose to nose. 'You are the handsomest baby in the world, you are! Yes you are!' He turns to Caitlin.

'He really does look like me, doesn't he?' he says proudly. Caitlin laughs.

'Which would make you the handsomest man in the world.' She put her arms around both her men and enjoys the feeling of rare contentment.

~

When Alex gets back home from work, Kelly follows her into her bedroom.

'Look I got you a present,' she smiles and hand Alex a bag. 'It's a top, a nice loose one, help you feel more comfortable.' Alex takes it.

'Thanks Kel, it's really nice.' Kelly sits on the bed with her.

'How are you going?' Kelly asks Alex.

'I just keep hoping it will all go away on its own. Like some dumb teenager, you know ...?' Kelly nods.

'Listen, what you decide, it will be the right decision for you. And if you do decide to have a baby, well, I'll be here to help you. And Evan,' Kelly adds as an afterthought.

'Evan!' Alex laughs hard for the first time in two days. 'What would you do?' she asks Kelly. Kelly looks at her and thinks hard.

'I really love Nathan and even if we broke up I think he'd be a great dad but ... I don't want to be a mum now. I'm not ready.'

Alex nods. 'You'd have an abortion,' she confirms.

'I don't know, maybe. I don't know. God, I'm no help am I?' Kelly flops back on the bed. Bloody hell.' There's short knock on the door and Gab comes in, holding out a book to Alex.

'Here, you go. Enlightenment on a stick.' Alex takes the copy of *The Dalai Lama's Words of Wisdom*. She closed her eyes and flicks through the pages, choosing one with a random jab of her finger.

'"The main cause of suffering is an egoistic desire for one's own comfort and happiness". What does that mean?' Alex looks up at Gab.

'Don't ask me, sunshine.' Gab find her spot on the bed. 'I bought you some choccy too. How are you?' she asks.

'I don't know, the only thing I seem to able to say right now is, "I don't know"!'

'What about Rex? Have you talked to him yet?' Kelly asks.

'No, I don't know what to ...' she catches herself. 'See?'

The girls look at her.

'OK, I know I'm being gutless, but I just don't want to have that conversation. To hear that horrible silence when he hears those words, "I'm pregnant."' Alex examines the ends of a strand of hair. 'I guess there is part of me that would like him to just rush back and announce he wants to marry me and it'll be happy ever after.' She pauses. 'But that is one thing I do know – that won't happen.'

37

The next day Alex sits and waits for the woman opposite her to finish filling out forms. She doesn't want to be here, this is the last place on earth she wants to be, but she's almost twenty-nine for God's sake, and she's a doctor. If anyone is going to do this thing right, then it's her. She's come to see a counsellor.

'So, how do you feel about being pregnant?' The woman smiles. 'You can call me Helen by the way.' Alex manages a weak smile back.

'Shell shocked,' she shrugs. 'I can't believe that I am in this position. I can't decide what to do. I'm twenty-nine. I've got a good job. I'm not poor ...' Helen nods and makes notes.

'What do you do, Alex?' Alex feels her cheeks flush.

'Um I'm a public sector worker.' Helen nods and makes notes, utterly impartial

'OK, and do you have a partner?' she asks, pleasantly mild.

'No, not any more.' Alex listens to her voice as if it is someone else's far away and in another room.

'And what are your feelings about the possibility of terminating this pregnancy?' Helen asks her. Alex stares at the wall.

'I'm not anti-abortion, but I feel guilty about me having one. At my age and my circumstances, when it comes down to it, I could support a child.' Alex tries to picture herself as a mother but try as she might the image won't come into focus. 'I mean, it's not like I'm seventeen and have no support.' She looks at Helen for affirmation.

'Actually, that stereotype is a bit of a myth,' Helen says. 'It's not about whether you feel you should be a parent; it's about whether you feel ready to be a parent. Do you?' Alex look from Helen to the wall and then back again and says the one thing she is definitely sure of.

'I don't know.'

~

'Spontaneous dinner party!' I call to Alex as she walks in the door. She looks appalled for a moment and then forces out a smile as she sees Jason, Caitlin and the baby are all here along with Nathan and Christian. Kelly gives a worried little smile.

'Oh, you're Christian,' Alex says, holding out a businesslike hand. 'Alex.'

'Hi Alex.' Christian looks at Alex the way men do when they first meet her, like she is very beautiful.

'I'll just get into my party gear!' she calls out cheerily and then almost runs into her room. She lies on the bed and presses the palm of her hand to her flat stomach. It doesn't feel any different.

'Angus – say hello to Aunty Alex.' Jason walks in the room and holds out baby Gus to her. Alex takes him, feeling the warmth of his small body against hers.

'Hello baby, aren't you gorgeous?' She looks into his big blue eyes and tries to equate what's going in her body with the small human being.

'How are you?' Jason watches her closely. They don't talk so much these days but he thinks he can sense that something is wrong. Something more than the whole Rex debacle.

'Not too bad.' Alex is carefully non-committal. 'Your baby is adorable.'

Jason sniffs the air like a connoisseur. 'Gus, my son, I think you've made a small deposit. I'll be back, You wait there and I'll be back.' He disappears out of the room.

Alex looks at Angus, who returns her gaze with measured concentration before breaking into a gummy smile. She feels her heart flutter.

'Are you smiling at me? I think you are? Because you are a funny little baby, aren't you? With a funny little nose, and funny little fingers and toes.' Angus giggles and grabs her finger with his fist, jamming it into his mouth.

'Stop flirting, you little charmer.' Jason returns and begins to change Gus. Alex watches, unable to stop herself from wrinkling her nose at the dirty nappy.

'So how is fatherhood?' she asks casually. Jason kisses Gus's tummy before fastening his nappy

'It's a little bit like falling in love,' he says sweetly and Alex can see how he's changed; besotted with his little baby boy.

'Dinner!' Kelly shouts from the other room. Alex watches Jason go and turns to look at her reflection in the mirror. 'It's the same as when I lost my virginity,' she thinks. 'I don't look any different.'

'Who wants booze?' Jason is pouring wine as Alex joins the party. 'Alex, Kel?'

'Not for me, please.' Alex tries to look like her answer isn't loaded with meaning.

'Can I have one?' Caitlin asks and she tugs Jason's sleeve as if she'd been forgotten. Alex looks around the table and suddenly deflates, like the day has defeated her.

'You know what? I'm so tired. I'm just going to go to bed, OK?' The conversation doesn't even break as she heads for her bedroom. Kelly and I exchange a glance and Kelly's tells me, 'Leave her be.'

~

Jason pulls Caitlin in close to him, his mouth travelling slowly downward between her thighs.

'Actually Jason, I don't really want you to do that.' She tramples on what little enthusiasm Jason had managed to muster.

'OK.' They look at each other and begin to kiss again. Jason thinks he might just be getting back into it when Caitlin pulls away.

'My arm's gone numb,' she tells him, pulling the limb in question awkwardly out from underneath him. Jason sighs and rolls away from her.

'This isn't really working, is it?' he says.

'No.' Caitlin looks at the ceiling, hiding her disappointment. The truth is she could tell that he wasn't really interested in her, that his attentions were merely dutiful; and Jason never had been very good at being dutiful.

'Let's leave it then, shall we?' he says, not sounding too disappointed.

'OK,' Caitlin sighs. Jason goes instantly to sleep, leaving Caitlin to stare at the ceiling, waiting for the sound of Angus's cry.

38

Gabrielle is dreaming about Dominic's hot breath on her neck, his long fingers entwined in her golden hair, his mouth pushing firmly onto hers ... when a knock at the door wakes her. She blinks into the half dark for a moment, waiting for the world to find its natural order. A small, hot part of her wonders if it might be Dominic on the other side of the door.

The knock comes again, louder this time and Gab is reminded of Mac. This guy she dated last summer who used to turn up in the middle of the night for hot, crazy sex. She smiles at the memory but she doesn't want to see him again; she's had her fill of being nothing but a sex object.

'Who is it?' she calls out.

'It's me, it's Alex.' Gab quickly opens the door and ushers her in.

'What's up?' Gab asks her, leading her back into her room. They climb into bed and draw the covers up close.

'I've made a decision,' Alex takes a breath. 'I'm going to have an abortion.' The moment she says the word Alex begins to cry, leaning into Gab and glad to have her arms around her.

'You're doing the right thing.' Gab strokes her hair and repeats, 'You're doing the right thing.'

'Then how come I feel so terrible?' Alex sobs quietly.

'Because the right thing isn't always the easiest thing to do, because this is the hardest thing you have done. But it doesn't make it wrong, not for you and not for any of the children you will one day have,' Gab tells her gently, squeezing her hand.

'You know tonight, Jason was over for dinner and he offered me a drink and I thought no, just in case I decide to have the baby. And now ... and now I can drink because I'm not going to have this baby, because this baby isn't going to survive, and I can't bear it.' Alex curls up as small as she can go, shielding herself from herself.

'Listen,' Gab tells her. 'When I look at Jason and his nice little family it does make me think about when I was pregnant. But I don't regret it, it would have been with the wrong person at the wrong time.' Alex lifts her head to meet Gab's eyes.

'So you don't think that I'll regret it?' she asks, in desperate need of reassurance.

'Not if you have really thought it through, which I know you have.'

~

When Alex emerges from her own room the next morning I'm waiting for her, waiting for her to tell me what I think already know.

'Tell me what's going on Alex,' I ask her quietly. She looks at me, trying to find a way to articulate to me what she can hardly explain to herself.

'I'm pregnant. I'm going to have an abortion,' she says finally. We stare at each other across the floor. I feel like I should go to her, hold her but I don't want to hurt her. She looks like she might break if I touch her.

'Are you all right?' I ask. She nods.

'When is … it,' I ask, feeling like I have to.

'Thursday,' she says, her eyes dark pools of sadness.

Kelly walks into the room and goes straight to her, putting her arms around her in an easy way that's barred to me. I try to think of something, anything else I can do to get Alex from here to Thursday, something other than hold her. If it's me, if I want to avoid feeling something or thinking about someone – something, I mean – then I just distract myself. I've spent pretty much most of my adult life in the practice of self-distraction. I'm an expert.

'Let's do something, just the three of us. Come, on?' I ask Alex, and Kelly looks at her hopefully,

'OK,' she says with a shrug.

I take them onto the roof top and make them Cuban drinks, I find my Cuban CDs. Alex and Kelly watch me as I run about, making everything as perfect as it can be.

'Umbrellas for the ladies,' I say, handing them both a big, beautiful cocktail. I grab Alex's hand and pull her onto my imaginary dance floor. Kelly watches with an anxious smile, worried that my plan might fail.

'Right, now the secret of Afro-Cuban dance is, of course, rhythm. It's all in the hips.' Kelly laughs and Alex rolls her eyes, looking self-conscious and awkward.

'You know, I'm not very good at this,' she says with a reluctant smile.

'That's because you've never danced with a professional, baby. Okay, follow me – I'll lead because I'm the man. I don't think even you can dispute that!' Alex laughs and lets me lead her through the music, the beats grows louder and the rhythm takes us over and for a while she is lost in its insistent melody. She's distracted from herself and the plan works. I catch Kelly's eye, and she mouths 'Keep dancing.'

'You, señorita, are magnificent,' I tell her in my best approximation of a Cuban lothario.

'Thanks, I didn't know you could do a Russian accent,' Alex teases like she would if things were normal.

And we dance and dance until we're too tired to think.

~

It's dusk when Alex leaves the party to go to bed. It's only when she closes her bedroom door that she realizes she could have run two marathons and still she wouldn't be able to sleep tonight. She sits on the edge of the bed trying to remember what it is that she is supposed to do and when it comes back to her the night comes crashing down on her head.

She has to tell Rex. She goes to the computer and logs on to e-mail. She carefully, slowly, types in Rex's e-mail address. She doesn't want to get it wrong, she doesn't want someone else to get his message, someone who doesn't know her – or worse, to have it returned with a little message reading 'undeliverable', which is kind of how she feels about what she must tell him, anyway.

~

'Dear Rex,' she writes. 'I hope you are enjoying it out there in the bush. I have to tell you something.

I'm pregnant and I have decided that at this time in my life I am not ready to be a mum or a single mum. I feel very sad about it but I can't see that any other option is viable. I know this will be upsetting for you but I wanted you to know, as in a way we are in this together, although I feel pretty much alone right now.

I am having the termination on Thursday.

Love Alex.'

~

Alex re-reads the note and winces at the cold formality, but what else is there to do? If she began to write how she really felt, she might never be able to stop and if all of that came out of her she's afraid there would be nothing left. Nothing left to put back together again. She presses the 'send' button and goes to bed.

~

Caitlin watches Jason getting ready for work, her eyes full of envy.

'I might be late tonight,' he tells her, without looking at her. 'I've got court tomorrow.' Caitlin's face falls.

'But I've got yoga tonight, I told you!' she says.

'Caitlin, can't you miss a week?' Jason asks her, like she's over-reacting.

'It's the first week,' Caitlin says. 'I was really looking forward to getting out!' she calls after him as he walks down the corridor. 'Since I got back I don't go anywhere! I am stuck in this flat, your bloody nanny in residence,' she shouts. Caitlin has discovered that subtlety doesn't work when you need Jason's attention. Angus screams his head off and gets it; Caitlin decided to try it too. Jason returns and looks at her.

'OK, OK. I'll bring work home. Jesus.' He picks up his briefcase and heads for the door, pausing to kiss the baby.

'Bye little Angus, bye baby.'

'Bye,' Caitlin says, but the door is slammed shut.

Some women wouldn't even notice if their husbands didn't kiss them goodbye. Caitlin is not one of those women. She feels like screaming now, but what's the point when daddy isn't here to hear her?

So when Jason pops home between court and office for a flying visit he's surprised to find that Caitlin isn't thrilled to see him. He's even more surprised to find her on her way out, with a cheerful Angus strapped into his stroller and chewing on a rattle. Caitlin has all of her bags packed and on the pavement.

'Where are you off to?' he asks, puzzled, trying to remember if she'd mentioned another visit to her mum's.

'We're moving out.' Caitlin looks at the road.

'What?' Jason can't quiet get with the game.

'There's no point in me staying.' Caitlin's voice is tight with tears.

'But Angus?' Jason asks before he can stop himself. 'But ... why, I mean?'

'Jason, you don't love me and it seems to me inevitable that we're going to break up. So let's do it now before Angus and I are really settled in here.' For a woman with a broken heart Caitlin is calm and dignified.

'What the fuck are you talking about?' Jason shouts at her, angry and afraid at the thought of losing his son once again. 'You're not taking Angus.' He tries to grab the baby out of his pram.

'Yes, I am, Jason, calm down,' Caitlin says. Jason tries to pull Angus out of the straps but in his anger he can't work the fastening. Gus begins to cry, his face a picture of fear.

'Jason! Stop it! Can't you see what you're doing? You'll hurt him!' Caitlin tried to pull Jason off the baby and he swings round, pushing her to the ground. For a moment they stare at each other.

'I'm sorry, I'm so sorry.' Jason begins to cry. 'Please, please don't take my baby away from me ...' Caitlin struggles to her feet and lifts screaming Angus out of his pram.

'I'm sorry. I'm sorry. Can't you see that I have to? For all of us. I'll call you about seeing Angus.'

The cab she'd been waiting for pulls up on the curb. Jason says nothing as he watches the driver pack the bags in the trunk. His family gets into a taxi and leaves him feeling the loneliest he has ever felt. Of all the things he's been through, nothing is as bad as having his boy wrenched from him. Nothing.

39

Alex has gone to the clinic with Gab.

Kelly is cleaning everything she can think of and has changed the sheets on Alex's bed. I have bought all the women's magazines that I can afford and I'm cooking. I cooking pretty much everything that Alex has ever liked in the last three years. We're doing everything we can, because really we can do nothing.

We watch the clock and wait, we try not to think about what might be happening to Alex now. We play Scrabble; I win. We play all the CDs we haven't listened to for over a year. We wait.

When Gab brings Alex in she looks pale and tired but she still looks like Alex. They haven't removed any part of her soul, although maybe it's still anaesthetized.

'Hi,' I say to her.

'Hi.' She gives me a little smile.

'How are you feeling?' I ask tentatively.

'Hungry,' she says.

'Oh good – I mean, I've cooked. Pasta and Napolenata sauce. Want some?'

'Thanks Evan. Yeah I'd love some.' Kelly takes Alex's bag from her hand.

'Come on, let's get you to bed. You can eat in there.' Kelly takes Alex away and Gab helps me prepare her a tray, the pair of us not looking at each other or speaking. Not wanting to say to each other what we can't say to Alex.

Finally we lay a picnic of pasta out on Alex's bed.

'How do you feel, Alex? I mean how do you feel inside your soul?' Kelly asks her. Alex thinks for a moment.

'Relieved,' she says simply and we all breathe out simultaneously.

'Thanks for the mags, Evan,' Alex says to me with a smile. 'It must have been tough for you to blow your whole monthly budget on me.'

'Oh yeah, but I figured I'd just borrow it back from you, tomorrow,' I tell her.

'What have you done today?' Gab asks me.

'Avoided the computer,' I say ruefully.

'Isn't that what you do every day?' Gab makes Alex laugh.

And that's how it goes on. The four of us sitting around on Alex's bed like it's the most normal place in the world to have dinner. Talking about our universe as if nothing has happened. Every now and again I can see a look in Alex's face I've never seen before. A sadness that hadn't been there yesterday.

~

For the first time in a long time Alex is having a dreamless sleep – until, that is, she wakes up and finds Rex sitting on her bed. She's pretty sure that she must be dreaming after all, but she sits up and rubs her eyes hard, just in case. He's still there.

'Hello?' she says, disorientated.

'Hello.' Rex pauses. 'How are you feeling?'

'Not too bad,' Alex says.

'I'm sorry I didn't get here before. I only got your e-mail this morning.' Alex nods, dumbly not sure if she should feel happy or terrified.

'Are you in any pain?' he asks her, his face in shadow.

'A bit, not too bad.' She looks at the window; it's dark. 'What time is it?'

'About nine. Look, I'm sorry you had to go through this alone,' he says. Alex listens to the warm timbre of his voice and relaxes. He doesn't hate her.

'Did I do the right thing?' she asks, all but begging for affirmation.

'Yes, whatever you decided was the right thing.' He sounds certain for her sake.

'What if it was you, what would you have decided?' Rex's head dips a little.

'I can't … You did the right thing.' He puts his arms about her and draws her against the warmth of his chest.

'I'm here now,' he says and Alex falls asleep feeling safe for the first time since he left.

When Alex opens her eyes in the morning Rex is watching her and she thinks she sees something there in his face, love maybe; but it's gone before she can be certain and she supposes it was just the remnants of a pre-waking dream.

'I have to go,' he says.

'I know, OK,' she tells him and she means it now. She feels as though this is the ending that she thought would never come. The conclusion she needed so badly.

Rex kisses her gently, pushing her hair out of her eyes one more time before he leaves.

40

Christian told me this story.

In 1962 there was a laughing epidemic in a place called Tanganyika. It started with some girls having a giggle. Then the giggle turned into a laugh, then the laugh turned into a guffaw, a cackle and before you know it, it spread across the whole country, village after village, lasting for six months. In the end they had to close the school. That's what Christian told me.

Nobody knows why it happened. Nobody knows why we laugh, either, we just do.

I have one theory. I think laughter is evolution's most sophisticated version of self-preservation. If we didn't see the funny side of things we'd all be dead by now. Suicide.

While I was waiting to hear from Lauren on whether or not there was any chance at all of me getting my novel published I wrote a short story. It took me thirty minutes and it was about a beautiful but heart-broken bird who'd forgotten how to sing, a lost and lonely bird, and how she'd finally found her way home. I'd written it half listening to the radio, to some programme called *Texture*. They were running a short story competition. It seemed liked fate to me, so I saved the story onto my laptop, attached it to an e-mail and sent it off. It took me less than three minutes.

They just called me to tell me I've won. They want me to go on the show tomorrow, to get the prize. Book tokens.

I laugh.

I'm looking forward to sharing my glory by generously letting everyone else buy a drink for me in the Fu Bar that night but by the time I get there Richie Blake is stealing my thunder and then some. Things are going pretty good for him. He's won a reader's poll in a women's magazine. He's getting noticed. Richie was happy and the best thing was he was sharing his happiness with his friends and we were happy for him, like good mate should be. Mostly.

I piped up with my story like a small knave at his princely court.

'So who's interviewing you, again?' he asks me benevolently.

'It's a show called *Texture*, the competition had over 2,000 entries,' I tell everyone so they know just how good I must have been to win (exclude the people who entered who probably can't hold a pen, the ones who wrote about their dogs, the ones who wrote about their exes and the ones who wrote about illegal sex and it maybe came down to about fifty readable stories, of which mine was the best; an achievement in anyone's book).

'This show called *Texture* – they ran the competition. This really could help me get published.' I smile. Everyone nods encouragingly.

'Isn't that a gardening show?' Gab asks, with a sly smirk.

'Yeah, maybe that's why you won, they think you're an ornithologist,' Richie jokes.

'Ha, ha,' I tell them deadpan. 'Why would I be on a gardening show?'

'As a gnome?' Christian pipes up. Everyone laughs, including the universe.

'Fine, mock my achievement,' I half joke. Richie leans forward into the group.

'I'm being interviewed next week too, as it goes,' he says.

'Oh yeah?' Gab asks.

'*Blabber*.' Richie name-drops the title of the hugely popular show onto the table like a winning hand of cards.

'Wow!' Gab.

'*Blabber*, that's so cool!' Simon.

'Richie Blake the big star!' Miranda adds. And on and on and on.

'So why is *Blabber* talking to you?' I ask, trying not to sound too mean-spirited.

'Because I am a fabulously talented actor destined to become the icon of our generation.' Richie grins. 'Why are what's-it-called … *Texture* talking to you?'

'Because I am a fabulously talented writer destined to become the voice of our generation – and without whom the icon wouldn't have two words to say.' Everyone laughs and nudges Richie. I am the winner.

'Oh, I've got two words for you.' Richie says mildly.

'What's that?' I ask.

'Your round.' A roar of laughter thunders into the rafters.

~

I'm waiting for Alex to come in from work. I've had a bit of a smoke and the edges of the room seem to be stretching very far away ever so slowly and then spinning back at me so fast I feel dizzy.

I practise cool stuff to say on the radio.

'I invoke, palliate and drive away the dead nightly …'

'Shit!' Alex turns on the all the lights, temporarily blinding me.

'I'm waiting for you.' I squint at her, the small part of me that's still sober listening to the slur in my voice and my garbled syntax. 'I mean, I am waiting up for you.' I correct myself slowly. 'Check you're OK.' Didn't mean to say that last bit out loud.

'You scared the shit out of me!' Alex lets go of the wall and walks over to me, assessing me for lucidity.

'I am here to help you see the funny side …' I tell her.

'You're in a drug warp, I know that much.' She's tired and angry at me.

'I'm on the radio tomorrow Alex, will you come with me? I won a writing competition and I want you to come with me, I can't do it unless you come with me …' I attempt a sweet smile but by the look on Alex's face I'd say it was nearer a leer. 'You are my muse after all,' I finish with some flourish.

'I'm going to bed,' she says with half a smile.

'Say you'll come with me first,' I sink off of the chair and onto my knees.

'Evan …' I watch her wavering.

'Come on, we'll hang out. We'll spend the day together. It'll be great, please come with me, I need you.' I think given a little more encouragement she might say yes. 'It'll take your mind off your uterus,' I say. She looks at me for a moment, her face a picture of opened-mouthed hurt and disbelief.

'Fuck,' I say to the empty space her sudden absence has created. I didn't mean to say that out loud either.

The floor begins to softly undulate under me. I decide to spend the night here.

~

I find I am looking at a table leg. From the way my head feels I'm fairly certain at least one of the table's other four legs has been buried deep into my skull. I lie still for a moment waiting for pieces of last night to come back to me. It must have been Alex that has murdered me; fair enough.

I pull myself into a sitting position.

Kelly is looking at me.

'You are appalling,' she says. 'I can't even talk to you.' She looks as if she's about to leave and then comes back into the room, bending her face down to meet mine.

'Do you even know what you said to Alex?' she asks me.

'Um?' I find I cannot articulate. She can't be bothered to speak to me any more and the door slams shut behind her. I wait for the pain to subside.

I drag myself onto my knees and head for the phone.

'Hello, Evan Wylde ... I'm supposed to come into today ... yes ... but I have flu, I can't come. Sorry. Yep, sorry. OK you can send someone out in a couple of days.' I don't really know what the teenage-sounding producer is saying, so I decide just to agree. I climb to my feet and head for the kitchen sink, running the cold tap into it until it is full.

I stick my head in.

'What the fuck are you doing?' Alex's voice reaches me through the icy water.

'Oh, hi,' I lift my head and shake drops around me. 'I'm committing suicide. I can't believe how horrible I was to you last night. I'll never laugh again so suicide is the only option open to me.' Cold water runs into my eyes. 'I'm sorry Alex, really, really sorry. Are we OK?'

Alex looks at me. 'Yeah, we're OK.' I'm not sure if she's saying it because she can't be bothered not to.

'Richie's on *Blabber* next week.

'God, I love that show,' Alex says flatly.

'He's on with Luke Kelly,' I add.

'God, I love Luke Kelly.' Alex lets a tiny smile soften her mouth.

'Yeah but I'm changing the accepted form of the novel, Alex. I'm like Kerouac. Someday people will appreciate me as a literary revolutionist.' I sigh hard, not seeing my own joke any more. Alex claps a heavy hand on my shoulder.

'No they won't, Evan, and if they do you'll be dead first.' I wince despite myself.

'If I'm not appreciated Alex, then it's your fault. All of it. The whole world. Everything, Palestine. India and Pakistan, it's all your fault.' Alex finally smiles.

'OK ... are you going to hang around me all day?' she asks.
'Yeah,' I tell her.
'Good,' she says.

41

Richie's already feeling pretty good about himself when he goes into Pia's office.

'You wanted to see me?' he asks confidently.

'Yes, I did, close the door.' Pia tells him. His confidence wavers and for a moment he feels like the little boy getting hauled up in front of the head for looking up the girls' skirts in class. He'd always wondered what the fuss was about.

'I assume you know that Josh is leaving?' Richie allows himself a self-satisfied smile.

'Yeah, reckons he's going to be the next Russell Crowe,' he laughs.

'Or the next Kevin Van Hentenryck,' Pia adds.

'Who?' Richie asks

'Exactly.' Pia's like ice. 'Well, Josh going has created a problem. We need a new hunk, Richie, a new heartthrob to set the teens' hearts racing. A star. Well, we think it might be you.' Richie can't help the excitement that lights up his face.

'Me?'

'How does it feel?' Pia asks him, with her best approximation of a smile.

'Great ...' Richie is speechless for once.

'OK, well, we have to test your demographic. Make sure the girlies love you, Richie, but in the meantime we'll start upping your profile. OK?' Richie suppresses a whoop.

'OK!'

'And no more of that refusing to discuss your love life bullshit, OK?' Pia's voice is knife-edge sharp.

'OK!' Richie feels a bit like he's just sold his soul to the devil, but he reckons he'll get over it.

~

Gabrielle considers her desk, which is littered with a hundred Post-it notes from Dominic. Now that it's out there, now that they've both said how they feel about each other, it's harder. She thought it might be easier, but it's harder because now they don't have the cover of pretending that nothing is going on between them. In fact, since they made the declaration that there is nothing go on, it already feels like an affair.

'That's funny,' Gab thinks. 'But not ha ha.'

They flirt with each other, non-stop. It's not really what they say so much as how they look at each other; the way Gab rests her hand on her hip, the spaces between them each drawing its own conclusion. Just waiting to be closed.

'I'm just going to that meeting uptown.' Gab stops at Dominic's door on her way out, the arch in her back just a little more curved, the weight of her breasts against her shirt just a little more pronounced.

'OK, well I guess I won't see you until tomorrow, then?' Dominic asks her, his eyes roving.

'Guess not.' Without even knowing it Gab's body issues him an invitation, a challenge that he couldn't refuse even if he had any choice.

So when Gabs finds Dominic waiting for her as she walks out of her meeting a couple of hours later, she isn't really surprised – not on a molecular level, anyhow.

'How'd it go?' Dominic falls into step beside her.

'What're you doing here?' Gab laughs.

'Waiting for you. I was just passing on my way to a drinks party down the road,' he says.

'How far down the road?'

'About ten K's …?' Dominic laughs. Gab stops and faces Dominic, feeling as if every inch of her skin is magnetized towards him.

'I should go home now,' she says, sounding unconvinced, raising her hand to hail a cab.

'Please,' Dominic looks at her, all pretence slipping away. The cab pulls up and she holds on to the handle, gripping tightly, feeling the weight of the future pulling her free of the earth.

'Come with me,' she says and Dominic gets into the cab with her.

~

For Gabrielle there is no kissing in the cab, no touching, no speaking even until they reach her apartment. She leads him in through the door and walks into her bedroom. Dominic follows her, pausing briefly in the bedroom to watch her as she lays on her bed, fully clothed, her hair spread out behind her on her the pillow. She holds out a hand to him.

In the last few seconds it takes for their lips to finally engage they both feel a lifetime pass between them.

Gab melts under his kiss, finding it everything she imagined it should be, imagining it is everything she finds it to be. Feels his fingers in her hair, the weight of him crushing her breasts, enjoying every moment of the reality of what she has begun.

She rolls on top of him, straddling him.

'I can feel you,' she whispers, enjoying her power over him. He reached up, his fingers finding their way under her shirt, searching for her breasts. Gabrielle feels like the most fabulous woman on earth, she rocks faster on his hips, leaning her mouth into his ear.

'I'll get a condom,' she whispers. Dominic shudders then, his fingers clench deep into her flesh and he is still. She looks at him; it takes her a moment to realize he has already come.

'Oh,' Gab says, not sure whether or not she should laugh and deciding not to.

'God, I'm sorry.' Dominic can hardly look her in the eye. In fact, he doesn't.

Gab rolls off him onto her back and looks at the ceiling, speechless. Dominic sits up and goes to the bathroom. He is in there a very long time. When he returns he looks guilty.

'I have to go,' he says, picking up his jacket. Gab stares at him.

'I can't help it, Gab, I have to. I'm late already ...' He checks his watch. 'I'm not going to apologize,' he begins.

'I'm not asking you to apologize!' Gab barely contains her anger.

'Gab.' He finally finds the courage to touch her again. 'What do you want me to do, what is it you think we should do?' he asks her.

'I know exactly what we should do. We should go back to bed. We should make love properly this time, and it'll be fantastic and tender and sweet. And then you'll stay the night and hold me all day long and then in the morning I'll make you breakfast and we'll go to the zoo. We'll do all that hopeless, pathetic bullshit that other couples do. You know why they do it? Because they can.' Gab finishes, out of breath, holding her throat closed tight to keep back any more tears. She'd always known it would be like this, but still she had to find out for herself.

Dominic brings her hand to his lips and kisses her fingers.

'Gabrielle I am sorry,' he tells her at last. 'Goodnight.'

When he is gone, Gab imagines it his him that is unbuttoning her shirt and releasing the catch of her bra. When she slips naked into bed she holds her pillow in her arms and goes to sleep dreaming that when she wakes up Dominic will be there.

When her alarm clock wakes her the next moment, Dominic isn't there and Gabrielle realizes that he never will be. She make a decision, the hardest she's ever had to make, a resolve she keeps all the way from her house to Dominic's office.

'Are you sorry I came last night?' he asks her, immediately. Gab can't hide her smile this time.

'Do you want to rephrase that?' she laughs, watching a flush spread over his cheeks.

'Do you regret it, I mean?' he says again, looking bashful.

'No, not for a second. But, Dominic, if we did this people would get hurt. Your wife, your children. You, me. Everything. I can't do it. I can't. It's not in me.'

'Gabrielle …' Dominic looks at her, his heart breaking in his eyes.

Gab stares at him a moment longer, feeling with every particle in her body that she wants him, wants to be with him and run to his side.

'But even then, I don't care that it's wrong, I don't care about my job. It's not even about your wife and kids. It's …' Gab can't bring herself to say the words.

'I said once to you that I couldn't just go to bed with you, that it would be more than that for me. Are you afraid you'll fall in love with me?' Dominic asks her, his voice rasped with emotion.

'I'm afraid that if I stay here that could happen, yes,' she says at last.

'I can't let you quit,' Dominic tells her.

'You can't stop me,' Gab says quietly. 'I'll have my letter to you this afternoon.' They look at each other a moment longer and then Gab turns and walks away from Dominic. In her head she's running in the opposite direction.

42

Jason sits at the bar, almost smiling. It's a work in progress. Since Caitlin and Angus left he's been the epitome of what it is not to smile, he's been the personification of the antimatter of laughter. He's been the dictionary definition of negative.

'Looking a bit more chipper?' I question him. He looks at Christian and they exchange a knowing glance. I briefly wonder if it's another Richie episode.

'I went to Christian's laughing club,' he says with a shy grin. 'It's total bullock but it sort of works.'

'I beg your pardon?' I say. Christian takes over.

'Well, remember those people in Tanganyika?' he says. I nod. 'Healthiest people on earth. When you laugh, even if you just begin to laugh, not for any reason at all, it makes you feel better. It lifts your spirits and soon you are laughing for real. It's good for your heart too.' I stare at him, wondering if he was on day release from an asylum when I found him at the bowling green. 'So anyway, every morning I go to the park and meet a bunch of people and we laugh for about thirty minutes. It's cool. The trick is letting yourself go, getting through that awkward first laugh.'

'You just laugh and you feel better?' I sink my beer and ponder.

Jason takes over the story. 'So I was telling him how my secretary found me at my desk, crying, and he invited me along. I thought, "Can it get any more embarrassing than blubbing in front of your secretary?" So I went.' In one easy stroke Jason glosses over the reference to how much he's missing his son. 'It worked! I do feel a bit better. Not like suddenly my life is perfect or anything, but that I can handle it.' I look from Christian to Jason and back again.

'No, see I don't think that's funny,' I say. It seems to me if life were that simple there'd be world peace and free love all round.

Richie swaggers into the bar and drop his flash mobile onto the table.

'Did I tell you that Pia says I'm going to be a huge star?' He cuts through our conversation with his razor-sharp ego. I look at Jason and then Christian.

'See, now that is funny,' I say, and everyone but Richie laughs.

~

Later that afternoon an anticipatory Richie marches into Pia's office.

'Pia, you've booked me onto *Blabber* with some grieving muso who's going to do a song about his dead dog. Even I can't compete with that.' Richie assumes the look of someone about to be huge.

'I'll unbook you. I was going to anyway,' she says, eyeing him. 'Your Q scores are back.' Her voice is devoid of inflection.

'Really?' Richie puffs up a little bigger. 'Great!'

'Not great,' Pia says flatly.

'What do you mean not great?' Richie asks her, deflating imperceptibly.

'You have two strong areas of appeal – ages six to fifteen and fifty-plus, but where it counts, Richie, you don't light any fires. You're too safe.' Richie looks at her.

'What are we going to do?' he asks her, still hopeful for a plan.

'We're going to leave where you are.' Pia turns her back on him and busies herself with some random piece of paper.

'But you promised ...' Richie begins.

'Richie, you're a "nice boy",' Pia says over her shoulders, with just a hint of sarcasm behind her voice. 'You appeal to kids and grannies. But you're not a star. You probably never will be. You can go now.'

Richie stares at the back of her head for a long moment, impotent with rage, fantasizing about stoving her head in with a staple gun.

He spins out of her office and into an uncertain future. He's finding it hard to see the funny side of the capriciousness of fate.

~

Across town, at almost exactly the same moment, Dominic opens Gabrielle's letter of resignation. A key slides out onto his desk with a note.

'My place, eight o clock,' the note reads. Dominic laughs for joy, his heart thundering in his chest. He knows that somehow this must end badly, that much is certain, but all he want is the promise of holding Gabrielle in his arms once again.

43

Alex had been working all day. Her laugh quotient for the entire shift was zero, nil, nada, niet and some other ways of saying nothing in a few more languages. I've been watching her face for about three years now. I know when Alex is down, sad and depressed but even then, even in her darkest hour, there's been something else there. Some dark, ironic humour bubbling away beneath the surface, some sense of the great big joke that the universe had written for her, the seed of a ridiculous idea growing in my mind.

But since the abortion even that has gone.

I lie on her bed waiting for her.

'Hello,' she says, looking at me, her face blank with exhaustion.

'Alex, will you come with me somewhere tomorrow?' I ask her.

'Another radio thing?' she says wearily.

'No, no I'm having lunch with some woman from there next week. But will you come? Say yes. Go on. Go on. Go on.' I work on the badgering premise, it usually works when all else fails.

'Oh yes, OK! Evan, let me get to bed, all right? I'm shattered.' I nod, satisfied, and leave her, wondering if it's possible for me to make things any worse than they already are.

Well, you know what they say … desperate measures.

~

The morning is almost cold but bright as Alex follows me through the park, still unsure about what we're up to. Eventually she picks Jason and Christian out of the crowd we are approaching; and then Nathan and Kelly too. She looks at me.

'What's going on?' she asks me suspiciously.

'It's a laughing club,' I tell her casually, as if I've just pointed out another tree.

'I'm going to kill you,' she whispers through gritted teeth, as Kelly greets her and Christian introduces her to the others in the group. They look pretty normal, definitely cheery. We all stand around and look at each other, waiting for the muse.

Slowly, like bubbles rising to the to the surface of some still water, we begin to smile at each other, then someone giggles. Just a little giggle escapes and ricochets off the group with carefree abandon.

I watch Alex; she is stony-faced. Then all at once Christian catches her eye and he laughs out loud. Alex can't help but smile, and neither can I and neither can anyone else. Before I know it I'm caught in the middle of a gale of melodious laughter and at its heart is Alex. She reaches out her hand and catches my fingers, her dancing eyes alight with meaningless joy.

I think if she could stop laughing she'd thank me.

~

In 1962 there was a contagious laughing epidemic in Tanganyika. Forty years later all over the world people are still laughing.

Nobody knows why it happens.

Nobody knows why we laugh.

We just do.

44

I'm lying on my bed imagining the fame and fortune that is sure to befall me now that I am the winner of *Texture*'s best writer of the year (category fiction). I close my eyes and visualize walking into that bookshop. Seeing all of these rows of books with 'Evan Wylde' printed just slightly larger than the title. The way that publishers do when the writer is bigger than the book, even. I imagine an admiring fan; she's maybe just around forty, with a bit of the look of an old flame of mine – Carmen – in her eyes. She's telling me she thinks it's fantastic. She offers me her body.

I wrench myself out of that daydream and back to the famous writer one. I should call Lauren, tell her about the competition. Or maybe I shouldn't, maybe she'd think that 'writer of the month' on some low-rating radio show is tantamount to the kiss of death for me. It's just that she's had the manuscript a long time now and I've heard nothing.

I'll have lunch with this woman from *Texture* and then think about calling Lauren.

Kelly wanders into my room and sits on my bed, looking exhausted. She eyes my reclining position with envy.

'You were like that when I left this morning,' she says.

'Yeah, I'm head writing. It's very draining,' I tell her, hauling myself up onto an elbow.

'Jesus, Evan, how do you pay the rent?' I shrug. That's one of those mysteries of life.

'So how was your day?' I ask Kelly, seeing shadows under her eyes. 'Shall I make you a cuppa?' She rolls her eyes in gratitude and sinks onto my bed.

'I'm so good at my job, I love my job. I love Peace too. I mean, I really love her, she's inspirational. I want to be Peace when I grow up.' I listen to her as I go to the kitchen and put the kettle on.

'Yeah, and she knows it,' I tell her. 'You work too hard, Kel. You never get any time off, you're on call twenty-four hours a day.

'That not true!' Kelly protests as she joins me in the kitchen. 'Today I saved the day again, I rustled up a string quartet out of the blue when there weren't any left in the whole of Melbourne and she thanked me and gave me tomorrow morning off! Just like that! That's the kind of woman she is – inspirational, but fair.' I turn to see Kelly looking out of the window, daydreaming a future where she is mentor to some other up-and-coming girl.

'You look done in,' I tell her.

'I am done in, Evan.' She sits up and takes the tea. 'But I am also fulfilled. Much like you must be after a whole day of lying down, I imagine.' She sips her tea smugly and takes it to her room.

'Don't tar me with your nine-to-five brush, baby. I'm a writer, we don't do office hours!' I call after her. Back in my own room I sit down at my laptop and finger the power button for a moment and then I go to lie down.

You may think I'm joking but this positive visualization thing, it works, trust me. If you see something hard enough, imagine it and will it, you can make it happen. I've just flown to England to pick up my Booker Prize by the time Alex comes in from work

'Busy?' She raises an eyebrow at me.

'Yeah, I'm …' I decide not to share this particular visualization at this delicate stage. 'I'm planning what I'm going to say to this Jemima woman tomorrow when I do my interview. Got to come across well, got to play the media.'

'And?' Alex asks me with a little smirk.

'How about, "I'm just trying to push the boundaries a bit, trying to speak for my generation because we need to be heard!"' Not bad for something off the top of my head. Alex gives me her 'I'm about to be funny' look.

'You did write a story about a bird for a local radio station, didn't you?' She laughs.

'It was a metaphor! Parable-type thing,' I say defensively. 'Alex, you don't get it. You've got to be seen in a certain way. Something new, a little bit of arrogance and attitude. You've got to stand out from the crowd!' Alex looks at my skinny white legs dangling from my shorts.

'Evan, I don't think there's ever any chance you won't stand out from a crowd.' She laughs at herself again and leaves.

To be misunderstood – it is always the artist's fate.

~

Gabrielle and Dominic were past that getting-it-together phase and were now in the getting-it-together-as-often-as-possible phase.

Post-coital and almost purring, Gabrielle pulls the warmth of his body hard against her and smiled.

'Want to order food in?' she asks, lost in a dream of her own construction.

'I have to go.' Dominic pulls away from her suddenly and she feels a chill raise goose bumps along the skin where he was.

'No.' She tries a teasing smile, letting the sheet slip down to her waist.

'Yes.' Dominic gazes at her appreciatively but he is unmoved. Gab sighs, suppressing the urge to pursue it any further, making herself stay firmly within the boundaries she knew would be set for her.

'I guess it gives you a chance to miss me,' she says with a sigh, pulling the sheet up under her chin.

'I don't miss you,' Dominic says, with a small smile. He drags the sheet away from her, leaving her bare under his gaze. 'I ache for you in my heart.' Gab winds her arms around his neck and kisses him, but still he pulls away.

No, he is gone. Gabrielle goes to the freezer and takes out a carton of ice cream, and takes it back to bed.

Gabrielle is trying to focus on what is in front of her, not why he had to leave or where he was going. But it was always in the background, just waiting.

45

I have been waiting outside this café for the last twenty-two minutes until I can be safely, fashionably late. I watch the girl that must be Jemima tapping her pen against her Dictaphone in annoyance, judging exactly when I should make my entrance. I decide the time is right when I see her call for the bill.

'Jemima, hi. Evan Wylde.' I steam to her tableside, hand held out in greeting.

'Hi.' She gives me a polite smile in return.

'Am I late? Sorry. Sometimes I just vague out, thinking about things. You know,' I give her my sweetest smile and settle back onto the seat opposite her, my arm flung over the back of the chair.

'No problem.' She looks me up and down, probably noticing my cut-price chic and tousled hair. I went for stubble, but it's a bit patchy and Alex said I looked like I was coming down with the mange. By that time, though, it was too late to shave so I'm hoping she'll think I'm charmingly uncaring abut my appearance.

I drink wine as Jemima reels off her set-piece questions.

'And finally, what do you think the young woman of today is looking for?' she asks me almost absently, gazing over my shoulder.

'What you mean, apart from me?' I laugh. She doesn't. 'Um, well smart, funny guys who know how to take care of business in the world and in the bedroom. And the park and the back of the car, against the wall out the back of he pub … A guy who's in touch with himself, you know?' I waggle my eyebrows. Jemima looks at me as if she can't imagine wanting to know anything less.

'Right, well thanks. It'll run on Sunday and Greg'll read out your story as you couldn't be bothered to come in and do it yourself …' She gets up to leave. I get the feeling I might not have made the best impression.

'Hold up a sec,' I catch her as she hits the street. She turns on me impatiently, tapping her feet.

'Yep?'

'Did I offend you in some way?' I ask her, only just coming up to speed with her attitude.

'Nope,' she lies hurriedly and turns again, but I step in front of her.

'How about another drink?' I ask her. She sighs and crosses her arms.

'Do you really want to have a drink with me, or are you just shocked your turbo charm hasn't work on me?' I stare at her, caught out.

'Jesus, you're tough,' I say. I can't help smiling.

'Listen, the interview is over and so are your fifteen minutes of fame. OK?' She tries to dodge past me.

'Is it me, or are you like this with everyone?' I block her path again, risking certain death.

'It's you.' She holds my stare, her eyes fizzling with anger.

'But you don't even know me!' I protest lamely as she shoves me aside.

'I know you!' she says as she walks away.

'How?' I protest starting after her. She turns on me.

'Because you're typical of your type. An arrogant, self-obsessed, vain wanker. Ergo NOT MY TYPE!' She shouts the last few words. My chin drops to my chest and I watch her disappear into the crowds.

'Christ Almighty,' I tell a shocked pensioner, 'I think I'm in love.'

~

'How'd it go?' Alex asks me without lifting her head from her book.

'She hated me!' I tell her, flopping onto the sofa.' Alex smiles.

'Really?'

'Yeah, I was charming and brash … or as she saw it, an arrogant and vain wanker.' I shake my head in awe-struck disbelief. 'Can you imagine?'

'Um, yes?' Alex laughs.

'Very unprofessional, I think,' I say with a grin.

'I think I like this girl,' Alex says. She looks at my mile-wide smile. 'And so do you, don't you?' I look at quickly for any fleeting trace of sadness, but I see none.

'Yeah, I think I do,' I say and I begin to imagine a way to get her to like me.

46

Alex is finding that whenever she gets five minutes to enjoy her wine and finish her book, something happens. This time it's Gab, looking glorious up to her neck, dressed up to the nines but her hair in disarray and her mascara staining her cheeks.

'Gab?' Alex steps aside as her friend wanders shell-shocked into the flat.

'I met his wife,' she says. Alex rolls her eyes and goes to fetch another glass of wine.

'Oh God, what happened? Does she know?' Alex puts a glass into Gab's hand, watches her down it and then tops it up.

'I went to this function with him. I know it wasn't a date or anything, that we couldn't be together, but just being in the same room with him, knowing that he was mine. That's all I wanted.' Alex nods and strokes her hair.

'I'm in the loo when this woman, not exactly the most glamorous person, starts talking to me, tells me I've got nice top on. I'm thinking that she looks the way I want to when I'm that age. Really self-possessed. Great clothes. You know?' Gab sniffs and finishes the wine again. This time Alex does not top her up, so she takes the bottle from Alex's hand and does it herself.

'We're coming out of the loo together and I see Dominic. I smile and wave at him and you should have seen his face, Alex. He looked at me like I was the creature from the black lagoon. It was then I realized she was his wife. We went thought the whole pantomime of polite introductions. I don't know how she didn't guess … It was hell.' Gab wipes angry tears away from her eyes with the heel of her fist.

'You knew he had a wife. That's what married men do. They have wives,' Alex says, forgetting what dangerous ground she is treading on.

'I know, intellectually I know it. But somehow it didn't seem real, she didn't seem real, until tonight.

'Yeah, I know, it feels like shit, doesn't it?' Alex says, hoping for some kind of final understanding from Gab, some insight on why it was she had an affair with Jason all those months ago.

'I'm not you,' Gab says bluntly, verging on sudden anger.

'What?' Alex is startled.

'I didn't know her! She wasn't my best friend!' Alex recoils from her.

'Oh, well that make you a much better person than me, then,' she says angrily.

'I'm not saying that.' Gab tries to rein her anger in – after all, it's not really Alex she's angry at.

'Oh but you are, Gab. Want to know how I could sleep with your boyfriend? I blocked you out of it and just focused on us. Sound familiar?' Gab wilts, sinking into the chair. Alex watches, trying to judge her mood, hoping to curb her own.

'I'm in love,' she wails.

'Yeah, so was I.' Alex relaxes, thinking the tension is over.

'Oh please, Alex. Dominic and I are something special. You and Jason … you were just a quick fuck.'

Alex looks like she's been slapped in the face. 'That's what you think?' Alex asks her best friend. 'You think I'd go, "Oh look, there's my best friend's boyfriend, he'll do for a quickie." Fuck you.' Alex takes the near-empty bottle of wine out of her friend's hand and stands.

'Maybe you just told yourself you love him, to feel better about it,' Gab sneers. Alex takes a deep breath and starts counting to ten.

'Maybe you should go home.'

Gab is more than little drunk and as she strides out of the apartment she struggles to keep her dignity balanced on uncertain legs. Alex watches her go and remembers how much it hurts to want someone else's lover. She would do anything to save Gabrielle from that pain. If there was anything that she could do.

47

I've been hanging out outside the radio station for a few hours now. Finally my patience pays off and Jemima appears. On her way out to lunch, I reckon.

I decide to start with self-obsessed.

'I just hoped we could clarify a few things,' I say, falling into step beside her. She jumps as I approach and then looks angry. On reflection, maybe my surprise attack wasn't the best way to put her at ease.

'Oh yeah, sure.' She quickly recovers her composure. 'What exactly do you want to clarify?'

I persist, despite her icy demeanour. 'Well, I thought it was important that I say that I thought it was important for my generation to be active in the world. Like Amnesty, which I am a big fan of.'

'Oh, are you. How convenient,' she returns, unmoved. 'I'll introduce you as "Evan Wylde – loves windsurfing and Amnesty."'

'I don't love windsurfing,' I say.

'I hate it when people do that.' Jemima ignores me. 'Attach a cause to themselves just for the sake of looking rounded.' She picks up her pace, leaving me momentarily behind.

'I'm not doing that!' I yell, dumbfounded. 'I'm an active member of Amnesty … well, I mean I did join a couple of years ago. OK, so my membership's lapsed few months back but, you know, I've got bills to pay and …' My brain finally gets my mouth to shut up.

'Well, whatever you're doing, we're done. Goodbye.' She turns into a busy sandwich shop and I ponder the merits of going in after her. The thing is, I don't want to come across as some self-obsessed, ego-mad stalker guy. I'm not that kind of guy. I have to find a way to show her that. A way that won't get me arrested for harassment. I turn on my heels and drag my feet all the way home.

~

Gabrielle tries to look Dominic in the eyes, but she can't seem to. He's gone from her mature Romeo to family man in one easy step.

'Gabrielle, I …' he begins, shutting the door to her office so that the other staff who have recently begun to exchange looks and whispers when he walks by can't hear them. The closed door fuels even more talk.

'You should have warned me,' Gab tells him flatly.

'It was a last-minute thing, how could I turn her down?' Dominic spreads his hands, looking like a man harassed.

'I feel like ...' Gab stares at him, unable to tell him exactly how she feels. 'It's just that she's so nice.' Dominic flinches.

'I know,' he says sadly.

'Don't agree!' Gab pleads with him desperately. 'Tell me she's frigid or a psycho or something ...' Dominic shakes his head.

'But she's not,' he shrugs helplessly. Gab pauses for a moment and then takes the plunge.

'Do you still love her?' she asks, her heart full of fear. Dominic looks at her unhappily.

'I love you,' he says, but it's what he does not say that hurts Gabrielle so much.

'Fuck.' She picks up some random piece of paper and leaves Dominic standing impotently in her office. She feels her colleagues' eyes on her back as she hurries to the toilets.

~

I look at the back of Alex's head and wonder if she can give me any tips on how to woo women, but then I think I might be pushing even my luck a little too far. She senses my gaze and turns to look at me.

'Did you charm her?' she says expectantly.

'Um, no.' I look embarrassed. 'She thinks because I'm well-read that I'm a wanker.' I sit down next to Alex, my whole body a gesture of my incomprehension.

'Well, you are wanker, but I don't think it's because you're well-read,' Alex tells me sweetly.

'Thank you,' I sigh, letting her friendly insult wash over me. 'If she really knew me, she'd go out with me. She'd like me, wouldn't she? Like all the other women in the world.' Alex rolls her eyes. As if she too hadn't been one of those women once. Almost.

'Maybe,' she says with a shrug. 'I tell you what, if I see her I'll tell her how great you are.' I look at her, seeing a plan formulate before my very eyes.

'You're a genius!' I tell my muse. 'I'll be right back.'

'Evan!' she calls after me, 'I was only kidding!' But it's too late, she's set in motion what must be maybe the best seduction plan since

… well anyway, it's a good one, top ten at least. Half an hour later and I return, holding out a piece of paper to Alex.

'She's a journalist, she has to believe in hard evidence,' I tell her. She takes the paper from me and looks at it. It reads: 'A True and Honest Testament to The Character of Evan Wylde.'

'Will you sign it?' I ask her happily.

'Am I allowed to read it?' she grins, skimming the words.

'Uh, if you want to. Anyway, do you think it'll work?' I skip around Alex like a kid.

'Well, can I take out this bit that says "and from what I've heard he is a tender yet powerful lover?"' Her eyes are brimming with laughter.

'No,' I say shortly, snatching the paper from her hands and heading for the door.

I mean, what does a writer have if it isn't his artistic licence?

48

Alex answers the door to Gabrielle.

'He still loves her,' Gab says as if she's entirely forgotten last night's exchange.

'I don't think we should talk about this,' Alex sighs, not letting her friend in this time, but Gabrielle pushes past her.

'Did you love him? Did you love Jason?' Gab asks her, staring at her hard.' Alex wonders just how much Gab's affair is getting to her. She makes a futile gesture.

'Yes, yes OK! I loved him.' Alex sits down like a leaden weight, remembering how she felt, chasing away that feeling she gets sometimes, the feeling that her heart is permanently doomed.

'I love him, he loves me and he loves her – how can that happen?' Gab asks her, tear-tired, wide-eyed and hopeless.

'You're going to lose this, you realize that, don't you?' Alex rubs her fingers across her eyes. 'You're the one who's going to end up abandoned, feeling sick with guilt about what you've done to them.' Gab stares at her.

'Them?' she asks in disbelief.

'Yes, them. They are them and you are just you. So he loves you, big deal. It's not going to help if he still loves her,' Alex says hopelessly.

'Don't act like you got hurt by fucking my husband and screwing up my marriage. You didn't!' Gab shouts, her anger indiscriminate. Alex opens her eyes and fixes them on Gabrielle.

'How can you think that I didn't get hurt? You know me. I was hurting people I loved, it was the worse time of my life.' Alex searches Gab's face, looking for some kind of benevolence.

'You still managed to get a few fucks in between all the anguish,' Gab lashes out at her.

'Listen Gab, you just don't have the moral high ground anymore.' Alex's anger rises with the pitch of her voice. 'Not while you're fucking Francesca's husband!' They hold each other's angry gaze for a moment and then Gab breaks away, hurling herself out of the door.

Alex blinks as it slams behind her and stares at the place where Gab had been for a few moments. I think Alex would cry if she had anything like tears left to cry with.

49

I hand-delivered my manifesto to Jemima's office (addressed 'To Jemima, the cross one') and now I'm watching the phone. Normally only girls watch the phone, but I'm introducing this female-orientated pastime into my life with the secret weapon girls have yet to discover.

Positive visualization.

When a girl watches the phone, all they do is whine miserably, 'Oh why doesn't her call me? Is the line out of order? Maybe he's lost his phone? He must be dead in a ditch.' All of which boils down to an unconscious form of negative visualization. Self-fulfilling prophecy, if you will.

I'm sitting here, imagining Jemima in a tight black suit (I have never seen her wear one, but there is always hope) dialling my number right now ... the phone rings. No, I mean the phone actually rings.

I jump and snatch it off the hook.

'Hello?' I say, fully expecting it to be someone collecting some kind of debt.

'OK.' It's Jemima's voice. I have conquered the universe.

'Really?' I say, just to make sure it isn't an hallucination.

'Really, your stupid declaration thingy has got me as far as a date. You'll have to keep me interested to stay on, though. Deal?' I can hear a smile in her voice.

'Deal. So, um, how about tomorrow about eight-ish?' I ask her quickly, before the magic wears off.

'OK, where?' she says.

'The Fu Bar? Do you know it?' I say edgily, imagining Simon letting me run a tab. Make it so, universe!

'OK, OK. See you there, then.' I put the phone back on the hook and look around for someone to tell. Alex wanders in.

'Jemima?' she asks casually, like she hasn't been evesdropping.

'Yeah, I willed her to phone me.' I ignore Alex's frown. 'We're meeting tomorrow in the Fu Bar,' I tell her.

'Good choice.'

'Yeah, I'll be more like myself there and she'll see the real me and love the real me and ...' Alex interrupts.

'Before you know it you'll be making tender yet powerful love to her?' I give her the half-smile she expects. As she looks at me I wonder exactly how it is we have managed to gather up the mess of US and bundle it kicking and screaming behind a tightly shut closet door. I want to ask her what she thinks about it but even the temptation of bringing up the subject rattles the metaphysical closet door handle, and I am too scared to. The last thing either of us needs right now is a resumption of that particular maelstrom.

It's just that I have the feeling that one day it will all come tumbling out again into our neat little lives.

~

Richie has made up his mind that he does not wish to be 'left where he is' as Pia put it, mainly because 'where he is' is playing some kind of verbally challenged village idiot with a Labrador. He has decided to trade in his ninety thousand dollars a year for something better – his old and lately neglected friend: his Integrity. He's going to quit and then that'll show Pia. Then when she's on her knees begging him to stay – begging him, mind you – he'll laugh in her face and leave her there, a useless, gibbering wreck. She probably lose her job because he'll tell them at the top that she alone is responsible for his departure.

'Um excuse me, Pia, may I have a quick word?' he says on the threshold of her lair.

'What?' She look him up and down like he's a troublesome insect that she will have to squash.

'I want to quit,' he says, conjuring up the emboldened mood that he developed en route to her office. She looks at him in disgust.

'Let me tell you, Richie, if this is some gambit to get me to change my mind on the character thing, it is ill advised. Very.' Richie draws himself up under her stare, thinking 'Remember Stanislovsky.' Things are not going quite the way he envisioned just at the moment, his positive visualization skills are being somewhat dulled by Pia's evil aura.

'I'm quitting it,' he repeats solidly, fully expecting his conviction to catch up with him any minute now.

'You have a contract,' Pia reminds him, deadpan. Richie decides to appeal to her better half.

'I know, but I have to be true to what I believe in, to my Integrity. How can you want me here if I hate it?' he asks, pulling his best lines out of his hat.

'Richie, do you think I really care if you hate it? I hate it, you hate it, the bloody tea boy hates it. It's the seventh ring of hell, but unfortunately for you, you signed a contract.' Pia sighs and looks at him in disgust. 'Look, you finish your contract and then you can go off and be Guy Pearce, Brad Pitt, whoever. OK? Because if you don't, let me tell you what the alternative is. The alternative is that we sue you for breach of contract. And you'll be paying us off for the rest of your measly, worthless two-bit acting career. In fact, strike that, you won't be able to afford an acting career, you'll be flipping burgers in McDonald's to pay my bills. Does that sound like you being be true to yourself. Does it?' Pia almost finishes her soliloquy with a wicked laugh. 'Just pull yourself together and knock your airy-fairy ideas on the head, Richie. This is soap world, not real life.'

'Shit,' Richie says. 'Shit.' As he thunders away from her he swears he hears her wicked cackle chase him down the hall.

He keeps walking out of the lot, gets into his car and keeps right on going until he hits the bar and Simon sets him a cold one.

'You don't look too good, mate,' Simon tells him.

'I wanted to leave the show, but I can't. Pia has me by the balls and I've got the feeling if I tried to go they wouldn't be coming with me,' Richie tells him. Both men wince.

'Oh well, have a big expensive drink, you can afford it.' Simon smiles.

'Yeah, you're right. Guy Pearce was in *Neighbours*. And Russell Crowe.' Richie cheers himself up.

'And Mel Gibson was in *Punishment*,' Simon adds.

'Yeah? Who else?' Richie is feeling better about soap. They look at each other.

'Um …' Simon racks his brain.

'There was …' Richie can't think of anyone else.

'Oh shit,' Simon says with a laugh. 'Who else is there?'

~

I watch them across the bar and wonder if I should try the 'Richie Blake from *The River* is my mate' card on her. I reckon not.

She's sucking on a tequila sunrise like there will be no tomorrow and eyeing me speculatively.

'I've got no time to waste on relationships that are going to suck,' she tell me right off the bat. 'I have this possible arsehole rating. Anything above five gets sacked immediately.' I look at her; some distant bells ring at the word 'relationship' being bandied about five minutes into a first date, but I let them peal. She's pretty and feisty. I think I can handle her.

'What rating am I?' I ask her.

'Four and half,' she tells me, with a glint in her eye.

'I knew you'd warm to me,' I say happily.

'No, make that a five,' she says, like I knew she would. It's OK, I'm learning how to play her – please her, I mean.

'You're a tough girl to go out with, aren't you?' I say, as if I relish the challenge.

'Oh yeah, but I'm worth it.' She gives me a cat-like smile. I lean over the table and look into her eyes; the tequila has begun to soften them a little.

'I can see that for myself,' I whisper and lean in to kiss her. The tips of her fingers stop my mouth.

'If you shit me, I'll rip you to pieces, OK?' she says with a sweet little smile.

'OK,' I say and brush away her fingers in pursuit of a kiss. She lets me taste her and she tastes of alcohol, warm and disorientating.

'I'm not going to sleep with you on the first date,' she tells me up front.

'Fair enough,' I say. 'What are you doing tomorrow?' Hey, listen, if it works, why change it? She laughs and kisses me back.

~

We want to be ourselves, be who others want us to be, be something the world will let us make a buck out of and be someone people want to love. No wonder it's bliss one minute and disaster the next.

50

Remember the butterfly effect? The chaos theory? Well, it's one I adhere to wholeheartedly and my bedroom is testament to this. I look around it, trying to imagine seeing it from Jemima's perspective, hoping it'll look like the kind of room she'll want to have unbridled sex in.

Tonight is date three (as it turned out she doesn't do sex on date two either), so I've invited her over here for dinner in order to cut out the middle part of the date and skip to the grand finale.

Sometimes disorder is the rightful order; people like Alex just don't get it. 'You're not seriously going to leave your room like this, are you?' she asks me in horror. 'I mean, at least change your sheets.' I examine my sheets closely and give them a sniff.

'That'd be pretentious,' I tell her. 'Jemima doesn't like pretentious.'

'Basic hygiene is pretentious, is it?' Alex looks dismayed.

'It's charming disarray,' I tell her as I hear a knock at the door. 'Excuse me, oh judgmental one, my lady love is here.' I open the door on a fragrant Jemima and usher her into the flat.

'This is Alex, Alex – Jemima,' They look at each other, each weighing up the potential of the other.

'I won't be a moment,' I tell her, 'I've just got to grab something from my room.' As I expected she follows me to the threshold and surveys the charming disarray.

She wrinkles up her nose.

'I bet you think this kind of grot is charming, don't you?' I nod hopefully and hear Alex laughing all the way back to her room.

~

Normally when you are first going out with someone you don't see anyone else but them, you spend every moment either with them or thinking about them. You don't spend endless nights sitting in alone because you can't bear to be away from the phone or because you've recently fallen out with your best friend over it.

Gab paces her flat, back and forth back and forth. 'I sleep with him, don't I?' she thinks. 'I have a perfect right to call him.' She quickly dials his number before she can change his mind.

'Dominic Hlasek.'

Gab resists the urge to hang up. 'Dominic, it's me,' she says, trying to sound light.

'Oh, g'dday mate.'

She strains to hear any affection in his voice. 'It's so noisy, are you in a restaurant?' Gab asks, unhappily.

'Yeah.' Dominic's voice is a study of disinterest.

'With Francesca.' It's not really a question.

'Yeah mate, if you're ringing about the Citytrans site, I should have some news in the morning.' Gab refuses to take the hint.

'Is it just the two of you?' she asks, hoping for some boring function.

'That's right mate.' Gab is briefly angry with Dominic for not loving her enough to lie to her, but then she supposes he is lying to Francesca. If he's honest with Gab, no matter how painful it is, then that means he cares for her more. She is winning the battle.

'I miss you. I love you.' She gives him the reassurance she needs to hear so badly herself.

'Those are my concerns too. I'll talk to you tomorrow.' Dominic ends the call. Gab closes her eyes and squeezes back her useless tears.

If she had a cat now, Gab would kick it. But she knows she has no one to blame but herself. She's fallen in love with a married man and when she invited him into her life, humiliation came right along with him.

~

I look at Jemima and Alex sitting comfortably across the table. A few weeks ago I would never have thought this possible. That's it OK for me to be here with Alex and another girl, another girl I like so much, and – more importantly – likes my writing.

'Despite everything, your story was great. I mean, it was a pretty obvious metaphor, the whole bird-as-woman thing, but it was the epitome of the modern woman's dilemma. To be alone and heartbroken, or settle for less than you deserve and be heartbroken. Quite insightful for a bloke. That's never going to happen to me,' she tells Alex.

'You're so right,' Alex says, trying to resist the urge to count how many times it has happened to her so far.

'I've got this one friend and she's been single for seven years!'

I try not to laugh as Alex gasps in horror. 'Seven years! I'd kill myself,' she says earnestly.

'She had her heart broken by this total creep.' She looks at me, sending me that same warning again. 'And ever since then she's just shut down.'

'I don't blame her, poor cow,' Alex says earnestly.

'And now there's this guy she likes but she just won't ask him out. She's paralysed by the fear of rejection,' Jemima tells Alex and together they go off on the merry tangent to girls' world.

'That's so terrible.' Alex pictures Jemima's friend and sees herself.

'It's such a waste,' Jemima agrees.

They both look at me then and I squirm uncomfortably.

'So let's get back to discussing the merits of my story,' I say with enthusiasm. Jemima smiles at me.

'Honestly Evan, there's only so much you can say about a bird story.' She stands up decisively. 'Lets go to bed instead.' Alex almost chokes on her wine and I feel a very uncharacteristic blush spread over my neck.

'All right,' I say, taking her hand. ''Night, Alex.'

''Night.' She watches us go, her face unreadable in the shadows.

51

Richie has just finishing re-reading his script for the tenth time. He's gathered up his courage and he's back on a mission to confront Pia in her office. If he has to stay where he is, then he wants where he is to be more than two scenes a show and hardly any lines.

'Pia …' he begins.

'Not now Richie, I'm due in a casting session.' This stops Richie in his tracks. Casting? Who?

'These scripts, they are full of rewrites?' He asks her.

'Very good Richie, ten out of ten for observation. And?' She makes a move toward the door, Richie blocks it.

'And? And I was supposed to have the main story line. I was getting Sophie pregnant, but now I don't even kiss her and then my "younger, better-looking" brother shows up! Ryan hasn't even got a younger brother!' Pia looks at him like he's some born-yesterday moron.

'This is soap-land, Richie. He has now.' She goes for the door again.

'But what's going on? I'm only in two scenes!' Richie won't let her pass.

'That's two scenes more than you wanted, right?' Pia tells him archly. Richie winces.

'But …' he tries to collect his thoughts.

'Don't you remember, this show is beneath you, isn't it?' Pia waits patiently for Richie to catch on.

'Are you writing me out?' Richie asks in horror. The penny drops like a ten-ton weight.

'Oh bravo. Yes, we're writing you out.' Pia waits for the news to sink in.

'But I've got a contract!' Richie is aware of how pathetic he's sounding.

'Yes, you do, don't you? One with a clause that says we can drop you any time you contribute to a drop in ratings or your Q scores fall off. Even old ladies don't like you now, Richie.' Richie can't think of anything else to say and she pushes him lightly aside and walks past him.

'Next time you might want to think twice about biting the hand that feeds you.'

Richie make a call to his agent.

52

'm sorry.' Gab looks at Alex across the table in the Fu Bar. 'I've just gone crazy, that' all. I'm sorry.' Alex smiles and squeezes her hand. 'I need you.'

'And me, I'm sorry too and I need you too.' They let a moment of relieved silence past between them.

'I wish I'd never asked him if he still loved her,' Gab says inevitably.

'You're better off knowing,' Alex tells her. 'This way you can take off your rose-tinted specs and see the reality of the situation.' Alex tries to open Gabrielle's eyes.

'No I'm not. Before things were much simpler. Now it feels like a competition,' Gab says.

'Yeah, and I bet he's loving it!' Alex takes a drink to drown her annoyance with Gab's blinkered attitude.

'So what's Evan's new girlfriend like?' Gab takes the hint and changes the subject, watching her friend closely for signs of jealousy. Alex thinks for a moment.

'She's cool. Really nice, you know, I like her ...' she trails off, thinking for a moment.

'And?' Gab interjects.

'Well, I just can't figure what it is about her that make me feel so odd. She's smart, funny, she calls Evan on all his cutesy little tricks ...' Gab laughs.

'She's the first woman he's been out with that's in your league!' she says.

'No, that's not it,' Alex laughs, but to herself she says, 'Well maybe.'

~

Kelly watches the clock, waiting for Nathan to turn up. Another Friday night watching other people have a good time while she waits for her boyfriend to have his mama desert. Another Friday night with Nathan round at his family's, shutting her out of his life. She's staring so hard at the hands of the clock that she doesn't notice Nathan until he's kissing her hello.

'Hi, gorgeous, how's your evening been?' Kelly reins in her smile and feigns coolness.

'OK, yours?' Nathan frowns a little at her tone, but lets it pass.

'OK. Too much chicken soup. You don't want another drink, do you? Come on let's go back to your place and ...' He reaches for her, pulling towards him and nuzzling her neck. Kelly breaks free of his arms.

'I don't know if I like this,' she says, determined to air her worries.

'Like what?' Nathan sighs and settles back on a bar stool as she picks up her jacket and bag.

'Well, you having dinner with your family and then turning up here, to see me when it suits you. I feel like your bit on the side!' Nathan laughs.

'I thought it did suit you?' he says, taking her hand as they leave the bar.

'It'd suit me better if I was at dinner.' Kelly tests the water.

'Kel ...' Nathan sighs her name.

'I just don't want to feel like I'm second best or something to be ashamed of.' Kelly pulls her hand out of his.

'I'm not ashamed of you, Kel! I'm happy and proud of you. I want to shout it to the whole world! In fact, let me do that right now,' Nathan stops dead in the street and coughs to clear his throat.' I, Nathan Lieberman, love Kelly Lewis!' he proclaims loudly; people turn and look at him, smiling.

Kelly melts into a giggle and drags him away, down the street.

'Stop it!' she laughs as he tries to break free of her embrace and shout again. She flings her arms around his neck and lets him kiss her, melding into the contours of his encircling arms and forgetting all her worries for the rest of the night.

The next morning Kelly brings Nathan coffee and scrambled eggs on toast in bed.

'Do you like bacon?' she asks him. Two crispy rashers are laid over her own eggs.

'Nope.' Nathan tries to read the paper, by now used to picking up on the none-too-subtle signals Kelly gives off when she wants to talk abut 'US'.

'Don't you? I love it. Do you think that people who convert to Judaism still get to eat it?' Nathan looks up at her briefly, resists the temptation to comment and takes a bite of toast.

'What do you want to do later?' he asks her hopefully. She pauses and sits on the edge of the bed.

'I've been reading on the internet about Judaism.' Nathan takes another bite out of his toast.

'Oh yeah …?'

'If you want to convert you have to study with a rabbi and answer questions in a religious court. It's called the Bet Din. I wonder what kind of questions they'd ask.' She hopes Nathan will be impressed with her research but instead he shifts rather uncomfortably in the bed like he's sitting on a field of crumbs.

'You seem to know more about it than me,' he says lightly. 'Do you want to go and see a movie tonight?' Kelly ignores his deliberate ploy. In her mind they have to get this sorted now, or they might as well have no future.

'Do you know any women who have converted?' she persists, pushing.

'A couple.' Nathan starts to get up, almost knocking his coffee flying.

'Could I meet them?' Kelly asks him. He bends and kisses her on the cheek.

'I'd better get a shower, I'm supposed to be partaking in a communal clear-up back at my place! Want to get going so I can be free to take my favourite lady out tonight!'

Kelly sighs. 'The big fob-off again,' she thinks. 'Why is it always the woman who has to initiate the conversations about a relationship and the guy who acts like he'd rather be at the dentist? Just once I'd like Nathan to turn to me and say, "Kel, I've been thinking about our future and where we're heading. I'd really like to discuss our relationship. Please don't shut me out …"' Kelly jumps as Nathan shuts the bedroom door behind him.

'Hell will freeze over first,' she thinks.

53

Richie tells Christian about his sacking from *The River* as he hangs off the edge of the bar, more than slightly the worse for wear. Richie likes talking to Christian; a straighter bloke he's never met, but the best thing about him is that all he knows about Richie is that he is a recently failed soap star whose ex is his kooky flatmate. He doesn't even know Richie is gay.

'It's my fault I blew it. I shouldn't have looked a gift horse in the mouth,' he says, cheerfully inebriated. Christian looms a little closer towards him, swaying slightly on his feet.

'Hey, what is a gift horse?' he asks Richie.

'Dunno,' Richie shrugs and giggles. 'To really add insult to injury, they've cast a male stripper to replace me! Can you believe that!' Christian nods enthusiastically.

'Yeah, more muscle, less trouble.'

'Well he'd better be the strong silent type!' They both laugh into their beers.

'You seem to be taking it pretty well,' Christian says.

'Well, I'm being positive. It frees me up to wait by the phone again. And anyway it's not as if I'm starting totally from scratch.' Richie downs another beer and decides to try a spot of method acting so that he actually believes what he's saying.

'So what happens to you? Freak gardening accident? Rapidly spreading cancer? What?' Christian asks. Richie gives him a wry grin.

'Brent the stripper tells me I'm adopted. I feel betrayed so I join an Indian monastery where no one speaks.' They both laugh.

'You're not going to talk any more?' Christian giggles.

'Mate, with the dialogue they gave me I think we can call me grateful!' Richie feels the hysteria of the beer and the suddenly script-free future rush to his head like a blast of pure oxygen. His legs tremble under him and he holds on to the bar for support and thinks of Mel Gibson for luck.

54

Gabrielle watches Dominic as he ostensibly checks over some notes she's brought him.

'I have to leave in about half an hour,' he says, glancing at the clock on his wall. Gab feels a little frown settle between her brows and makes an effort to smooth it out. She must be one hundred per cent beautiful for Dominic all of the time. He can't see his golden girl looking even slightly frayed around the edges, or else he might give her up and go back to his golden woman for good.

'Oh?' She tries a playful tone. 'Big shot meeting is it? Excuse for a piss-up with the brothers?' Dominic shakes his head and for a second she catches his glance lingering on a photograph of his children.

'No, Francesca and the kids are going to her mum's for the night. I want to get home before they go and say goodbye … to the kids.' A smile radiates from the centre of Gabrielle's being until it reaches the very corners of her mouth.

'So you can come and stay with me tonight?' she says, happily expectant. Dominic blinks at her.

'I don't think so,' he says gravely. He seems surprised she's even suggested it.

'But why don't you think so? It's perfect, I'll wear something slinky, cook you a fabulous meal and then we can have wild sex anywhere and any way you like it …' Gab says, dropping her voice and mentally checking off her list for any other attributes the perfect woman should have. Talk about the footy after, maybe?

'No Gab, I can't. Francesca thinks I'm at home. I should be at home.' Gab's face freezes at the sound of his wife's name.

'But we never spend the night together,' she says with a small voice.

'Sorry,' Dominic says simply, indicating discussion over. Gabrielle wishes this was like any other relationship. She wishes she could scream and shout at him for being so thoughtless, for not caring enough, but she knows that she can't. She knows that if she is to keep him for good she must walk a tightrope of restraint, must only be a good thing in his life. She has to wait ever so patiently for

Francesca to find out, and to drive him away into her arms with her menopausal histrionics.

'OK, sure,' she says with a brittle smile.

~

Kelly can hardly contain herself. Just before she reaches Nathan's family home she stops and inspects her reflection in a shop window. She's wearing her best grown-up dress and her sensible but feminine shoes. She look herself in the eye and assesses herself as potential daughter-in-law material, for tonight she is having Friday night dinner with Nathan and his family. Weeks of Chinese water torture nagging have finally paid off. As her nanna says, 'If at first you don't succeed …'

She knocks on the door, measuring each beat so that her knock comes over as sensible and well-rounded, the knock of a potentially fabulous mother.

When she see Nathan, her eyes light up. She takes a step toward him and he takes a quick step back.

'Come in!' he says brightly, maybe a little over-loud. His mother emerges from the kitchen and stands there for a second, looking at Kelly.

'Mum, this is Kelly,' Nathan says amiably. Kelly wonders at his tone and tries to interpret it. In her mind that introduction was missing 'The girl I've told you so much about. The woman I love.' Or something. But still, maybe things have to be super-formal on Friday night dinners.

'Hello Kelly, lovely to meet you,' Mrs Lieberman says sweetly. Kelly resists the urge to curtsy.

'Hello, Mrs Lieberman. I've brought you flowers.' Nathan's mum takes them with an approving smile and Kelly racks herself up her first point.

'And this is Jonathon,' Nathan tells her as she walks into the dining room. Kelly tries to catch Nathan's eye but he seems preoccupied with every inch of air space except the ones between her forehead and her nose. She hadn't expected anyone else; she'd thought this was a kind of welcome-Kelly-into-the-fold dinner.

'How are you?' she says to Jonathon, feeling her nose decidedly out of joint.

Reality dawns on Kelly as the meal progresses. Nathan won't look at her at all. Ms Lieberman asks her what she does for a living – what she, Nathan's, girlfriend does! It all becomes clear. Nathan has never once mentioned Kelly to his mother, never once except about tonight, and she's pretty sure he hasn't told her that she's his girlfriend. In fact, she's certain.

Kelly had expected this evening to be a night of wonder, for something – some kind of shift – to happen inside her when she heard the words of the Torah being spoken, for a completion of a stage in her journey with Nathan to take place. Tonight she was to become a part of his greater sum. A transformation that she knew was inevitable if they were ever to have a future that did not exist wholly in her imagination.

'Well, I'd better get going,' Kel tells Nathan at the earliest opportunity, desperate to be on her own, to let her anger and disappointment out from behind her polite smile. Nathan walks her to the door and after a quick look around whispers, 'Can I meet you at your place?'

Kelly wants to say no, but she wants to talk about this even more. 'Yes,' she says and she goes to kiss him, but he side-steps her so that her mouth lands chastely on his cheek.

Everything had appeared rosy to Kelly before. She loved Nathan, she couldn't wait to meet his mum and experience a Shabbat dinner and now it all looked completely different. The rose-coloured specs had shattered.

She went home and waited for Nathan.

When he arrives he is her lover again, his arm instantly around her waist, kissing the top of her head, leading her to her bedroom with quiet murmurs and caresses. Kelly wants to let everything go under his touch but pulls herself away.

'Nathan,' she says in an even tone that belies her raging feelings. 'Why did you set the whole thing up so that I wouldn't look like your girlfriend? Making sure we arrived separately, left separately, inviting another "friend".' She holds his gaze and watches as his whole demeanour deflates.

'I didn't,' he says without conviction.

'Nathan! Stop treating me like an idiot!' Kelly would raise her voice if it wasn't for the thought of Alex trying to sleep and Evan trying to do whatever it is he is doing with Jemima.

Nathan sits up and takes Kelly's hand in his. He thinks for a moment and begins.

'It's just that I didn't want to say you were my girlfriend because if I had my mother would have had a thousand bloody questions and I didn't want to put you through that! You don't know her Kel, she come over all sweetness and light but when it comes to the women in my life she's as stubborn as a mule. I don't want my mother to be part of our relationship.' Kelly stares at him, wondering if he can hear what he's saying to her.

'You invited me there and made it very clear that I wasn't your partner! Have you any idea how insulting that is?' Kelly finds herself close to angry tears. 'I thought you wanted me to come because I was important to you and you wanted me to meet your parents!'

'Well, you were wrong,' Nathan says bluntly.

'About which bit? Kelly asks in a small voice.

'I didn't want you to meet my parents, OK? But you kept on and on about it so in the end I invited you around. It was the only way I could think of doing it.' Kelly looks at him as if she doesn't know him. Nathan has never hurt her like this before; she senses the beginning of something, maybe even the end.

'I'm sorry, OK? I'm sorry I hurt you.' Nathan pulls Kelly onto the bed and kisses her. She lets him hold her because she needs someone to hold, but as she pretends to sleep she wonders, 'What sort of an apology was that? He should be sorry because what he did was wrong, not because he got caught out.' It's a long time before Kelly's tightly closed eyes relax in sleep and even then she dreams for what is left of the night.

55

Gabrielle spends most of the morning sending e-mails to Dominic persuading him to cancel his meetings up in town and have lunch with her instead. She wants to sit somewhere in public with him, liking the way he looks at her in front of all those other eyes.

Eventually the mail comes back that reads, 'OK, OK. You win.' Gab looks at her watch: 12.15. There doesn't seem to be any point in starting any work now. She looks at the pile of unread and unprepared reports on her desk. Since this thing with Dominic began she has done hardly any real work. Gabrielle, who used to be so proud at being so good at her job and now ... she ponders on the impact Dominic has had on her life for a while and then she decides the retouch her make-up, ignoring that nagging little doubt that she isn't acting like herself any more.

At lunch Gab takes Dominic's hand across the table. She can feel that half of him wants to pull it away and tuck it neatly under the table, but that the other half is keeping it there by sheer force of will. She is telling him about the first love of her life, about Jason.

'And so I was married for one day,' she finishes, passing all the remembered anguish off with a little smile. In comparison to the current state of heart it seems like a walk in the park.

'Are you divorced?' Dominic asks. Gab laughs because she always forgets that bit.

'No, no, but we will get round to it one day.' She pauses, lowering her eyes over a glass of wine. 'What about you?' she asks.

'I don't want to get divorced, not ever.' Gab is shocked by the bluntness of his answer.

'Never?' she asks.

'No, I don't think so. I don't know.' Gab looks wildly around for something else to focus on.

'Then what are you going to do with me?' she asks.

'I don't know. I really do love you Gabrielle, but I've got a whole life with Francesca and the family. I can't break that up and I don't want to stuff you around either ...' Dominic looks so sad that

Gabrielle is easily able to push away any unkind thoughts – such as that he was pulling off his 'genuinely nice man torn between two loves' routine a little too frequently.

'Let's not talk about it.' She gives him the let-off. 'Let's enjoy what time we have together today.' She decides that she doesn't have to listen to stuff that doesn't fit into her view of the world, or at least how she wants it to be.

~

Kelly is just in the middle of saving Peace Piccardo's life again when Nathan shows up in what would be her lunch break – if she ever had time for a lunch break.

'I've got some news!' he tells her by way of a greeting. She stares at him. It takes her a few moments to let go of her frantic search for 240 gold chairs by tonight and another second to remember she is angry with him. Kelly is surprised that her anger has burnt for so long – longer than forty-eight hours now. Normally Nathan's sweetness has melted all her cross words in her mouth before she can say them.

'Have you?' she says.

'I've been promoted! Head of the department!' He beams at Kelly, sure of her approval, so when she doesn't give it he looks like he's been slapped in the face.

'Oh. That's good,' Kelly says and returns her gaze to her PC. 'You know what, I'm really a bit busy at the moment. Peace forgot to book the chairs for The Directors Guild Annual Dinner and Ball. It's their fiftieth anniversary, so the chairs have to be gold. There are 240 gold chairs in Melbourne but they are at this wedding just out of town. A wedding on a Monday and with gold chairs – what are the chances of that? Anyway, at the moment it looks like I'm going down to Ikea with 400 cans of spray paint.' Kelly keeps talking over the cracks in the conversation, over the things she doesn't want to say, or want Nathan to say.

'Kel,' Nathan finally butts in. 'A bit of excitement wouldn't go astray.

'Well then, go and tell your mother,' Kelly snaps. 'Like I said, I have a crisis with chairs, or maybe that doesn't mean anything to you either.' Nathan stares at her.

'Are you still angry about that?' he asks in a wearily condescending tone. Kelly pushes her chair back from her desk and walks out of the open-plan office and into the corridor. Nathan follows her.

'I'm so hurt about what you did. Are you ashamed to be my boyfriend?' she asks him at last.

'No, Kelly! No.' Nathan tries to hold her but she slaps his hand away.

'Are you ashamed to be going out with a black woman?' she challenges him.

'No! I'm proud of you Kelly. I just didn't want my mum to know, that's all,' Nathan says, hearing his own contradiction too late.

'What if we ended up getting married? Would you tell her then?' Kelly can't stop herself rushing headlong into the future in an attempt to divine it.

'If we decide to get married then I'll tell her. But we're not getting married, are we?' Kelly senses that Nathan's patience with her anger is wearing thin.

'Apparently not,' she says.

'Is this what this is about? Getting married?' Nathan asks and for a moment Kelly wonders if all their problems up to now have been about good old-fashioned male commitment phobia and nothing to do with Jewishness at all.

'Am I a stepping stone until you meet the right woman?' Kelly says bravely.

'No, you are not a stepping stone,' Nathan recites.

'Would you marry a non-Jewish woman?' Kelly persists.

'I don't know, I have never thought about it.' Kelly turns away from him to hide her tears. So in almost a year together, the thought of marrying her has never even crossed his mind?

'Can you go please?' she says over her shoulder, sounding as cold as she can.

'Why?' Nathan lays a tentative hand on her shoulder and she shrugs it off.

'I told you, chairs!' she almost shouts.

'OK, OK. I'll talk to you later, OK?' Kelly starts to walk back to the office.

'OK.'

'I love you Kel, OK?' Nathan says as he watches her retreat.

'OK,' she says and although she feels it she does not say it back.

~

Alex has brought her work up onto the roof because Jemima is downstairs. And she can't put her finger on why she feels a bit odd around Jemima, who is a perfectly nice woman, the kind of woman Alex gets on with really well, but anyway she does. And it's not jealousy so it must just be 'one of those things'. She's forgotten her charts and is gazing at the horizon when Christian comes onto the roof, a tray of plants in his hands. He looks at Alex for a moment and takes a couple of deep breaths. Alex is the kind of woman who is way out of his league, more beautiful than he deserves, really clever and funny. He remembers that he's the kind of bloke everyone likes and that it is probably all right to go and say hello.

'You working?' he asks, feeling stupid. Of course she's working, no one reads that stuff for fun. Alex smiles at him, a breeze whipping her dark hair across her face for a moment.

'Sot of, half-heartedly. Well, not at all to be honest.' She laughs and Christian hopes the blush that had begun to spread up his neck can be mistaken for a touch of sunburn. Alex looks at his plants,

'Plants. I wondered whose garden this was. It's great, just what we need around here.' She hauls herself out of the chair and walks over to watch as Christian begins putting the plants out.

She crouches next to him, and Christian tries to remember what he's doing as the skin of her bare arms brushes against his.

'That's fantastic, what is that?' Alex gently picks up a leaf.

'This is a Monstera Deliciosa,' Christian tells her, admiring her touch with the plant. 'It grows a fruit you can eat, but you have be careful because of these little black things. They are sharp, like razor blades.' He chances a look at her face and finds her smiling at him.

'Do you often work up here?' he asks banally, wondering if he should follow up with, 'Don't I know you from somewhere?'

'No, not really. Evan is downstairs being impressive with a girl,' she says, stretching herself straight. Christian watches the fluid movement with half-disguised admiration.

'Listen, I could pot you one of these up if you like? They grow indoors fine too' Alex smiles with genuine pleasure and Christian feels his heart pick up a little speed.

'OK, cool. Thank you!' she smiles.

'No worries,' he says. She gives him one last smile and then picks up her books and goes back downstairs. Christian watches after her. It's his policy to never to get involved with women he is friends with, especially not with someone as complicated and unavailable as Alex seems to be. Or maybe that makes her just perfect.

56

Gabrielle is ill, a cold that might possibly turn into the flu. She blames Dominic, she blames him for not letting her sleep at night whiles he sleeps peacefully by his wife or not letting her eat while he goes out to fancy restaurants on special occasions with his wife; for not letting her think about anything, anything else at all, but him.

She's obviously got a bit run-down.

She picks up the phone and calls him.

'Hi, look I feel awful. Can you drop in on the way home with some Panadol and some fruit juice?' She can hear Genesis playing in the background; he must be in the car already.

'Sorry Gabrielle, I'm almost home now,' he says, with a slight edge to his voice.

'But please, I'm really ill. I need someone to look after me …' she pleads, her voice thick with mucus.

'Look I can't, OK, I'm sorry darling. I'll call you in the morning.'

'Fine.' Gab hangs up the call and tries not to cry because she knows it'll make her nose even more red and she can't afford to have a red nose while Francesca's is so perfectly pert. She dials Alex's number.

'It's me, I'm really sick can you bring me some Panadol? Oh thanks, you're a doll. See you in five.' She put down the phone and wonders if it's possible to asphyxiate yourself with a cushion or if you'd pass out just before you finished off the job. Gab shakes her head to try and free it of some of its congestion and dabs Nivea on the end of her nose.

~

Alex lets us in with the spare key.

Gab is sitting on her sofa amid the detritus of used tissues. I try not to look like I've just come across the scene of a nasty accident and I quickly rearrange my face.

'Hey,' I tell her. 'You don't look so bad.' It's a total lie. Alex goes to the kitchen and comes back with some water and hands Gab the pills.

'You poor baby, want me to you make you a hot drink?' Gab nods miserably.

'I brought you a video,' I say, going to the telly. '*Reservoir Dogs.*'

'Don't you have another video?' she says grumpily, but I let it pass because she's sick.

'So, apart from the obvious, how are you?' Alex puts a steaming hot cup of lemon and ginger tea on the table next to Gab.

'I rang Dominic and asked him to come over but he said he couldn't. He had to get home,' Gab sniffs. 'You always have an excuse when you're married. If he wasn't married I'd have chucked him by now.' Alex put an arm gingerly around her infectious friend.

'Gab, where do you think this will end?' she asks.

'When he leaves his wife and comes to live with me,' Gabrielle says doggedly. I turn away from her, silently seething.

'And the chances of that happening are …?'Alex asks her.

'Nil, nada, niet,' I want to say. But I bite my tongue.

'One day.' Gab doesn't sound too convinced. 'I mean come on, I'm the younger model. I always win, eventually.' Alex sighs and brushes a soggy tissue away from where she is sitting.

'I'm just scared you are going to get hurt. And he's got everything, he's got you, the wife, the kids …' Gab waves the conversation away.

'Can we talk about something else?' She turns her attention to me. 'Evan, you're pretty quiet. What have you got to say?' I freeze. I'd hoped they had forgotten I was here.

'I haven't got anything to say,' I tell her, focusing on Mr Pink and Mr White having a fight over tipping.

'Obviously you have. It's you. Never in three years have I known you not to have something to say about everything.' I sigh and meet her eyes.

'OK, I can't understand why a woman as beautiful and as brainy as you is putting up with this. He's fucking two women and he's loving it. What's the phrase – he's having his cake and eating it too? I don't reckon he's worried at all. He's just hoping that it will go on as long as possible. That's what I'd be doing. It's win-win for good old Dominic.' There, I've said it. Now that I've said it I wonder if I can sneak out the front door without anyone noticing. Alex looks from Gabrielle to me and back again.

'Well, he's not you,' Gab says at last and she sinks deep under her blanket and even deeper into denial.

~

When Kelly gets home from work Nathan is waiting for her, sitting on her bed. He has put a vase of fresh flowers on her bedside table and he's holding a package on his lap. Kelly looks at the flowers and then at him. She feels too tired of being angry.

'Hi,' he says tentatively.

'Hello.' She sits next to him on the bed.

'The flowers are nice,' she says by way of encouragement.

'This is for you,' Nathan holds out the package. It's a dress, a beautiful dress that Kelly has been coveting for the last couple of weeks. She's touched that Nathan remembered it, remembered her size. It's a thoughtful gift.

'I'm really sorry about what's happened,' Nathan tells her and she assumes he means everything.

'OK.' Kelly accepts his apology.

'I've been over to see my parents and I've told them you are my girlfriend and that I'm very serious about you.' Kelly swallows hard.

'OK,' she says quietly.

'I think in the back of my head I'd always thought I'd marry a Jewish girl,' Nathan says, by way of some kind of explanation.

'Nathan, if this is going nowhere you have to tell me. I mean, look at us: we're different.' Nathan catches her hands in his and looks her in the eyes.

'I do want to be with you,' he says. 'This is going somewhere.'

'Thank you, thank you for saying that.' Kelly falls into his arms with grateful relief. They both sleep very deeply.

~

Gabrielle and Dominic sit in the middle of the park as far away from anyone who might see them as they can get. Gab thinks it might be funny to pretend to look for bugs and secret cameras but she's still too weak after the flu and anyway what she has to say isn't amusing. She's very aware of the faint pinkness that still blushes the edges of her nostrils and her chapped lips, still rough after several applications of Vaseline.

'I don't want to see you any more,' she lies.

'Oh.' Dominic didn't expect this. He expected another difficult conversation about what is going to happen, but he didn't expect this.

'When I got sick and you wouldn't come I realized this is how it's always going to be. I'm always going to come second.' She waits then, her ultimatum issued.

'It not as simple as that,' Dominic tries to say and she's glad to hear the pain in his voice. 'I've been with Francesca for a ...' The past suddenly hits Dominic in the stomach and temporarily winds him. From nowhere his son has landed in his lap.

Gab tries hard to cover the emotion on her face as she see Francesca approach them with the other kids.

'Hi! What a surprise.' His falsely bright tone make Gabrielle want to vomit.

'We've been to the dentist.' Francesca looks at him closely and then at Gabrielle.

'Well, I'd better get back to the grindstone,' Gab says brightly, forcing herself not to run from the scene of the crime.

She can hear the small talk going on behind her as she hurries away, only the kind of conversations that families can have: 'How was the dentist? Did you go on the tram? No, you can't have a new pair of trainers for every new filling.'

But what she can't see is the dawning realization in Francesca's eyes about everything that's been going on. All the odd little moments, the hastily ended phone calls over long trips to the bank, suddenly fall into place.

As she shepherds her children back home she feels a tiny crack open up in her heart and it begins to break.

57

The earth travels around the sun at 29.8 km per second, always has done always will do until it gets sucked into a black hole, or blown up by a giant asteroid, or nukes, or both. At least, that's what the scientists tell you. They tell you that day follows night and hey, let's face it, for most of the time you can even see that it's true. For the last few days, over a week in fact, I have been able to see that that is true. The day is done after a steady twenty-four hours, Kelly comes and goes to work, Nathan arrives in the evening and they retire early to her room. Alex goes in and out on shift work, watering her mini triffid that Christian gave her every day, even though it doesn't need it. Jemima seems to have been more or less living here, and I have been more or less having the most sex I've had in months and feeling pretty glad about it too. And it's all taking the usual sixty seconds per hour to get done. Super.

But just when you think you know exactly what to expect your world gets kicked off its axis and flies out of some cosmic window at ten billion miles per hour and nothing you thought was true is certain any more.

Kelly has cooked us dinner; it's pretty simple, curiously vegetarian fare. She sets it on the table and gives us all a carefully constructed look of benevolence.

'Yum, Kel,' Jemima tells her. I like the fact that Jemima likes food. I've never been able to stand women who feel guilty about eating.

Kel gives her sort of knowing smile and pats her on the arm. She's off on one.

I catch Alex's eye and raise a brow at her.

'What do you reckon? I reckon she's leaving her job.' Kelly looks at me and rolls her eyes.

'Nah, she's had another fight with Nathan, she's thinking about which present she wants him to buy as a making-up gift this time round.' Kelly squints sternly at Alex, who giggles like a naughty girl.

'No, I know that look. The last time she had that look the apartment was filled with dodgy vitamins. Kel, what is it? Are you going to redecorate with the principles of feng shui?' Alex and Jemima laugh and Kelly leans back in her chair shaking her head at me.

'I know! Kel's thinking of becoming a Buddhist nun and you'll need the lounge for chants and meditations.' We all look at Kelly, ready for her news.

'Close. I'm thinking about becoming Jewish.' She looks from Alex to me. We look at each other.

'God,' Jemima says.

'Well yes, he's involved.' Kelly smiles.

'I love you Kel,' I tell her, awed, inspired by her endless ability to throw a gigantic spoke into the wheel of her own life. Alex reaches for the wine bottle as though another glass might help her to see reason.

'Is this because of Nathan?' she asks.

'I'm not saying I definitely will, but if Nathan and I are to have future then I'll have to think about it.' Kelly shrugs like she's discussing changing her hairstyle. Alex and I both know her well enough to know that even changing her style would elicit month of preamble including having her cards read and meditations. 'You see, being Jewish is not just about religion, it's a way of life, a cultural commitment. For Nathan's children to be Jewish the mother has to be too. I'd have to be.' Alex looks as though she is biting her tongue.

'Kelly,' I say. 'There's someone you've forgotten in all of this. Someone who's been very good to you over the years ...' Kelly's face floods with anxiety.

'Who?' she asks me.

'Someone who you've known for a long time, an old friend who's made you happy, and bought you gifts if you've been good. And if you're Jewish you'll have to abandon that friend.'

'Evan! Who!' Kelly looks alarmed.

'Santa Claus, Kel. No more Christmas for you, my girl.' I had expected her to laugh, but instead she looks even more disturbed.

'But for love ...' she begins uncertainly.

'Love, schmuv,' I say, pleased with my attempt at irony. 'If you're talking religion then it has to be something you believe in, not something you do to please your boyfriend.' Kelly nods thoughtfully.

'Kelly, I can hardly bear to say it, but he's right. You don't just change religion like a pair of knickers, do you?' We all stare at her in horror.

'It's the wine!' she shouts and she giggles into her hand, it make me smile to see it.

'One more thing you haven't though of Kel,' Alex chimes in. 'The Easter Bunny.' Kelly shrugs.

'That's just chocolate,' she says.

'Exactly,' Alex says and we all laugh again. Alex is getting pretty funny lately.

~

While we are discussing the magical healing properties of chocolate Gabrielle is sitting staring at her TV, her hair scraped back, her worst clothes on, indulging fully in her status as ex-mistress dumped for a frumpy wife. When she hears a knock at the door she resent the intrusion of life into her timeless subsistence. It's much harder to feel sorry for yourself when someone else is around.

She opens the door to Dominic.

'Oh hi, oh good, hi. Hello. I'm so sorry, I do want to be with you, I don't care how, just as long as I am,' she says grateful to him, happy to drop her ultimatum in thirty seconds flat. 'Look, about what I said …' She is stopped mid-sentence by the look on his face, and then she sees his luggage.

'Oh. Bags. Big bags. Two big bags.' She look into his face and sees that something terrible has happened, something terrible and wonderful all at once.

'I just filled them up. Is it OK?' he asks her.

'Is it OK?' she asks him. 'Come in, just come in.'

Gabrielle can't hide the feeling of triumph as she ushers Dominic into her home (maybe their home) and sets him down on the sofa. She sits on the floor opposite him, crossing her legs.

'I shouldn't have come here, I should have gone to a hotel, I'm sorry,' he says, He looks shell-shocked.

'No, no. I'm glad you are here. You are meant to be here, it's the very place I want you to be.' She takes his hands. 'What happened?'

Dominic pulls her up to him until she is kneeling in between his legs.

'You happened. You, Gabrielle,' he whispers and then he kisses her.

58

Alex has swallowed some chlorine-filled water and is spluttering.

'I beg your pardon?' she finally manages to say to a radiant Gabrielle.

'He's left her! He stayed last night! This morning we got to cuddle up and we had breakfast together. His bags are at my place. There are shirts in my wardrobe!' Alex finds herself wondering if there is any justice in the world but quickly suppresses the unkind thought.

'He left his wife! For good?' She can't help asking.

'Yes, of course for good. As of today I am no longer having an affair. I am having a boyfriend.' Gab beams, bursting with victory.

'Well. That's great.' Alex's uncertain tone has nothing to do with the latent feeling of jealousy that she chased away. She is really worried there are still more tears to come.

'Oh, be happy for me Alex,' Gab says, in a voice bordering on anger. 'I love him and this is what I wanted. I have to make it work.'

Alex smiles at her friend. 'Well, then, you will.'

~

I bump into Miranda in the hallway as I leave in search of cheap but excellent coffee. She's standing there stock-still, open-mouthed.

'Hi there, M. Are you thinking of taking up busking as one of those statue acts? If you are, can I just tell you, you suck.' She comes to life as she hears my voice.

'I've got a rollover from Pores Afresh!' she says, waving a bit of paper at me.

'Hooray! What's a rollover?'

She jumps up and down. 'It means they are running the ad for another rotation and it means, more importantly, that I get eight thousand dollars!' I jump up and down with her.

'Do you want breakfast?' She hooks her arm though mine.

'Can I have really expensive, really good coffee?' I ask her.

'Anything for you, Evan.'

I'm feeling quite sage-like today, so it's just after my last croissant that I say to Miranda.

'You know what this means, don't you?'

She nods happily. 'New underwear and my roots getting done,' she says with a mouthful of buttery crumbs.

'No. Well, yes. But also it means that fate has handed you an opportunity take control of the creative process. You can be the creator, write your own work ...'

'You mean write my own one-woman show?' she asks, her eyes glowing at the thought of it. I hadn't quite meant that, but I decide to take credit for the idea.

'Exactly. Written by you, for you. You can make it happen, Miranda. You have the power.' Miranda licks her fingers and picks crumbs off her plate.

'Yeah, and just think how much it'll piss off Richie, she says laughing.

We take a taxi home because we can and because Miranda is suddenly filled with the muse to write.

'Come on, come on,' she urges the cab driver. 'I'm being creative. I don't know when it might wear off!' We part at her apartment door, laughing and breathless and I'm still uncertain if she's serious or not.

'Fare thee well, fellow writer,' I tell her, clapping a hand on her shoulder. 'May the gods be with you.' She nods seriously.

'Evan, when I've written a bit can I bring it round to you to read?' she asks, sweetly demure. I can't help feeling like a big shot.

'Well of course. I'd be glad to share my expertise with you and guide your fledgling talent.' She grins and practically shuts the door in my face, she's so excited.

I just hope I haven't created a monster.

It's only two hours later when the knocking at the door is so loud and so insistent that I'm fairly sure it must be the cops. I take a deep breath and resist the urge to flush my weed down the loo.

'Yes?' I call through the wood.

'Evan! It's me, let me in. Let me in!' I open the door to Miranda, who looks slightly flushed and breathy. Pretty sexy actually.

'What have you been doing?' I ask her, intrigued.

'Writing, you idiot. Look!' She holds up a heavy ream of A4 thick with type.

'You've written all of this today?' I ask her, taking it. It really has writing on it.

'Yeah! I'm on fire and anyway it's easy. You make an awful lot of fuss about nothing.' I raise an eyebrow at her but I can see she is buoyed up so I let it ride.

'OK, got to go!' She runs out of the door. 'More writing to do!'

I close the door and look at the pages she has given me. Well, if they are any good I can always plagiarize them I suppose.

It seems like eons later, spent in some kind of literary purgatory, when Alex taps me on the shoulder. I look at the clock; apparently it's less than an hour.

'Do you want to come for a drink with Kelly and me?' she asks. 'Ooh, what've you got? "A One Woman Show by Miranda Lang". What's that?' I look at her dolefully.

'The clue is in the question,' I say.

'Wow! Miranda's written her own show. Cool! I had no idea she was working on anything like this!' She takes it from my hands.

'That's because she only started this morning,' I say with a heavy heart.

'Any good?' she asks brightly.

'Yeah, it's great,' I say, thinking that Miranda will be able to take some small comfort from the fact that I am a terrible actor.

'Really?' Alex asks me uncertainly, catching my tone.

'It the most terrible piece of unbelievable rambling emotionally confused and pointless crap I have ever read. So, as far as you or anyone else is concerned, it's great.

'You have to tell her the truth,' Alex tells me. 'Just dress is up a bit … tell her she's made "a great start", but be constructive.'

I sigh. 'See, you don't get it. Constructive would be: "Tear this thing up then burn it, then have it ground into antimatter and never darken my door again." That would be positive.' Alex gives me one of those smiles reserved especially for my over-dramatic moments.

'Just ease into telling her gently, then,' Alex says if she's the expert. You break the death of a close relative to a few people and suddenly you're the expert.

'Oh I see, is that's what you do, is it? When you read my stuff, do you pretend to like it?' I say.

'Yeah, that's right. I pretend to like it. Lauren pretended to like it. Jemima pretends to think it's the best thing since sliced bread … it's all a big conspiracy.'

I watch her go back to her room under the cover of finding a top to wear out and tell myself that she's only joking.

Or is she?

~

I didn't go out with Alex and Kelly in case I bumped into Miranda in the bar. Unfortunately, Miranda didn't got out with them either, because when they called round they told her I was in reading her play. So now she's here, looking at me, like a baby deer unaware it is caught in the dazzling light of a juggernaut.

When did I become the expert? Lock myself in my bedroom for a few years with a computer and suddenly I'm the go-to-guy for literary criticism.

'Well?' she looks at me and twiddles her hair expectantly.

'Well, Miranda it's a great start,' I tell her convincingly. She reads my face quite plainly.

'It's shit, isn't it?' she sighs, and collapses back on to the sofa, going cross-eyed as she looks at the tuft of hair she's tugging.

'Well, yes, it is shit. But you know, it's a good effort and writing is a craft, isn't it? You didn't just become a wonderful actress overnight, did you? You practised and studied and worked hard.' Miranda screws up her mouth and looks at me sideways.

'Keep talking,' she says. I think I might offer my bad-news-breaking service to Alex. For a small fee I could hang around the relative rooms waiting for the reaper to visit.

'Well there are other ways of doing this, Monkey.'

Miranda raises an eyebrow. 'Other ways, Tripitaka?' she asks.

'Yes. You could try writing a song, or make poetry ... maybe a spot of rap,' I suggest.

'Let's face it, master, it's like the old Chinese saying: "The blonde Actress, she write like shit."' I'm glad she's taking this lightly.

'Then you know what you should do, Monkey? You should go see other people's plays, find the right one for you and put it on. You are an actress my child, go forth and act.' Miranda's face breaks into a picture of delight.

'Evan, a lot of people say you are an up-yourself easy-life, but I just want to say I respect your craft and I respect you.' She hugs me hard and plants a lip-gloss sticky kiss on my cheek.

'What people? What people say that?' I ask her as she heads for the door.

I told you. It's a conspiracy.

59

Since Nathan broke the news to his mum about Kelly he's been less keen to go home than usual, as his mum's caring enquiries ('It's not nagging, dear…') about his job, his house, how much he's eating, how long she's got left to live to enjoy grandchildren, have increased two hundred-fold and now exclusively focus on 'I'm sure Kelly is a lovely girl, dear, but have you really thought this through?' So for the first time in months he's not having Friday night dinner at his mum's. He's having it with Kelly. He'd sort of hoped for a takeaway and a night of passionate carefree love-making. But Kel's been on the internet again and she's prepared him her own cyber-version of a virtual Shabbat meal.

'Light two small candles,' she reads aloud from a print-out. 'And say a simple prayer thanking God for a time to rest, relax and reflect.' She looks at Nathan and he nods encouragingly.

'Um, thank you God for this time to … rest, relax and reflect. Amen.' Nathan swallows his smile. 'Is that OK?' she asks him earnestly.

'Absolutely.' He nods.

'Right. "Spend the evening talking about spiritual things" … OK, did anything spiritual happened to you today?' Nathan looks at his feet under the table and composes himself.

'Well, I really enjoyed walking through the park to get here today, the sky was really pretty and the park had a good vibe. Even so, it was one of those times when arriving is far better than the journey.' Kelly smiles, delighted.

'And you?' Nathan asks.

'Well, I did have an amazing day. I've been really thinking about what I believe in. I mean I must believe in something, it's important, isn't it?' Nathan watches her in the candlelight.

'What do you believe in, Kel?' he asks her softly.

'I believe in love and I believe in you,' she says simply and for the moment, at least, it seems as if that is all they will ever need for ever.

~

Gabrielle is waiting for Dominic to come home. He's taken his children to see *Star Wars* for the ninth time (or something). She has pulled back her unwashed hair and taken yesterday's tracksuits out of the laundry. She is sulking again, and this time because he belongs to her. She doesn't want to be jealous of the time he spends with his children, in fact she's damn well disgusted by herself, but somehow the way she loves Dominic seems to have almost consumed the Gabrielle she thought she was. Before he came to live with her she couldn't bear him not being with her and now he's moved in she can't bear him going out of the door.

'This must be what love really feels like,' she says out loud. 'As if you're going insane, as if you can lose everything about yourself in just longing for the other person.'

When she hears a knock at he door she hopes it's Dominic home early and that he's forgotten his key.

It's Francesca.

'He's not here,' Gab says, closing the door as far as she can to cover up her scruffy appearance.

'I know, that's why I'm here. I need to talk to you.' Francesca looks drawn. The glamorous image Gabrielle has created for her looks frail and worn. Still, Gab knows she mustn't let her get to her.

'Sure, come on in! Have a glass of wine, why don't you?' Gab flings open the door, her voice hardened with an edge of sarcasm. 'At least I have a flat stomach,' she thinks as she lets Francesca in.

'I suppose you're wondering why I'm here?' Francesca looks as though she's gathering her courage.

'Yeah, it did cross my mind.' Gab sits in a chair over the arm of which Dominic has left a sweater. She picks it up and folds it deliberately.

'I wanted to see where you lived, where he lives, I suppose,' Francesca says, sitting down heavily. She pauses and take a painful breath. 'Do you realize that my life, the life of my children, has been turned upside down this week? Dominic and I have been married for twelve years; twelve years and two children. That's a long time, don't you think? I suppose you can't even imagine what it's like for us. I don't suppose you even care …' She speaks softly, as if she doesn't even have the strength for anger.

'Look,' Gab forces herself to be tough. 'I really don't need this right now …'

'No, you look.' Francesca's change in tone is shocking. 'If you have a relationship with Dominic, you have a relationship with us.

We come as a package. Had you even thought about being a step-mum?' Francesca hits home. Gab shakes her head slowly, wishing she'd been able to lie better and more quickly.

'I'm taking it one step at a time,' she says, aware of how defensive and immature she sounds and wondering how this burnt-out middle-aged woman has managed to get one over on her when she wasn't looking.

'Still,' Francesca pauses and looks at her hands.' I can see how having stepchildren would be preferable for a career woman like you. It must have been quite easy for you to decide you don't want children.' She lifts her gaze to meet Gabrielle's in a silent challenge.

'Look, I'm sorry for your pain but frankly, whether or not Dominic and I decide to have children has nothing at all to do with you.' Gab is horrified when Francesca laughs.

'No, you're right. It's all to do with Dominic.'

Gab stares at her. 'What are you talking about?' She barely manages to refrain from dragging this woman out of her home by her hair.

'He hasn't told you, has he?' Francesca gets up and goes to the door. 'He had a vasectomy seven years ago, so if you ever want to have children you'll have to find someone apart from my husband to have them with. Goodbye Gabrielle, good luck.' Francesca closes the door behind her, leaving Gabrielle clinging onto the stem of her wine glass, counting the seconds until she can scream without Francesca hearing her cries echoing down the corridor.

~

Alex arrives ten minutes later.

She hands Gabrielle a bar of chocolate.

'Have you ever talked about children?' she says after Gab has finished telling her the story.

'No, but that's not the point. The point is, when was he going to tell me? When we'd been together six months? Two years? Five?' Gab opens another bottle of wine.

'Well, sometimes they're reversible.' Alex gives her half-hearted encouragement.

'I mean, imagine if I was with him for a couple of years and then it was all, "Oh this is perfect, I love you, let's have a baby" and he's all, "Sorry love, no can do, I've had the snip." What then? I'll tell you what then. My biological clock will have seized up and I'll be a barren old maid!' Gab wails.

'Come on, Gab, you're not even thirty yet. And it's pretty early days to discuss kids. He only left Francesca a few days ago.' Gab wipes her hand roughly over her face.

'But you should have seen her face. She comes in here all frail and wounded, and then lands that on me. The woman's a genius, caught me totally unprepared,' Gab says bitterly. 'Am I a bad person, Alex?' Gabs asks. 'A marriage wrecker; dad stealer? Is that who I am?' Alex pauses for a moment.

'No, you're person in love. That's all,' she says.

'Yeah and it is love; it's real love for the first time in my life. The real deal movie-style love.' Alex smiles and gives Gab a hug.

'Oh, I'm sort of jealous, I want to be in love,' she says sadly, forgetting for the moment that she is.

Alex slips quietly out of the door when Dominic comes in. He takes one look at Gabrielle's tear-stained face and he rushes to her side.

'I saw her, when I dropped off the kids. She told me what happened.' Dominic loosens her hair from its tie and runs his finger though it, brushing away her anger.

'I bet she loved it,' Gab sniffs.

'No, she feels old and ugly and foolish.' He pauses, feeling sorry he has hurt the woman he once loved so much. 'She was crying, and the kids were watching me making their mummy cry ...' Gab draws backs from his embrace.

'I'm sorry, all I ever think about in this thing is you and me. I haven't wanted to admit there was ever anything else to think about, but of course there is.'

'It's not your fault. I admit I never even thought about the vasectomy. Of course you'll want to have children one day, won't you?' Dominic asks her.

'I think so,' Gab says sadly.

'Let's have a drink.' Dominic pours more wine and holds her close. 'We'll work it out one way or another,' she says and Gabrielle feels safe and a little drunk in the crook of his arm.

~

Somehow Alex, Kelly, Nathan and I all end up together on the roof.

Kelly has spread a blanket on the ground and we're all lying down looking up at the sky. The stars are out, shining brightly above the glare of the city's lights.

'Look, see, there's a beak; going round, you see his head and that big star there is his eyes ...' We all stare at the sky trying to make sense out of the cosmos.

'My grandpa showed me how to find an emu in the sky when I was seven. If you try too hard you won't see it, you just have relax then suddenly it will come,' Kelly explains.

'Oh yeah!' Alex sees it first. 'Look and there's its legs!'

'And there's its tail!' I say, even though I can't see it.

'Evan, emus don't have tails,' Alex tells me.

As Alex as I engage in a discussion of the anatomy of emus Nathan takes Kelly's hand and says softly.

'You don't have to become Jewish for me, Kel.' She smiles and squeezes his hand.

'I know. And I know that I can't change what I am or take on another person's faith. My faith is in me and it's who I am. I'm still trying to figure out who that is.' They look into each other's eyes for a moment and then bury their faces in a cloud of stars, feeling the rush of falling though space to who knows where.

60

Christian is telling Kelly a joke about Gandhi. It sounds like a pretty funny joke, but just before he gets to the punchline Jemima pulls on my shirt with the kind of persistent insistence that is usually followed up with, 'Evan! You're not listening to me!' It is this time too, and I look at her.

'Yes I am,' I say. 'You said you were going to get off now, but that you'll see me tomorrow.' I shrug and turn back to Kelly and Christian, who are laughing uproariously.

'That's hearing, that's not listening. OK well, I'm going. I'll see you tomorrow?' she says and kisses my earlobe.

'OK,' I say.

'Tomorrow night?' she presses.

'OK,' I say again.

'I might be a bit late but I'll be there before nine,' she says, her record apparently broken.

'OK.' It's a hat trick from Evan Wylde. I watch her walk out the bar and weigh up her extremely cute walk alongside the fact that's she's becoming ever so slightly grating.

'I hate that,' I say to Christian. 'Why do people need to make an appointment whenever they say goodbye? No one just says goodbye.' Kelly rolls her eyes at me and goes to the loo.

'She's your girlfriend,' Christian says reasonably. 'That's what girlfriends do.'

I look at him for a long moment.

'She's not my girlfriend,' I say carefully.

'It's a security thing,' Simon leans over the bar. 'A psychological reinforcement that absence won't beak down the relationship.' He nods sagely.

'She's not really my girlfriend,' I repeat, feeling a familiar sensation of commitment claustrophobia creep up on me. 'We're just going out and we've got this … "thing" going. That's all.' I knock back some beer, pleased with my rationalization.

'That means she's you're bloody girlfriend. You sleep with someone, you see them more than three days a week, they have a toothbrush at your house. She's your bloody girlfriend mate, might as well admit it.' Christian grins at me like a schoolboy who's just found out that his teacher is afraid of mice.

'Not fully,' I say uncomfortably. The discussion subsides as we watch a very tall, very good-looking woman lean in against the bar. She has the kind of skin that looks like it fits her perfectly. Some people, you know, look like they've stretched it a little far, or some-times that they've shrunk a little thin for it. But hers was smooth and golden as a crisp apple.

She looks at the bar, feeling us admiring her as she waits for Simon to bring over her beers.

'Hello,' she says at last, looking me in the eye.

'Hi,' I say back, trying to maintain an air of mystery and to suppress my foolish grin of pleasure. She looked at me and not the big-muscles gardener. She picks up her beers and shoots me one last look as she strides back to her table.

'I love a woman who drinks during the day,' I say out loud.

'Oh, do you love me, then?' Kelly settles back onto the bar stool.

'Kelly,' I tell her. 'You know I do.' I glance over at the beautiful woman's table again and sigh. Jemima might not be my actual girl-friend but even so there's that thing that make it terribly impolite to go after another woman whilst I'm seeing her.

Women really hate that. Unless …

~

Jemima did turn up at exactly eight fifty-five tonight, we drank two bottles of wine and for half an hour she and Alex discussed the reasons why men aren't able to think of two things at once and whether or not our commitment phobia is genetic while I tried to concentrate on the telly and block out their babble. The harder I tried not to listen the louder Jemima talked, sending me badly disguised messages.

It was after two when I got up and started to write. I sort of knew this would probably piss Jemima off and to be honest if I had been on my own I'd have waited until morning to start.

'What are you doing?' she mumbled, sitting up, her hair in disar-ray and sleep smudged around her eyes. 'You know I've got to be at work by eight-thirty, don't you?'

'Do you?' I said absently. 'I've got to get this idea out; I can only think of one thing at a time. If I don't write it down now, it'll be gone.'

'Couldn't you write it on a note pad like normal people?' she sighed, fully awake.

'No, I don't have one,' I said letting my irritation at her presence surface.

'Evan, everyone has a note pad.' She looked at the clock and flopped back onto the pillow.

'Journalists have note books; writers don't,' I told her, spinning on my chair to look at her. 'There's a really big difference. You churn out hack work to a deadline. I create.' I pressed on, hopeful that it might be this easy. She was angry but she swallowed it, refusing to rise to my bait.

'OK, OK, whatever you say. But I need to sleep now. Have you finished?' I nodded, defeated, and logged off my computer. When I got back into bed I turned my back on her and lay awake until dawn deciding what to do.

~

Kelly looks at my sleepless face as I pad into the kitchen, feeling fraught with low-level unreasonable anger. Relationships are great but why isn't there some kind of hassle-free built-in get-out clause at the get-go? Why all the angst at the end?

'You look like shit,' Kelly tells me sweetly. 'You could at least have washed your face.

'Jemima's in the bathroom,' I say resentfully. Kelly catches my tone and raises an eyebrow.

'I thought I heard you two last night. Arguing, were you?' She pours a cup of coffee and hands it over.

'Yeah, it's because she's a woman and women can only think of one thing at a time – actually, strike that, only one thing all of the time. Commitment.' Kelly huffs her disapproval, thinks briefly of her own obsession with Nathan's commitment to her and decides not to disagree.

'Well, I know one thing. Arguing in the middle of the night is bad.' She purses her lips and looks likes she's sucked a lemon.

'I know,' I say. 'It's just not happening, Kel.' I sigh like I am admitting a defeat. Kelly's face transforms from maternal know-it-all to empathetic confidant.

'What? I thought she was perfect for you,' she cries, sotto voce.

'I did too, and then last night the more we talked the further away we got.'

'But I ...' Kelly begins as Jemima walks in and chooses to ignore the abrupt halt in the conversation in favour of pretending everything is OK.

'OK, better go. I'll see you tonight?' she asks me brightly and I almost feel guilty.

'Yeah, OK.' She winds her arms around my neck and grinds her body into mine as she kisses me. To the average layman it would seem like we were a match made in bed, but you and I know she's showing me what I'd be missing out on if I let her go. What women never get is that no matter how sweet they may taste there is always the possibility that there is someone out there who tastes even better. Or sometimes that there has already been someone whose sweetness they will never match.

'You big hypocrite,' Kelly says to me when she is gone.

'What? That was all her,' I shake my head and search out cornflakes. 'We're just different – she's got this TEN-YEAR PLAN. I don't even know what I'm doing this afternoon.' I shrug, as if any couple had ever needed a better reason to split up.

'So you're different.' Kelly thinks about her own situation again. 'That can be what make a relationship great if only you let it ...' Her voice trails off into a momentary self-reverie.

'I think she's too Paul McCartney for me,' I say, shaking my head. Happily I see that I've pulled Kelly back to earth with my deliberately offside tackle.

'Paul McCartney?' she asks me, perplexed.

'Yeah, Paul shitted John so much that John broke up the band and did his own thing,' I tell her as if I'm explaining that the world turns.

'But Paul broke up The Beatles, didn't he?' I stare at her, caught out by own my half-knowledge of the Sixties pop scene.

'Look, the point is they shitted each other, all right? Jem shits me. Our creative partnership is over. Now I'm going back to my room to write my equivalent of "Yesterday", OK?' Kel shrugs.

'OK – just as long as it isn't "Mull of Kintyre",' she says with a giggle.

Paul, I'm with you, man. You write one duff thing, they never let you forget it.

61

Alex lets the ice-cold white wine hit the back of her neck and imagines it numbing out her vocal cords, even though she knows that such a thing is anatomically impossible.

'I'm turning into an alcoholic,' she tells Simon with a resigned calm. 'Ten minutes after I leave work and I'm knocking back the booze. Drinking alone, it's the first sign.' Simon puts on an expression of mock hurt.

'You're not alone. I'm here,' he tells her. She grins at him as Christian enters the bar. 'And now Christian is here, all workmanlike.' Simon admires him.

Christian smiles a greeting and lean against the bar, still dirty from a day in someone's garden. It's a look that suits him: kind of rugged but also vulnerable.

'Hi,' Alex says self-consciously.

'Look at me. Knock off work and ten minutes later I'm in the bar. Can't even be bothered to home and get changed.' Alex and Simon exchange a smile.

'I know exactly what you mean, same here.' Alex and Christian look at each other, aware how different they are and enjoying it. In the spirit of her recently re-invented manifesto Alex decides to get to know Christian better, because she has decided that she must open up her mind to different things and different people, even if they are people she wouldn't normally choose. And after all, he does live next door, so it's kind of a convenient place to start.

'So, do you want go and sit down?' she says in her friendliest agenda-free voice.

'Yeah, cool.' Christian tries not to look like he's too excited.

The evening passes quickly and when Alex looks at her watch she's surprised to see it's almost eleven. Christian has entertained her more than she thought possible.

'So you left school. And then what?' she asks him, genuinely intrigued.

'Travelled for a bit, did my VCE at night school. Came top in my class, first time ever.' He gives a self-deprecating grin.

'God, I'd have loved to have done that. Four months after I left school I was at university. I've been working ever since. That's what I don't like about me.' Alex follows up her comment with a downward cast of her lashes and a little shrug.

'Hey! You're beautiful. You're a doctor. You're smart, you're making money ...' Christian catches her gaze on its upward journey and holds it.

Alex feels the quantity of wine float her inhibitions.

'Beautiful is good.' She says her thought aloud and then laughs, embarrassed. Christian shifts a little in his seat.

'I could never do what you do, though. For one it takes someone really tough to do your job and for another I need to be outside.' Alex looks at his callused hands and smiles to herself.

'I reckon your job is pretty tough,' she says.

'Nah. You find out what you want to do, it's a piece of piss. I love it.' His face is open and complication free.

'You do love it, don't you?' Alex takes pleasure from his pleasure.

'You bet. Can I get you another drink?' he asks. And she nods her assent.

As Alex watches him make his way to the bar she wonders at how it can be possible to have so much in common with someone who should be so different. One moment happens and the great gulf that convention says should be between you gradually closes up.

~

In contrast, there are times when you feel as if your closeness is a bond that can never be severed until one day you wake up and you and the love of your life are standing on opposite sides of the Grand Canyon.

'It's awful.' Gabrielle has been arguing with Dominic for about as long as Alex and Christian have been together in the bar. 'You should just move her in here and we can all live together.' She goes to the fridge and finds half a bottle of white at the back. It's two days old but she's not much bothered as she pours herself a glass and downs it. She doesn't offer any to Dominic.

'Gabrielle don't be silly ...' Dominic is becoming very tired of placating her.

'She's doing this on purpose! Why don't you see it?' Gab refills and empties her glass in one fluid movement.

'Doing what? What is she doing?' Dominic is exasperated.

'The phone calls on the hour every hour; Chloe's got trouble at school, Jack's got a middle ear infection. You have to go with her to her brother's fortieth. On and on and on and on. When does it end?' she demands.

'They are my family, Gab.' Dominic's patience runs out into a cold anger. 'They never end. You should know that. They exist.' Gab sighs and up-ends the bottle until the last drop finds its way out.

'I exist,' she says quietly.

'And I thank God for it. Please Gab. Come on, let's go out. Let's be happy.' As he says it Dominic knows he is asking for the impossible.

'Don't treat me like an idiot! I'm not your daughter! You can't just kiss it better and make it go away. I hate your wife. I hate her!' Gabrielle throws her wine glass into the sink and hears it shatter before she runs into her bedroom.

Dominic looks at the closed door for a moment and gathers his energy. This fight has a long way to go yet. Somehow his beautiful golden girl seems very far away.

~

Alex has followed Christian up onto the roof, exhilarated by the unplanned act of spontaneity under the stars. Christian crouches down to show her his plants.

'This is Flame Vine, *Pyrostegia venusta*. Beautiful, isn't it?' Alex watches his fingers gently hold the delicate leaves with the utmost tenderness.

'What's this one?' she asks, quickly shaking herself sensible.

'Bellflower, *Campanula carpatica*. There'll be purple flowers all over here.' He sits back on his heels and imagines what it will look like.

'Sounds like an anatomy term. We learn hundreds of Latin terms.' Alex says.

'We learn thousands,' Christian boasts gently. Alex likes his humility. She picks up his hand and runs the ball of her thumb over his knuckles.

'This joint is called the *Metacarpo phaylngeal*.' She turns his hand over and lets her thumb run down to the base of his, knowing she is leaping into the unknown and liking it. 'This here is the *Abductor polici brevis*.' Christian is perfectly still under her touch. Alex swallows and finally her eyes meet his.

'You are beautiful,' he says.

~

'You say you love me, but you don't show it to me. It's just words, words words.' Two floors down Gab paces the floor.

'Gab …' Dominic finds it impossible to reason with her.

'Love is about being together, being proud of each other. Showing the world you've chosen each other. That is love.' She stops dead in front of him.

'I know what love is, Gabrielle,' Dominic tells her, his weary demeanour making him look older than he is.

'Well, you have a funny way of showing it. "They" count more than I do.' Dominic regards her beautiful angry face for a moment

'It's different,' he tries again. The last time.

'She will never let you go. You won't let her let you go,' Gab says with conviction as if waking from a dream.

'Do you want me to move out?' Dominic challenges her. She looks at him.

'Do you?' She turns away from him, unable to look him in the eye.

'Gab?' he says again.

'Yes,' she says. 'Yes I do. I am tired of being angry and hurt all the time. Unless you can promise me that you will always put me first I want you to go.'

Dominic walks out of the door.

62

Alex opens her eyes and sees that her ceiling has new crack in it, one that runs from the left-hand corner to just over the window. And now she comes to think about it, her curtains seem to have been stolen in the night. She sits up abruptly and looks around the room feeling the panic of those few moments before you remember what you did last night. Finally she looks down at her sleeping companion.

Christian's big blues meet her.

'Hi,' he says with a shy smile.

'Um. Hi. Look, I've got to get going …' Alex doesn't know why she feels so panicked by the situation. It's not as if either of them are seeing anyone, they're both free agents etc. etc., but she does know with total certainty that she doesn't want a single one of her friends to find out about this.

'Christian!' Miranda's voice is just outside the door. 'I'm in a good mood today and I'm making brekky. You want some brekky?' Alex stares at Christian, shaking her head.

'I don't want … I don't think we should …' she stutters. Christian smiles and nods his understanding.

Standing outside the door, Miranda checks her watch.

'You're normally up hours ago,' she says. 'Big night?'

'Ah, no. Just fancied a lie-in.' She can hear the sound of hurried movement on the other side of the door. Miranda stifles a laugh – maybe he was indulging in early morning masturbation. She shuts her eyes tight on the image, counts to ten and opens the door.

She looks suspiciously at him standing stock still in the middle of the room, wearing only his jeans. She notices the unruly state of the bed and there is something else – maybe the trace of pheromones in the air.

'You've had someone in here!' she exclaims, a delighted smile on her face.

'No, no I haven't.' Christian is aware that he is a bad, bad liar. It's one of the things women love about him.

'Big liar.' Miranda confirms his status. 'I'll do those eggs for you.'

'Okey dokey.' Christian stares at her pleadingly, waiting for her to leave. She considers challenging him again and then decides the neighbourly thing to do would be to leave the room so he can sneak whoever it is he's got in the wardrobe out without her seeing.

'OK, eggs in five minutes. I'm just going to grab a shower first, OK?' She kindly absents herself to the bathroom. Christian smiles at her and Miranda uses all her willpower for the day not to peek through the gap in the bathroom door to see who it is who has seduced him.

~

It has not escaped my notice that Alex didn't come in last night. She didn't come in and she isn't back yet. I stare at the door, waiting for it to open. Just moments before I scoffed at Kelly's dead-in-a-ditch speech but now the image is stuck in my head: Alex's face, dead white in the dawn, her hair streaked with mud, her eyes dark and staring deadly, I can't get rid of it …

'Hi.' She closes the door behind her and assumes a studied air of nonchalance. She's been shagging all night.

'How was it?' I ask her, easily able to mask any trace of relief in my voice with the strain of sudden unexpected jealousy.

'How was what?' Alex attempts.

'Alex, you have a great big mat of tangled hair just at the nape of your neck.' Kelly giggles.

'Oh, well that's nothing. I just stayed with a friend from college. He was only here one night and well, it's nothing.' I gloomily watch her pour a coffee. It's much, much easier to forget our moment has passed when it's only me seeing someone else.

'Anyway, I need a shower,' she says and she scuttles to the relative safety of her room.

Before she can escape there is a frantic knocking at the door.

'Alex! Alex!' Kelly opens the door to Gabrielle, her face swollen and blotchy. Alex takes one look at her and leads her back to her own flat.

~

'It's as if a light suddenly went on in my head,' Gab says to Alex, who is now making her a cup of herbal tea. 'I think I'm going to vomit. I tried your mobile all night, and I phoned the flat. Kelly said you weren't back. Where were you?' Gab tries to keep the accusatory tone out of her voice but finds she can't.

'I was ...' Alex considers telling her closest friend everything. But somehow she can't, not yet. Not now, at least, when Gab's heart is so shattered. 'Staying with a friend from college. It was spontaneous, you know.'

'You? Spontaneous?' Gab manages a weak smile. 'No, I don't know. Trust you to be spontaneous the night I throw Dom out. I must remember to check your whereabouts the next time I ruin my life ...' Her bright tone dissolves quickly into tears.

'Gab, Gab.' Alex sits down beside her, handing her the tea. 'Don't be silly. You haven't ruined your life.' Gab holds the hot cup close to her chest.

'No, I haven't just ruined my life. I ruined everyone else's too,' she sobs. 'I feel like a complete idiot. It's like I've been sick. Delirious, you know? And then suddenly the fever's gone and I can see I've got someone else's infertile husband who is probably almost old enough to be my father in my bed. Yuck.'

'I don't think he's quite that old,' Alex reassures her.

'I know about married men, I just thought we were special. I love him. I do love him, oh God I love him!' Gab looks at Alex, her face a picture of despair.

'He didn't love me enough, Alex. What am I going to do?' Alex takes the steaming cup of tea out of Gabrielle's shaking hands and pulls her into a hug.

'You are going to take one day at a time, drink a little too much, eat a little more than usual but still lose weight. Not bother to use conditioner on your hair, go to the newsagents without mascara on. You might kiss a few people you shouldn't and not avoid certain types that you should. And then one day you'll wake up and it will all be better. One day sooner than you imagine.' Alex kisses the top of her head.

'You think?' Gab says quietly.

'Oh yeah, one day. But right now we'd better get back to the crying, because we can't start on the booze until at least midday.' Gabrielle sobs heavily into Alex's shoulder.

63

Traditionally, men are not very good at ending relationships with women. Over the millennia they have invented three basic ways of achieving separation. The first is the rarely used 'I just don't think it will work out between us' speech. It takes a brave man and a noble one to confront things in this way. This is the cleanest break by far and the one women always tell their friends they would have preferred, given a choice. But by nature men will do whatever they can to avoid a scene, even in private, and so they are compelled to enter into all sorts of artifice to eventually make the whole thing much worse than it needs to be and upset and emotionally scar everyone much more than they need to be.

The second way, and a very popular choice amongst the brethren, is to be as horrible as possible to the woman in question in the hope that she will get tired of being treated so miserably and finish with you, thus empowering her and absolving you of all responsibility for the break-up. However, the flaw with this plan is that women seem to have a endless capacity to stay in love with total bastards and often, instead of breaking up, you end up getting married by accident.

The third way is an oft-neglected technique and, indeed, one I would have overlooked if it hadn't been for Kelly clarifying for me what I had evidently been groping towards in the dark, if you see what I mean. I slept with another woman. In fact, she's still sleeping off a night of unbridled passion in my bed right now, her long legs tangled in the same sheets that Jemima and I slept in the night before (and for several nights before that, as it goes). That's right: I have slept with another woman. Not just any woman either – the woman from the bar with the perfect skin. I think I can say it was an enjoyable encounter for us both. It wasn't planned, it just happened. I saw her, she saw me, we liked each other, we made each other laugh and one thing led to another. I just thought I'd let it go and go back to being as horrible as possible to Jemima until she got sick of me when Kelly switched on the lightbulb that was hanging over my head.

'I know exactly what you're doing,' she said to me, gravely, as I ushered lovely-skinned Larissa out.

'No you don't,' I said, thinking she was referring to my offering to buy Larissa breakfast so that I could get her out of the flat. Luckily, she was late for work as it was.

'It's pretty bloody obvious,' Kelly said. 'Jemima may have a ten-year plan but she doesn't deserve this.' Kelly shakes her head disapprovingly.

'What are you talking about?' I said, genuinely confused.

'That now you'll go and confess to her and she'll be forced into finishing with you and then that's it – you're out of the relationship and you haven't really had to talk about it.' Kelly looks furious, she's thinking about Nathan again.

The lightbulb went on. Ping.

'Kelly,' I said. 'You are a genius.' Kelly's face filled with horror as she realized what she had done.

And this is the fantastically neat third way. I confess, ridden with guilt, to Jemima later on. She will be upset, but she will admire me for my honesty (see Break-up Tactic One) and then finish with me whilst retaining the moral high ground and her dignity.

And no one is badly hurt.

~

I look around the bar, glad to see that the lovely-skinned Larissa is not out tonight. Her presence would have complicated things even more, because not only would I have had to implement plan three on Jemima, I'd have had to have distanced myself from Larissa too ('Finishing with a woman, subsection A (1) 'One-Night Stands': ignore subject until subject gets the message).

Jemima sees me across the bar and waves a cheerful greeting.

'Wow, you're all here tonight,' Simon says to Kelly, Alex and I as we order a round. 'I'm flattered.'

'I'm here on business,' I tell him.

'You're disgusting.' Kelly shoots an evil look at me. Alex gives her a questioning look. 'He's breaking up with Jemima.' She sits back on her stool. Alex doesn't know about Larissa. I don't know why, but for some reason I don't really want her to know.

'Why?' Alex ignores me and asks Kelly.

'They have nothing in common. Basically she's a really nice girl and he's a sex-addicted pig,' Kelly says lightly without as much venom as she might have used.

'Oh,' Alex says, shaking her head at me. 'Fair enough.'

I shrug at them and, catching Jemima's eye, I nod my head to a relatively quiet section of the bar, an empty booth. She smiles at me and heads over to it, looking forward to an intimate tête-à-tête. For a moment I find my resolve wavering and I consider trying plan one instead, but then as I get near I know that I'm just not a plan-one kind of guy.

'Jem, I've got something to tell you,' I say to her immediately. I can see by the look in her eyes she's hoping it's the 'I love you' speech.

'What is it?' she says with a half-smile.

'Well, I feel really bad. It's just … I don't what happened but I slept with someone else.' I get the words out as quickly as I can and watch her for a reaction.

Her face is completely blank.

'It wasn't supposed to happen, you know, one thing led to another and …' I fill in time while I wait for her brain to come up to speed with her ears.

'Right. Well, my God.' She gives me a shocked smile. 'Well, thanks for telling me. OK,' she says, nodding like one of the dogs you get in the back of cars.

'I'm sorry,' I say, thrown by the absence of an incandescent rage. 'But I know you'll probably want to end …' She interrupts me

'I just didn't know it was that kind of relationship, I mean we never said, did we?' It's my turn to look blank. 'But you know, it's OK, we can have sex with other people. In fact, I have a date tomorrow night; I didn't want to tell you because I thought it would hurt you. But now we've got all this out in the open I feel much better about it.' She holds my look. 'Thanks Evan, for your honesty. I'll probably go back and finish my drink now, OK?' She smiles at me and makes to leave.

'Hang on,' I call after. Did she say she's met someone else? 'Hang on! That's not what I meant! I didn't mean we should have an … it was a one-off! I don't want you to go out with someone else! Just me! Jem!' Alex touches me on the elbow.

'How did it go?' she asks.

'She's going to sleep with another bloke!' I say, full of remorse and jealousy.

'Isn't that a good thing?' Alex asks me.

'How could she do that?' I stare at her, and from somewhere, probably my dad, comes the expression, 'Hoist by your own petard.'

'All of my relationships with women end up failing,' I say to Alex.

'No shit, Sherlock,' Alex mumbles, but I hear her.

'What?' I challenge her.

'Well, Evan. You just don't treat women very well,' Alex shrugs and looks as if she is really keen to drop the subject.

'What do you mean I don't treat women very well? I'm always cooking, aren't I? I've been told I'm not bad at cunnilingus either,' I tell her indignantly.

'I'm just saying, if you changed the way you treated women, things might work out better ...' Alex trails off, clearly unwilling to say what is really on her mind.

'What!' I demand.

'Well ... you didn't treat me very well,' she says, dropping her hand onto her knees. 'I mean, it doesn't matter now, but you professed your love for me and then sent me three postcards in three months. Explain that.' I stare at her, feeling uncomfortably ill at ease.

'I told you, I thought about you all the time,' I say, all thought of Jemima's impending infidelity temporarily banished from my head.

'Maybe, but I didn't know that, did I? Anyway, I kind of got off the point.' Alex takes a sip of her drink. 'I'm just saying that sometimes you treat women badly and it causes them pain.'

'Never deliberately.' I shrug.

'Really?' Alex says. She picks up her keys and leaves me to think about Jemima and her date for tonight.

64

This morning the first thing Kelly realizes when she opens her eyes is that she hasn't seen Nathan for over forty-eight hours. That over two days have past without them seeing or even talking to each other. Since the moment she ran into him in the café, just after Sam died, they have seen each other almost every day and they have certainly spoken every day. Kelly was so sure about his love she didn't even remember to worry about it. Now she's kicking herself as she hurries down the street; to forget your superstition is tempting fate too far.

'If positive thinking can cure cancer,' Kelly thinks, 'then it can save a relationship. Whatever Nathan has taken two days away from me to think about, it can be overcome. Aboriginal and Jewish people have a lot in common. We are both historically nomadic, both spiritual races who believe in symbolism. The Tarot. That sounds like the Torah, which is a good sign.' She comes to an abrupt halt outside the clairvoyant she has been rushing to see. She takes a deep breath and prepares to meet her future.

'I need the full hour,' she tells the clairvoyant expectantly.

Despite paying the full whack it is only forty-five minutes later when Kelly wanders back into the street, her head full of symbols and questions. The Tarot indicated choices, the clairvoyant told her. Emotional Fulfilment or Change. To find the true way Kelly must look for divine signs.

As she walks home she stares carefully at everything around her, looking for more signs.

She reaches the apartment block's main door. She has seen a little yellow dog scurrying along, alone, carrying a newspaper, but she's fairly sure it isn't a sign. She goes to see the only person who she knows will be in.

Miranda opens the door dressed as a schoolgirl.

'Oh,' Kelly says dumbly.

'Don't worry, it's a costume, maybe. For the play. Come in.' Kelly does come in and stands stupidly in the middle of the room.

'Nathan has gone all silent on me,' she says. Miranda watches her.

'And now I've got to look out for signs.'

'Road signs?' Miranda asks.

'Divine signs. Ones to tell me what will happen between Nathan and I. I've got a really bad feeling though and no signs yet.' Kelly wrings her hands. It is the first time Miranda has ever seen anyone do it.

'Kelly, calm down. Nathan is totally in love with you,' Miranda says, missing the significance of the forty-eight-hour absence.

'Is he?' Kelly ask her, desperately wanting it to be true.

'God yeah, head over heels. But men never show anything. I lived with a gay man for years! Never knew till he gave my other mate blow job!' Miranda smiles super brightly.

'What did you do when Richie told you he was gay? I think being gay and Jewish are similar kinds of obstacles in a relationship.'

Miranda frowns. 'Well, being gay is a pretty big obstacle in a hetero-sexual relationship, yeah,' she says, confused by Kelly's reasoning.

'So what did you do?' Kelly persists.

'What could I do? I let him leave. But neither Richie nor I had a choice in the end. Nathan does.' Kelly lets the truth sink in and she sighs hard. Somehow it would be easier if he did have to choose, because she's got the feeling he can't choose her.

'I still think there's hope. The clairvoyant seemed to think there was hope,' she says, ever the optimist. Miranda looks at her and decides to try and take her mind off it.

'Come and look at my body stocking,' she says. It's the only thing she can think of to say.

'Sure,' Kelly says, but she hasn't really heard her.

~

Later she sits on her bed, looking at the swirls in the centre of a sunflower as she picks off the petals.

'He loves me, but not enough. He loves me, but not enough,' she says rhythmically. She is waiting for Nathan's knock and so she isn't surprised when he does arrive, his gentle face transformed with anxiety. She leads him to her room and closes the door. She lifts her chin and waits.

'Kelly, I'm sorry I haven't called for a bit. I've been trying, really trying, to find a way round this; it's just not possible. We've got to stop seeing each other.' Kelly hears the words and finds it almost impossible to keeps the clairvoyant's hope alive in her heart.

'I knew you were going to say that,' she says. 'Why? Why do we have to stop seeing each other?' For a moment Nathan looks as if he doesn't know but then he remembers.

'Because this is impossible. No matter what happens we're still in the same situation. I'm Jewish, end of story. I can't deny who I am any more than you can.' Kelly clenches her hands together and tries her hardest to believe in hope.

'Why can't loving each other be enough?' she asks him.

'It just isn't enough, not against history, tradition – a million reasons that are not going to go away.' Kelly swallows hard.

'So I have to go away instead?' Nathan can't look her in the eye. 'When did you decide all this, in the last couple of days?' she asks.

'No, Kel. I didn't decide it, I just sort of realized we couldn't ignore it, not any more. You said yourself, we both have to know what lies in our future, we can't go on dragging out something that has nowhere to go … I'd better go.' He looks at her for one aching heartbeat and then turns to the door.

'Don't go,' Kelly pleads in a small voice.

'I'm sorry Kel, but I have to go.' Nathan can hardly speak. 'This thing is too big. But I do love you. Remember that I love you.'

Kelly sits on her bed, letting the hope numb her heart. She can't see any signs in here, not even in the corners of her room.

Alex has been waiting on the other side of the door for a few minutes. When she hears nothing at all she gently pushes open the door.

'What happened?' she asks.

'The inevitable, apparently,' Kelly tell her, looking shell-shocked.

'I'm so sorry, Kel.' Alex sits besides her on the bed.

'It's not over yet,' Kelly says, as if in a dream.

'Really?' To Alex it looks about as over as it can get.

'Nope, there's hope. My cards say so.' Alex nods and lets it go.

'That's good,' she says instead.

'Nathan loves me. I have to believe in that.' Alex thinks of Rex, the last time she saw him, and then of Gab feigning illness in bed next door. She decides not to tell Kelly that sometimes love isn't enough on its own.

'It doesn't matter what he's said, I'm just focusing on the positive energy of what he feels.' Alex takes her hand.

'OK,' she says. 'OK. Do you want anything?' Kelly

'All right, I'll be next door.' Alex gently closes Kelly's bedroom door behind her and looks at it for a long moment. She tries to guess how long it will be before Kelly wakes up from her dream.

~

I listen carefully as she tells me everything Kelly said to her.

'Will you keep an eye on her? I'm on shift in thirty minutes.'

I nod. 'How is she really?' I ask.

'In denial. It's weird how different people handle break-ups. I go to bed, Gab gets sick and Kelly reads the Tarot. What do you do?' she asks me out of the blue. I stare at her.

'I don't know really,' I say.

'Well just watch her, OK?' she says.

'Well look, this'll cheer her up.' I hold up a postcard. 'It's from Will. I found it at the back of the mailbox downstairs.

'Oh good,' Alex says. 'That will cheer her up.' But some kind of intuition tells her it might just not.

~

'"Still in Tennant Creek working for a miner digging dirt in the middle of the desert. It's great."' I read out loud to Kelly, who's curled up on her bed looking at the ceiling.

'Do you think he's got someone out there?' she asks tentatively.

'I dunno. No,' I say carefully.

'I think he has. Why would he stay in one place if it wasn't for a girl?' she asks me. I get the feeling that my answer is terribly important.

'Because he loves digging in the desert. You know Will, he's mad for manual labour.' She gives me a little smile and picks up a desiccated sunflower. After a few moments of silence I realize she's finished talking to me.

65

When the grapevine finally delivered news of Gabrielle's break-up to Jason he packed Angus's change bag and took him round there straight away. He wasn't sure if she would want to see him, but he knew he had to see her, to make sure she was OK.

'Hi, I brought you food,' he says as she opens the door, holding out two Tupperware boxes of home-prepared pasta.

'Jase, God! Thanks!' Gab looks tired and her cheeks are hollow but he's relieved to see that she's not gone totally ga-ga.

She opens the lids of the boxes he brought and puts them in the microwave.

'When did you become all kind, caring and sensitive?' she says to him. 'More importantly, when did you learn to cook?' Jason laughs good-naturedly and puts Angus down on the carpet. The baby looks around him for a moment, working out which almost-out-of-reach objects he is certainly not allowed to have, so that he can put himself in mortal danger by going after them. Jason caches him just as he pulls himself up onto the glass coffee table and reaches for a pair of nail scissors.

'His mother, then him in quick succession.' He smiles and kisses Angus on the top of his head before setting him down for another adventure.

'How are you and Caitlin now?' Gab asks casually.

'OK, actually. I didn't love her and she pretended to love me, thinking it would make me love her back. But it didn't, it just gave me the shits.' They both laugh.

'You poor thing,' Gabs says, feeling a little jealous that Jason is so over the aftermath that she is still struggling with.

'Well, I got Gus out of it all, and he's the best thing that ever happened to me.' He looks at her. 'The best thing is I didn't fuck up, anyway. And Caitlin and I are OK now, we got out of it before we hurt each other too much. We're all about this little man now!' Jason sweeps Angus away from the VCR just as he is about to post Gab's discarded earrings into it.

'Can I ask you a personal question?' Gab asks him.

'Yeah.' Jason looks a little uncertain.

'Did you love Alex?' she says. He thinks for a moment, hefting Gus onto one shoulder and then the other.

'No. I was obsessed with her for a while. But no, I never loved her.' Gab is glad to know that.

'I wonder if I'll ever be this cool about Dominic one day,' she says, noticing that she can say his name out loud without the sound of it killing her.

'You will be. How's it going at the office?' Jason asks her.

'He's transferring – Francesca's idea. I'm acting head of the department, which would be OK if it wasn't for the fact that all the women in the office hate me and see me as a home-wrecking slut. And all the men look at me as if I might be worth a go.' Gab tries to laugh but it sticks in her throat. 'So I've pretty much had flu ever since.' She serves up the steaming pasta and sets a plate down on the low table. Angus reaches out for some and squeezes it happily between his fingers.

'My God, you have to change everything when you have a kid, don't you?' Gab says, moving the plates onto the breakfast bar. 'Lucky I'm too slack-arsed to warm up the plates.' Jason laughs and straps Angus into his buggy before joining her at the counter.

'You should try a gesture of reconciliation; make the first move by showing that you want to resolve the tension. They are probably just testing your mettle.' Gab smiles at him, surprised at how comforted she is by his presence.

'When did you get so wise?' she asks him.

'I'm telling you Gab, a baby changes everything. You're not just living for yourself any more. Hey, how's the pasta? It's my signature dish!' Jason laughs.

'It's delicious!' Gab exclaims, and for a moment she lets herself imagine what it would be like if she and Jason had never broken up and if Angus belonged to her as well as him.

66

Kelly's been waiting at the school gates for Nathan. The children rush by, happy to be free of the bells, and she waits while they dwindle to a straggling few. Finally other teachers pass her by, giving her an odd glance; and then, at last, Nathan appears.

As soon as he sees her his face lights up in an involuntary smile. Kelly clings on to that fleeting expression as she watches him compose himself.

'I wasn't expecting to see you,' he says as he reaches her.

'I wanted to see you. To see if you wanted to see me. You did,' Kelly says smiling.

'Is this another one of your tests?' Nathan asks her, exasperated by his own pain.

'No, I wanted an honest reaction from you. I think you are afraid to show how you feel.' Nathan closes his eyes momentarily and then begins to walk away from her.

'Maybe my honesty just isn't what you want to hear,' he says harshly, with a huge effort of will.

'No, no. It's just that I can't believe that we aren't meant to be together.' Kelly catches his arms and stops him. Nathan blinks back tears, avoiding her eyes.

'Kelly, it's over. Fuck. We have nothing left now except for this … this huge difference that hangs over us. I'm sorry. Really sorry. I have to go.' Kelly stands stock-still in the road, feeling him leave. At last the world comes into focus around her and the first thing she sees is a sign. A road sign. It reads: 'Dead End. No Through Access.'

Kelly begins a slow walk home.

~

'We're over, for good,' Kelly tells Alex as she wanders into the apartment. Alex puts down her blusher brush and follows her into her room.

'Kelly, come with me to Miranda's play,' she says, one cheek perfectly flushed and highlighted, the other as yet un-made-up.

'I can't. I don't want to do anything. I don't want to breathe.' Kelly lays on her bed.

'I know, but you have to come. Please.' Kelly doesn't look at her.

'Why?' she says.

'Because otherwise I'll have to go on my own. Evan and Gab are already there doing stage stuff. In fact, if you don't come I'll have to stay here with you. And we'll dissect our lives and our fucked-up relationships and get really angry and probably drunk when instead we can go and watch Miranda's play and then get drunk with people who love you. Especially when your stupid prick of an ex-boyfriend acts like a stupid prick.' Alex runs out of breath at last. Kelly manages small smile.

'He's not stupid,' she says. 'But he is a prick.'

'Come on, let's get our public faces on and get out of here.' Alex holds her hand and helps her up off the bed.

~

Applause thunders around the hall and Miranda stands in the spotlight, her face glowing with achievement. She was fantastic, she was fabulous. Tonight she showed us why she wants to do this, why she needs to act. She needs to act because it's in her very blood. Just the way I want to write.

She's still high, higher than a kite, when we all pile into the bar and get the drinks in. I look around at my friends. Miranda's shining, luminous and complete, Alex sits back, the remoteness that has become part of her since the abortion only faintly visible now. Gabrielle and Jason whisper over a sleeping Angus; Gab's sorrow sits in every plane of her face and each angle of her body. Kelly smiles at Miranda, so happy for her that she can almost forget the massive effort of will it has taken to master her own unhappiness, just for tonight. Richie sits a little back, glad it went so well tonight, but a little jealous too. And Simon watches him, wondering. Christian is the last to come into the bar. He avoids looking at Alex and claps Miranda on the shoulder.

'Good one,' he says happily.

'You know what we need?' I say to the group at large.

'What now, Evan?'

'Go on, enlighten us.'

'You'd be the one to know.' And various other ripostes greet me.

'We need a goddamn party!' I shout, and a cheer goes up and rattles the roof. A cheer full of joy and hope, love and despair, all in equal measures.

67

Thing have been a little unusual in the last couple of weeks since Miranda's play opened; it's as if time has picked up speed and is hurtling us ever nearer to some unknown destination. All of us seem to be fraught with tensions; some mysterious and secret and others as plain as the break of party day.

Kelly and Nathan haven't exactly broken up. I mean, they aren't together any more. Kelly is frequently to be found crying quietly in her bedroom, clutching a card or pressed flower that Nathan gave her – they aren't a couple with a potential future any more. No, they just see each other every day and sleep together most nights.

It started out with comfort phone calls, each one turning to the person they would normally turn to in times of pain and crisis and then it became 'meeting' in coffee shops and eventually bars, the last-ditch attempt to find a solution on being apart. And then it was sleeping together just to be in the shelter of each other's arms and sometime during that night of unbearable tension, it was the best sex they have ever had. Doom-laden, hopeless sex. The ultimate in romantic eroticism, especially for a young woman who's a star-crossed lover even when she's single.

Alex and I have done our bit. Exchanges cynical glances, mentioned to Kelly that maybe it's not the best idea to drag it out this way, but Kelly just looks us and says, 'I know, I know. It's going to end tonight. Honestly.'

Gabrielle has sort of reconstructed her life, just teetering on the brink of total independence for the first time ever in her life, but little things conspire to pull her back to the past. During the after-show drinks, Jason was struggling to pack up all of Gus's things with the sleeping baby over one arm and his nappy bag in the other. 'Christ, Caitlin'd kill me if she knew I had him in a bar gone midnight!' he told Gab, who lifted the weight of his son from his arms. She felt the baby's warmth again her chest, his face nuzzled into her neck and for a moment she let herself dream again of how it might have been if things hadn't gone so terribly wrong. Jason caught her look and in that exchange she knew he wished things had been different too.

She wasn't sure if it was the comfort of familiarity she was seeking or if her hormones wanted to hang on to that baby for a few more hours, but anyway Gab offered to help Jason take Gus home, and she stayed the night there with him.

They didn't have sex together that night. When they got in Gab laid Gus gently in Jason's bed, stroking what little bit of hair he has back from his face.

'God I'm pissed,' she whispered to Jason.

'Me too. You can stay, if you like?' he said. 'I … I mean, I'd go on the sofa.' Gab smiled at his awkwardness and lay herself down on the bed next to the sleeping Gus, watching the rise and fall of his chest.

'Let's all sleep here together,' she said quietly. Jason laid down on the opposite side of Gus and they linked hands over the top of his head. It was the best night's sleep any of them had had in months.

~

Richie's finding his new career of waiting by the phone to be even more of a strain lately, ever since Simon fell out of unrequited love with him and in unrequited love with some Irish bloke about to leave for home. Instead of mooching around over Richie, Simon hums 'When Irish Eyes Are Smiling' instead and leaps to pick up the phone call at extraordinarily early or late times of the day. In fact, Richie is pretty sure they've been having phone sex, and somehow it's put him off using the handset.

Richie didn't realize how much he missed having someone in love with him until there wasn't anyone there. And it doesn't help that he's dwindled his ninety thousand dollars' worth of savings down to one thousand dollars and counting. He should tell someone really, but he just can't get round to it.

~

Miranda's play has had great reviews. She even got on the local TV news. 'Pores Afresh model reveals hidden acting talents' ran the shout line under her picture.

'My talents aren't hidden, I act in that commercial. Hey Christian! Don't I act in the commercial?' she said to her flatmate as we watched the TV.

'Yeah, you act real cute,' Christian replied and she hit him over the head several times with a cushion. But even so her agent has had plenty of calls for her since then. And then one day, she got a call asking her to take the show to the Edinburgh Festival.

'I'm going to Edinburgh!' she hollered happily. 'Who can lend me eight thousand dollars?' Richie avoided catching her eye.

~

Alex and I have been helping Kelly help Simon plan the party. First off Alex got moody with me for suggesting we should have the party at our place.

'Alex,' I said to her, 'what will best take Kelly-party-planner-professional's mind off Nathan when she gets in from work and all she has to think of are the dark, lonely nights? I'll tell you – party planning.' I was pleased with the simple genius of my plan.

'That would be a good plan if it wasn't for the fact that Nathan is here most nights?' She had a point.

'Alex,' I said. 'What little sense of adventure you had has dwindled entirely away.'

'Listen, do you remember the last party we had here? Gab found me and Jase in the broom closet, it all kicked off and everyone was miserable for weeks afterwards?'

I smiled. 'I wasn't,' I said, with a shrug.

'Well anyway, I'm superstitious about it, we've only just got that rug cleaned and anyway Simon the party king of the world wants to have the party at his place and if Kelly is over there helping him then she's not going to be here moon-eyed over her requited/unrequited love with Nathan, is she?'

She had another point.

~

Alex has blossomed. Something has happened to her to just clear away the shadows and the sorrows in her eyes. She's up all the time, she clearly feels good about herself, about her job, about the way she looks. Maybe it's because over the last few weeks she's seen she's not the only one who fucks up big time in the personal department. If I could talk to Kelly about anything apart from Nathan she'd tell me it looks as if Alex is in love – and if not in love, at least getting some from somewhere.

~

As for me, I have been living a version of *A Christmas Carol*, only it isn't Christmas, and so far there have been no carols.

First off, I was out getting some fresh air in order to help me write better when I bumped into Carmen. Carmen beautiful divorcee with two kids who I fell in love with last year – just after she finished with me, as a matter of fact. I slept on her doorstep for two nights. The Ghost of Evan Past.

'Hey, it's my writer guy.' She smiled at me. 'How's it going?'

'Well, I might get published. Someone's got my work right now. I'm waiting to hear.' I'd been waiting to hear for ever, it seems. 'How are you?' I remembered to ask her.

'Pretty good, life is settled down. I'm content. I'm happy.' So there we are, chatting, when who should walk by but Jemima – The Ghost of Evan Present.

'Oh. Evan.' This woman had pure hatred written all over her face.

'Hi Jem ...' I said uncertainly. 'How are you?'

'Well, I'm not too bad now.' It's clear that up until now I have been ruining her life. 'I had to go away for a bit, but I worked it out in the end. You are a total shit, by the way.' She gave me one last deadly look and disappeared.

'Up to your old tricks again, Evan?' Carmen said with a wry smile. I shrugged innocently.

'Can't think what I did to her,' I said.

'Used her, maybe? Maybe more interested in the thrill of the chase than all that relationship hassle that ensues?' I shuffled on the spot.

'I guess,' I said and a shadow passed over the sun.

'You are a bit of a manipulator, you know, Evan. A bit cruel. That was one of the reasons I thought we should end it.' She kissed me lightly on the cheek and then disappeared like a bubble bursting.

'But you said it was because I was too young?' I called after her, but she had evaporated into the morning crowd.

I wouldn't have worried about it too much if it wasn't for the fact that I ran into Lauren – The Ghost of Evan Future – waiting on my doorstep.

'Evan,' she said, with a smile.

'Hi Lauren, how's it going?' I saw my future in her hands.

'Look, my boss won't run with this at the moment. I'm sorry.' She handed me back my chapters. 'Keep working on it. You have got potential.' I stared at my work as she turns away.

'Lauren, hold up!' I said. 'This isn't because of ... because of what happened with us, is it?' She smiled at me.

'Because you're an egotistical prick happy to use other people's lives as a mean to distract you from you own emotionally crippled life?' she said. 'No. Don't worry, it isn't. It just isn't what my company is about at the moment. You should try other publishers. I reckon you've got what it takes in the long run.' I looked at my work sadly and then back to where Lauren was standing – except there was no one there now.

'Kel, am I an egotistical prick and an emotional cripple?' I asked Kelly when I opened the front door.

'Well, put it this way. Yes. But I love you, mainly because I don't love you, if you know what I mean …' she said pleasantly.

'OK.' I didn't know what to think, so I went to bed instead.

When three ghosts appear and tell you things, then, well, you should try and work it out, shouldn't you – buy a turkey for some kid with one leg or something. At least take a good look at the kind of person you are.

Or you could just party so hard you kill all the brain cells that remember the experience and try and get laid instead.

~

When you think of it, parties are the basic social model moment of humanity. They start when you're at playgroup giving out invites to your mates and they continue until you don't know who you are any more, let alone your guests, trying to smile through the smoke of a hundred birthday candles. Some parties are dull, some are wild. Some change your life and some you can't ever quite remember. I'm going for the last category of enjoyment.

Alex came off a twelve hour stretch just as we are leaving for the party and she reckons she is only staying for half an hour.

'Yeah right,' I say to her, giving her an 'E' before handing one to Kelly and then popping mine. 'Once this comes up baby, the whole night will seem like it's only half an hour long.' Miranda and Christian meet us in the hallway and I looked round my crew, all exceptionally beautiful and happening.

'You people are all very fine,' I say to them. I show Miranda my small plastic bag full of joy. 'Want any?' I ask her.

'Ooooh, our hero,' she says and when we head out into the night we are all ready for whatever this party may bring.

Gabrielle arrives with Jason. She's already a little bit pissed and now she's here she's knocking back tequila shots, hopeful that if her and Jason keep drinking they won't have to do anything as difficult as talking. Jason, on the other hand, is trying desperately to get a word in edgeways when she takes a breather from the booze.

'Simon, my good man,' I confront the host. 'May I say a finer party set I have rarely seen. A bath full of ice and booze, a kicking DJ and a very good selection of the single female variety. That's what I like about gay blokes. They've always got a ton of good-looking single girl mates.' Alex shakes her head at me in disgust and goes over to Gab.

You can tell it's a good party when the walls vibrate with the bass beat, when the floor shakes in time with the people dancing and everyone has to shout to be heard.

Kelly slides down onto a sofa next to Miranda.

'Hey, chick,' she says.

'Hey. What are you thinking about?' Miranda asks her.

'She is so great,' Kelly says, before clapping her hand over her mouth. She hadn't meant to say that out loud

'What?' Miranda leans in closer to her. 'Can't hear you. It's the music!' she shouts.

'I said isn't the party great? Kelly laughs.

'See that girl over there,' Miranda nods at a slim, dark-haired girl, all twisting hips. 'She just told me she had a threesome with another girl and a bloke.' Kelly wrinkles up her nose and gives the girl the once-over. 'What do you reckon?'

'Bullshit, I reckon,' Kelly says.

'Would you ever do it?' Miranda asks. 'I would with two blokes, sure. Maybe with another girl and a guy. It would depend on who it was. I mean, who would you choose?' Miranda flutters her eyelashes. 'I'd choose you Kel, you're so sexy,' she giggles, but Kelly flushes a little anyway.

'And I'd choose you. But what about the guy?' They both look around the room, their eyes passing over an assortment of men who just aren't quite …

'Will,' they both say together, laughing.

'Oh well, he's in … where is he? Middle of nowhere that's where, so deal's off.' Both girls feel a little bit relived and a little bit disappointed at the same time.

~

I'm watching Gabrielle and Alex dancing; it's beautiful. They are beautiful – I mean, ordinarily they are both super-special girls, but tonight, right now, caught up as they are in that halo of colours, they are exactly what beautiful means. I catch Alex's eyes and smile at her. I want her to know how beautiful she is.

'You should dance with Evan,' Gab says charitably.

'No I shouldn't! Fuck!' Alex exclaims.

'He's a great dancer,' Gab tells her within my earshot. 'He was really good in Cuba, he danced like a motherfucker, really. You should travel, Alex. China. Alex, you should go to China.' I dance around their periphery for a moment more, but Alex is too into the groove with her friend to take any notice of me, snake hips and all.

Through the smoke and the crowd I see Nathan arrive; he scans the room, looking for Kelly and as soon as he spots her he makes a beeline.

Nathan leads Kelly away from Miranda into Simon's bedroom. Miranda huffs out a sigh as she watches her drugs buddy leave.

Kelly watched Nathan close Simon's door.

'Do you care about me?' she asks, the pills and booze making her brazen and brave.

'Kelly, I never stopped loving you,' he says. 'I miss you so much that when I don't see you I spend most of the day just wishing my heart would stop beating.' Kelly raises her face to meet his and he kisses her, a long, sweet kiss full of love.

'Oh, God, Nathan. I've wanted this so much. For all the pretence to be over and for you and me just to be back together again, like we used to be,' Kelly whispers, her voice thick with emotion. 'If you want that, I know, I just know that we could overcome our differences in the end.' She feels Nathan stiffen in her arms.

'Kelly ... I ... that's not what I meant,' he says awkwardly, pulling back from her. There are shouts from the other room as a favourite track comes on. The volume is kicked up and the water in Kelly's bottle vibrates.

'I miss you, Kelly. I can't help wanting to see you. But we can't get back together, not like before.' Kelly stares at him like the sun has risen in her eyes ...

'So what are we doing here, then?' she says calmly. 'You're killing me.'

'I don't know,' Nathan tells her, shaking his head.

When Kelly pushes her way into the thronging mass of people, Alex sees snapshots of her expression captured by the strobe-lighting and goes to her side, the lighting effect making it all seem like she is an impossibly long distance away.

'Kel, are you OK?' Alex asks her.

'I'm fine. It's funny how getting out of your head makes you see things the way they really are, isn't it?' Kelly spins away from Alex into Miranda's arms.

~

Nathan is staring at the wall, wishing he was more wrecked than he is, when the door pushes open slowly.

'Kelly, I'm so glad you … oh. Rachel.' Nathan stands and smoothes down his shirt for the daughter of his mother's quilting circle companion. 'Hi, I didn't know you were at the party.'

'Oh yeah, I know Simon from my Pilates class.' Rachel shrugs and gives him a small smile. 'I just wanted a bit of peace and quiet and a joint,' she says.

'Oh right, well I'll be off then.' Nathan heads for the door, but she catches his arm and takes a step closer to him, pressing her breasts against his chest. Nathan fights the somehow sickening image of his mother's approval.

'Why don't you stay and have a drink with me?' she asks softly.

Nathan can't think of a reason why not.

~

When Jason looks at Gab it's as if the music softens and the lights dim before her radiance. He sees her break away from Alex and dance on her own for a moment, a hundred pairs of male eyes admiring her.

'Gab.' He is at her side in a beat. 'I want to talk to you about something.'

'Jase!' she yells with a giggle, throwing her arms around him. 'Whadyasay?'

'Gab, I need to talk to you!' he shouts.

'What?' Gab gestures that she can't hear him and points at the speaker.

'I need to talk to you!' he yells in her ear. She looks at him blankly. Finally he takes her hand and leads her toward Simon's bedroom.

'Let's just find a place we can have quick chat, OK?' he says

'OK,' she says. He opens the door to Simon's bedroom.

'Oh shit,' he says, closing it again. 'Shit.' He looks at Gab.

'What?' He stares at her. 'What?' She barges past him and opens the door herself. For a moment she can't quite believe what she's seeing and then she realizes that it's not an hallucination. She sees

Nathan leaning against the wall, his head thrown back, his mouth opened, and some girl she's doesn't know with her head between his legs.

'Ohhhh,' he moans.

'You fucking bastard,' Gab shouts. Nathan's eyes pop open and he pushes the girl away.

'Fuck you!' Rachel sits on the floor, her hair in her face, wiping her mouth with the back of her hand. 'You ungrateful fucking bastard. And who the fuck are you?' She turns to Gab. Gab storms into the room and drags her up by her hair.

'No, who the FUCK are you?' she shouts. 'Get out, get out of here now!' Rachel stares at her open-mouthed and then at Nathan and then grabs her bottle and leaves.

'You'd better go,' Gab tells Nathan, her rage making her temporarily sober.

'Gab please, I don't …' Nathan get up, buttoning his trousers.

'Just go, OK. Just go.' She stares at him as he walks past her. Jason comes into the room and closes the door.

'My God,' Gab says. 'Kelly and Nathan were so happy together. If there is no hope for them, then it can never work out for anyone, can it?' Jason sits down.

'That's what I wanted to say, Gab,' he says.

'What?' She sits down heavily on the bed .'Do you think I should tell Kelly? I sort of think I shouldn't. It would kill her. Let's agree not to tell her. I'll tell Alex, she'll know what to do.' Jason takes her hand, hoping it will stop her talking.

'Gab!' he interrupts her. 'I have something I have to say.

'Sorry, I just can't believe it … sorry what?' Jason drops his long rehearsed preamble, fearful of more interruption.

'OK … I've been thinking about this for a long time, Gab.' He looks at her, trying to read her face. 'I believe that there's one person for everyone. The one, you know? In all our troubles I've never changed that. Never.' The silence between them make itself heard in amongst the throb of the music.

'Do you remember the last party?' Gab says. 'The day we got married, the day I found out about you and Alex?' Jason drops his gaze to his knees.

'Yeah, I'll never forget it. It was the best and the worst day of my life. I will always regret everything I did to fuck us up, Gabrielle, but

I'll never regret marrying you. I did it for the wrong reasons then, sure, but I want to make it work now for the right ones. I know we can make it.' Gab's eyes fill with tears and she blinks them away.

'I don't know, Jase ...' she pauses. 'I don't know. I'd be lying if I said I didn't love you any more. But I don't know if it's enough. I don't know that it can ever be enough again.' Jason nods.

'OK, I understand. Will you think about it?' Gab nods slowly and bends to kiss him softly on the lips.

'I will. I'll think about it.' Gab's face becomes a picture of concentration. 'Jase?' she says tentatively.

'Yeah?' he asks, holding his breath.

'I think I'm going to chuck up.' Jason rushes her to the bathroom and holds her forehead and she vomits.

'You must really ... love me ... to do this ...' Gab tells him, between gags.

'You know I do,' he says, rubbing her shoulders.

~

I'm watching Alex dancing with Christian. She is dancing with abandon; in the past, Alex only ever danced with abandon with me. Usually if you should chance upon Alex on the dance floor, both of her feet are rooted to the ground and her shoulders barely move. I'm watching her dancing with Christian, twirling back and forth, running her fingers through her hair, tossing her head back and closing her eyes with a small, pouty smile playing on her lips.

Kelly comes up to me and flings her arms about my neck.

'Evan, you think I'm worth more than a shag, don't you? Don't you?' I don't think I've seen Kelly this drunk before.

'Oh, course you are Kel, you're worth a million pounds at least,' I tell her, worried about how she is swaying with my puny neck as her only anchor.

'Good. Do you want to sleep with me? Oh no, sorry, I forgot you're in love with Alex.' She giggles and totters into a group of dancers knocking tequila shots back from a bottle as they dance. One of the girls greets her with a chick scream and they hug each other tight and begin to talk closely, holding each other's shoulders for safety.

I look at Alex and decide she wants to be dancing with abandon with me.

'Your hair looks great,' I tell her by way of an opener.

'Yeah? Christian said that too. I'm never washing it again.' She sways towards me, toppling a little and I catch her in my arms. For a second I feel the memory of her kisses as if they were real.

~

And then it all goes black.

Everything shuts down, the music, the lights the party. A few of the dancers keep up the tempo, unable to stop themselves and a few lighters click on.

'Come on Simon!' I shout into the gloomy melee. 'You're messing with people's heads here!' I hear Simon swearing and muttering somewhere behind me

'OK, we have lift off!' Simon's voice comes out of the black and the party cranks up again, nought to sixty in ten seconds.

Kelly looks around for the friends she was with a few minutes before.

And she sees Will. She blinks hard, twice. Pinches herself and then chucks a bit of water from her bottle into her face.

'M–,' she says. 'Miranda …' Miranda looks at her and follows the point of her finger.

'Fuck,' she says quietly to Kelly and they hold hands in reverential silence. Neither one of them has had a prayer answered before.

'Will!' Gab rushes into his arms with the renewed vitality of someone who's cleared the toxins from her system and is ready to start again.

'Hey, Gab.' He laughs and hugs her tight. Eventually all of us are around him, shaking his hand, patting him on the back, kissing him frantically if you're Kelly and Miranda. We are all there except Richie, who doesn't seem to have been around for while, when I think about it.

'You guys are so out of it.' Will states the obvious, shaking his head with a grin. 'Seen Richie?' He scans the crowd.

'Not for a while, he's off somewhere with his boyfriend.' Kelly links an arm through his and swings on it.

'I really want to talk to Richie,' Will says. Miranda takes his other arm.

'OK, I think I know where he is,' she says, winking at Kelly. 'Follow us.'

~

Will finds himself in Richie's bedroom, neat as a pin and just as pretty. Kelly reclines on Richie's bed whilst Miranda lights two of his lavender-scented candles.

'You know, Richie reckons he's pretty much straight acting, but you know what? He had these candles before we split up. If only I'd read the signs! She makes a mock-dramatic face and pushes Will onto the bed.

'We'll just wait for him here, OK?' she says softly. Will starts to feel kind of mellow, the spliff he had on the way here combining nicely with the 'E' he took just after he arrived.

'We can have a private smoke, invitation only,' Miranda says softly, taking a joint out from behind her ear.

'Cool,' Will says, looking from one girl to the other. 'Can't wait to see Richie, you know, get things back on course.' The girls ignore him.

'Why don't you relax,' Kelly says, gently pressing him into a reclining position. Will looks at them again, suspicion finally making its way into his consciousness.

Kelly flops down beside him

'Hi,' she says.

'Hi,' he says. She kisses him, a long, deep kiss. Will is starting to enjoy it when he feels something else. He opens one eye and sees Miranda kissing his chest.

'We've decided to kidnap you and make you into our love slave,' Miranda purrs before taking her turn to kiss Will on the mouth.

'Oh, right.' Will can think of nothing more to say, especially as Kelly's hand has travelled to his fly and begun to unbutton it, one button by one.

~

Now the power's back on I go back to plan A. I want Alex to be with me tonight. I want everyone to see that she is my best friend.

I catch her making her way through the dance floor.

'C'mere,' I say, grabbing her wrist. 'Give me a smoochie!' She breaks free of my grip.

'Evan! Back off,' she half laughs, but she looks tired.

'Come on ya hot chick, give old Evan a snog.' Before I know what has happened I'm sitting on the floor and it feels like my face has exploded from the middle out.

Alex has punched me.

'Oops,' she says with a giggle. The party-goers cheer. Alex leans down and takes a look at my face. I'd scowl at but I'm concentrating on not crying.

'You really copped it,' she says with a chuckle. 'A deviated septum.'

'A broken nose!' I say.

'No, don't overreact. You'll be OK once the stinging wears off.' She pats me on the head and goes back to dancing. She goes back to dancing! She just assaulted me and she's dancing!

I ask you.

Richie appears in the doorway with Nick.

'Evan, mate, you look like shite,' he says.

'Alex broke my nose,' I tell him. He clearly doesn't believe me.

'This is Nick, he's ... um. Well, I've been seeing him for a bit.' I shake Nick's hand.

'G'day mate,' I say gruffly.

'All right, sorry about your nose,' he says. I notice Richie take Nick's hand and start to lead him towards his bedroom. It's pretty weird, but it's OK.

~

Riche pushes open his bedroom door and sees Miranda, Kelly and Will sitting on the bed as prim as three little maids.

'Will!' Richie is so surprised to see him he doesn't notice the look on any of their faces.

'Mate!' they greet mid-room and hug hard.

'I've missed you, you know,' Will tells him. 'I'm sorry I didn't say goodbye before I went. I'm sorry we fell out. It was stupid.' Will says what he travelled all this way to say.

'Me too.' Richie becomes aware of Nick standing slightly tense just behind him. 'Oh shit, Nick – this is Will, my oldest mate. Will, Nick my ... I've been seeing him for a while.' Will shakes Nick's hand. For another few moments everyone stands around in Richie's bedroom trying to edge around the various sexual permutations it affords.

'Right, well, we're off to party,' Kelly says at last, with a flushed giggle.

'Yep, see youse.' Miranda skips after. Richie looks at Will. Will looks at Richie and says: 'Women eh? Who can figure 'em out?'

Richie grins at Nick. 'Don't ask me.'

Will chuckles to himself as he makes his way back to the party. Whatever he had expected on his stopover back here before he went on his travels again, it had never been that.

I'm looking at my nose.

It doesn't hurt so much and it looks all right actually, so I take a big bandage and stick it on with the ends of some plasters. I don't want Alex thinking that she has hurt me bad – after all, all we want from life is to do the right thing, or have the right thing done by us.

'Hi,' I say to Alex, with a sort of sore, throat-raspy voice, on the general principle that poorly people need some kind of highly visible prop.

'Hi,' she says with a little smile and pours herself a glass of water.

'And?' I say to her crossly.

'And?' she says happily. Merry even.

'I think you might know what I'm saying. It's been a day and a half. I've waited, with good grace. And now I think it's time.' I cross my arms over my chest and wait.

'No,' Alex says lightly.

'No?' Alex you are going to apologize right?' I can't believe this, not from Alex.

'What for?' she asks me breezily.

'My nose!' I wail.

'Oh, it means that much to you, does it?' she says.

'Yes. It's the right thing to do. The right thing is the only thing to do.' This a relatively new discovery on my part but anyhow it seems like a good one.

'But you know Evan, I think it's just all part of life's rough and tumble and that you should learn to roll with the punches. You know, take it on the chin.' I hate it when Alex gets all cutesy.

'Why don't you feel guilty?' I ask her, annoyed that my injury isn't going to get me any mileage at all.

'I don't know; I just found the experience somehow freeing.' Alex pauses and looks around her. 'Maybe I've wanted to hit you for a very long time.'

I stare at her, aghast. It's the first and I hope the only time in my life when I feel that I have legitimately been able to use that word.

Aghast.

~

Gabrielle believes that forty-eight hours is the minimum time needed to have a hangover, and although she can sort of feel the last of the toxins being pushed from her system, she's not quite up to speed yet. So when she opens her front door to Jason she can't quite place why she's a bit uncomfortable about seeing him

'Thought I'd take you to breakfast,' Jason says, wondering whether he should have given in to that urge to buy flowers. Gab furrows her brow. Whatever her worry is, it's still lurking at the back of her mind.

'OK, I guess I can handle food again,' she says with a smile. 'I'll get changed.' Jason watches her go into what used to be his bedroom and calls out to her.

'Some party!' he says.

'Yeah, what I remember of it!' Gab laughs and Jason does too until something worries him.

'You don't remember it?' he says.

'I remember bits of it. Evan's nose, Miranda and Kelly dancing like lap dancers. That's it really. I was out of it.' Gab returns, looking refreshed and beautiful.

'Do you remember what we talked about?' Jason asks her tentatively.

'Yeah sure,' Gabs says with a bright smile. Jason lets out a sigh of relief. 'We talked about China. Or was that Alex?' A dark cloud passes over her face. 'Oh fuck, I remember Nathan and that girl sucking him off. Yuck. I wish I'd forgotten that.'

'So you don't remember talking about us?' As Jason struggles to get the conversation back on track, another thought strikes him. 'Or is it that you don't want to remember?' Jason tries desperately to cut to the chase.

'Jason!' Gab sounds intrigued. 'You were there too. Tell me,' she says with a simple smile and Jason is convinced that she really doesn't remember.

'Um well I said that …' Jason looks at his feet. 'These things are much easier to say when you're pissed,' he says with a wry smile

'What! Just say it!' Gab give him an exasperated look.

'Well, I said that I …' A knock at the door interrupts them. They watch each other for a beat and Gab sighs.

'Excuse me a moment please,' she says as she swings the door open.

It's Dominic.

'I've left. For good this time. I just want to be with you,' he says. Gabrielle shakes her head and wonders if she's still coming down.

'You've what?' she says to the mirage.

'I love you, Gabrielle,' Dominic says. Gab reaches out a hand and presses him gently on the chest. Yes, he is real.

'Um … hi?' Jason interrupts the moment.

'Oh fuck, Jase. Sorry, I forgot you were here, um … oh God, breakfast. We were going to have breakfast, weren't we?' Gab looks from her erstwhile husband to someone else's.

'Do you still want to do that?' Jason asks her, knowing the answer.

'I … don't think I can,' Gab says. 'I'll call you, OK?' Jason sidles out past Dominic, barely managing to keep his curses to himself.

'OK, just …' he looks pointedly at Dominic. 'Just take care, OK?' Once he is gone, Gab lets Dominic in.

'Are you happy to see me?' he asks Gab defensively. Gab sits down and gives herself a second to find out what she feels.

'Yes, yes I am. But … I'm not going through the same thing again. You can't stay here,' she tells Dominic. He hides his disappointment badly.

'I know, I have a hotel room. I'll stay there while you decide what is best.' He stands to leave. 'I'll call you, is that OK?' he asks, almost shyly; it break Gab's heart.

'Yeah. That's OK.' Gab goes to the door with him and lets him kiss her on the mouth. She feels the sensation of his lips on hers and she tries to memorize it, to cling on to it, just hoping that everything will be all right.

~

I watch Alex making a sandwich.

'I could press charges on you,' Alex says.

'I'm sorry? You could press charges on me?' I say, aghast. (Oh no. Again.)

'Yes, because you were sexually harassing me. That whole "Give me a smoochie" thing. Harassment. Case closed.' She grins before she take a bite and talks through her food. 'You should apologize to me – but because we're friends I am prepared to overlook it this time.'

Kelly wanders into the room.

'Hi, how are you two doing?' she says with a smile.

'We're doing OK. Alex has an apology issue but I think she'll overcome it in time and with counselling.' Alex waves a hand at me as if to chase off a bothersome insect.

'Where are you going today?' she asks Kelly.

'To the movies with Nathan. We sort of broke up again at the party but then he called yesterday and so we sort of decided to go to the movies, but only as friends.' She beams at us both and we both know that Kelly has rewritten the dictionary definition of 'friends' to mean 'painful-non-relationship-that-seems-to-drag-on-and-on-with-no-conclusion'.

'Oh, OK.' Alex is short. 'Have a nice time.'

'I will!' Kelly calls on her way out.

'I could sue you,' I say, getting back to the issue at hand.

'Shit.' Alex looks angry.

'It's OK. If you apologize I'll drop the charges.' She shakes her head.

'No, it's not that. Gab told me she saw Nathan getting sucked off by some girl at the party and now I don't know if I should tell Kelly or not.' She runs her fingers through her hair. 'She'd feel so hurt. Maybe he'll just tell her, you know, feel guilty and own up.' She looks at me hopefully.

Nope, Nathan is a man. That whole feeling guilty thing and owning up is for chicks. The only time men do that is when they want to break up with a girl and on recent history I'd say Nathan is having a hard time implementing that particular plan. You should tell her.' Alex sinks into a chair.

'I can't. I don't know. Oh God.' Alex looks miserable.

'I wish you hadn't told me,' I say petulantly. 'I hate knowing stuff I'm not supposed to. I'm a strictly need-to-know kind of guy ...' I watch Alex grab her bag and keys.

'Don't you want to clear this apology thing up before you go to work?' I ask her.

She looks at me, narrows one eye dangerously and takes a swing. Even though I know she's kidding I cover my face with my hands and duck.

'Mind my face,' I yell, involuntarily cowering.

Alex is gone. I think I can still hear her laughing down the hallway.

~

After her shift is done Alex finds a message from Gab on her phone: please come round. When she arrives, Gab hands her a coffee.

'Dominic's back,' she says, with a shrug that belies the significance of her statement

'What? When?' Alex takes a sip of her coffee when it's still too hot and it hurts her mouth.

'This morning, he just turned up. Bam! He's left her. Again.' Gab take a strand of her hair and winds it round her fingers. 'He says it's different this time, but I don't know. I can't go through that again. I won't.'

Alex watches her over the rim of her coffee cup, trying to work out what she is really thinking.

'Then just tell him that he's missed his moment, that you've moved on,' she says, as much as a challenge to Gab as a piece of advice.

'Yeah, yeah I will,' Gab says, but she sounds uncertain.

69

I look at Christian, sitting at the bar quietly enjoying a beer, and point at my nose.

'She still won't apologize. I mean still!' I am incredulous. Christian smothers a laugh.

'Have you ever been hit by a woman?' I ask him, feeling oddly proud and anguished all at once.

'No ... well, yes. When I was in grade four this girl used to hit me all the time. Used to drive me crazy and no one'd believe me. Then, one day she goes, "If you kiss me, I'll stop hitting you." So I did.' Christian takes a long draft of his beer. 'Make Love not War,' he says.

I hang on his every word.

'You think that's why she won't apologize, because she wants to kiss me?' Suddenly everything begins to make sense and that moment we missed all those weeks ago almost looks like it could be coming round again.

'Well ... no, that not what I meant ...' Christian begins.

'It makes sense,' I jump in excitely. 'We've got all this history. She's never been able to just grab me ... and then there was Rex and ...' Christian looks abashed.

'I don't think that's it, mate ...' he says lamely.

'No, see. You don't know her like I do. Maybe this is her way of finding a way to tell me that she wants me again, it's like a build-up and explosions. Sexual into violent.' I smile, suddenly happy.

'Or she was just drunk and kind of flailed out?' Christian suggests, but I ignore him. Him and Alex have hardly ever said two words to each other. Now I know exactly what she meant by hitting me.

The universe has given us another chance.

~

When Alex got back for Gabs she was worried that one of her best friends was on the brink of ruining her life forever; when she came across Kelly and Nathan necking like there's no tomorrow in the kitchen she can see that another one is heading the same way. 'Don't they know,' she thinks. 'It's my job to be the fuck-up queen around here and I'm not abdicating.'

'Hi,' she says loudly, looking at Nathan who goes pink when he sees her. He must have known Gab would tell her about what she saw.

'Hi. Listen Kel, I have to go. I'll see you later,' he says.

'Oh hang on, hang on. I have to get you that book. You have to read it, you'll love it. It really seemed to me that it was about us!' she runs off to her room.

'What are you playing at?' Alex asks Nathan coldly.

'Are you going to tell her?' Nathan asks. 'I never meant it to happen. It just did.' Alex looks at him for a long moment.

'I don't want to,' she says. Nathan breathes a sigh of relief, 'But I will. If you don't, I will.' Nathan's mouth opens and closes stupidly.

'But I ...' Alex looks at the door, listening for Kelly's bustle.

'For me, not telling her is the same as lying to her. And I won't lie to my friends. You have tell her.' Nathan look as though he has just been given the death sentence.

'I do love her, you know, I just don't know what's happening,' he says miserably.

'I know, I know you love her. I know you are basically a good guy. That's why you have to tell her,' Alex says, just as Kelly bustles back into the room.

'Tell me what?' she says, picking up on the tension.

'Tell you that I've read that book and it was crap,' Nathan says with a smile.

'Oh Nathan! You could have said! It took me bloody ages to find this!' Alex leaves them laughing and kissing in the kitchen.

~

Gabrielle is still waiting for Jason to tell her what he told her at the party. She sees him as she enters the Fu Bar and goes to kiss him.

'Hi, I'm sorry about this morning ...' she says, looking kind of sheepish.

'That's OK. How did it go?' Jason manages to ask her.

'Um, I don't know. I can't believe it. Anyway, what were you going to tell me?' Jason doesn't need to look at a cosmic clock to know that his time is running out real fast.

'I wanted to tell you that I still ...' Dominic arrives out of nowhere and kisses Gab's cheeks.

'Hello,' he says, sounding all too familiar as far as Jason is concerned.

'Oh hi. Listen, Jason was just about to tell me something ... Jase?' Gab look back at Jason expectantly. He backs down.

'It's OK. It's nothing, it can wait,' he says. Gab touches her palm to his cheek for a second and leaves to find a table with Dominic.

'Fucking fuck,' he says into his beer.

For a long time, they just look at each other. Finally, Gabrielle says, 'I don't think I can do this, Dominic.'

He watches her eyes, looking for signs of deceit. 'Gabrielle, to decide what you truly want in life, it's a terrifying decision to make. To act on it? That's a courage that very few display. But I have. For you, I finally have.' Gab listens to the timbre of his voice and watches the arch of his fingers as they arc in syncopation with his voice.

'You want me?' she says softly.

'Of course I want you. I turn my back on everything, everything except for you.

'You hurt me,' she says sadly. Dominic looks at Gabrielle and sees his impossible dream drifting away from him.

'I know, I was a coward. But I want you, I want you,' he whispers.

Gab leans across the table and lets herself fall into the moment and kisses him in a way that makes the whole bar watch.

Alex stops dead when she comes into the bar. She exchanges a look with Jason. She thinks for a moment and then walks over to Gabrielle and Dominic.

'Hi,' she says, breaking their kiss with her greeting. Gab avoids meeting her eyes.

'Hi, how are you,' Dominic say awkwardly. Alex's disapproval is palpable.

'Um, I'll just get us a couple of drinks,' Gab says to him with a smile and Alex walks back across to the bar with her.

'What are you doing?' Alex says, incredulous.

'I think it's really going to be different this time. I do.' Gab's voice ends in a rise, as if she is asking her friend a question.

'Gab? Really?' Alex makes her view perfectly clear.

'No. It's not, is it? It's always going to be the same. Oh God, I don't know. I love him. That's the problem, I love him.' Gab looks across the bar at Dominic, who waves at her and blows her a kiss.

'That's always the problem,' Alex sighs. 'Well, you have to do what you have to do. Just be careful, OK?' Gab squeezes Alex's arm and goes to Dominic's side.

70

'Bloody men.' Kelly stomps around the living room, kicking things, picking things up and putting them down for no apparent reason. 'I can't believe it. What is wrong with men, Evan?' She looks at me accusingly. I guess the cat must be out of the bag.

'Oh, you know about Nathan, right?' Kelly storms past me on her next angry lap of the living room.

'He promised he'd be here at seven at the latest and then … Know what about Nathan?' My mind catches up with my mouth and I back-pedal furiously. 'Um, that he's Jewish?' I try to cover my looking like an idiot.

'Evan?' Kelly scrutinizes me and stands right in front of me. I wonder if I am about to be hit by a second woman.

'I don't know,' I say. 'Look Kelly, I'm not involved in this. I'm an innocent bystander, I know nothing.' If I thought I was in deep before I've just dug myself in six feet and handed the shovel to Kelly.

'You are going to tell, Evan, we are friends,' Kelly growls at me. Her body language, her eyes and her intonation are saying that we are exactly the opposite of friends.

'That's just why I can't tell you. Friends don't hurt each other.' I hammer a nail into my coffin.

'Evan, what is going to hurt me?' she cries. 'Is Nathan fucking someone else?'

'NO! No, no. Look, Gab saw him getting sucked off by some girl at the party, that's it, OK!' I say at last, thinking that at least that isn't as bad as fucking someone else.

Kelly stares at me, her anger and rage dissolving into hurt.

I forgot. As far as girls are concerned, it is as bad as fucking someone.

'Kel, I'm sorry. Look let's have a hug?' Kelly doesn't move.

'Gab knew and she told you?' she says, her voice fragile.

'Well no, Gab told Alex who told me. And I didn't even want to know,' I add.

'I have to go to for a walk now,' Kelly says quietly and she turns on her heel and walks away like an automaton.

~

Gabrielle is halfway through dinner when suddenly she gets a vision of her head looming above the a toilet bowl and the feeling of Jason's cool hand on her forehead.

She puts down her fork.

'You must really love me to do this,' she said to Jason. And he said, 'You know I do.' Oh fuck. Gab looks at Dominic, the colour draining from her face.

'What's up?' he asks her, a little panicked.

'I suddenly don't feel so hungry, will you take me home?' Gabrielle makes her excuses and sends Dominic back to his hotel. She has to think.

She rings Jason

'Jason, I remember. I remember what you said,' she tells him in place of a greeting.

'Ah, right. OK then,' he says. 'And?'

'I don't know,' she tells him. 'I can't really think. It's like suddenly two things that I thought I had wanted for so long are mine and I just don't know if I want them any more.' She pauses. 'I'm sorry, does that sound cruel?' Jason swallows hard.

'No, I … just want you to be happy, Gab. I want what's best for you, and I understand if that's not me – I mean, if anyone fucked it up it was me. But listen, if you decided to choose Dominic, you have to be certain because if you are wrong he could really hurt you.' Gab looks at the photo of her and Jason she has always kept by the phone.

'I know, thank you.' Gab picks up the picture and puts it away in a desk.

~

'Don't you want to hit me any more?' I ask Alex. She is brooding, waiting for Kelly to get up; anticipating the fall-out.

'No. I don't want to do anything you,' she says miserably.

'I'm sorry I told Kelly but she practically had me in a headlock!' Alex draws herself up and sighs.

'It's not your fault. It's mine and Gabs'. We should have told her. I might have known you can't leave it to some dumb-brain man to fess up.'

I meekly let Alex vent her anger at my kind. 'It's hard trying to do the right thing,' I say to her wisely. 'Which is why right now would be a good time for you to apologize about my nose.'

'Don't get all cocky, Evan, I'm still cross with you,' she warns me,

I balk at the injustice of it.

'Why can't you just do it,' I plead with her.

'Maybe I just don't want to give you what you want,' she says sniffily, looking at Kelly's door. I remember Christian's story about the girl who hit him until he kissed her.

'Are we still talking about my nose,' I ask her, with a smile.

'If you hadn't whinged on about it constantly, begged for it, you might have had it by now.'

I can't keep this grin from spreading across my face, which in turn infuriates Alex. 'So I'd have had it by now, would I?' I say to her, raising an eyebrow.

'Why are you grinning like a retard?' she says to me.

'Don't worry, Alex. I understand.' This pisses her right off.

'Oh shut up Evan,' she says banging around, the tension of waiting for Kelly building to an unbearable pitch.

'I was talking to Christian and he told me. I know your little secret.' Alex stops dead and looks at me.

'No,' she says and I see she is genuinely alarmed. 'No way. No you don't. Fuck it.' She heads for the front door and exits. I listen to the slam reverberating around the flat. Alex should just let herself feel the love – I mean, what's the point in denying us? Only a fool would do that.

~

About fifteen minutes later she comes back in, with the kind of smile I only like to see on display on my own face.

'What?' I ask her.

'Look, I'm sorry I walked out on you like that,' she says softly, almost girlish. 'I just got flustered, I don't really know why. It's the strangest thing.' I let myself smile back at her. I think she's beginning to come out of her denial.

'You don't know why?' I ask her, intrigued.

'No, it's just so odd. It's like when I hit you … I just don't why I did that.' As Alex shrugs, her arms darts out and she gives me a dead arm. 'Oh see, like that, I don't why I do it?' She tips her back a little as she shakes her head. 'It's a mystery.

I rub my arm.

'Maybe you want some physical contact, explosive physical contact,' I edge a little nearer her, wanting to close the space between us but still a little wary of that right hook.

'Are you flirting with me?' Alex purrs and she cuffs me round he head. I duck ineptly

'Do you want me to?' I say smoothly as she punches me in the shoulder; this time it really hurts.

'Alex, stop it,' I say, trying not to sound annoyed.

'I can't help it, Evan. I just get this weird compulsion. What could it mean, I wonder? Do you think I want to fuck you and I just don't know how to say it?' I catch her wrist mid-strike.

'Oh, Christian told you,' I say, irritated to be caught out. Alex laughs and twists out of my grip.

'Why do you want this apology so much anyway?' she says. I look at her. I wonder.

'Maybe because I thought if I battled with you something might happen between us,' I say. Alex's face quickly falls.

'Nothing is going to happen between us,' she says flatly.

I look away from her and pick up the paper. When you realize the moment really has gone – and what's more, gone forever – it's like a terrible anticlimax. The end to dreams you hadn't even let yourself have.

Alex bites her lips and then says.

'I'm sorry for punching you at the party, Evan.'

I smile sadly. 'Really, it was nothing – all part of life's rough and tumble.' I try to lighten the lead weight moment.

'Exactly. I don't know what you were whinging about ...' Alex's voice trails off.

'Always have to have the last word,' I say deliberately.

'Always,' she says with a half smile.

'Exactly.' I continue the game.

She pauses, letting me win this at least.

'Kel told me she punched Nathan's lights out. I think that relationship is over once and for all. I bet Nathan will regret that moment for a long time to come. Shame really, 'cos Nathan is a good guy, really deep down, and he did love her.' I nod in agreement.

'One dumb thing can change your life for ever,' I say, but I'm not talking about Nathan and the moment weighs heavily on my heart.

'Is there anything you regret?' Alex asks me carefully. I look at her and for the first time in a long time I decide to do the right thing. To say what I need to say with no ulterior motive, just because I know that at some point I have to say it.

'I'm regret going away and I'm sorry I didn't come back earlier,' I say, holding her gaze, showing her my honesty with my eyes. 'What about you?'

'The same,' she says, without hesitation. A long moment of silence passes between us and then Alex breaks into a smile.

'C'mere,' she says.

'Why, want a hug?' I say playfully.

'No, I want to slap you.' We both laugh.

71

Alex is feeling jangled and uncomfortable when Gab arrives at the door, and she is glad to see a friend who can take her mind off it, for although she is absolutely sure that she is at the end of something, she can't help feeling in her heart as if she is at the beginning. Unfounded optimism isn't usually part of Alex's emotional repertoire and she's not really sure how to handle this intuitive feeling that everything is going to be all right. Kelly would tell her to go with it, and so she tries her best to let go of her control and see what happens.

'My divorce came through,' Gab says as she walks in, holding up the papers. 'This morning, I'm sitting there and Dominic's over and we are having a dreamy time and then this. The divorce. Dominic thinks it's a sign. New beginnings, starting afresh and all that bullshit.' Gab looks blankly at Alex.

'And isn't it?' Alex asks with a shrug.

'Well yes, except Jason told me he still loves me; never stopped, apparently.' Alex sighs. Typical.

'Quite a week you're having. Let's hope the rest of your life's sweethearts don't turn up in hope of a reunion too, especially not that kid with the ginger hair and the bad breath. What was his name?' Alex struggles to keep the hint of envy out of her voice. Why do her lost loves never re-emerge hoping for a second chance? 'So do you still love Jason?' she asks carefully.

'I do, I think, but you know when it comes down to it … I want to have a baby with a man who's never had a baby before. I want to travel places with a man who's never been there before. I want us to discover the world together. I want a partner not a … not a …' She flounders, winding her arms through the air as if they might find the right word waiting there.

'Experienced tour guide.' Alex finishes for her.

'Dominic's given up so much for me, though,' Gab says sadly. 'I can't just say, "Oh well, I've changed my mind", can I?'

'Well,' Alex says. 'What you have to decide is can you give up your dreams for him or for Jason and if you can, are you sure you won't end up hating them for it, eventually?' For some reason Alex thinks of Rex and her heart turns over.

Gabrielle looks at Alex, her face a perfect description of indecision and agony. Alex can't help but smile.

'What?' Gab says, returning her smile instinctively.

'It's just us.' Alex giggles a little.

'What?' Gab's face mirrors her friend's.

'Well, look at us. Have you ever met such a pair of fucking fuck-ups in all your life!' And both girls roll onto the sofa laughing, and they keep laughing until the tears run down their cheeks.

~

As Gab walks into the Fu Bar to meet Jason she mulls over her last conversation with Dominic again and again.

'I would have done anything for you,' she told him. 'But the moment's gone now and sometimes you have to accept that and move on. It's just too late.' She had watched Dominic's face crumple and every one of his years showed in it at that moment.

'I have nothing without you. I've put my whole life on you,' he had said, and Gab had felt ever so slightly angry and suffocated.

'I did that once too. It wasn't enough then and it isn't enough now,' she'd said. 'It's just too late for us.' Dominic had looked lost and alone when she left him.

'I know,' was the last thing he had said to her.

~

'Jase.' She smiles brightly. He is sitting at a table with a bottle of champagne on ice and his papers spread out over the table.

'Hi.' He smiles at her, a brave, sweet smile – the smile of a friend, she thinks.

He pours out two glasses of champagne and hands her one. They lift them in a toast.

'To new beginnings?' they say together.

'Are you ready?' Jason asks her, handing her his best pen.

'I'm ready,' she nods and they give each other one last smile as man and wife before they sign their divorce papers.

72

The first lie I ever told, or remember telling, was to my mum when I was four or five years old. I came in from the yard and she looked a bit glum and I thought, 'I know what'd cheer her up.'

'Mum,' I said, pulling at the hem of her skirt. 'You'll never guess who I just saw!' I remember jumping a little bit as I got more excited with the story I'd made up for her.

'Who, sweetheart?' she asked absently. I think she was peeling potatoes.

'I saw Jesus floating in the sky, I saw him go behind a cloud,' I said happily. I knew how much Mum liked her religion.

'Evan Wylde, you wicked, wicked child. How dare you lie like that? Now go to bed at once.' She'd slapped the back of my legs and sent me packing. Of course, at five years old I had believed in Jesus and I fully expected to run into him floating about one day, so I'd never imagined my mum would have caught my story out. That was the first time that I learnt that some people call some stories lies and some lies are considered works of literary art.

I've been practising the art of both ever since.

I'm scouring my cookbooks, looking for the perfect meal to cook Alex tonight, when I see an intruder in the flat.

'Bloody Jesus!' I scream as a strange woman walks out of Kelly's room.

'What! What are you screaming at!' she yells. I stare at her; it is Kelly, only in a blonde wig. A really long, peroxide blonde wig.

'Your hair,' I say, before I can compose myself.

'You hate it, don't you?' Kelly asks with such despair that I choose to lie.

'What do you mean by "hate it" – if you mean that I really dig it, then you're right. It really suits you. I mean, I wouldn't normally see you as blonde, but it looks good.' I see my little white lie stoking the embers of Kelly's dwindling confidence. This is the defensive lie designed to be used when you're caught unaware. Often a very weak and transparent lie, but if it's to someone about their appearance it is usually accepted without question

'Really?' Kelly looks at me hopefully. 'Because I don't want to look stupid or anything.' This lie can have a number of parts.

'No, I love it. It's great,' I tell her enthusiastically. That was part two.

'You don't think it's too blonde?' Kelly goes for affirmation.

'I think it's not blonde enough!' I say sincerely. And that was part three.

Kelly looks at me and then back at herself in the mirror.

'Not blonde enough – really?' she says. What is it about lies? Are they just social lubricants, useful because they make life run more smoothly? But maybe their value is more sinister. Maybe lies help us present to the world something that we're not.

~

Alex is showing the world she is a confident, professional woman, not looking for love but happy to invite it in should it manifest itself. She's doing all of this when she bumps into an old college friend who is doing exactly the same thing.

'Kereth!' Alex beams, her pleasure genuine. 'My God, how are you! You look good.' Kereth smiles. She's thinking the same thing about Alex but choosing not to say it.

'Good, just back from a year in "the smoke".' Alex frowns at her. 'London! It was great,' Kereth tells her, 'but now I'm back here chasing a man!' Kereth giggles and Alex smiles at her.

'Wow, gossip.' Alex frowns as her beeper goes off. 'Shit, well look, let's catch up, OK?' she says as she backs away from Kereth. 'I'll call you!' Kereth waves her agreement and then Alex turns and runs.

'What's up?' she says to the nurse as she arrives in casualty. 'A little girl, five years old, suspected iron overdose. Her mum's pregnant, she thinks she ate her supplements mistaking them for sweets.' Alex steels herself, knowing that it could be very bad, even fatal, for the child.

'Fuck,' she says to herself before she composes about her the air of a professional and competent woman who's going to do her best for this little girl. Only this time it's not a pretence.

'Hi, I'm Dr Christensen.' Alex briefly shakes the distraught mother's hand. 'OK, we need to intubate her. I'll need some help.' The nurse takes the mother gently by the shoulder.

'You should wait outside now,' she says. The woman stays rooted to the spot. 'Don't worry it's going to be all right.' The nurse tells a professional lie. 'I'll get one of the intensivists,' she says to Alex as she guides the woman into the corridor.

Alex senses help enter the room. She looks up and see Rex. She tries to blink away the hallucination, but he is still there, his face serious and intent on the little girl. Alex pulls it together.

In silence they work on the child.

~

With her mother installed by the girl's bedside, Alex comes out into the corridor and sits for a moment, rubbing the back of her neck, trying to take in everything that has just happened. Finally she becomes aware of Rex standing beside her.

'How is she?' she asks, not daring to look at him.

'Not so good. We're having trouble keeping her blood pressure up.' Alex holds her head in her hands.

'You never get used to kids dying,' she says exhausted.

'She might not die,' Rex's hand hovers over her shoulder for a moment and then withdraws

'But it doesn't look good.' At last Alex looks at him.

'No. Look, page me if anything happens.' Alex nods and pretends she is not watching the love of her life leave the room.

~

Her shift is over but she can't bring herself to leave so she makes her way down to the residents bar, remembering that feeling of intuitive optimism that had begun a while back and has been buzzing round her head ever since. Could Rex be something got do with it? The bar is busy and Alex sees oyster woman, Jennifer, heading a committee for the hospital swimming gala – barely dressed, as usual.

'Oh, Alex.' Jennifer spots her. 'Glad you can make it, I've put you down for the fifty metres, all right?' Alex stares at her and nods, not exactly sure what she's agreeing to.

'Fantastic.' Jennifer smiles and returns to her clipboard.

'You too, huh?' Alex jumps as Rex joins her and hands her a glass of cold water. She hastily arranges her face into a smile.

'Fifty metres too?' she says. He nods. For a moment, they both listen to Jennifer discussing the novelty race.

'So have you been back for long?' Alex asks, terrified that he will say yes.

'No, just since yesterday actually. No rest for the wicked and all that …' he shrugs and shifts in his seat.

'Good experience up there?' Alex questions him, doggedly upbeat.

'Yeah, hard work, but good,' he says. He looks like he has got something else to say, something difficult.

'Are you feeling OK … about the termination?' he says at last. Alex looks at him, and tries to find the truth in her heart.

'I am. But I still feel sad. You know, I'd have liked to have had a little boy that looked like you.' For a moment Alex wonders if she had been too honest.

'Yeah, I know,' Rex nods. 'I feel sad too. I think about it, I think about you – a lot …' he shrugs, at a loss to add anything more.

'Do you?' Alex asks him She is somehow glad that he feels it too, because now she isn't quite so alone. When you've been through something as big as Alex and Rex have been through, there's no place for lies any more. You've laid yourself bare already, there's no point in covering up any more. To have that closeness with someone, even when you may seem so far apart – it's special.

~

Of course, Alex forgot the meal I was cooking for her. She couldn't have known that I'd prepared fresh mussels in a cream and mustard sauce followed by braised lamb with a honey and ginger marinade. She probably just thought I was doing pasta. She probably never guessed that I'd lit two candles and set the table for her; she must have thought we'd eat it in front of the telly like we usually do when it's just us. She didn't know that I had wanted to use the evening to show her that despite everything, despite all those weeks since the taxi cab kisses, that all the time I've been in her heart and in her life that I am still her friend, whatever may come. I wanted her to know I will always be there for her.

But then Rex showed up and she didn't, not until I was on my way to bed and then all she could talk about was Rex, Rex, Rex …

The neo-nihilist manifesto states that we are liars and truth is the greatest and most original lie. Put more simply – fuck everyone. It's all bullshit and I hate the world and everyone in it.

73

Alex is swimming alone, lost in her thoughts and the water when suddenly her daydream is made flesh.

'You'd better keep at it,' Rex says to her, smiling.

'What do you mean?' She can't help but act coy around him.

'Because you're not going to beat anyone at the gala, not if that's the best you can do.' Alex smiles and feels the water running off her body in rivulets as she stands in the water.

'Don't you worry. I'm working up to peaking for the big race.' She is flirting with him. Rex's eyes drink her in.

'You look good, Alex,' he says. Alex is flushed, but she maintains her smile.

'OK, well, see you later,' Rex says, as if he doesn't really want to leave, and he swims away.

'Will I see you later? 'Alex wonders and that delicious feeling of anticipation begins to build in her stomach again.

By lunchtime she's feeling positively upbeat when she runs into Kereth in the canteen. They greet each other and agree to share a table.

'Soooo,' Alex grins at Kereth. 'Tell me about this man, then.' If Alex was honest she'd say that really she doesn't give a toss about Kereth's love life and that she wants Kereth to talk about it only so she can have her turn next and dissect this morning's conversation with Rex in detail.

'Well, that's why I'm here. He's actually a doctor here.' Alex raises her eyebrows.

'Really? Do I know him?' Kereth giggles.

'You might – Rex Mariani?' Alex stares at her.

'Really?' she says dumbly.

'Yeah, do you know him? We went out for a bit before I left and we sort of stayed in touch while I was away and anyway, I can't get him out of my head and now that I've come home we've decided to give it another go.' Alex lets this information sink into her stupidly happy brain. Of course it couldn't be a happy ending for her, who was she kidding? Stupid-fucking-dumb-ass intuition.

'So anyway, I think we're ready to make a real commitment to each other,' Kereth finishes.

'Well, that's good,' Alex lies. 'That's really great. Do you know I've just realized that I've got to get up to ICU. I'd better go.' It took Alex three lies and one deep breath to get out of that room.

~

We're all at home, the three of us, watching TV and trying not to look at Kelly's wig, all pretending to feel things that we don't.

'Are you coming to Miranda's "Goodbye I'm off to Edinburgh" party?' Kelly says, twiddling a nylon strand of her hair. She's pretending she's got attitude.

'I can't, I've got the hospital swimming gala,' Alex sighs. She'd give it a miss except the only thing she has left is the thought of beating him. It's not that he was two-faced exactly, it's just that he told her she looked good when he should have been telling her he was on the verge of being engage to little Miss Smug Kereth. Alex had forgotten that she never actually liked her very much.

'Oh well, I'm going. She's got a cool band in and I think she might sing. Evan?' I jump. I was pretending to watch a documentary on the space shuttle, but really I'd been brooding on my failure to shore up the closeness between me and Alex, closeness that had been absent since I'd come back, if I'm really honest.

We all hear the knock at the front door and we all look at it like it might be Fate. None of us moves.

'I'll go,' I say at last, feeling a heavy-hearted prescience as I head down the hallway.

'Is Alex in?' It's Rex the ex.

'Wait here,' I say. 'It's Rex,' I tell her. Alex is rooted to her chair. She looks at Kelly and then at me and then down the hallway.

'Oh just go and see him!' Kelly gives her a whispered order. Alex pulls herself slowly to her feet.

'You know what, that wig has changed you,' she says and I can almost see her armour herself for her last encounter with Rex.

'Hi,' she says, smiling tightly.

'Hi, look I've just seen Kereth.' Alex raises an eyebrow. 'I didn't know you knew her.' Rex looks embarrassed. 'She told me what she'd been saying to you.' He looks at his feet. 'It wasn't true, none of it,' he says at last. 'I mean, I went out with her once, but not now. That bit is all in her head.'

Alex looks at him, her heartbeat growing louder in her chest. 'OK – well, it's none of my business anyway,' she lies again.

'I just wanted to make that clear to you, that's all,' Rex says, holding her gaze with his beautiful brown eyes.

'Why?' Alex challenges him. He backs down.

'I just didn't want you thinking something that wasn't true,' he says.

'Right, well, I'll see you later then,' Alex says and she lets him kiss her on the cheek before she closes the door.

74

'm watching Miranda up on the stage with her mates the band Butterfly 9. She looks radiant, happy and anticipatory. Kelly is by my side, resplendent in her blonde wig. Simon's behind the bar and Jason and Christian, Gab, Richie and Nick are all here. All of us except Will.

Oh, and Alex.

'Thanks for coming to my party,' Miranda breathes into the mike. 'You're all invited to come and see my show. I know it's a bit of a long way to go, but if you do come I'll definitely get you tickets.' Miranda laughs sweetly at her own joke.

'So enjoy the party and I'll see you when I get back!' The band kicks in with some swinging guitar pop and Miranda's soft voice fills the bar.

~

Right now at the swimming gala Alex and Rex are on the edge of the pool waiting for the starter gun. Alex shakes her arms and legs like an Olympic swimmer and Rex gives her a little smile. 'Good luck,' he mouths at her. She refuses to let it unnerve her.

'Go!' Jennifer starts the race.

~

Simon looks at Richie and Nick necking at the bar and rolls his eyes. When I look at him I can't see that Richie crush in his eyes any more. In fact, he looks happy to be free. He bends across the bar and speaks into Gabrielle's ear.

'How's your love life, love?' he asks her, nodding at the necking couple.

'Perfectly uneventful,' Gabrielle smiles contentedly. 'How's yours, Simon?' He look at her and purses his lips.

'Well, there was something going on, but I've got the funny feeling that it's recently deceased.' He shrugs and is glad to find that the thought isn't as devastating as it might have been.

'Jason!' Simon hands him a drink. 'Please break the drought – someone around here has to be getting some!' He looks at Richie and Nick still clenched in a pash. 'Someone apart from Richie, that is.'

'Only if you count doing it with yourself as getting a bit!' Jason says cheerfully. Gab splutters her giggles into her drink and hits Jason in the chest.

'Just stop it right there,' she tells him.

~

Alex pushes herself as hard as she can, she resists the urge to lift her head out of the water and look for Rex, and she swims the race of her life. Her finger touches the side two seconds after his. As she rises out of the water she hear Jennifer's voice over the tannoy.

'And the winner is Rex Mariani!' Alex sees Rex at her side, laughing with joy. He leaps out of the pool and stretches out his hand to her. She takes it.

'Alex.' Rex holds her wet arms and over the noise of the cheers he says, 'I don't love Kereth. I love you.' Alex blinks at him, uncertain of a word she has just heard. She holds her breath as if she were still underwater.

'And would the winners come to the podium, please?' Jennifer's magnified voice interrupts the moment.

Rex leads Alex by the hand and they climb up onto the winners' podium. He climbs into the tallest block and helps her onto the second-place block. Alex doesn't even notice who take takes third. As the crowd cheers them on, Rex takes Alex's hand and pulls her on the first-place block alongside him.

'I've been waiting six months to kiss you again,' he tells her and he does – a short, sweetly soft kiss.

'I've been waiting all my life to kiss you,' Alex tells him and she melts into his arms, certain that if she never has to breathe again it won't matter.

~

Kelly closes her eyes as she listens to Miranda sing, so when she hears someone's voice in her ear she jumps.

'I like your hair,' the voice says. She turns around to look at the guy. He's pretty cute.

'Thanks,' she says, and she winks at me. As an expert I can tell the guy isn't lying.

'Can I buy you a drink?' he asks her.

'Sure,' she says happily.

I watch my friends talk about the love they have and the love they don't have and I wonder.

If you love someone and pretend you don't, is that lying? Is that lying because you've been letting yourself live a lie? What can you do when the truth – the real truth – is that the woman you love loves someone else, and you know that this time you really did miss your chance?

I've been lying to you. I've been lying to myself. I still love Alex; I never stopped.

It's as simple as that.

Also available from Channel 4 Books:

SEX TIPS FOR GIRLS Flic Everett	0 7522 6510 5	£6.99
24 HOUR PARTY PEOPLE Anthony H. Wilson	0 7522 2025 X	£9.99
PUMP UP THE VOLUME Sean Bidder	0 7522 1986 3	£9.99

Also available from Pan Macmillan:

DIRT MUSIC Tim Winton	0 330 4925 7	£10.99
PUBERTY BLUES Kathy Lette	0 330 48945 3	£6.99
RELIABLE ESSAYS Clive James	0 330 48130 4	£8.99
LOVESONG Nicky Gemmell	0 330 37293 9	£6.99
THE NEW GIRL Emily Perkins	0 330 37601 2	£6.99

Available from all good bookshops. You can also order copies directly from Pan Macmillan Book Service By Post by calling 01624 675137.